"... Lynn lies beneath her caresses as though she walks in a woods where all the foliage is new, where light shines through levels of light green, dark green, where tendrilled ferns blow in the wind and trees with various barks rise smoothly toward the sky, with strands of cloud lightly blowing over. She moves there with no effort of her own. She moves there as though she is herself the wind moving among flowers whose smell she has never known, whose colors blow before her and around her, under and above her, orange and yellow and tulip red, and there is no ending to it and no beginning and she doesn't understand nor need to know but only to be there and hear Ruth's voice and know that it is Ruth and that they are together entirely beautiful."

Lovers in the Present Afternoon

by

Kathleen Fleming

the NAIAD PRESS inc.

1984

Printed in the United States of America
First Edition
Second Printing, June 1987

Cover design by Tee A. Corinne

Typesetting by Sandi Stancil

Library of Congress Cataloging in Publication Data

Fleming, Kathleen, 1931–
    Lovers in the present afternoon.

    I. Title.
PS3556.L446L6 1984   813′.54   83-19413
ISBN 0-930044-46-0

For B
with my love

for R
life-giver within the shining hours

and for women everywhere who work to understand
themselves and dare to effect change.

I want to thank Jane Rule whose encouragement and help with this manuscript were invaluable. I also want to thank the many friends whose warmth and enthusiasm kept the book alive.

ABOUT THE AUTHOR

This writer's earlier works, including a novel, a collection of short stories, articles and poems, were published under her married name. Divorced, she is now publishing as Kathleen Fleming. She has done her writing and teaching on the West Coast, in Europe, and on the East Coast where she now lives.

PART I

1

The thick July heat is not cooled by the momentary rain. Pressed against the passenger door, Lynn lets the rush of damp warmth spray against her face. "That therapy stuff is your kind of game," Tony says, "not mine." He ups the speed of the windshield wipers and passes a double trailer truck. The *sssss* of water from the truck's gigantic wheels slashes up at Lynn and she closes the window. "Are we almost there, Mommy?" Lori leans into the front seat to ask. "Sit down!" Tony snaps. "Get her out of here!"

"Lori, settle down. See the airplane over there?" Lynn points to a low flying jet. "Maybe Gramma is on that one!"

"Damn it! Christy, keep her still — I can't see a blasted thing!" Tony swerves into the fastest of the three lanes.

"Here, split this," Lynn says, handing a bag of M & Ms to their older daughter. "Tony, you have to get over to the right." She points to the airport sign.

"Christ!" he says, trying to maneuver.

Lynn watches cars cut in and out, alert to warn Tony as he crosses. As they slow on the exit ramp, Lynn stops monitoring the traffic and studies Tony. She likes the way the silver is streaking the black of his thick, curly hair. "But it's not a

1

game. We need help," she says softly. "The kids do. We do, hmm?" She extends her hand toward him. Don't push too hard, she tells herself.

"That's a matter of opinion," Tony answers. He flips on the radio, jerks the dial to the helicopter report on parkway conditions, lets his hand fall into hers between them on the seat. "Actually," he says, squeezing her hand for a second, grinning at her, "isn't it pretty silly at the age of forty —" he glances sideways — "to think and talk —" he puts his hand back on the wheel, laughs and lowers his voice to the tone of a dirty joke — "about your potty chair?" He lets his scorn burgeon to a great guffaw. "Come on," in an instantly conciliatory tone, "admit it."

"It depends, I guess," she says, thinking, why did I tell him that? Knowing she has pulled on a smile the way she pulls on the same dress every day because it's hanging there and comes by habit to be on her.

"Shh," he says, concentrating on the announcer's information, and "Shhhh!" again as though she'd tried to interrupt.

Lynn takes pen and paper from her purse and jots a note for her next session with Julia: "Therapy stuff . . . your kind of game." She puts the paper back in her purse, feeling already the warm rigor of Julia's presence when they work together in the quiet little office where Lynn goes for help once a week. He's right; I do like to figure things out with her and he would hate it. Snared by this admission, Lynn crosses and uncrosses her cramping legs and rolls the window down again.

Later, as they cross back through the airport parking lot, Lynn says, "Why don't you sit in front with Tony?" knowing her mother won't.

"No, no, you sit with Tony," her mother answers quickly. "I'll sit with the girls. They came all this way to ride back with me, didn't you?" She puts her arm around Lori as they settle into the back seat. "Why, you're a chocolate child! Did you just arrive from Africa?"

"Not my side of the family! Must be yours," Tony says, grinning at Lynn's mother who laughs and shakes her head. Lynn sends a disapproving frown toward Tony and quickly gives Lori a kleenex with which she wipes away the chocolate.

Closed into the car, wedged into summer airport traffic, moving slowly toward the exit, Lynn feels submerged in a tunnel of humidity below the surface of the air they regularly breathe.

"It's like a miracle, being here!" Her mother leans forward to put her hand on Lynn's shoulder.

Lynn wills herself not to pull away, wills her voice to hold even as she answers, "It's great to have you here. Was it a good flight?"

"Fine, and look what I have for Tony!" Lynn's mother draws back with the girls and rummages through her bag. She pulls out a miniature bottle of bourbon and gives it to Christy to hold, saying, "Lori, see if you can find another one for Daddy in the bag."

"Did they think they'd get you high?" Tony asks, laughing over his shoulder.

"The stewardess was having a good time herself is what I think."

"How come you got so many, Gramma?" Lori holds three more.

"I guess I look like the partying kind," Gramma answers, laughing. "Oh, Lynn, look what else I have."

Lynn turns. Her mother takes a packet of snapshots from her purse. Lynn watches her arthritic fingers fumble at the rubber band as she tries to extract one. "This is Anthony reading when he was three. Remember how he loved that bear book?" She hands the photo to Lynn who sees Anthony looking up from his book with an intrepid smile. "How is Anthony doing?"

Lynn cringes at her mother's sickroom tone. "He's okay," she answers, and thinks, you should tell her now and get it over with.

"Did he do all right in school this year?"

The silence flickers palpably through the car like circus flashlights responding to the clown. Lori breaks it first. "Anthony doesn't go to school any more, Gramma. But he reads more than Jon and he's writing a book."

"We took him out of school this winter," Lynn says.

"Out?"

"He wouldn't go," Tony interrupts. "We didn't take him out. He refused to go."

Her mother's voice shifts key into her it's-serious-enough-to-talk-to-a-man-about tone. "What do you think, Tony? Do you think he should work for a while?"

"He won't work," Tony answers. "He thinks it's enough to hate Nixon. He's superb at that."

"He's having a hard time," Lynn says, more to Tony than to her mother. Then to change the subject, she says firmly, "Let me see the rest of the pictures. Christy, tell Gramma about the French club."

Christy dutifully begins to speak, "We have this letter exchange with kids who live in France."

Lynn tunes out, sifting through the pictures in her hand. There is Tony at a merry-go-round with Anthony and Jon; Christy on a horse at the farm where she learned to ride; all four children under the Christmas tree when Lori was newborn, Christy with her mothering smile, holding Lori as though she were a doll. Where was she really? Lynn stares a moment, hearing in the back seat Christy's helpful voice, seeing in the photo Christy, six years before. Among the bright colors of her mother's recent visits, Lynn finds a faded sepia snapshot, taken by a street photographer, dated 1941.

It shows her mother in a broad-brimmed hat walking on a city sidewalk; Lynn, about eight years old, in a plain dress and a sweater that is too small, is walking beside her. Her mother's arm hangs stiff between them, her mother's hand grips Lynn's. Her mother is watching her and Lynn is looking down.

Lynnanne sits very still, hands gripping the side arms of the barber chair, thighs sticky against the slick leather underneath. Her mother and the man are talking. She watches them in the mirror: as though on a movie screen their mouths move, their arms gesture, the man's hand moves quickly about the girl's brown hair, scissors flash, combs flick. Outside the window in the mirror the red and white currents of the barber pole twist and twine inexplicably in motion and in place.

In the mirror the man is listening and talking, listening, and his hand is somewhere behind the child's head. Another white-smocked man passes near them in the mirror. Then all the faces explode into agitated noise.

"You're skinning her!"

"Hold still! Hold still!" Slapped against the mirrored girl's neck, a towel soaks itself red: "Why didn't you say something?"

"It's the gauge on the clippers, set too close for her."

"It's not your fault," the mother says to the barber. "It's all right," she tells the girl in the mirror. "It doesn't hurt now."

Lynnanne sits as her mother told her, keeping quiet, holding still. The man in the mirror cleans the neck of the girl in the mirror, tapes on a bandage, and brushes her shoulders off with a whisk broom. Her mother's lips in the mirror move, her mother's hands give money to the man, her mother's face smiles goodbye to the man. Her mother's hand takes her own hand firmly and leads her out, on to the grey sidewalk, past the barber pole with its swirling red and white, white and red.

The rain has stopped and the heavy July heat closes in on them when they turn off the expressway and slow down near their home. Her mother sighs deeply, leans forward to put her hand on Lynn's shoulder, "Has it been this sultry all the time?"

"There's been a lot of rain," Lynn answers. She thinks of the sweaty smell of Jon and his friends, the sweet thick stench of pot in their clothing and their voices intermeshing like heavy smoke that you can't walk through until someone yells or blasts with the Woodstock record and the air clears and there is space for an hour until it all begins to gather in again. "Jon's friends have come to practice and all the kids have stayed in a lot this summer," she says with a bemused laugh.

Still leaning forward, her mother speaks to Tony, "Teaching this summer, Tony?"

"Um," he answers, looking over his shoulder as if he has to watch the traffic.

Lynn fills it in. "And he's been asked to chair the Department of Romance Languages at the University of New Hampshire."

"That's wonderful, Tony. I'm not surprised. I wish it weren't so far away is all."

"He's also finishing up his book on Dante and getting a paper ready for an Italian studies conference in the fall." Tell her now about vacation, Lynn thinks, or you won't ever manage to do it and she'll end up going along. Tell her now. "But if you'll watch the house for us, he'll take a little time away from work the end of August."

"Why doesn't Gramma come too?" Lori asks.

Lynn blushes and pulls away from her mother's breath. "Lori, Gramma does better in the house than in the woods; it'd be pretty uncomfortable there for her."

"Oh, I don't mind staying behind; you need some time to yourselves," her mother says, with the hurt in her voice like a fingernail down a blackboard. "But I hope you won't miss seeing Billy! They're coming through on their way to Europe."

"When?"

"I'm not sure. I've got the calendar in my purse." Her mother sits back to open her bag.

Lynn says, "Never mind. We'll do that later. We're almost home."

"Is Uncle Billy bringing Tammy?" Lori asks.

"Oh, yes! And Jimmy and Barbara!" her mother says.

Turning into their development, Lynn's nearing-home-apprehension rises in her like the flush of a quickening fever. She listens for — sirens? The screech of brakes? What she hears is the usual afternoon droning of slow sprinklers, back and forth, and a power mower on the corner.

"Gramma, that's my new three-speed," Christy says, pointing.

"There's Anthony! Can he be that tall?"

Anthony is standing, slightly slumped, his long straggly hair circled by his headband, leaning on the mailbox. Something is wrong.

As they pull into the driveway, Tony calls out, "Open the garage door, Anthony!" and waves toward it as though the boy needs sign language as well.

"Oh, Anthony, my goodness, how tall you are!" Gramma calls out the window, pulling the door handle before they've quite stopped.

Anthony comes to the car, grinning at his grandmother. "Hi, Gramma," he says, bending down to kiss her as she starts to climb out.

"How's my basketball player?" she asks, taking his arm.

"I kinda quit that," he answers, blushing.

"Hey, open the door!" Tony gestures impatiently.

Lynn takes a bag and starts toward the house. Anthony goes to raise the paint-chipped door. "Uh, Mom," he says over his shoulder.

"Anthony, get those bags," Tony says.

"Mom."

Lynn turns back, questioning with her glance.

"The door's locked, Mom. Jon had a tantrum. He's really crazy!"

"Shhh," Lynn says, with a warning glance toward her mother. "Locked?"

Tony is already at the door, banging, ringing the bell. "How come you locked the door?" he yells at Anthony.

"He didn't," Lynn says, "Jon's inside."

"For Christ's sake, what's going on?" Tony thumps on the door.

"How long has he been in there?" Lynn asks Anthony.

"I don't know. He threw a bunch of stuff around and I took off and he locked me out."

"Jon wanted to come along to meet you," Lynn says apologetically to her mother, feeling guilty for leaving him at home. "Jon," she calls at the walls, the windows, of the unanswering house.

Tony walks rapidly around the house. She hears him pound on the back door and shout, "You open this door right this minute, Jonathan! JONATHAN! Damn your stupid hide, open up!" Thump! Thump! Thump! "You just wait'll I get my hands on you! You just wait!"

In the front yard her mother leans on the car, her lips in a resigned and suffering smile. Lynn watches her and feels sucked under. Lori and Christy wait it out under a tree. The front door opens and Jon comes out, wearing jeans and a Woodstock T-shirt; he ignores the rest, going to his grandmother. He holds out his hand to take her arm and kisses her hello.

Lynn sees Tony, sweaty and livid, charge around the house. He breaks stride, seeing his son escort his grandmother gently through the doorway. Lynn and Anthony move after them, carrying her luggage.

2

"Okay, that was a good start. Smooth and careful. Now go down to the corner and take a right." Lynn adjusts her safety belt and watches the street ahead, the intersecting streets.

Anthony's foot on the gas pushes unevenly. The car jolts forward. Lynn says nothing. At the corner he stops abruptly. The motor dies. He fumbles, pushes the gas, grinds the starter.

"When that happens, just stop. Take your time." Lynn is tense but she holds her voice at a comfortable pitch. Behind them a car honks. "They can wait or they can pass you. Take your time. Lots of accidents happen because drivers get flustered by some idiot honking behind them. You know how to start the car. Put it in neutral and start it just like you did before."

Anthony looks over his shoulder at the car behind them and then starts the engine. He tries to go forward in neutral and the motor dies.

Lynn smiles at him. "It's okay. Start over again. Then shift and go, when you can. Don't forget to look first. You've been sittting here a while. Take a right. Watch that little girl on the bike. Always keep your eyes open for kids on bikes and dogs and cats — and never swerve without looking around even if a dog runs in front of you."

"I could never hit a dog, Mom." Anthony frowns.

"Go straight at the light. It's okay. You can make it."

"Pigs! Pigs!" Anthony's peaceful voice is suddenly harsh and angry. He looks after a police car going in the opposite direction.

8

"Hey, cut it out. You just drive, okay? Slow down about here for that light ahead, then if it turns, you can still stop."

Later they stop for milk shakes. "I want a chocolate shake. Here, you can have whatever you want." She hands him money and waits, watching herself watch him as he orders, jokes with the girl behind the counter. Contradictions. The school psychologist said, "He shouldn't find contact sports easy but he does; he shouldn't get along well with girls, but he does; so then he shouldn't hate school but he does."

In the back seat of the car next to theirs, two teenagers lie in one another's arms. A middle-aged couple walk by and shake their heads. "This isn't your living room, you know!" the man yells at them as he pulls out.

"Make love, not war!" Anthony shouts back.

Lynn blushes and laughs. The kids in the car don't notice anything.

"Seriously, Mom, why do people get so mad about that?"

"I don't know, Anthony. Scared, maybe? As far as I'm concerned if people show love that's a pretty happy thing. As long as they're honest with each other. And use birth control!" She hesitates a minute, finishes her milk shake, and adds, "That's the boy's responsibility just as much as the girl's, you know."

Anthony nods. This is not a new conversation between them. For years on Sunday mornings she's stood at the stove making pancakes for the kids and for years they have talked about everything. Tony usually reads the paper or sleeps late. She wonders if he ever talks to Jon and Anthony about sex; she thinks probably not.

"Now take us home. It's time for Christy's piano lesson."

"My, don't you look like the tropics though?" her mother says, on their way out the door.

"It *is* summer," Lynn answers.

"But you wear shorts in stores? It's hard to get used to. Christy, are you as musical as Jon?"

"She's not as interested as he is — yet," Lynn says.

"They got it from Tony. Anyway, they certainly didn't get it from you!" Her mother laughs. "Remember? You can't say I didn't try though."

"No, you tried." Lynn forces a smile. She remembers herself rigid at the keys, fingers brittle, striking at random.

"Does Tony play much?"

"No, he doesn't have time any more." Abruptly in her memory Lynn hears Tony's eager playing of Mozart while Anthony crawls rapidly across the floor; when did Tony stop? Before the year in Italy? He hasn't played since then.

"What a shame! Maybe hearing Christy will make him start again."

They drop Christy at her lesson and go to the store. "Now let me get the chickens — and I suppose there has to be beer — I wish Billy wouldn't always have to drink. I think it's a problem for Diantha, I really do."

"I'll get the groceries, Mother."

"Then I'll just duck into the bakery and meet you at the car."

Going up and down the aisles, glad to shop without her mother there, Lynn remembers:

In the evenings, in the narrow house, Lynnanne sits at her mother's dressing table and watches in the mirror as her mother takes strands of hair and spins them into curls, wets them with water from a glass with air speckles on its side, and fastens them tight against her scalp with bobby pins. In the morning her mother combs them out. At school the other girls comb their own hair and Lynnanne watches them. Every night the girl in the mirror holds still and waits and when her mother is finished she gets out of the mirror and goes to her desk to write.

Her mother's room is filled with piled debris. Her bed is layered with books, candy boxes, magazines, extra pillows, a jewelry box, a shawl, a bedjacket, writing paper, a box of letters. These things leave barely room for her body to lie, propped up with pillows. Next to her bed is a nightstand with a radio on it, a bottle of aspirin, pens, pencils, an alarm clock, a prayer book, a Bible, and more letters. Next to this is the dressing table which has three mirrors that bend to face one another. Every night Lynnanne watches the girl inside the mirror whose face is bounced and tipped from one glass to the other. The wood is dusted with old powder and there are perfumes, lipsticks, colognes, hairpins, brushes, combs. Across the room is a bureau with no surface space showing through, on which stand photographs of Billy, Marsh, and Lynnanne, her mother's father, sister, nieces, nephews, and jewelry boxes, stacks of library books, Ladies' Home Journals, newspapers, with postcards stuck along the edges of the mirror.

Sometimes her mother lies with a washcloth on her head, a wash basin beside her on the floor, her voice a muffled sound rising from the bed. The room is thick to enter; Lynnanne feels the shock waves go out from her steps to shake her mother's bed as she goes in. She walks across the room, trying to put her feet down lightly.

"Would you bring me a cold washrag?" The voice is weak, apologetic.

Lynnanne takes the damp washcloth from her mother's outstretched hand and goes to the bathroom where she runs cold water on it, folds it, squeezes it fairly dry, and returns to the woman in the bed. She stands beside the bed, unable to breathe. The closed-in room, dark, is clogged with airlessness.

Lynnanne angles her arm behind her head, leaning on the wall, legs askew.

"Don't raise your arm like that, Lynnanne. Keep your hands at your side. And straighten up. Don't slump."

"Anything else?" Lynnanne asks, dropping her hands.

"Maybe a little hot milk with soda crackers and two aspirin after while?"

"When?"

"Whenever you have time."

"I don't want to wake you up." Lynnanne runs her hand over her chin.

"Oh, never mind, bring it now. Don't pick at yourself." Lynnanne takes her hand away from her face.

"You want to keep yourself pretty. You have such nice skin — keep it clear and smooth for the man you marry."

On the way to bed, Lynn stands before the mirror in their bedroom. Tony is in the shower. She stands, naked, turning before the glass. She moves her hands slowly up and down her arms and thighs, feeling a new smoothness, savoring the new tightness. She has lost almost fifty pounds during the therapy and is now within five pounds of her ideal weight. This new image in the mirror is startling to her; she still expects to see the body she has carried around for twenty years. She walks to the door and locks it, turns on the radio, and puts on a dim lamp in place of the bright ceiling fixture.

She lies in their bed then, thinking about her body, thinking out from the inside where she is used to being, to the outside where she now likes to go, feeling with her hands the shape that she now is. She runs her hand across the sheet where Tony will soon lie. She is practicing a new way to wait for him. She takes all the thoughts about house and children and stacks them in a corner of her mind to be taken down next morning. She thinks about her body, his body, the water stroking his naked chest, thighs, penis, hoping her excitement will excite him too.

"I'll need the car tomorrow; we're interviewing that guy from Berkeley and I have to go to lunch with him." Tony is wearing plaid pajamas. He sits on the bed beside her.

"I'll have to bring it to you at noon then because I promised Mother I'd take her to the library and I have to pick up Billy and Di at the station at ten o'clock."

"You know, I'd like just for once to keep the car all day."

Lynn wishes she weren't naked, lying there below his conversation. "I'm sorry," she says.

Tony sighs and sits against the headboard. He crooks his arm behind his head, saying, "It would help to send Jon away to school."

Lynn pulls the sheet up around her shoulders. "Now, you mean?"

"Yes, in September."

"I don't think he wants to go."

"I know I don't want to pay for it."

"Let's get him to a counselor."

"I don't think counseling will do the trick. I think he needs authority and I want him out of here."

"No, you don't." Lynn puts her hand gently on his leg.

"I *do* want him out of here. I'm fed up with the two of

them. Anthony won't do a damned thing if it isn't a demonstration and Jon's traded brains and talent for a gui-tar and a joint!" Tony strums an invisible guitar and then lifts his right hand to his lips, thumb against first two fingers as though holding a joint. Lynn obediently smiles. Tony lets out a heavy laugh.

"Give them time – they'll come out all right."

"Oh sure they will. When I'm six feet under!"

"You look pretty healthy to me," Lynn grins.

"Let's see how healthy you look," he says, and pulls the sheet off her. He sits looking her over from head to foot. "You're getting skinny, lady," he says, lighting a cigarette.

"You know, Mother hasn't noticed. Today at the book store Mrs. Foster said, 'So, you'd better stop before you fade away altogether!' and my mother said, 'I thought you'd lost weight but you're so hard to keep track of – up and down, down and up.' " Lynn smiles wryly.

"What were you doing in the book store?"

"I got the new Masters and Johnson."

"I wish you'd get your sex books someplace else."

"It's a perfectly respectable book to get. All the best people read it." She laughs at him.

Tony grinds out his cigarette and slides down so he's lying on his back beside her. "Come here, and demonstrate your book larnin', woman." He puts out one arm and pulls her over on top of him. His lips close over hers and his tongue moves into her mouth.

Her anticipation siphoned out of her by the conversation, she deliberately moves her hand along his leg, closes her fingers on his penis, strokes its soft shape into hardness, and opening her thighs to him, turns over on her back.

He raises himself over her, enters and thrusts in and out, in and out. She feels the regularity of the thrusting and tries to recapture the tremors she felt while he was showering.

Her mind wanders in search of a printed passage somewhere, a word picture of a man pushing a woman backwards on the grass, coming down on her with such intensity that neither knows nor cares if anyone should pass, man and woman throbbing with the accelerating beat. She feels his pace quicken and a flicker of feeling pulses around her clitoris like the snap of a porch light flicked on and off.

"Did you come?" he asks.

"Yes," she says, "good night."

"Good night," he says, turning away.

Lynn snaps to her feet and wakes, hearing her own voice calling, "I'm coming, Lori." In the dark she finds her robe and unlocks the door with a quick rush of guilt; did Lori try to come in and find their room locked? They have never locked their door before. Going down the hall to Lori's room, she finds Lori in bed, turning restlessly. As she enters the room, the child calls out, "Mommy, Mommy!"

"I'm here, Lori. Go to sleep."

"I'm thirsty, Mommy."

"Okay. I'll get you a drink."

"Also, I'm hungry."

"Can't you wait till morning?"

"I don't think so. I'm very hungry."

"Okay. I'll bring you something to eat. Now hush."

Lynn goes downstairs to the kitchen and returns with a glass of milk and a peanut butter sandwich. Lori sits up in bed and takes the glass. "Thank you."

"You're welcome. Good night, Little Bear."

"Would you stay?"

"I'm tired. I'd like to go to sleep myself, Lori."

"Just until I'm through? Please?"

"Okay. I'll sit on the stairs, all right?"

"Until I'm asleep?"

Lynn sighs. I'm doing this all wrong, she thinks. "Until you're asleep. Good night, now." She leans down through the smell of peanut butter and kisses Lori's cheek.

Sitting on the stairs, Lynn leans her head against the bannister. The house is very still. They're all home, asleep, she knows, and breathes deep, feeling the comfort of their safety. When Lori's breathing is deep and even, Lynn returns to her own bed. At least they don't tumble in beside us any more, she thinks, and laughs quietly, remembering one winter before Lori was born when the other three were all little and would come, one by one, until in the morning they were one tangle of legs and arms and curly heads. So how did we get in trouble?

she thinks, and begins the recapitulation, starting with Anthony as a gentle little boy reading everything when he was four, loving baseball when he was eight . . .

Sleeping, she wanders down a long corridor with bars on both sides. Children are calling her and she cannot reach them all; some are behind bars, some are not. She gathers up the ones that are not and runs with them. They must reach the door before it's closed. She stumbles but rights herself and gets to the door in time. "Tony?" she calls, "Tony, get them." Tony is at the wheel of a car, with a map held up in front of him so he can't see the road. He's driving faster and faster. The children in the back of the car start to open the door and Lynn asks him to put the map down but he points to the lines up and down and across and starts following one with his finger. "That's not the road, Tony," she says, slowly and clearly. "Those are latitude lines."

He laughs and she realizes that they're not; they're longitude lines. She's studying it with him and the car is going off the edge of the road and she can't make a scream come out nor reach the wheel which is spinning out of reach.

3

"Has she learned to cook yet, Tony?" Her oldest brother, Billy, leans heavily on the kitchen counter, watching Lynn.

"Reasonably well," Tony answers, grinning.

Lynn puts the biscuits in the oven, wipes her forehead with her arm, and turns to the stove to check the chickens frying in the deep cast-iron pot that once was in her mother's kitchen on the farm.

Billy pours himself another bourbon. "You like it here?"

"It's near the city. We're comfortable," Tony replies.

"Yeah, that's great. Thanks for putting up Di and the kids. It's real good for me to have a place to put 'em while I'm running around in town." Billy's face is flushed and he runs his hands through his grey hair as he laughs a thick deep laugh. "Good for my wallet, too. You folks can do the same when you come out our way."

"Billy, what are you doing out here? Learning from Tony how to help in a kitchen?" Their mother laughs and pats Billy on the back. "Better watch out or Di will get ideas and that'll be the end of you! Can't I help, Lynn?"

"No thanks, we're about ready to sit down."

"Do you want Billy to find chairs?"

"I'll locate some." He takes a long swallow of his drink.

"Iced tea?" their mother asks, tapping his glass, laughing her quick worried high-pitched laugh.

"Definitely iced. Iced to a T. Correct."

"Did you want those biscuits in the oven much longer, Lynnanne?" her mother asks.

Lynn whirls to take them out just short of burning. "No, they're ready. Want to put them on the table and sit down?"

Lynn puts the chicken on a platter and starts for the dining room. From the living room beyond she hears Lori's voice, "I'll tell if you don't stop!"

Her mother's voice follows, "Oh, you don't want to be a tattle-tale, do you, Lori?"

Lynn sets the chicken next to Tony, says, "Start serving yourselves," and goes to the living room. She finds Jon and Lori in a tangle on the floor with the dog squiriming out from under both of them.

"What's up?" Lynn asks.

From across the room Lynn's mother's eyes lock in on Lori.

"Nothing," Lori says.

"Let's go eat," Lynn's mother says. "Um, um, doesn't that chicken smell good though?"

"Jon?" Lynn keeps him back as her mother and Lori go to dinner.

"She was *riding* Pal. So I showed her how it feels to have someone ride on you, that's all."

"Oh Jon!"

"Oh Jon! Oh Lori! you mean. That child is a genuine menace."

"Let's go eat. And you just remember how much bigger you are than she is and take it easy, you hear?"

Billy's arm encircles Lynnanne. Controlling her hand with his, he punches her face with her fist projecting from his own. "Quit hitting yourself! Look at the dumbbell beating herself up!" He laughs.

Lynnanne twists, pulls, but cannot break away. "Stop it," she whines, her voice rising, rising as the pain persists.

"Hush," their mother says from across the room. She is making apple jelly. The rows of jars stand full, their amber filtering the sunlight. She moves toward the jars with a pan in her right hand; steam rises from the pan.

"Cry baby, cry, put your finger in your eye," Billy chants softly next to her ear, and her fist is pushed hard against her cheek, against her eye, " 'cause your mama gave your papa the biggest piece of pie."

"You two go outside to play," their mother says, "before he hears you. And Billy, didn't he tell you to saw up the cord wood today?"

Lynnanne twists free and runs from the room. Their mother's set lips and barely rearranged eyebrows lay silence on her as the liquid paraffin pours into each jar, sealing, sealing.

At the edge of the cornfield where the ferns grow lush and tall she hollows out a green space where she hides, curling into herself like the fronds of the ferns. It is quiet here. She watches the patterns of sunlight moving on the ground as the wind sways the ferns and above them the cedars, firs.

Billy's hand shoves aside a fern, breaking its stalk, and the sudden rush of sunlight stabs her eyes. "Hello, boy," he says, crouching beside her, his bulk awkward in the space sized for herself alone.

"I'm a girl," she says, squinting up at him.

"I say you're a boy."

"Girl."

"Look like a boy to me. Got pants on."

"I am too a girl."

"Prove it."

"No."

"See. You're a boy all right." He pulls a long spear of grass and sucks on it. "I can see that."

"I am not either."

"If you aren't, show me."

She pulls her overalls down and arches toward him, her panties stretched taut across her stomach.

"Boy all right," he says, grinning down at her. "A boy if I ever saw one."

"Girl, girl, girl," she says, shoving her panties down, revealing the bareness of her thighs, her hairless mound. "Girl, girl, girl."

His weight topples her backwards to the ground and his body, heavy on her, holds her there.

"Get off," she says.

"In a minute," he grunts, "I have to make sure you're not a boy."

"Get off," she whimpers.

"In a minute," he mutters, loosening his fly, "in a minute."
He prods her thighs, her pelvis, with his hardened penis.
Pinioned, she feels the blows against her legs, against the place
between.
Far up the trunk of a near fir tree a woodpecker beats the
bark. She knows from her father the sound, the red, black,
white of its wings and head. Her mouth, wanting to call out, to
tell, opens, gathers air.
"Shut up!" Billy says, his voice a panting hissing in her ears,
hot and near, heavy and hard.
She sees her mother's warning eyes and feels the paraffin
congeal on her lips.

Lynn is reading her poetry to an auditorium that is nearly
full.

I always know
who it is I love:
this is the rock
on which my private house
is built.
When they love back
my house has windows out.

Tony and some friends are in the front rows and she sees
various university people that she knows. Her voice is sure.

In the country where I lived
when I was small
no one ever yelled at all.
My grandfather grew old,
stayed
in the antique poster bed
with the high radio beside
and died
and all so silently
I barely knew which day
and no one I saw cried.

Lynn checks the back of the auditorium once more to make
sure her mother hasn't sneaked in; she did not feel well and was
left at home, resting.

> My father lost his mind
> day after gradual day
> and went away
> and no one ever yelled
> or drank
> or cursed
> or fisted, hit at walls.
> My brothers went to war—
> we sold our farm
> moved to the city
> house like every house
> down the many housed block.
> My mother wept
> when the troop train pulled away
> but on no other day.

*The bareheaded boys with wavy hair, still wearing jeans
or cords, laughing, calling back, sucked through the narrow
doors of the already pulsating train — and then in the back
seat of Aunt Agnes' car, her mother cries, her hand on Lynnanne's, gripping; Lynnanne lets her hand be held beneath the
weight of her mother's hand, holds it still as though she's
trapped under a fallen tree, until she can hold it there no
longer; sweating with shame and guilt not to be comforting
her mother in her need, she pulls away and presses herself
against the rainstreaked window of the car.*

Lynn remembers that then there were three years without
them, of bringing her school friends home to stay over, three
years of playing first-base and basketball and tennis, of tourna-
ments and trophies . . .

> And they came home.
> And in our settled house

we went our ways.
Everyone moved steadily
in parallel.

Lynnanne is in the living room of the narrow house. Christmas week, 1945. Billy pulls her down on his lap, his hand closing on her thigh just above the knee, his other arm around her waist. Twisting loose, she feels his gun in holster? She is fourteen. She knows he will not go back to war, will have her flat again, be above her pounding against her, and she numb and powerless to throw him off.

"It's like a wonderful dream; I can't believe he's really home again," their mother says, bringing food to the table, laying her hand on Billy's shoulder where the sergeant's stripes are sewn. "Can you, Lynnanne?"

. . . and woke at night
to bats
clawing my hair
in dreams.
My mother never thought to ask
what it was I feared.
The house contained us
like a great cocoon.
Bats hung in daylight hours
a husk of corn
gathered into a silent dark
and moths spun dusky sheaths
to garner lack of sound.
I learned
from what I feared.
I hanged myself
up from those sagging floors
rigid and still.
I said that's how my body grows.

Lynn moves the papers about on the podium and says, "I think I'll end with an elegy for my father."

December is a hard cold month to die:
at eighty-two my father chose today
to send me coasting distant hills of snow
my hands in icy mittens
without shape and past control.
The cedars down the slope
spread webs of glistening light
and once my fear was fact—
the sled that dropped me faster than delight
caught on a stump—
I crossed dark air
to crash against the rocky ground
I had forgotten lay
beneath that crusted white soft snow.

I wonder if this man's death belongs to me.
My father's died.
I know
I know my father's died
as though I say
that's what he's doing now
and what will he do next year
this father who has died?

A child trusts her father to remain.
I was so young
the year he went away
that all my grieving now
is childlike:
I ponder
curious, prod the bruise.

Disabled by an old and misplaced war
a military funeral's granted him,
too far away for me to go.
I imagine bugles blowing
old men standing stiff
a coffin borne:
a 1918 film
jerky and rough.

As Lynn reads she is aware of Tony in the second row. She has read several love poems dedicated to him, and now, as she reads the long lyric to her father, she is focusing on Tony, his head tilted downward as he listens, his hand already holding the cigarette he can't light up in the auditorium.

May grass run wild
where his bones lie—
may honeysuckle trail
from the sky down fir and pine
and sun and rain
contain the various webs of green
the cedar weaves
to catch the glistening light.
This precarious human line
moves, lyric,
as simply as the waves of sound,
steady, fierce as a laser beam.
I owe this man my life:
I owe him love—
not mine for him
but mine:
I love.

Lynn looks directly at Tony but he is looking down. She hesitates a second, wanting him to meet her eyes. He does not and she finishes the poem. The applause is long and loud; suddenly less assured, she moves down the stairs to meet people in the aisle who shake her hand. "My father was also in an institution," an older woman says, tears shining on her cheeks. "That's a beautiful poem. Thank you for it."

"Would you come into the city and do a reading for us?" The woman who asks is New York suave.

Lynn feels herself altering as she answers, "No, I'm sorry, but I don't go off for things like that. I have four kids and I stay pretty close to home."

"Do you have a book out?"

"I don't have time to send my poems around. I've had a novel published though." Lynn blushes and adds, "I think the most important thing is to get the new writing done so that's what I try to do."

Tony comes back in from having his cigarette outside, hands her the keys to the car. "You were great! Don't forget to pick up Lori — I have to meet a class. See you later." He is gone and as she moves out slowly, through congratulatory looks and remarks, Lynn remembers his head tipped down and does not know why she is still wishing he had looked up, does not know what the reluctance in her is to leave the campus, pick up Lori, go home to prepare dinner, as though the reading were not yet completed, as though she has something more to say.

4

"Can I help?" Marie and Marty sit at the table watching Lynn cook.

"No, thanks, not right now. Go on, tell me about the kids," Lynn answers, separating the romaine leaves as the water takes the specks of dirt away.

"Where was I? Oh, yes, so Nicky went to the Marine recruiting station and tried to sign up. Do you even believe that? His father is out running teach-ins on Vietnam and there's Nicky pounding on the door of boot camp." Marie sips her wine. "Wild."

"Look, he doesn't understand a thing about Vietnam. He's just the usual going crazy fifteen. Honest to God, do you know anybody's kids who are okay?"

Jon and Nicky come in and go to the refrigerator to take out cokes. "Mom, give us a ride tonight — Nicky brought his guitar — okay?"

"Sure."

Marty grins. "This place is like Grand Central Station just like it always was."

Lynn smiles at him and checks the spaghetti sauce. "Does Nicky still play in a group?"

"Does he ever! You want to know what they call themselves?"

"Probably not."

"Ready? 'The Leap and Buffalo Hide'!" As Marty turns his wide open smile toward her, Lynn remembers sharply how he delights her.

25

"Hey, where's Tony? Excuse me a minute." On the way upstairs in search of Tony, Lynn passes Anthony carrying a Vietcong flag. "And where are you going?"

"Nowhere." He laughs and steps aside for her to pass.

"You'd better put that thing away."

"They're all pretty right-thinking people," he says, "except for Nicky. He's a real reactionary."

"Give him time," Lynn says, going on up the stairs. "But I think we can do without that flag this weekend. And Anthony, don't let Lori get left out all the time, okay?"

"Sure, Mom."

She enters their bedroom and finds Tony sitting at the desk playing solitaire. He does not move as she comes in.

"Hey, where are you?"

"Right here."

"Aren't you coming down? Marty and Marie are in the kitchen."

"So?"

"Don't you want to come down and talk?"

"You don't need me. I'm bored."

"But you like Marty and Marie."

"Don't tell me who I like. They're okay but I'm still bored."

Lynn puts her hands on his shoulders, massaging, saying, "Well, come down and be sociable anyway. They hardly ever come out to visit."

"Um," he says, laying a seven of hearts on an eight of spades and turning through the deck again, three by three.

Lynn leaves the room, calling back to him, "Supper will be ready in about fifteen minutes."

Laughter rises over the table like the steam from the spaghetti Lynn sets in front of Tony. He is pouring wine and mimicking a fellow graduate student of twenty years before, "Let it breathe, now, Martin, let it breathe."

Marty and Marie are laughing and Marty says, "Remember when Holbrooke took his orals and dreamed the night before that he had to dive into his baby's plastic swimming pool?"

Lynn circles back to the kitchen for the garlic bread,

answers the phone as she goes through, and coming back, hears Tony's voice, nostalgic, "Remember Gladys Murdock in Chaucer painting her toenails?"

"Can I help?" Marie asks.

"No, thanks, that's it," Lynn answers, setting down the bread and starting to serve salad.

"And we lost our fellowships and went out mowing lawns that summer. Remember the first one — we said we'd 'do it' for twenty dollars and he made us prune and water and fertilize and weed and God knows what else?"

"And Duane and Alice were always dropping by to see if we had something to eat?"

"And Zweitzer and his Cliff notes?"

Lynn refills the bread baskets. She is remembering the graduate school years, the long days of baking and cooking with a baby on her shoulder, passed in the glow of being a new mother, discovering with delight how children grow. At night she wrote. She never went to the campus.

"And that bitch, what was her name? — Michelle Leandre — asked me one day, waving her lorgnette in the air — 'But what does Lynn *do* all day?' I told her she was writing a novel and running a house and taking care of two little kids." Tony laughs and pours more wine. "But what does she *do* all day?"

"Come to the beach with us?" Nancy asks, standing at the open door with sunshine all around her.

Lynn doesn't know how. She holds the baby close against her shoulder, wondering what she'd do with him in the sand. "No, thanks," she says, "I have to clean the house today."

Nancy, old college friend of long nights of wine and poetry and walks in Riverside Park on spring afternoons, looks at her in disbelief. "You're turning into a cow, Lynn," she says with fury.

"No, I'm not," Lynn answers, holding the baby tight. "You don't understand." Tony does not want them to be friends; he doesn't like Nancy's husband, Eric. Lynn doesn't know how to be daytime friends, how to get to campus with the baby in her arms; there is no money for a sitter; they have no car; dizzy, Lynn sits down in the rocker, cradling the baby.

"Come on, we'll get you back before Tony comes home."
Nancy tosses her black hair toward the blue sky and water.
"Come on."

"No, I can't."

"Okay, and lock your door so you won't get raped!" Nancy
spins and is gone, slamming the door, leaving Lynn with the
baby, rocking.

The kids leave the table in a jumble of scraping chairs and
last snatched bread.

"What's your new novel about, Lynn?" Marty turns to her,
lighting his pipe. "And do you have a publisher?"

"People," she answers, laughing. "And no — I'm just on the
first draft."

"GIVE ME AN F, GIVE ME A U, GIVE ME A C, GIVE
ME A K!" shakes the room, obliterating conversation.

"Turn it down!" Tony yells.

Jon runs through, followed by Nicky carrying the Vietcong
flag in his hand.

Anthony comes running after them, yelling, "You'd better
give that back!"

Tony leaps up and grabs Anthony by the arm, snarling at
him, "Get that goddamned rag out of here! I told you to get
rid of it!"

"Power to the people!" Anthony shouts, twisting away to
run after the others.

"Ho Ho Ho Chi Minh!" Lori chants, running through after
them, detouring to the table for another piece of bread, throwing back at the adults, "Down with Tricky Dick!"

"Not that you politicize them early or anything," Marty
says, roaring with laughter.

Tony is flushed with rage. "Anthony does, not me. I wish
he'd join the Marines. I'll pay Nicky whatever he wants if he
can talk him into it!"

Marty and Marie laugh. Marie turns quietly to Lynn, "Are
you getting any help?"

"Yes. I have a marvelous therapist."

"She's marvelous all right," Tony interrupts. "Anthony is
an unemployed drop-out! That's pretty marvelous. Hey — did

you hear about the woman who went into a coma when Eisenhower was president? She wakes up ten years later, opens her eyes, and says, 'How is Eisenhower?' The doctor thinks she's a little out of it but he says, 'Eisenhower is fine, fine.' She says, 'Thank God, thank God.' So the doctor says, 'What's so important to you about him?' And she says, 'I've lived in terror that Eisenhower would die in office and we'd have Nixon for president!' "

Their laughter is grim. "That isn't even funny!" Marty says. "How *are* we going to get that bastard out of the White House?"

"God only knows."

Marie speaks reluctantly, "You know, ever since Chicago I've been wondering what it was like in Germany — was it like this? When we saw those policemen clubbing those people marching in the street — did people sit around and watch in horror like we did that night and not know how to stop it?"

"Turn over," Tony says, "and I'll finish faster."

Lynn moves her body so she is lying face down under him; she turns her face toward the window as he enters her, stares out the window at the summer night sky, summer full moon.

He works at finishing: and she is lying still, and it follows the day of driving kids, shopping, driving her mother, stripping beds, washing, folding, stacking clothes, sweeping up, settling fights, cooking, washing dishes; she is lying still, staring out the window at the moon, the turning sky above the conveyor belt on which she is carried through space summer day after night after day, lying still, holding herself in place, moving with the throbbing of the conveyor's motor, throbbing, throbbing, as she is lying flat and still.

"Sorry I'm slow," he says, strain in his voice.

"That's fine," she says, too tired to try to invoke pleasure.

Later, as he, released and relieved, turns on his back away from her, she says, "A lot of men would like to take a long time."

"Umhm," he says.

She gropes for a reassuring thought. "I'm glad my mother isn't going with us to the lake. She said she'll call my brothers; maybe one of them will be in the city on business and come out ι͘o see her. Then I won't feel so guilty about leaving her behind."

"If you don't keep Anthony out of my hair, I won't stay at the lake, I'll tell you that." His tired voice slides between them like a clammy sheet from which she shrinks.

Awake, Lynn lies alert. Jon's stereo is on, its beat reverberating against the floor beneath the bed. "If you don't keep Anthony out of my hair, I won't stay," stays in her mind like a piano phrase marked repeat; she does not know how to get past the two dots that mean repeat.

She sleeps and wakes to stare at the moon, clear and low in the sky. A tree's side branches feather its pale yellow. She lies awake. The moon moves slowly past the branches of the tree into the open sky.

The road that runs past the farm is a two lane road and in the dark the trees cross branches overhead to leave almost no sky, except for a patch straight ahead where the road lifts upward and the triangle of sky mysteriously changes content (now moon, now none, now stars, now moon again) as the pickup moves toward it, turning, with the narrow winding of the pressed asphalt.

Lynnanne stares ahead watching the road, watching the trees, then stares at Marsh, watching his hand on the wheel, watching his foot on the pedals.

"Will you?" he asks, his other hand reaching toward her.

"No," she says.

"Yes, you will. You let Billy lots of times — let me."

"No."

"Then look out!" he says, his voice sliding smoothly toward her along the seat, and the road ahead disappears into black.

She cringes. "Don't, don't!" In that black second she feels the truck start to plunge toward trunks of trees, scrape boulders, and sink, spin, hurtle into the long ditch that dips beside the road; it will flip over and over downward toward the gully where it will crash to a crumpled bloodied stop.

Silken his voice in the dark, laughing his voice in the dark,

"Want the lights on? Just say the magic word and on they go!"

Her voice comes from the wreckage in the gully, "All right, all right," and the lights beam instantly along the road ahead, still there, unwinding into the silent night.

Turning from the window, Lynn lays her hand on Tony's back. The beat of the stereo thumps the mattress from below. It will be good on vacation, she thinks, we will make it good.

It is heavy, hot. Tony is moving on top of her in the bed in the rented room near the beach their first vacation, their first married year. He laughs. "Even when we're sunburned?"

She nods, smiling. This is Tony, she reminds herself as the rhythm intensifies; don't let what Billy did mix you up; lie still; enjoy; this isn't Billy, isn't Marsh; this is Tony whom you love: you chose Tony to love. Lie still. Enjoy.

Afterward they lie apart, sweating, talking. "Tell me more about the army," she says. "What did you start to tell me last night?"

"Nothing," he says. "Some awful things happened in the army. You wouldn't want to know."

"Yes. I want to know everything that ever happened to you." She strokes his back.

"Once the guys dragged me along to a whore house . . . I'd never seen a prostitute before . . ." He lights a cigarette and grinds the match out in the ashtray between them in the bed.

"You were just a kid. What was it like?"

"The woman was all mascara and heavy smelling powder . . . she was disgusting. That's enough." He drags slowly on the cigarette and blows the smoke toward her in a sudden spurt. "There are some things I won't ever tell you, Lynn."

"Why?"

"There are things I just don't want you to know."

"But I want to know, Tony."

"Not everything. Anyway I don't want you to know." He pats her shoulder and laughs an embarrassed laugh. "I don't want to know everything about you either. Now let's go to

sleep." He takes a long deep pull on the cigarette and then shoves it into the ashes, twisting it out, and turns away, closing his eyes.

The summer heat is thick and wet along her smarting skin. She is dizzy with its heavy pressure closing in on her. Follow the bouncing red ball, follow the bouncing red ball: things I don't want you to know, things I don't want you to tell: follow the bouncing red ball.

5

"I'll be ready to go in about ten minutes," Tony calls from the bathroom.

"Okay." Lynn is changing the sheets on their bed. "Who shall I ask for Labor Day weekend?"

"Nobody."

"Come on. You don't want us to go anywhere, do you?"

"Right."

"Well, we'll be back from Pennsylvania and there are a lot of people it would be nice to see before the school year sets in."

"Name one."

Lynn goes to be bathroom doorway and leans there, smiling at him. He is wearing his pants and undershirt as he shaves. "How about the Johnsons?"

"He's a bore. Have them if you want, but you won't see much of me." He looks at her obliquely in the mirror. "I said I don't want anybody."

"How about Tina and Jeff?"

"I can do without amateur night at the shrink's."

"Martins?" Lynn knows already what he'll say, and he does.

"Let Anthony go there if he wants — they'll lecture us on the war all day. Rant, rant, rant. I can't take it."

Lynn goes back to making up the bed. Pulling the spread into place she thinks of an old friend from graduate school, newly divorced. "How about Tim? And maybe Jeanne and Carl?" She stands in the bathroom doorway, holding the dirty sheets.

"Look," Tony's hand moves in steady slashes down his cheek, stroke, stroke, stroke. "I don't want a bunch of people shacking up in my house, all right? Last time Tim was here he seduced Shirley – remember?" Stroke, stroke, his hand moves, and then the short chin strokes, shrup, shrup, shrup, and he lays down the razor and sloshes water on his face. "She was here as my guest and he had no right to take advantage of her."

"Maybe Shirley seduced Tim–" Lynn has always liked the smell of the lather, the look of the newly bare face. She smiles at him in the mirror. "They're adults, Tony."

"I nearly tripped on them in the living room in the middle of the night – *my* living room. Forget it. I don't want you to invite Tim to my house again. Period."

"I'll just ask Jeanne then."

"I'm ready. Let's go." He grabs a shirt and buttons it on his way downstairs.

"Want to go for a swim with us today?" she asks, following him.

"Have too much to do – don't forget to pick me up."

"Isn't Anthony coming, Lori?" Her mother leans her hand on Lori's shoulder as they are walking toward the car.

Lori shakes her head, looking back toward the house. "He thinks the water's dirty," she says.

"But it really isn't – he's being silly," Lynn says and hopes her mother will let it go.

"What a shame, he'll miss having a good time," her mother says.

Jon and Christy and their friends are in the car already. Her mother sits in front and Lori wedges herself in next to Christy. As she pulls out into traffic Lynn sees in the mirror Lori's small body next to Jon's. "Don't squish Lori," she says over her shoulder, laughing.

"Be sure to tell me when you've had enough," Lynn says to her mother.

"Tell me before you go in swimming, Lori," Lynn says, and lies with her eyes closed. The kids scatter along the beach.

Lynn's hands grope beside her in the sand, her fingers close on pebbles, smooth and warm. Turning them slowly in her fingers, she feels the sun's thick warmth all along her body and almost falls asleep.

Twirling the stone, twirling the knob: the knob is on her high chair. The high chair is unfinished wood and until she is eleven, she is skinny enough to sit in it with the tray thrown back. Because they are short of chairs, whenever there is company they put her there.

Twirling knobs, twirling . . . and she is farther back, farther, way under the sunlight's warmth, down, down, to another chair; there is a tray here too, on the low potty chair, and knobs on a wire, and all of space, the fields, trees, voices, sky, concentrated, reduced in size to fit that tray where her hands are allowed to be, to twirl the knobs, to finger the spoon, to smooth the wood, to lock her fingers on her fingers, to trace the crevice around the edge and back again.

Others move above, about her, free to enter the space that is hers, free to roam distant space. She is held there. She cannot leave her seat behind her tray with the knobs to twirl. She is held there. She has no legs, only hands. She is low, near the floor, and other people begin with legs that stretch upward into bodies that go free, that bring her things and have faces that speak and turn away and come and go. She watches.

What is out of reach of her own hands she seizes with her eyes. What is out of reach she hears and carries back cradled in her ear to hear over and over in that place that has no motion where she has no legs. She waits. She watches. She floats in space up toward the moldings, out the windows, in and out of cracks in the woodwork and the floor. She has her favorite graining in the wooden floor, her favorite routes along the curling straightening amber, orange, purple in the patterns of the rug. Anchored, she lets herself drift into the bodies that cross her field of vision and she goes with them out the doorway that is denied to her.

What she discovers, she arranges to use the way she wants when she's alone. She has there in the tray all manner of voice, all manner of movement, shrunken to fit the little circus ring, and there with her own fingers, her own hands, she spins, twirls, the little wooden spools on the little steel wire, and she cheers the red one on the left, denies the yellow one on the right, favors the blue one in between, and spins, spins, the little wooden balls that are skewered there before her as she is pinioned there herself, separated from whatever lies below her waist, knowing that whatever that part is, it is not hers to touch, it is not hers to move, it is not hers to know: it is not hers.

Carefully Lynn brings herself back to the beach and the presence of her mother. Calculatedly, she opens her eyes and studies her mother who is reading the newest historical novel. "When I was little, was I easy to keep still?"

Her mother's fingers hold tight to her book. "You were a good little thing."

"Yesterday I was talking to a friend of mine and she said her two year old is driving her crazy . . ." Lynn hears her own voice, shaky and contrived. "He won't hold still two minutes. I wondered how you managed."

Her mother's voice is matter of fact, on guard but not alarmed. She stares out across the water as she speaks. "When you were little I was cooking at your grandfather's house. We were there two years, I guess, and I did all the housework. Every morning I'd put you in your little potty chair in the corner of the kitchen and you'd stay there, poor little thing, until lunch time."

"Didn't anyone object to a potty chair in the kitchen?"

"They didn't even know that's what it was!" A smile flickers over her face. "I set you there and spread a blanket all around your middle, to the floor, and they never knew the difference."

Yellow bead, red bead, flat bead, round. Twist, twirl, spin, slow, stop. No way to move. Nothing beneath the blanket allowed to move. Air above, blanket beneath. Air to feel with the fingers, blanket to feel with the finger tips. The world begins with a blanket for a floor and you move by spinning with the fingers the little red and yellow balls; you move by

*following free people's dresses, pants' legs, as they come and
go. You get things from far away by reaching up your arms,
your hands, by waiting, by naming things that people bring
as they come and go.*

Lynn holds her voice extremely level, not to let anything
slide off on either side. "What kept me sitting still?" Remembering her own children at one and two, in perpetual motion,
her own abandonment of all other activity so they could explore and she could protect them until they began to have good
sense. "Why didn't I climb out?"

Opening her book again, hands trembling slightly, her
mother's voice gives back, not sure she ought, but dropping the
words behind like a token in the stile to get through to be let
out, "I tied you there."

Lynn leans on one elbow, watching Lori dig, half in water,
half in sand. Lynn's legs tense and she flexes toes, flexes calves.
"And after lunch, where did you put me? You must've had
more chores."

"First you had a nap, then you went in the playpen. Until
your grandfather came home and took you out. You could see
out the window from the pen. You used to watch for him
coming up the walk and then you'd start jumping up and down.
He loved that. He spoiled you — any time you cried he said,
'Find out what this child wants,' and then you'd get it. Her
mother laughs a deprecatory laugh. "I guess he didn't ruin
you for good?"

Lynn smiles toward her. "I guess not. I manage pretty
well." She lies down again, closing her eyes. Her first memory
is of her father rolling a wagon of blocks across the floor to
her. Christmas. She is on the shiny smooth floor of her grandfather's house.

The floors at the farm were rough, the wood splintered
and worn, smelling like the firs outside the house. Sitting, the
space above stretched high to the rain mottled ceilings of the
farmhouse.

The way she sits is the way she always sits but the sunlight

*through the windows is different. The cracks along the floor
are not the usual cracks. Her brothers come at her from above.
Their hands are on her. She looks up and around her at the
strange walls, strange corners of the room; she looks for someone who is not there. Both boys are there and she is looking up
past them, looking for someone who is not there and their
hands are on her and they are over her and around her and she
cries and her eyes search but do not find the face she is looking
for.*

She feels a blow: hard: and a woman is there.

Lynn snaps up as Lori calls, "I'm going in to swim now,
Mom." Lynn nods at her, stares at her and beyond her at the
water, blue and flecked with foam and blue again as the small
waves splash lightly on the shore. Dream or memory, she
wonders, feeling the vivid certainty of the blow, of the boys'
faces there above her, circling. Her mother grabbing her up out
of the potty chair? Or pushing her back to tie her there when
she tried to escape? Tied there, as though given to her brothers,
made their captive, trained to hold still.

"Have you had enough?" Lynn asks her mother.

"Pretty soon," her mother answers. "But they haven't."

"They can stay. I'll take you home and come back for
them."

"Are they safe here?"

"Sure. I'll wait for Lori to finish her swim and take her
along for the ride. I'm going to have a quick dip, okay?"

Lynn swims out and then turns to swim parallel to the
shore, soaking into her vision the green of the trees, the blue
of the water and sky. When she stands to walk ashore she sees
the boys around a mound like ants working on their hill. They
are burying Lori. Only her head is visible. She is holding her
face very still. Lynn watches their flying arms, their intent
faces working above Lori, with a steady appraising look.

Lynn's face smiles at them but she tenses and has to resist
telling them to stop. She can feel the weight of the sand, feel
Lori relinquishing movement. "Ready?" Lynn asks her mother.
"Lori, want to ride along with us? I'll get you a Good Humor
on the way."

"Bring us some too," the boys say.

Walking toward the car, her mother says, "Your neighbor with three little boys in a row was telling me how wonderful you are."

Lynn laughs.

"I don't know her name. She said whatever is wrong, you always know what to do." Her mother laughs a little mocking laugh. "You always said you'd learn when the time came how to run a house and take care of children. Remember? You said you could read and you'd learn what you wanted to learn. You didn't want me to teach you anything . . ." Her mother puts her arm on Lynn's, leaning heavily. They stop to rest and Lynn, wanting to pull away, holds very still.

That night, lying quietly in bed side by side, uncovered to the heat, Tony says, "Let me rub lotion all over you."

She smiles at him. "You've been reading Masters and Johnson."

"Why not?"

"Okay. Let's try it. I'll have to buy some."

"What else would you like? Shall I get some feathers?"

"I doubt it." She laughs uncomfortably.

"Why not? A feather brushing across your nipple might be very exciting."

"Would you like to get a king-sized bed?"

"Does your shrink recommend it?" His voice caustic.

"We haven't discussed it." She laughs. Julia said last time, "How old are you, Lynn?" and Lynn answered, "Thirty-nine," and Julia smiled cheerfully and said, "You and Tony have many years of good sex ahead of you then." Lynn smiled and nodded and wondered why it was still in doubt in her own mind.

"I'll bet you haven't!" Tony says sarcastically.

"No, really. We talk a lot about the kids. And about my childhood — all that stuff — it turns out my father saved my sanity, for instance."

Tony is quiet. Lynn decides not to start on that.

Tony leans on one elbow and looks down at her. He traces her nipples with his finger tip. "Do you talk a lot about us?"

"No. What was it Julia said once?" Lynn puts her hand on

Tony's shoulder, turning herself toward him. "She said, 'No need to dig up the landscape.' "

Tony nods, satisfied, and they stop talking as he takes a condom from under his pillow, slides it on, saying to her, "This is a new kind. They're supposed to be sexier." He pushes into her and begins to thrust.

Bolt awake. Three o'clock. Lynn swings quietly out of bed and goes to check Lori. The bed is so flat that Lynn's chest has a flickering cramping chill as she thinks Lori is mysteriously not there. She is, arms lying curved against the summer air, dolls, books, a half-empty box of crayons scattered along her bed and floor, her right hand loosely holding her music bear. Lynn does not bend to kiss her though she wants to; Lori sleeps lightly; any touch will wake her, unlike the boys and Tony, who can sleep through anything.

Lynn goes downstairs, sees no light under her mother's door. She passes the sleeping dog. In the kitchen she gets a glass of juice. Three years ago I would have had ice cream, she thinks. She stands so she can see her new thin reflection in the sliding glass doors. He is reading the sex books, she thinks, and smiles. We'll make it yet. On vacation we'll have time to play. Without my mother in the house it'll be easier. I'll get a new nightgown and new thin slacks. I'll relax and let him rub me all over if that's what he wants to do. Walking back through the living room to the stairs, she picks up the Masters and Johnson from the end table where he left it. She turns on the lamp, sits down and starts to flip through the pages again. To her surprise she is fascinated by the medical drawings and the detailed descriptions of the physical. Bodies, she thinks. I had an actual body when I was a child.

My mother put that body in a chair and tied it there. 'Patty cake, patty cake, baker's man, bake me a cake as fast as you can. Pitty patty polt, shoe the wild colt, here a nail, there a nail, let the rest go free?' Surely those are not the rhyming words. 'Pitty patty polt, shoe the wild colt, here a nail, there a nail, pitty patty polt?' She stumbles. Aunt Nell used to do that with Lori and Christy and Jon and Anthony, one after the other, when they'd run to her and crawl up into her great soft lap. Their Great Aunt Nell who forever for sixty years carried her huge flowered bag of knitting, ready to settle anywhere and let the needles flash as she listened, as she talked, ready to say, "Oh, the little scamp," whenever a child went wrong, or "Little rascal, he's all tired out." But Lori and Christy and Jon and Anthony all ran free. Never a play pen. Never held back. Aunt Nell.

"You kick like a wild colt, your mother tells me," Aunt Nell says to Lynnanne, age ten, on a summer day, lake water outside, in a cabin in which they are about to share a bed.

Waking with her legs in mid-air, thrashing, exploding out of the nightmare where the creatures surround her, where she cannot escape, cannot move, Lynnanne discovers herself waking in possession of legs that ache, and will not hold still, legs that she scrunches up tight against herself, as though if she sleeps in a hard enough knot nothing can intrude and she will be safe from the crawling, slithering, clawing creatures that pursue her through the night.

In college, lying awake one lonely freshman night, it occurs to her quite naturally that she can lie down to sleep without tightly curling up her legs, far from the tall and narrow house where she lived with her brothers on one side of her and her mother on the other, in the bedroom with no lock, into which they came at will, in that house where her father never lived at all.

Standing at the city window the first day in the narrow house, Lynnanne, ten years old, sees the woods. They stretch as far as she can see, cedar and fir and pine, maples and alders, leaves smoldering orange, yellow, amber in the sun. She runs downstairs, out toward the street. Concrete. Sidewalk. Street. Concrete path, concrete steps. And the house, stucco, rising narrow and tall.

"Where're you off to, kid?" Billy calls after her.

"I'm going to walk in the woods," she says, already unsure.

"Woods?"

"I saw woods from the window."

Billy laughs. "No more woods, kid. You're a city slicker now."

She stands on the hot concrete, sun beating down, near an isolated hydrangea bush. She still sees the trees that she saw through the window the way one sees a searing light after the light has gone. Her eyelids open, close again, and open. There is the neighbor's house. And another house. House after house and square after square of cracked concrete.

She finds her way around the four walls of the house, unwinding it the way she would a ball of twine until she is back to the concrete in the front. Her mother and the neighbor watch her awkward route. "I was looking for the woods," she says.

"I'm afraid there are no woods," the neighbor says. "But there's a park about ten blocks away."

Lynnanne knows she glimpsed the woods, real sun-pierced and wind-moved trees. But they are gone. Words in her head delete them from the yard. Her eyes relinquish what she cannot find as though she's turned her head away and can turn it back again whenever she should choose.

Carefully she focuses on the steps to the porch. Inside the house the sunlight too is gone. She gropes to find the stairs.

Lynn closes the Masters and Johnson. Walking upstairs, she stops again to check Lori. Seeing her shape barely lifting the patterned sheet, the slight rising as she breathes, Lynn remembers the boys at the beach piling the sand around Lori. Their forms loomed large above hers. Just like my brothers and me, she thinks. She is as little as I was. They are as big as Billy and Marsh were.

Lynn stands immobilized, seeing as on an enormous movie screen her own brothers and herself. She has never known it in point blank physical terms before. She has thought about the bribes, the arguing, pleading, ordering, her entrapment. She has thought about her own confused taking flight — leaving her body there for them while she went out the window, over the trees, eyes shut tight, taking herself far, far from the bed, far up and out and away, leaving only her body in the bed, on the grass, in the car, on the floor.

Suddenly she sees it in physical dimensions: not converted into words, not converted into shadows. She sees Billy, huge, his erection huge, battering a small and slender child, as he says, "Just takes a minute, don't hurt you none . . ." "Hold still, spread your legs, hold still a minute, can't you, come on . . ." and the words are not the point after all. The boy-man is enormous on the girl-child; his frame, his arms, legs, overpower, his bulk encompasses, his organ pounds, bludgeons, deadens the fragile quivering feeling hidden deep in the small girl's groin. He does not only negotiate, plead, parley, arrange, outwit, bribe, blackmail, shame, coerce the figure in the frozen frame of film. He obliterates. His weight tumbles her to the bed, pinions her on the floor: his penis is a battering ram and she is flattened by it like a rabbit on concrete beneath a hurtling rolling roaring tanker truck.

HOW COULD MY MOTHER NOT HAVE KNOWN?

HOW COULD SHE LET THEM?

Lynn stands silent. Her voice stays locked in her throat. She screams the only way she knows to scream, far within, in words that echo only in her own hearing, sounds that boomerang from side to side, knocking against her bones, her flesh, ricocheting from heart to lung to pelvis, back to heart.

HOW COULD SHE NOT KNOW?

HOW COULD SHE TIE ME, TRAIN ME TO HOLD STILL AND GIVE ME TO THEM AND NOT KNOW?

HOW COULD SHE REFUSE TO KNOW?

She stands now, cold in the marrow of her bones, struck down by the simplicity of what she sees, feeling like that child felled by weight, held down, not by collusion, not by capitulation, not by surrender to entreaty or to need, pinioned not by collaboration but by brute strength, crushed into the bed, ferns, hay, dirt, against the concrete cellar wall, blotted out, and every time it was done again, obliterated once again, and over and over and over with the throbbing throbbing throbbing

throbbing throbbing beating of the hard hard "Come on, kid, give me a break . . . I've got a hard-on . . . don't be a prick-tease . . . you've gotta help me out now, look . . . I've got a hard-on, kid" hard-on of the talking walking down-from-Jack's-beanstalk-sky brother that was from the beginning then the towering crashing power-generating huge sky-tall house-wide thunder-heavy giant brother-giant thrusting against her numb immobile child's thighs — thrust thrust thrust thrust thrust his giant giant cock.

6

On the way to the lake in Pennsylvania, Lynn watches the deep woods go by. Her breath comes easily here. Alert, she stares far into the woods, watching for deer, for small and running creatures: wild. She watches near, far, farther, as the trees streak brown and green, hard trunks, soft briars, leaves.

"If you want me to drive, let me know," Lynn says. "My God, it's beautiful." She reaches across the seat to take Tony's hand. "Remember when we headed West the first time together?" she asks, smiling at him.

"Umhm," he says. "Well, at least we've got a better car this time." He grins at her sideways.

"Seventeen years ago this summer. Anthony, you were little," Lynn says into the back seat, "the first time we drove this route."

"Nothing was polluted then," Anthony says.

"Oh sure, Hiroshima was after you were born, right?" Jon strums his guitar, intoning, "Pure, pure, everything pure until the day I was born . . ."

"Shut up! It's not funny, Jon! Look at the water in that swamp!" Anthony waves his arm toward the woods.

"Watch it!" Jon pushes his arm away.

"I'm pointing at something!" Anthony says, pushing back.

"You two start a fight and I'll leave you right here by the side of the highway!" Tony turns around in his seat to shove whatever arm his hand encounters.

"Don't, Tony! You drive, I'll take care of them," Lynn says, turning around in her seat. "Anthony, be careful of the guitar. Jon, you know he won't hurt it. Tonight we can sing some of the old songs . . . Daddy can teach them to you. Do 'It's the same old merry-go-round' for them!"

"Mommy!"

"What, Lori?"

"I need to go to the bathroom."

"Oh Christ!" Tony says. "I told you to go at the last gas station."

"I did!"

"Daddy will find a place when he can, Lori. You can wait a while, can't you?"

"No."

"Tony, you'd better stop the first time there's a station."

"We're on the parkway; there aren't any for fifty miles. She'll have to manage."

Christy is sleeping in the corner next to Anthony. Lori starts to climb into the front.

"Not while we're moving, Lori," Lynn says. "I've told you that. If Daddy had to stop suddenly you'd get really hurt."

Lori tumbles into the front seat between them. "My tummy hurts," she says.

"Do you have to throw up?" Lynn asks.

"Keep her up there," Jon says.

"Probably that water she drank at that place," Anthony says. "It was all murky."

"Right. And little green men were swimming in it." Jon starts strumming the guitar again.

"Knock that off, Jon," Tony says over his shoulder. "Save it for the campfire."

"I'm glad you're bringing your guitar, Jon," Lynn says. "Who wants something to eat?" She starts to get out a bag of sandwiches.

"Give me one," Tony says. "And don't mess up the car — you got a garbage bag back there?"

Trunks of trees pass: whunk skip skip whunk whunk, whunk in uneven bursts. Lynn hands out food and watches the highway markers for a moment for the regularity and then again stares off into the trees.

Uncle John on one side, her father on the other, Lynnanne snuggles safe. "Want to steer?" Uncle John asks, and she puts her hand on the wheel next to his big hand.

Her father says, "As I was going to St. Ives, I met a man with seven wives; each wife had seven sacks; each sack had seven cats; each cat had seven kittens; kits, cats, sacks and wives, how many were going to St. Ives?" Lynnanne turns it over and over in her mind, watching the fields touched with snow pull by on either side, knowing that for all the wild processions of cats and fiddles, kings and pipers, and the pussycat just back from London, of cock horses winding mysteriously toward Banbury Cross to see the Great Lady upon the white horse, there is only one pilgrim going to St. Ives and that is her Aunt Nell who asked her the riddle first, who is deep deep soft in her front and smells of dried flowers in the fields in spring.

"Only one, Daddy. One is going to St. Ives." She pushes into his side, serious and pleased.

"Can't fool this child at all," her father says. "You just cannot pull the wool over her eyes." His arm folds her to him and his laugh rumbles from inside him and spills around her with the sunshine sparkling off the fields and trees.

"Hey, let's put the canoe in!" Anthony tries to help as Jon starts hauling it into the water, its hull scraping sand.

"Watch it!" Tony yells at them. "Those things break! Wait for me!"

Anthony steps back, dropping his end of it. Jon continues to pull at it, yelling at Anthony as he lets go, and Tony charges toward them, yelling.

Lynn is unloading the car. Christy is helping her and Lori is running toward the lake. "Lori, Lori, wait a minute!" Lynn calls after her. She catches up with her at the water's edge. "There are rules around lakes, you know. You don't go in swimming alone. You always tell us if you're going in the water. And if you go out in a boat, you tell us first, and you wear a life preserver, and you don't do that alone. Okay?"

"Okay."

"Christy, you stay out here and watch her."

"Lori, come have a ride!" Tony wades out by the canoe.

"Where are the life preservers?" Lynn asks.

"Next time," Tony says. "We're just trying it out right here near shore."

He tries to climb in and the canoe rocks. "Maybe I need my suit on first?" Tony asks and laughs.

Jon wades out next to him. "You get in like this," he says, and starts to throw one leg over.

Tony grabs at him, saying, "Let Lori go first," and the canoe tips over. Knee deep in water, Tony and Jon stand arguing about what went wrong. Lori starts to cry.

"Come on, Lori, I'll take you for a swim," Christy says.

Lynn sits on a boulder out from shore. Her feet hang down into the water. Her thighs are warm against the sun-warmed stone. She strokes the grey grains of the rock with her right hand, fingering patterns of mica and feldspar. She looks carefully at her slender arms, her thighs. She moves her feet back and forth in the water, watching the motion of her legs. She puts her hands flat against the surface of the boulder, one on each side, tips her head down to study her body in the new blue swimming suit, then tips it back to let the sun strike full against her face, neck, breasts.

I am thin, she thinks, the way I was always meant to be. Even after I gained weight, she thinks, I felt like I was thin on the inside, waiting to come out. I moved like someone who was thin — who told me that? Someone meaning to reassure me. Fifty pounds gone. Fifty pounds picked up in the first years of the marriage. Afraid to lose it until the therapy. Gone. God, it feels good, she thinks, bending forward to look eagerly for her reflection in the lake. I move now the way I want to move. She slides down into the water and swims away from shore, relishing the smooth water gliding past the rhythmic movement of her arms and legs.

She looks across the lake, watching Tony and Lori in the canoe. They're too far away to identify but Lynn has watched them go from the time they left the shore. She studies the large figure and the small one and smiles. There is some movment in the figures. Lynn tenses, treads water, watching. She feels Lori hit the water, feels her arms thrash up toward the boat, sees the boat teeter under Tony's lunging as his arms reach down toward the child . . . and knows it's only happening in her mind.

Lynn climbs back on the rock. Standing there, she strains to see across the lake; she makes out the canoe growing larger, coming smoothly toward her across the quiet blue, the two figures clearly defined, steady in their places. She sits again, cradling her knees in her arms, waiting, seeing Tony as she thinks Lori must be seeing him. Lynn smiles.

A shiver moves through the long expanse of bark and wood underneath Lynnanne. She feels it in her thighs. She straddles the trunk, watching her father push, pull, push, pull the cross-cut saw. Sawdust sifts downward at each end of the thrusts. He leans into the motion, hat shoved back on his sweating head, circles of wet moving downward in great arcs below his armpits as he works. The sunlight glints on the metal of the saw and sprays the ground, the trunk, with flickering light. When the saw's teeth have almost broken through to air, the chunk falls of its own weight, ripping the last thin sheath of wood, shredding the bark. Her father sets the saw against the trunk, bends to get his water jar from the shade. The sweat glistens along his jaw and neck. He gives her water in the tin cup and she drinks.

"Hey, Mom, what's for lunch?"

"I'll be there in a minute, Jon. Soup and sandwiches; I'll fix it for you." Lynn watches the canoe, now safely close to shore. When he has a chance, she thinks, Tony is fine with them, and adds without meaning to, particularly while they're little. She hears his voice drift across the water, deep and clear;

she likes his voice. He should sing more, she thinks, surprised that she has forgotten how he used to sing in the Bach Society; there isn't one since we moved, she thinks, that's why.

"Mom," Christy comes to sit near her on the rocks. "Can I have the canoe when they're through with it?"

"Not by yourself – maybe Anthony will go with you."

"Mom, I'm perfectly safe by myself. Anthony is tippier than anyone."

"It's safer if two of you go though."

"Mom, everybody's starving."

"Okay, I'll be right there. Go set the table and lay out the sandwich stuff."

Lynn holds her eyes on the canoe as though if she were to turn her back and go into the cottage, it would after all tip over and Lori would go under just off shore.

"Give it here!"

"I'm just going to – hey! watch it!"

The boys' voices escalate and Lynn, throwing one last glance toward the canoe, runs toward the cottage. Jon runs out with a scrap of paper in his hand, Anthony right behind him. "Give me that!" Anthony yells in a desperate voice, as Jon throws it in the lake.

Anthony is about to shove Jon in when Lynn runs in between them. "Anthony," she says, and he stops, giving her a wild look.

"Mom, he threw a valuable paper away."

"You can fish it out again if you really need it," she says. "Jon, don't ever do that again."

Lynnanne leans against her father as he rests. "Tillicum means friend," he says. "Hi. You scookum tillicum."

"Hi. You scookum tillicum," she answers.

"And clattawa—" he scowls at the world around them, "means, Get out!"

She leans, safety-belted to him by his salty smell.

Underwater earth shines rich and sparkling and the sticks of wood embedded there glint, streaked with sun, draped with lake weeds and wide-leafed plants. Lynn strokes past channel-ings of light and turns on her back to float while staring at the trees that edge the sky, the clouds that move along the tops of trees. Far across the lake a mourning dove calls and is answered back. Lynn breathes deeply, slowly, strokes, strokes, and remembers.

Tony is swimming near her. "You know," Lynn says, "it's funny. I keep remembering more things about my father. He taught me to swim. I'd forgotten, but he used to take me down to the lake at my grandfather's and he took me once to this river near the farm. There were thick weeds along that river and he showed me how to float on my back . . ."

"Uhnhuh," Tony says. "You look like you're having a good swim. I'm going to take Christy out in the canoe. I don't want her going off with Anthony." He swims away.

"Let them go," she calls after him but he swims toward shore and out of earshot and she again floats on her back, watching the clouds drift.

He still doesn't want me to tell him any of it at all, Lynn thinks, and holds her breath and swims again under the sun-speared surface of the lake, where minnows flash silver through weaving grasses and her body moves newly smooth and free as though her father's hand still steadies her, holding her lightly so she will not notice when she has swum free.

7

Lynn sits dripping on a towel, looking up at Tony. He stands shaking water from his ears. He rubs his hair briskly, and looks acorss the lake. "Where's Lori?"

"Christy walked her over to the ice cream stand."

"Tonight," he says, with a mock leer, "let's go skinny dipping."

"Okay," she answers, smiling.

They lie on a blanket to dry out. Strands of sound from Jon's guitar drift toward them from the cabin. Lynn knows Anthony is out in the canoe. With the children safely scattered, she can relax. She savors the slow warmth of the sun; she turns her head on her arms, smelling her wet skin. She lifts her head to look at Tony. "How're you doing?"

"Okay."

"Relaxed down to your toes?"

"Not yet."

"Takes a while. It's good to be away together." She puts her arm around his shoulder. Light gusts of wind break the sun's warmth. She closes her eyes, listens to the uneven lapping of the water along the shore. She edges closer to Tony, kisses his shoulder, presses her breast against his arm stretched out by his side.

"Hey, don't," he says, startled.

"The children are away," she answers, laughing.

"But there *are* neighbors, you know."

"So? We're legal, remember?" She rubs her breast harder on his arm.

"Hey, you over-sexed vixen, lay off." He grins and pulls away. "I'll take care of you tonight."

Lynn lies apart from him, watching the leaves sparkle in the sunlight, twist in the wind. She closes her eyes and imagines them together in the night. He holds her close and kisses her long and hard and his hands are all over her like the wind, and the warmth of his body matches the warmth of hers and they draw together the way the sunlight draws her flesh toward itself with gradual but certain rises in intensity. Urgently Lynn wants Tony's touch: she sees that he is sleeping and goes for another swim.

That night Lynn stands beside the water, hesitant. "Look at the stars!" she says.

"Marvelous!" he answers. "Come on, let's go." He heads straight out from shore, doing a fast crawl.

Lynn pulls off her clothes and steps into the shallow water by the shore. It feels smoother than in daylight but colder. She shivers, looking for Tony who is already far out in the darkness.

"Come on," he calls. "Chicken?"

"Yes."

"Come on in — I'll warm you up."

She forces herself to fall forward for the first immersion. She does a rapid breast-stroke out from shore, then turns on her back. Used now to the water she finds the stars straight above her a new mystery. She breathes slowly, letting the water under her, the stars above, transpose the moment into something she has not known before.

"Hey," Tony says, giving her a pat on the thigh as he swims on, "come here."

She swims beside him toward shore. They stand and he pulls her against him, passing his hand down her back, pressing his bare body to her own. Their bodies are cold and wet. "Look at the stars," she says, but when they both look up the sky is more brittle than before, the water colder on their legs, their shoulders chilled by the slight wind.

"Beautiful," he says.

"I'm cold," she admits. "Let's go in."

Back in the cabin, in bed, he says, "You have magnificent breasts." He passes his hand over them gently. His voice hardens: "Don't you dare ever give them to anyone else." He plays with one nipple. "Tomorrow I'll get a can of Instant Whip and squirt it on your nipples and lick it off again," he says.

Later, feeling him thrust in and out, she wishes he hadn't said that. She doesn't know what else she wishes he would say. She remembers how her body felt, lying beside him in the sun, and wishes as they lie together that it would feel that way now.

They stand by the lake together. Lynn puts her arm on Tony's. She waits for him to speak.

This vacation is a special time for Lynn. In her therapy she has worked to be free of her brothers' shadows, her mother's constricting hand. In these woods that echo her father's loving presence she feels her new self take hold, as though this time by the lake were the culminating moment of her therapy.

She stands now, feeling thin and strong and happy, eager for Tony to embrace her new presence, to sketch his blueprint for their new life, ready to bring her new strength to match his as they start to build together.

"I'll try," Tony says, in a tired voice, "but I don't know if I can make it."

"Make what?"

"Everything. Life," he says, with a shrug.

Tony stands in the cabin door, calling to her. "Come on, we're going to play poker."

Lynn leaves the shore and goes into the cabin. They all sit around the table waiting for her. She watches herself lay her reluctance to one side, like taking off a coat, to join them. The smoke is thick over the table and the faces around it are intent. "I'll deal," Tony says, putting aside his cigarette, and the cards come at her, one by one.

Jon and Tony are packing the car. Lori and Christy are on

a walk with Anthony. "It won't fit in that way, Dad. You'll break it!" Jon's voice is rising.

"I won't break it. Give it here."

"I'll hold it all the way myself!" Jon yells.

"Fine! Take the fucking thing! Shove it up your fucking ass!" Tony yells back.

The car sputters to a start and guns off down the road. Jon comes into the cabin, redfaced, cradling his guitar.

"Where's your father going?" Lynn asks, keeping her voice quiet over the panic roiling in her stomach.

"The maniac didn't say," Jon answers.

Last night of vacation, she thinks, walking toward the lake to wait for Tony to come back, and sheer disappointment rises in her throat like bile. Tony has never charged off like this before. What if I wait and he doesn't come back? Lynn thinks. What if he simply disappears? What if he leaves us here without a phone, without a car, and doesn't drive back up the road, doesn't write, just disappears? She sees the moonlight delineate every twig and leaf, etch each branch against the star-bright sky. She looks from tree to tree and back again at the silent lake.

Lynn listens for Tony's car but there are only the usual noises of the woods at night. She walks up and down the shore, Tony's voice fading in and out like a distant radio broadcast.

Manhattan. 1950. "If people are so stupid that they destroy the cities, I don't want to live," Tony says, standing under a new air raid shelter sign. "Civilization doesn't deserve to last if people wipe out the centers of culture and learning . . ."

Lynn answers, "I want to live. I do. I'll hide somewhere and start a new civilization."

His voice, pale and contemptuous and envious, comes back at her, "You would want to live—" and with a strange, harsh laugh, "you like to live."

Seventeen herself, writing, always writing, she saw him first at a piano and thought he meant to be a pianist or a composer. She wanted to help him become whatever he wanted himself to be; she wanted to save him from any feeling of defeat if he could not do all that he might want to do. She went with him to plays because he loved the theater; she went with him to concerts to be with him when he was his most intense.

Lynn sits on a rock by the lake, tears in her eyes. Where did he go? Where is he? Why can't I reach him anymore? She remembers on the trip to Italy his lying beside her at night, face hidden in the dark, telling her hour after hour of the poverty, the cheating, the decadence where there had been glory, had been magnificence. He sank into despondency, night after night. "Nothing matters," he told her in that foreign darkness. "I don't love you, nothing matters any more. I don't love anyone."

"You do love us," she said to him, holding him in the dark, "you do."

It is just before their wedding. They are alone in his apartment. "I don't want to throw myself in front of a subway train," he says.

"Of course you don't!" Lynn answers, astonished.

"But I may have to, Lynn. You don't have to marry me."

Lynn answers, "I love you, Tony. Of course I'm marrying you."

It flickers through her mind like a subtitle in a film flashed white on grey, too briefly for her to read: Everyone's been told and that makes it too late to ask him what he means, too late to check out that strange note in his familiar voice.

"I love you," she says, "I love you and I want to marry you, and I'll always love you, Tony," and she knows she is promising to pull him back from whatever dark concrete tunnel or hurtling train he ever finds darkening his way again.

It's been ten years, she thinks, and almost ten more years after that. She feels decades turn, a cycle ending and another one beginning. She tries to understand why they're not lying together in the cabin, planning the year ahead in some new way, savoring the last night of their vacation.

The soft silence of the lake is broken by the car's engine far down the road. For a moment Lynn is not yet ready to see Tony and wishes it were not their car's headlights slashing willow and alder trunks, not his footsteps marking his return quite yet.

He goes directly into bed where he lies as though water-logged. She follows, speaks as she lies beside him, "Why is it so hard, Tony?"

His back to her, he answers in a low voice, "Look, I told you I would try."

"But what is wrong?"

"I don't know. I just know I'm tired, that's all I know."

"Did you enjoy it up here at all?"

"Of course."

"Then what's the matter?"

"Let's get some sleep, okay?"

They lie in silence. Some creature rustles through the leaves outside their window. The moonlight streaks the bed with pale light.

"Tony, why won't you get help?"

There is silence. Her body lies near his, her arm over his shoulder. His breathing is his waking breathing. She waits.

"I don't want to, all right? You like that sort of stuff. I don't. That's all. I'll do it my way."

"Your way isn't working."

"Maybe your way isn't working either."

"I've learned how to change. I love you, you know. I want us to be happy. Why won't you try?"

"Look, we have to get up early." Slowly, dragging his body over so he faces her, he says, "Good night," and touches her lips with his, then lets his weight settle into the bed again.

In the dream the river that runs into the lake is crystal, waves sharp as fragmented glass. It is mountain cold on her feet and flashes sunlight back against the bright blue air. Lynn and Tony are there with the children who are young. Tony is carrying Lori piggy-back and Anthony is playing with stones at the water's edge. Jon and Christy are throwing rocks into the water. They have come to buy a house. This house is large and beautiful. Lawns spread out on every side. They didn't realize before that the house has waterfront, and seeing that it does, Lynn knows they can't afford it. They continue looking at the view.

Tony sets Lori down at the water's edge and leaves alone in a canoe. Anthony has put sticks in the water like a fleet and Tony paddles through them, scattering them with his oar. Lori watches this and starts to cry.

Far across the lake the canoe is reduced in size over and over again as it nears the other shore. The shadows begin along the ground beneath the evergreens, rise up their trunks, darken their green boughs, and Lynn takes all the children into the house, which had become the cabin, to put them all to bed.

In the night outside, lanterns swing, throwing irregular shadows toward the cabin. Lynn crouches in the doorway watching a cacophony of light: flashlight beams, lantern arcs, one set of headlights parked far down the road. Voices, whispers, shouts match the ragged movements of the lights. On the lake small lights move slowly like the eyes of great creatures hunting through the night.

Lynn starts to awaken, legs cramped: for a moment she is crouched beside a wood range, watching the moonlight on the walls, listening for her father's voice outside the cabin, listening for his footsteps among the tramping of work boots. Then she knows it is Tony who went off in the canoe and she thinks, we have to tell them we don't have the money for this place, and then she knows that Tony is lying there beside her in this cabin in this bed and they are not househunting but going home the next morning to the house they already own.

Lynn slides out of bed quietly and goes carefully out the door. Walking toward the outhouse, she carries the flashlight, unlighted, in her hand. Once there, she flashes it carefully all around the seat before she sits. Then she hurries, anxious about bugs beneath the boards. On the farm the outhouse door hooked shut but the boys could poke a stick through and lift that hook. Lynn now shines the flashlight beam around the walls, watching for spiders in the webs along the top and down the sides.

Going out again into the woods, for one minute as she turns toward the cabin she thinks she is again back on the farm, returning to the house. Thirty years back to lilacs and Marsh shouting, "Anti anti over!" as the ball disappears over the barn roof and Billy runs, knowing which way to go to catch it as it lands, leaving her to stand, watching, lost, not even knowing how to get from one side of the barn to the other, not knowing the course of that ball once it is out of sight.

She was eight when her father left in 1939. "He will be back," her mother said. Lynn remembers her father's hat and jacket, workshoes, unused in the back hall. Her brothers began to do the milking. No one named the place to which he went, the hospital. Once her mother said, "He breathed gas when he was a soldier in the war in 1918. It made him sick."

Lynnanne walked in the woods and waited. Outdoors she felt close to her father's presence. She walked by the stream where the underbrush was lush and thick under the alders; she walked on the hills where fir and cedar trunks rose high; she walked when the sunlight filtered through the thickest green and when it shafted straight down through barren jagged ice-bright twigs. She walked with snow blowing lightly on her face and with the wind fierce against her chest. Even later after his death, wherever she travelled, not knowing or caring why, given a chance, Lynn walked in the woods again as she had walked as a child in the elusive ancient shadows of dark rain. Caverned within herself she walked in the woods and waited.

"Outside to fight! No fighting in the house!" their mother says.

Outside, with her father gone, Lynnanne is Billy's prisoner. "Kidnapped," he says, and ties her to a tree. She waits, hearing her brothers' voices fade in and out. Watching the rope pull tight against her skin, she twists and pulls, then waits.

Marsh comes and lets her free. "Run away from him!" he whispers hard into her ear. "Run away from Billy. I'll head him off. Pick my side. I'll help you get away!"

She runs, tripping over vines, through briars, hears Billy and Marsh thrashing through the woods behind her. Scratched by the underbrush, she runs, trusting Marsh, frantic to escape from Billy's ropes.

Later, pine needles underneath, Marsh leans hard, presses her to the ground, pants into her face, "Hold still, hold still, you gotta, you're my prisoner now!" Lynnanne knows it doesn't matter which one's side she's or nor which one wins.

8

"Brandy?" Lynn watches Tony hand the glasses, amber glowing in the firelight, to their company. Jeanne, their psychologist friend from Boston, smiles up at him from the raised hearth where she sits, cross-legged.

Guests move around the living room, finding their after dinner places. Lynn ducks upstairs to say goodnight to Lori and coming down the stairs again, hears Tony's voice, mellow, talking to Jeanne and others by the fire. "I took them myself last time," he's saying.

Lynn moves across the room to join them and settles on the floor near the fire; she watches the flames flicker around the log and among the kindling. "I admire that," his colleague says. "I've never actually gone myself."

"I march a lot," Jeanne says, "but I keep thinking of the Berrigans and I wonder if I should be in jail instead." She sips her brandy.

"You're of more use out," Lynn says.

"I don't know. Someone asked Daniel Berrigan, 'What will become of my children if I go to prison?' and he answered her, 'What will become of them if you don't?' "

"Were you in Washington on May Day?" Tony asks Jeanne, gathering nostalgia.

"Yes," she says. "Where I was it stayed quiet. You?"

"We ran into trouble. Troops coming. We looked down this long avenue and saw them moving toward us, and you could tell it was hopeless to walk against them, but Anthony ran ahead and we followed him a ways and then I took Jon back. It was hours before we all got together again. That damned tear gas burns like hell."

There is a moment of respectful silence. Lynn watches Tony as he talks. His voice carries his listeners up the block, across the street, next to the barriers, past the police, back to his friend's apartment where they stayed. His tone is smooth and proud; she ponders it. Like the glaze on a still and frozen pond his tone: she lets herself glide on it like an ice skater as Tony's voice waves her on; abruptly she crashes through, plunging into the icy memory of a scene two weeks before:

She is washing dishes after supper. Anthony is talking with his father. It is the night before a demonstration Anthony is planning to attend. Lynn is thinking that this is good for Anthony, he has met students at these demonstrations; he begins to have friends again for the first time since he left school.

Suddenly Tony is yelling down at Anthony, "And if the war ends tomorrow? You'd be out of luck then, wouldn't you?" Rage and contempt hurtle down at his son who buckles under the avalanche and yells back with fear and ritual rage:

"Stop the murders! The murderers must be stopped!"

"Why don't you get off your ass and do something real, Anthony? Don't just sit there and rot! Demonstrations aren't life, for God's sake!"

"What an experience to have shared with your sons, I envy you that, Tony," his colleague says, as Tony's voice continues, calm and assured.

Lynn sees Tony, the benign father, stare silently into the fireplace. She wants this to be the real Tony: Tony, taking the boys to scouts; Tony reading stories at night out loud on trips; Tony, laughing and interrupting his piano playing to lift the crawling Anthony onto his lap while finishing the sonata.

The raging contemptuous Tony confounds the caring

paternal Tony and the two images hover before her as though she lacks binocular vision, and though each is sharp and clear, there is no process in her that will allow the two to fuse. She turns away and joins the others in the kitchen.

"Hey, Tony, come to the beach with us!" Jeanne shouts.

"No, you go ahead. Somebody has to work, you know."

In the car, Jeanne asks, "Is he avoiding me?"

"You? No, you're one of the few people he likes these days."

"What's the matter, Lynn?"

"I don't know." Parking at the beach, Lynn says, "I really don't know, Jeanne."

"You look terrific, thin woman! The therapy goes well?"

"It's the best thing that ever happened to me." Lynn walks along the water savoring her physical movement through space in a way that is still new to her. "You know, I'd thought a lot about my life and all, but I never would have gotten it straight alone. It's like I had all the pieces before — like jigsaw puzzle pieces — and I'd looked and looked at them — but Julia says, 'Try putting that one there next to that orange one . . .' and suddenly the whole thing comes together. It's incredible." Lynn bends to pick up a handful of stones and slings them, one by one, into the waves.

"And Tony?"

Lynn turns to face her, unsure of the question.

"Tony and therapy, I mean. Will he?"

"Won't touch it with a ten-foot pole."

"Too bad. How is he doing with the boys?"

Lynn stares out across the water. Where the gulls touch down near shore there is a shallow place. They seem to stand on the surface of the water there, dipping their beaks for shellfish.

As Lynn drives Tony to campus, he says, "They're a pair of cop-outs, is what they are!"

"They're your sons. They need you."

"They should've thought of that before they screwed everything up. They're a fine set of failures. And they'll

corrupt the girls before they're done."

"Tony! They're kids, having a hard time."

"When I was as old as Anthony I'd been in the army a year already. Who had a hard time?"

"It's too bad you did! It would have been better if someone had helped you, Tony."

"Not necessarily. I grew up."

"They're your kids and you love them. They need you."

Tony swings out of the car and turns toward his building, giving back to her like rabbit punches: "Look! Loving is a contract! They've broken the contract! I don't love them much any more. They've forfeited it!"

She tries to tell him what she wants to be true. Desperately she throws after him, "You do love them, Tony, you do." He does not look back and she, watching him cross the grass, feels like an outfielder way out who has thrown the ball hard to the second baseman who has already pivoted and missed the play.

"He tries, Jeanne. I guess adolescent boys are hard for fathers."

"Does Tony fight with Anthony?"

"They argue. The don't fist fight, if that's what you mean."

"That's good. Anthony seems very vulnerable. It would be too bad if he had to be physically afraid of his father."

"No, no. Tony withdraws mostly."

Turning the corner of the living room, Lynn sees the screaming pair falling toward the floor, sees Tony's contorted face as he wrestles Anthony down and pins him with his weight, sees Anthony wrenching himself trying frantically to escape.

"No, I don't want to kill you," Tony says, with a wild laugh. "I love you, you crazy kid. Do you think I'd bother if I didn't love you?"

"There've been a few times. Jon and Tony both have explosive tempers. They throw things — both of them. But with Anthony it's usually talking." Where was that scene? Lynn wonders. Why did it happen? Anthony had done something . . . torn up something . . . school books. That was it: he'd torn up his school book. Why did Tony have to knock him down? The words or the act — which should she tell Jeanne Tony meant? She heard the yelling and the thumping as they threw each other around the living room, and she ran from the kitchen where she was making dinner, ran to see, and then stood, not knowing what to do, what to say, where to put herself, and ended up back in the kitchen, making dinner. She doesn't tell Jeanne about that day.

She stands, looking out across the water, letting it hit her that she is telling about Tony all the time now, telling Jeanne, telling Julia, telling, telling, and that instead of being with Tony, talking and understanding with him, she is puzzling and explaining about him, trying herself to know about him. She could explain to anyone that he is wrong, show scene after framed scene to persuade anyone that he's no good: is he then no good? she wonders and it is like going under the big waves, smashing against the sand, and coming up, mouth full of sand and salty froth. "Enough," she says to Jeanne. "How is your world, old friend? Your turn to tell."

Leaving Jeanne at the airport, Tony pulls back on the parkway and heads for home. Lynn says, "I wish Jeanne lived closer."

Tony says, "She seems happy. When is your mother leaving?"

"Next week, probably."

"You might think about asking her to stay to watch Lori after school if you find work." He lights a cigarette with the lighter and seems to Lynn to focus on the task for a long time. "I want you to find a job."

"Oh?"

"I want you to be self-supporting." He continues deliberately, letting her know that he has thought it all through and has more to say. "I also want you to make your own social life. From now on, don't accept invitations for me. I'll make my own arrangements."

"What does that mean?"

"Just that."

"If we're invited to dinner what am I supposed to say? 'I'll come and I'll see if Tony is also free?' " Lynn laughs a dry laugh.

Lynn keeps words moving back to Tony the way she hits back table tennis balls; she can return and return almost any smash but she herself only wins a point when the opponent's ball goes wild. She cannot smash.

"Yes. Actually I don't care what you say. But don't make any plans for me. And don't make any commitments for me to other people."

"I really don't know what you're talking about."

"It's not so complicated. I told you I'll try but I'm not sure I'll make it."

Is this the subway scene again? Is he threatening to leap? She wavers, wanting to pull him back in her own arms, not wanting to lose her balance. Guilty at shying away, she says, "You won't go see a therapist?"

"No, I won't."

"That makes no sense."

"Therapy isn't everybody's God, Lynn. It's yours. It isn't mine."

As he says her name she feels they're in touch for a fraction of a second. It's gone before the sentence ends. She tries to answer. "It's not my God. But it does help."

"You."

Words move like waves back and forth, seeming to be invested with meaning as well as sound, and Lynn watches, listens, and knows the movement is illusion and underneath nothing moves, nothing goes from one of them to the other. Underneath is a vast dark expanse of water that separates them and that holds each under a silent weight. Syllables go from each like bubbles that rise to the surface and burst, leaving little rings of froth to drift away. It's hard to breathe under the pressure, sunken there: Lynn opens the passenger window wide and leans her head slightly out to take the air full tilt.

As though the sprockets have ripped the film, Lynn watches scene after jerking scene. Tony drops her at the train station and keeps the car. In the city she fills in form after form. She looks at the interviewer and knows it's useless. Too old, too slow, too out of touch. Her clothes are wrong, her hair is wrong, her voice is wrong. Her experience is wrong. She's written but not published enough. She's taught but not for pay. She's organized but without a position. Everything she has ever done, she discovers, doesn't count.

Nearing home, she wonders if Jon cut out of school again; she sees him in a hazy room, sharing a joint, practicing with his group. She wonders if Lori will miss the bus again and need a ride, if Anthony, off at a demonstration, is all right, or is coughing his way through tear gas, or worse, lying at the edge of a street with a concussion from a policeman's club. She knows Christy will come home as usual and move through the house carefully, step by bent over step, the way a tall person enters a room in mid-film showing, trying not to break the projector's beam.

Lynn dozes, then looks out through the dirt-glazed train window at the lined-up cars, each with a woman at the wheel, waiting for men to come back after working in the city. She half-dozes again, wondering which station this is, which Tony is meeting her or she is meeting, home from which conference at which campus. Tony with the angry face denouncing old Professor Cullers? Tony with the snide smile putting down old Esterbrook? Tony with the eager face, praising Professor Malloy before they moved to the new campus where Tony joined Malloy's department, or Tony later, mocking Malloy as he had before mocked all the others?

The train's movement carries Lynn through time to Tony's youngest face, nostalgic and eager, telling her about his relatives as he took her to his home for the first time. His mother sat in the center of the living room: ornate vases, a sofa with lace doilies on its back and arms, a carpet with rust and orange flowers against dark green; his mother a cross between Picasso's Gertrude Stein and the traditional Japanese woman with fan, holding her fancy cup; Lynn with a walk-on part moving toward her, moving away, knowing herself assessed and dismissed in the same moment. Later Lynn thought, there was no fan, we must have spoken. But in her actual memory no words were exchanged; there was only a flashing on-stage encounter, silent and severe, with Tony, observant, as the only audience.

As though his mother then, and later when she cursed the marriage, sprayed them with a thick veneer of plastic, they never made contact with his old community. Before they lived near his mother, Tony's face lit up when he told Lynn stories of his childhood. While they lived there however, they were estranged from all the relatives. Because Tony wouldn't go near the Church? Because his mother's friends dropped by for tea and found Lynn playing with Anthony on the floor in an untidy house? Only after they'd moved on to the next campus, when they returned for a visit, only then did Tony take the children to his old uncle's store, let the nostalgia in his voice match the smile on his face in the presence of the old man who held out candy to the kids, smiling and calling to his wife that Tony and his fine young family must come home with them for dinner that very day.

Lynn lifts her head from the sleepy blur of towns, the one with the walk along the river, the one with the park with the caged raccoons, to see this present train station, in this last town where they live in this most recent house, near this most recent campus.

The car is there, and getting in, she watches this Tony's face as he asks her, with a deprecatory laugh, "Get a job?"

"No," she says, "not quite."

It is as though this is the relief he needed. "Too bad," he says, smiling, pulling into traffic.

"I'm going back to school to be a teacher," she says.

"You always said you never would."

Lynn doesn't answer that out loud. To herself she thinks, 'And thought I never would, never would, never would, with the rhythm of the train she has just left.

9

Lynn looks up from baking cookies. The decorated windows of the kitchen are steamed up from the spaghetti boiling on the stove. Christmas carols are blasting from the stereo. The car has just pulled into the driveway. Jon gets out and begins to untie the tree from the top of the car. Christy and Lori get out to watch. Tony is giving Jon directions Lynn can't hear, but Jon is not obeying. They move toward the house and through the living room, voices rising.

The tension is like some airborne fungus choking light and muffling sound. Lynn wishes guests would arrive: they bring quick talk or jokes to hold in front of them like machetes to chop their way in and out. She thinks, we just push aside the heaviness like jungle vines that spring back into place.

"You're going to break the bottom branches, Jon!" Tony says. "Turn it around!"

"It's already in!" Jon says, setting it upright in the living room. "Which way do you want it?"

"It's a beautiful tree," Lynn says, wiping her hands on a towel.

"We'll have to cut off the top," Tony says. "Get the saw, Jon."

"Why, Daddy?" Christy is taking ornaments out of the big carton.

"It won't fit is why. Remember the year we had the giant pine?"

"That was the year we went on the sled to cut the tree," Jon says.

"Me too?" Lori asks.

"No," Jon says, "you weren't born yet. Christy was little."

"And your mother made gingerbread men for every kid in town," Tony says, laughing, looking toward Lynn.

It is like an invitation to the dance, Lynn thinks. "Remember when Daddy made the cradle for your dolls?"

"Let's sing carols," Christy says.

Lynn turns off the stereo and says, "You start."

"Where's Anthony? He has to sing, too. Anthony!" Christy goes toward his bedroom.

"Never mind Anthony," Lynn says, but she knows it is already slipping. As though she has in her hands a lifesize glass globe with all of them within it, and snow falling as they shake it, as they sing, as they ride a sleigh with bells jingling and horses tossing their festooned manes, and her hands cannot hold it, cannot keep it from falling, she watches the whole scene crash.

"That's the wrong saw, Jon."

"Daddy, Anthony won't come. Make him come."

"Don't try to hang that there, Lori!"

Smash! "Christ, Lori, now look what you broke. That was one of the most beautiful ones, clear from Mommy and Daddy's first Christmas, wasn't it, Mom?" And Lori running crying from the room and Tony taking the saw from Jon who stomps toward his room as Lynn smells burnt cookies and hears Anthony intoning, "Ho Ho Ho Chi Minh" and Tony shouting, "Shut up, Anthony!" as Christy tries to start up "Silent Night."

Lynn stands at the sideboard with Christy. "Here are the place cards," she says, "put them around."

"Should I put Uncle Billy next to Daddy or next to Gramma?"

"Next to Gramma, I think."

"Mommy, what was Christmas like when you were little?"

"We lived on the farm, you know. There was lots of cooking and we got a tree from our woods and we sang carols and it was like this," Lynn pauses, "but not so many presents."

Going into the kitchen to check the turkey, Lynn hears

her own voice go on. It is like a tape she has put on, that does not connect with any human voice.

What if, she thinks, at table I were to say, "Hey, Billy, remember how you used to fuck me all the time?" Would they laugh? Would everyone go on reminiscing about the good old days when people were poor but cared for one another? What if I said, "I'm going to sue you, Billy?" Why not? she thinks, smiling her non-smile smile; someday some woman *will* sue her stepfather or uncle or brother or whoever it was that stalked her day and night. "Get the napkins on, Christy? Then you can pour the milk."

Lynn sets more hot rolls and more dressing on the table, and turns back to the kitchen for more milk. "Hey, Thing, while you're out there, fetch us some more wine," Billy says.

From the kitchen Lynn hears the old exchange begin. "Remember when Lynnanne asked what a dumbwaiter was and you said, 'You are'?" their mother asks.

The laughter starts and she goes on. "And the cat's stomach?" Billy guffaws and one of the cousins asks what the story is.

Lynn, walking back in, feels her face produce a smile. "They called me 'The Thing,' " she says, accusingly, to no one in particular, and the people at the table do not respond.

Her mother is speaking to Tony and Billy, with everyone listening, ready to laugh again. "One night they were teasing her at dinner and she told me to let her eat in her room or she'd get a cat's stomach." Everyone laughs and Billy holds up his glass for more wine.

"What I said was," Lynn says, speaking to the children, filling wine glasses as she talks, "that scientists had discovered if a cat is surrounded by barking dogs while she eats, her stomach reacts and she gets an ulcer."

"Did the little cat get an ulcer?" her mother asks, laughing.

"No, I didn't get an ulcer," Lynn says, and knows there is a smile on her face.

"She was spoiled rotten! Tony, it's remarkable how you've

straightened her out," Billy says, grinning broadly down the table.

"Remember all the dolls you had?" Her mother looks at Lynn now with an imploring look. "Every Christmas poor Agnes brought you another doll."

'Poor,' Lynn knows, because Aunt Agnes is now dead and never had any children. She brought them toys and cakes and once an ice cream cake for Lynnanne's birthday and once some goslings and once a baby goat. "I remember," Lynn says to her mother.

"*I* remember," Billy says, "how her room was stuffed with toys and how she got away with murder."

"The boys," her mother says to Tony, "didn't think I was strict enough with her."

"Strict? She had her meals in her room like royalty." Billy tips up his glass and reaches for the bottle.

Lynn, listening to them talk about her as if she were not there, continues to put food on children's plates, to carry dishes to the kitchen, to fix dessert. She checks the clock, planning to wrap presents as soon as she's done the dishes, planning to set the dough for Chirstmas morning rolls before she wraps the presents. She remembers retreating to her room. That was in the narrow house, after the war, and she could not swallow when she sat with them.

"Lynn, aren't you going to sit still one minute? It's Christmas Eve, you know." Her mother follows her into the kitchen, smiling sadly at her.

"I've got a lot to do tonight, that's all."

"I know. I wish I could help. It's been just wonderful to be here, you know."

Lynn holds her voice even. "I'm glad you could come."

"It's nice at Billy's too. Di is sweet. It's just never the same as with your own daughter." Her mother's face is melancholy brave.

"I wish things had been calmer for you here," Lynn says. "Next year will be better. Anthony will be doing something by then."

"He's happier, I think, than he was last year," her mother says.

"Lots," Lynn says.

"Well, I just won't think about leaving," her mother says, with tears in her eyes for a moment.

Lynn remembers the rabbits, skinned, their hides stretched to dry, that Billy strung up around the shop when he was seventeen. Her mother goes back into the dining room. My mother's been here six months, Lynn thinks, pouring herself more wine. She'll be here again six months next year. Six months is enough, she thinks. I have a right. She is quoting Julia's words to herself, invoking Julia's certain voice. From the other room she hears her mother, "Jon, are you going to play carols on your guitar? Tomorrow night I'll be gone, you know."

Scraped dry, pulled taut, the rabbit hides' hairs quivered in the wind.

Tony is in bed. It is one a.m. Lynn is sitting on the floor of their bedroom wrapping the last gifts.

"About through?" Tony asks.

"Almost."

"Who's going to watch Lori when your mother's gone?"

"I'll get a sitter if the other kids aren't home."

"I don't want her left alone with Anthony."

"What?"

"You heard it. I don't want Anthony affecting her any more than I can help."

"Anthony is very sweet with her and totally protective."

"He thoroughly brainwashes her."

"Anyhow, it shouldn't be a problem. I don't have classes that late most days. When I have an evening class, Christy will sit."

"Just be careful about using Anthony."

Lynn lifts the presents in her arms and starts out the door. "We need air," she says. "We are all crowded in too close, too tight. That's one of the problems. It'll be better when I get a teaching job."

"You're already gone too much," he says.

"Graduate school takes time, remember?"

"You could've done something easier."

"Like what?"

"Like take in typing or sell by phone from home."

She laughs and turns to go. Glancing back at him, she realizes that he is serious.

"To distance is to kill," he says.

"We need air."

He does not answer. She stands, one foot in the familiar house where it has always been and one foot lifted toward a great ship which sails in a world outside. She feels the reverberations of the ship's engines on the sole of her foot as she starts to board. The foot still holding to the house falters. Lynn feels her balance hover above deep waters, strange and cold.

She watches Tony turn in bed, pull the covers around his shoulders, and settle toward sleep. As always on Christmas Eve, she is making sure that everyone there will wake up to find whatever he or she most wants beneath the tree. She leaves to finish wrapping presents.

The house is very quiet. Lynn arranges the last presents underneath the tree. She takes down the stockings and fills them with candy canes, nuts, chocolate Santas, little toys, joke gifts for the older kids. She hangs them up again just where they were.

She sits then in the completed scene. The only lights are the colored ones among the branches of the tree. Outside snow is falling. She didn't notice it begin.

Everything is done. Everything is right. Everyone is sleeping, safe in bed. The dog guards the front door. The cat is by the hearth. Cards from their friends hang on the fireplace. Lynn stares at the stockings, the tree, lights, tinsel, and through the lights and tinsel and fir boughs at the snow beautifully whitening the darkness of the night. She looks at all this as she has looked at it every Christmas Eve for the nineteen years since she and Tony were married. She waits for that special peace and happiness to fill her, to rise in her with its special mystery and delight. She stares and waits and staring, knows that it is not happening at all. Every component is there, but her stare goes through and on into the night, as though nothing is apprehended by her vision, as though she stares through a facade, a cheap storefront display that barely registers peripherally.

She chants to herself: Tony, Anthony, Jon, Christy, Lori: Lori, Christy, Jon, Anthony, Tony. The snow is beautiful, she adds: the tree against the snow, the silence of the falling snow, the quiet of the house.

Somewhere beyond her vision, where her gaze is not locked into this sightless stare, she thinks there are Christmas scenes that she would like to have again. She names them to herself: the magical turning of the figures on the music box under our first tree; Tony's hair covered with snow in the quarter snapshot booth . . . Anthony on his first trike next to Jon in the fire engine; the little golden trumpet . . . Christy snuggling her big doll, everyone singing "Jingle bells, jingle bells, jingle bells . . ." Lori's face this year seeing Santa Claus, not sure but not yet certainly unsure . . .

. . . The smell of fir and cedar branches hung along the frieze in the living room on the farm, the cinnamon and nutmeg smell of my mother's baking, the frothy sweetness of candy boiling up. the stocking full . . . the red wagon brought home on top of Aunt Agnes' car with Daddy saying it's a new machine for milking . . .

. . . The sleigh bells before dawn louder louder louder while I held still not to be known to be awake, listening as Santa came close and then went farther far far far and then the silence once again, so in the morning when I saw the presents, saw the stockings filled, I remembered again the darkness before dawn and the wonder of the clear and distant ringing of the bells.

Lynn catalogues back to the beginning when her father rang the sleigh bells in the night, when she was four, to this afternoon when she saw Lori sneak the presents she made at school for Tony and herself underneath the tree. Lynn catalogues and waits to be persuaded.

Failing this, she thinks of joining Tony, of crawling in with her Chirstmas-Eve-successfully-arranged-fatigue, it being three a.m., and feeling his familiar body warm and close. She thinks of whispering, "Merry Christmas, Tony," and turning to give him a special kiss, wanting from him a special Christmas love.

Lynn stays a long time in the living room, staring out the window at the falling snow. At last she rises, unplugs the Christmas lights, and goes slowly up the stairs to go to sleep. She looks back once from halfway up the stairway. She sees exactly what a camera would see: a living room, a window, a decorated tree.

Likely, she thinks, it will go on snowing until dawn. Suddenly exhausted, she does not take off her robe when she goes into the bedroom. Lying down, she thinks that there was something else she meant to do. In a minute, she thinks, she will remember, or someone will call and she will swing out of bed and go to handle it, whatever that last detail was that will ensure that Christmas morning everything will be right for everyone.

PART II

10

The morning sun, still low above the horizon, spears across the beach. Lynn stares into Ruth's hazel eyes and it is as though they move together along the wind cooled path across these dunes and blowing grasses toward evergreens and fern, and do not turn back. "How come I always have to look into the sun to look at you?" Lynn asks, leaning on her elbow in the sand.

"Again?" Ruth laughs; her short black hair blows around her face. Their hands are touching.

"Yes, again."

"Want to walk?"

"No, don't move. Not yet."

"Lynn, what is with us?" Ruth's eyes darken. She frowns and falls on her back on the sand.

"Like what?"

"Every morning I can't wait to see you. What's happening to us?"

"We're friends."

"Not like any friends I've ever had before."

Two fishermen in high hip boots walk past them, carrying poles and buckets. Ruth pulls her hand away from Lynn's until they've passed.

Lynn looks across the water for a moment, then back at Ruth. "Do you want to spend less time together?"

"That's the trouble. No, I don't." Ruth leaps up and runs along the beach.

Lynn stands and jogs after her. She feels as if she could run forever on that sand in that sunlight with Ruth.

"We're headed for trouble, Lynn." Ruth twirls to confront her.

"Look," Lynn waves at the beach, gulls, sky. "What trouble?"

"I don't know," Ruth smiles reluctantly and they walk together, hands brushing, toward the car.

Lynn sits at a table in the University Library. It's between classes in the afternoon. Every morning she practice-teaches in a high school an hour from home. Christy gets Lori and herself off to school; Jon takes care of himself and Anthony sleeps late, then goes to a part-time job in a pizza parlor. Lynn drops Tony at the campus on her way to the high school. Later she goes back to campus; after her last class they go home together. She doodles a list in the margin of her notes: supermarket, cook dinner, clean up, pack lunches, have coffee with Tony; give Jon a ride to his friend's and Christy a ride to chorus; grade a set of papers; plan classes for the next day; put Lori to bed; and at ten o'clock, Ruth. She tries to read the text but finds she is scribbling Ruth's name in the margin of her notes. She fights off her feeling for a while and then takes out a sheet of paper and her pen to write a poem to Ruth.

She soars, glides, sky-dives. What courses through her goes directly to the page. She balances in space, spinning earthward, pulling out of the dive and following the air currents up toward the sun to break into serene flight, and then levelling out to let her breath return, let the rush of blood catch up with her heart, pounding, her dizzied vision of the whitening sky.

"For Ruth, with love," she writes and signs. Then she tucks the paper in her purse and heads for her next class, the excitement of the poem palpably around her as she walks.

In the narrow house no one ever speaks about her father. There are no pictures of him around the house nor on her mother's bureau. Lynnanne has a small snapshot of him in her room.

Lynnanne lives somewhere between the trees on the farm and her school. She walks the three straight blocks to school and home again like an ant on a well worn path. She does not know how to go any other place.

At night she hunches up her legs and fights off beasts, sweats her way through long dream-vines and screaming, runs, while hordes of sharpwinged highscreaming bats dive down at her.

At first the teacher frightens her. She is small and dark and darts about the room, her quick voice striking out at random. The playground is concrete with iron fences all around it. At recess she leans against the building waiting for the bell. A blond girl with curls says to another girl with braids, "I'm going to see John. Want to come, Lynnanne?"

"Who's John?" she asks, and they both howl with laughter and run away to tell the others among whose giggles Lynnanne drowns.

The teacher throws words and numbers to her and she fastens herself to them and floats. "I'm sending you to the junior high in January. You're too smart to sit around here any longer," Miss Dahlquist says, abruptly, one day during math.

"That certainly speaks well for the teachers in your old country school," her mother says.

In January, Miss Dahlquist asks the class to write letters. "Write me a real letter about this year," she says. "Tell me the truth."

Lynnanne sits, straight pen in hand, ink open in the well, remembering how she was at first afraid of this quick woman, and then how she came to be eager for the words Miss Dahlquist flung toward her. Lynnanne walked the rungs of what she understood, word after word, number after number. When she slipped, going from rung to rung, she hung over the swirling space below where creatures clawed up at her and nothingness absorbed her falling body in that unreal sphere where her brothers always lurked, a menace that could not be named to anyone.

Lynnanne writes of her first shyness and fear and then she writes, "And now I'm not afraid of you and I don't know why I ever was. Now I love you and I always will."

She slides the letter under the classroom door after school, afraid to be there when the teacher reads it.

The next day the teacher thanks her for the letter and takes her out into the hall to ask her why she ever was afraid. Face to face, close enough to touch, Lynnanne can neither think nor speak. She panics and is still.

On the farm Lynnanne watched her father slit the bark of an apple tree until it lay gaping, bleeding sap. Then he took a branch of another tree, also fresh cut, and held it to the first. He soothed the wound with grafting wax and bound it up. That, he told her, would make something new begin to grow, something that had never been before.

Watching her teacher's eyes, Lynnanne knows the letter is like that, her own words are like that; she herself wrote words that are between the other and herself like the grafting was for apple trees. She has the power to put on paper words that slash and heal, letting new sap run free so that new trees may grow.

"But that can be said of any of us, can't it?" Neil, Ruth's husband, asks rhetorically of the people at the table. Someone has just suggested that Blacks have had obstacles to learning.

Ruth is serving soup. "No," she retorts, "it can't. We've had a tradition of learning in spite of obstacles. That's quite different."

Lynn watches her quick sure movements as she serves, watches her face flush with the argument.

"But Ruth, you can't mean that we haven't, most of us, overcome obstacles!" Neil looks as though she has interrupted him and he is pausing to correct her before going on.

"No, she doesn't mean that!" Lynn leaps to her defense. "She means that historically most of us came from traditions that not only allow learning but encourage it to the hilt; we've had language and ideas since we were born. Blacks weren't legally allowed to read or write — to learn was a crime! — and they were deliberately separated from others of the same tribe to kill language and religion and communication!"

The men look at Lynn indulgently. "We're not forgetting that," Tony says, "but how much mileage can they get out of it? It's been a hundred years. Besides, we're talking about lowering the standard of higher learning altogether when we talk about open admissions. We're not talking about restricting *access* to Blacks, only about making them come up to standards. What good does it do them if you just pretend they're getting a higher education?"

Ruth disappears into the kitchen for more soup and Neil nods and takes it up. "Exactly. We'll have incompetent surgeons killing us all off if we don't require genuine intelligence and learning."

Lynn, focusing on Ruth, hears her answering a phone call in the kitchen. Ruth's tone alerts Lynn and she slides out of her chair to go see. "We're not saying to do away with qualifying examinations, Neil, we're only saying to make exceptions for entrance to people who've been deprived," Lynn says, moving away from the table.

"And where do you stop? Where is your argument taking you?"

"To get the soup!" Lynn laughs and enters the kitchen.

Ruth's face is white. Lynn puts her hand on her shoulder silently, waiting to hear. "It's Nate. He's hurt. He's unconscious. They're not sure what happened." Ruth puts her hand in Lynn's for a long moment. Then she goes to the living room.

Ruth stands by Neil and the table quiets as she speaks. "Nate's in the hospital."

Neil is on his feet. He grabs Ruth's thin arms as if to hurry the information out of her by shaking her. "What happened?"

"He fell wrong going over the hurdle. They're not sure."

"Leg?" Neil pounds at her. "Back? Ruth, what's broken?"

"They don't know yet, Neil. They just got him out of X-ray. Let's go." Ruth turns toward the door, turns back, scans the people in the room. "I'm sorry. Go on eating."

There is a murmur of concerned dissent. Neil echoes her,

"Yes, eat. Just make yourselves at home. Is he conscious?"
Ruth, in the open doorway, throws back, "No, he's not.
Let's go."

Tony comes around the table and puts his arm around
Lynn's shoulders, "He'll be all right, Lynn. Don't worry.
Remember when Jon fell off the roof and we thought he'd
broken everything and it turned out a nose bleed was the only
thing wrong with him?"

People laugh nervously and begin to tell stories about their
children's near disasters. "Ruth would really hate her cooking
to go to waste," an old friend says, and everyone nods and
begins to eat.

Lynn watches Tony pouring wine and laughing and thinks
how good it feels to be all together like this, depending on each
other for comfort when it's needed, best friends. She goes to
serve the rest of the dinner, knowing it's too soon for Ruth to
call.

During dinner they are alert, expecting news. Neil phones
just before dessert. Lynn takes the call. "He's conscious now.
He'll be all right. He tore a ligament and they think that's all."

"That's wonderful!" Lynn feels relief surge through her
body as she goes to tell the news.

"Neil's coming home," she says. "Ruth's staying there a
while."

Later, on their way home, Lynn says, "If you don't mind,
I think I'll go by the hospital and make sure Nate's okay."

"He's fine; Neil said it's just a ligament. I'm really beat,
Lynn; let's go home."

"You don't have to go, Tony. I'd feel better if I knew."

"Go ahead then." Lynn feels the anger between them in
the car. "You can never quit, can you? Nothing's ever enough
for you."

"What do you mean?" she asks. But she knows what he
means. And she knows that she does not want to quit, that it
is not enough, until she can see Ruth's face at peace, can know
that she is all right.

11

As though she whirls in the center of a rock tumbling chamber, Lynn cooks, serves, clears, washes, phones, and maneuvers to prevent collisions through the dinner hour. When Anthony has left for a strategy session for the next march and Jon has been dropped off to practice with friends, Christy goes to her room to study, and Lori finishes her bath. Lynn feels the tumbler decelerate.

"Shall we walk around the block?" Tony asks.

"Sure," she answers, and tells Lori she'll read to her when she comes back.

Lynn puts her hand on Tony's arm as they walk. The lawns are still winter flat and the trees are not yet caught in a sheen of green although she can see buds swelling if she looks at the branches carefully. Her hand feels distant from herself, resting on his arm. The dog runs ahead. Probably Pal is as worried as any of us are about the jagged vibes that fill the house, Lynn thinks. Do dogs fake contentment? Lynn studies the houses that they pass. In every house a woman who watches the kids; in every house a man who comes home to dinner. In every house a woman straining to make it work?

"I don't want to go to dinner at the Zellman's Saturday night," Tony says.

"I told them we'd come."

"So tell them we can't. You can go alone; I don't care."

The dog looks back over her shoulder to see if they are following. A neighbor loads his kids into his car and drives away. Lynn bends to pick a blade of grass as an excuse to take her hand from Tony's arm. "You have to work on the linguistics article next weekend?"

"Yes. I'm reading galleys for my *MLA* article tonight and tomorrow night and that puts me behind – we have a long meeting tomorrow afternoon." His voice becomes strident and he walks faster as they turn into their driveway. "See you later." He heads for the car.

"Work well," she says. "I won't call the Zellmans until tomorrow night – think it over." She stands watching the car pull out, feeling a certain relief, as though all the machinery has shut down now and she can allow herself to be off duty. Lynn goes to read to Lori.

After the book Lynn kisses the child goodnight and starts out of her room. "Mommy, my throat hurts."

"Oh? Want a drink?"

"Umhm."

Back with the drink, Lynn again says goodnight.

"I think I have a temperature, Mommy. If I have a temperature, do I have to go to school?"

"No. But I don't think you do. Now you go to sleep. I'll put on a record for you – want *Sound of Music*?"

"Yes. But I want you to take my temperature."

Lynn fights off the rising urgency. "Okay, I will." Shaking down the thermometer she hears the quiet opening of the front door downstairs. Ruth, she knows. All the patience of the day is gone. "Three minutes and that's it, Lori. Leave it on the table – I'll check it later."

"No, I want to know tonight." Lori's voice begins to rise.

Not a fight at bedtime or she'll never go to sleep, Lynn thinks, and reining her whole body in, she answers, "Okay, I'll wait." She turns on the record player and stands by the window studying the branches of the nearest maple; the buds bulge with hidden green.

"Okay, let's see. Normal. Absolutely normal. Now sleep well." Lynn pulls the blanket up around the child's shoulders, puts her teddy bear next to her, and kisses her again.

Lynn holds herself back from running down the stairs and goes with a deliberate step. She finds Ruth standing at the bookcase. She wears jeans and a dark shirt; seeing her, Lynn can for a moment neither move nor speak. Then she says, "Hello."

Ruth pivots to face her. "Hello, hello," Ruth whispers. They walk, holding hands, to the sofa where they sit close to one another.

"It's a beautiful poem," Lynn says, meaning the one that was in the mailbox in the afternoon.

"Do you think it works?"

"Yes. Let's look at it." Ruth opens her notebook and hands the whole thing to Lynn, who turns the pages gently, reading a few lines here and there. "You've written a lot of poems in the past three months — you know that?"

"Yes. Crazy, isn't it?"

"Why?"

"I'm not a poet . . ." Ruth shrugs.

"You write good poems!" Lynn smiles at her.

"It's a passing aberration."

Lynn stops to reread a poem:

The Boarder

The Yellow-Star-Law decreed:
he moved into our house
one day
into the back room—
Mother complained:
the smell of sardines,
how he seldom bathed—
yet she was somehow glad
he was there

And I, the child
loved the crown of his tousled gray hair,
jealous of the beautiful children
who left him to me.

He spoke to us of Historic Cycles,
and far China's ultimate rise

when "It" was over—
we talked of our promised land, America.
His knowing gray eyes, however
spoke of Death
while Mother divided our rations
pretending normalcy.

When sirens wailed
and incongruous bombs
fell around us
we sat in the darkened hall
away from the windows.
Mother fussed and paced.

But he and I sat huddled:
his stories of Greek gods and heroes,
of wonderful beasts
and snatches of Mozart operas
spun their loving cocoon
around my fright—
and I slept.

No one is left
to tell me
whether he held
in his protecting arms
another strange child
in terror
as cyanide gas filled the showers.

Lynn tightens her hold on Ruth's hand and is silent for a
while. "I can't get over this one. It's a very powerful poem —
you know that?"
"I don't know."
"It is."
Ruth goes to the stereo and puts on a Mozart Quintet.
She stands there as Lynn continues reading.
"Do you want coffee or wine or something?" Lynn looks
up at her back.

Ruth shakes her head. Then she turns to face her. "I've lost ten pounds this month." It's a matter-of-fact statement.

"How come?"

"I can't eat."

"That's the effect I have on you? Could we reverse roles?" They both laugh but Lynn is laying this new information beside what she already knows of Ruth; she ponders. "Is it because you're writing and talking about all this?" Lynn waves at the poems, meaning Germany, Nazis, her moves from house to house and finally her escape, the roundups, the death of those who stayed.

"I don't think so. No." Ruth walks toward her and sits down again. "I think it's knowing you."

"Well thanks." Lynn laughs. "I'm getting you tea and toast."

"No, I don't need anything."

"Humor me, hmm?" Lynn goes to the kitchen, and has in her mind a collage of the child Ruth, standing at an apartment window, staring down at soldiers in the street, straining to leap the hurdles in gym as the Nazi teacher motions the class through its routines, locked in the sealed train without food, stomach cramping from fear and hunger meshed into one spasm. She takes the tea and toast to her and sits close to her again, wanting to shelter that child, keep her from everything that hurt and frightened her. "How did you come through so beautifully?" she asks.

"I just came through."

"You're very beautiful," Lynn says.

Ruth sets down her tea. "Stop," she says. "It's hard enough to eat."

Lynn smiles and reads silently while Ruth eats. The first poem in the notebook is about a round-up. Fear hangs from the leaves of the trees, sputters up from the scuffed dust of the street.

Ruth interrupts her reading. "How did *you* come through what happened to you?"

"Me?"

"Yes, you. Those stories about your childhood are devastating."

"Nobody tried to kill me," Lynn says.

"Maybe worse what they did to you."

"No."

"I used to feel guilty about being alive," Ruth says, quietly.

"I think everyone who got out alive must have," Lynn answers.

"Why me? You know. Once I tried to kill myself. Maybe just because I couldn't figure out why I should live when they all died."

"God."

"It's all right. I didn't do a very thorough job." Ruth laughs. "I was twenty − it probably had nothing to do with the war. Everybody gets suicidal at twenty, don't they? I calmed down and got married."

"Did you talk to Neil a lot about it?"

"Neil?"

"Yes, you remember − the one you married." They laugh.

"No. Neil never asked. Whenever the kids asked about Germany during the war he gave them a lecture. He tends to think he knows more than anybody else about things."

"I see."

"Actually you're the first one to ask me who I am."

"Then it's high time," Lynn says, and they sit again in silence until the quintet ends.

Lynn puts on another record and sits again with Ruth. These bands of time separate day from night and night from day. On weekend mornings they meet at dawn to walk the beaches and the woods. School nights they meet in the late evening to read one another's writing and to talk. Like the strip of metal that unwinds around the key on coffee cans these bands of time exist, pulled from the fabric of their ordinary days. These bands curl tight around them, then swirl them away into one another's lives, both past and present.

"When did we start holding hands?" Ruth asks.

"I don't know. The first night we read poems, I think."

"Let me see what you wrote today, Lynn."

Lynn slides her poem into Ruth's hand and waits, serious, for her response. Nothing that happens between them is without impact. Their shared astonishment at this is part of their frequent and intent looking into one another's eyes.

The back door clicks shut and they yank their hands apart. Ruth's face is sharply questioning.

"Tony," Lynn says. "Jon came home a while ago and Anthony wouldn't be home this soon. Tony'll go right to bed."

"And you'd better go right with him," Ruth says, snapping shut her notebook.

Lynn stands and goes into the kitchen where Tony is pouring himself a drink. "Ruth and I have been working; want to join us for a nightcap?"

"No thanks," he says, and starts for the stairway. "I have an early lecture in the morning."

"I'll be up soon," Lynn says to his back.

"Good night, Ruth," he calls down from halfway up.

"Good night," she answers.

Lynn pours two glasses of wine and goes back into the living room. "No, I'm leaving," Ruth says, her voice brisk.

"No, wait a minute. You weren't ready to go yet."

"Dammit, you *belong* up there with him. *I'm* the intruder. I'll let myself out." Ruth wrenches away from Lynn's light touch on her arm.

"I don't want to go up there with him. He's already asleep."

They stand staring at one another, taut. "He'll leave you, Lynn."

For a moment their eyes lock. Lynn has always told her children, "Whatever your friends' parents do, *we* will never get divorced." That certitude has wrapped the years around itself and has become the pearl that she has always pointed to with pride: "I have a good marriage," she said to Julia at the first session.

"Remember how you told me you couldn't spend time with me on weekends or much otherwise because your family takes all your time?" Ruth challenges her, turning toward the door. "He will, he'll leave you, and that's not what you want."

Like a comet the possibility: Tony might leave her. Lynn sees the streak and then the sky is dark as it was before with its usual stars and moon.

"No, he won't."

Between the day's demands that are great agitated ocean waves, and the calm inlet that she shares with Ruth there is a sucking riptide; for a moment Lynn is torn from the air, whirled into darkness, water plunging down her throat.

Lynn knows she will not relinquish Ruth.

"It's all right. Tonight he's tired. When he wants me, I'll be there. I'll go up and say good night if you want me to. But you stay — tomorrow night you can't even come over, remember?" By the time she finishes the speech Lynn herself believes what she is saying and her voice is steady, sensible. I'll be right down."

"You have to know for yourself," Ruth says, and yields, walks back to put on another record.

12

"The whole class wrote about the weekend. Friday night the terrible five got drunk and they dragged bushes into the middle of the parkway and set fire to them and hid to see what cars coming up fast would do! I'm reading this to the class and Andy is standing on the window ledge ready to jump!" Lynn is dropping lasagna into boiling water as she talks. "I didn't know if he was on something or not . . ."

"I don't want to hear about them," Tony says, taking the drink he has just poured and leaving the kitchen.

So what do you want to hear? Lynn wonders, making salad, what do you want to hear? I used to save everything to tell you. When Anthony was little I used to put him in the stroller and meet you every day or wait on the porch if it was rainy.

Miss M. is going down the porch steps, having come to visit on her way home from school. She has brought a sweater that she knit for Anthony and a new Camus novel for Lynn.

"He's a happy baby," Lynn says to her.

"He should be — he's got the most brilliant woman in the state all to himself all day," Miss M. answers. The smile she turns away with is a rueful smile. Lynn holds the baby close against her breast and smiles back.

But then I didn't notice her smile, Lynn thinks. Only now.

Only now I understand her words. Then Anthony and Tony
blocked out the sun for me, held so close, so tight, I couldn't
see any world beyond them, like hands up close against the eyes
block out all light.

So what will I talk about at dinner? And does it matter?
"Suppertime," she calls.

Watching Tony chew, her food is like barium. She does not
dare x-ray her unwilling body as she listens, swallows the chalk
lasagna silently, and clears the table.

The school counselor looks carefuly at Tony. "And what
about yourself? You're a professor. Would you say you always
think it through before you act?"

Tony laughs expansively. "No, I'm not a rigid academic,"
he says. "I fly off the handle sometimes myself."

"Ever throw anything?"

Tony laughs again. A note of pride enters his voice. "Occasionally I have," he says.

The counselor pauses, looking from Tony to Jon and back
again to Tony. "You tell me Jon flies off the handle and throws
things and you yourself do the same thing but when you talk
about yourself you laugh it off and when you talk about Jon
you consider it a heavy offense. How come?"

Tony frowns, then laughs, caught out. Lynn sneaks a look
at Jon and sees his relief. I never thought of that, she thinks,
and feels a wave of gratitude for this young man.

"How many schools have you been in?" he asks Jon.

"Six," Jon answers.

"That's a lot of adjusting to ask of anyone," the counselor
says. "Jon has shown remarkable ability to handle new situa-
tions and to control himself. You folks have one of those self-
contained nuclear families — that makes it hard for kids. Do
you have strong family ties?"

"Yes, but they're far away," Tony answers.

The counselor nods. A self-contained nuclear family? Lynn
has always thought of her family as thoroughly attached to
friendships and relatives but as he says it, she recognizes that
they do not have any strong family ties except for her own

mother who stays many months each year with them; Tony doesn't think they have strong ties either but it sounds better to say we do, she thinks. 'I care not seems,' she thinks, where is that line from? No, 'I know not seems.' And they are smiling and shaking hands and thanking one another and leaving the building as Jon disappears into the halls away from them.

Hamlet, of course, she thinks, walking to the car. Everything always comes from *Hamlet*, someone once said at a cocktail party, and that isn't so, but lots of things do. We were never cocktail party people though. Faculty dinners, yes. And a network of friendships. We did both shuck off our families.

"Now we've played 'Let's Get Daddy,' what's left? Tonight he'll get together with Anthony and learn to make bombs. I just hope when he throws one, it hits that nincompoop!" Tony says, pulling out of the high school parking lot.

Lynn moves as on a multi-level bridge. On the top deck, open to sun and wind and the spring sky, Lynn and Ruth walk together. On the middle deck Lynn is wedged in among heavy traffic. No one in the long lines of cars notices her tension as she runs the house, attends classes, student teaches, entertains.

On the bottom deck, closed in with Tony, movements are ponderous or random. "I'm going to Chicago for the summer session. Want to come?" he asks.

"I don't think it makes sense to move the kids for a month."

"Six weeks. No. Maybe I'll take a job there. Or maybe you should come without the kids and we could agree to be totally free — you fuck around with anyone you want and I'll fuck around with anyone I want."

"That's not what I've ever wanted. Is that what you want?" Lynn watches him the way she'd watch a drunkard at the wheel.

"No — you're the one who wants more sex."

Thoughtfully Tony leans above her, head resting on his elbow, staring at her pubic hair. She, naked, lies watching him.

"They say," he says, moving one hand to touch her, to stroke her thigh, "that female genitalia have a particularly exotic taste." One of his hands pushes her thighs apart. "I read an article on it this week." He moves his body so he is sitting next to her, still looking down.

He has never kissed her below the waist. He has seldom put his hand below her waist. She watches him study her and does not know how to speak.

"It's too bad there's no way for you to sample it," he says, with a wry laugh.

Lynn lies still, waiting. He has set out to experiment. He moves the way a mechanic moves, sliding under the car at the right angle, arranging the naked bulb so it shines up correctly into the elevated engine where it waits for his wrench, his screw driver, his exploring fingers. He is more awkward than that. He moves, she thinks, like the young intern who assisted at one of her deliveries, who stared at her as the chief obstetrician lectured him, and waited to see what would happen, not knowing how to touch, where to put his gloved and sterile hands.

"I don't want to hurt you," Tony says, again leaning on his elbow above her.

"You won't hurt me," she answers, straining to keep a smile on her face.

From the beginning he has had two refrains: one, "I don't want to hurt you," and the other, "I'm sorry I'm taking so long." She moves uncomfortably inside her head now, hearing the lines as in a round, trying to escape the words, but her body does not move, her legs held as steady as if they were in stirrups, spread apart as he has placed them, quiet, as he leans, perusing her.

Tentatively he touches with his fingers the inside of her thighs, parting them so he can see as he lowers his head to her. Then like a frightened diver in a sudden spurt of daring he pushes his head against her legs, disappears under water. She doubts that he can breathe. His tongue is against her vagina, his head against her thighs. He burrows. He lifts his head at last, shaking the water off from the long time under, gulping in the air.

"I feel like I raped you," Tony says.

"Don't be silly," Lynn says, ruggedly holding to the smiling she is doing.

Tony stands, dispassionate, looking down at her, then turns and goes to the bathroom where she hears the water flowing to wash it all away.

Rape, she thinks. When they cornered me they always argued until they got their way. Worse than rape, that steady, chronic use. Rape is a single moment of attack.

Out of the bathroom, he walks uncertainly toward the bed. "Would you like me to do that again sometime?" Behind the casual voice his strain, his summoning of nerve, his fear, his sweating, down in the dark spread-eagled fear, surround her.

"I don't know," she says, standing up, "we'll see." Another focused frame slams into place.

13

One afternoon at Ruth's no one else is home. They've finished grading papers. "When will Neil get back?"

"Not until midnight. He's not leaving Washington until five or six. When do you have to go?"

"In time to cook dinner. But I can come back for a while about nine."

They sit on the sofa in the living room. Ruth smiles, bemused. "We've never stopped holding hands."

"I know."

"It feels so right. For you too?"

"Yes."

Ruth stands, goes to turn the record, walks across the room to a window and draws the drapes, comes back, draws the drapes on the window next to the sofa, sits again and folds Lynn into her arms.

Lynn expects it to be awkward. It is not. She and Ruth are holding one another and it feels right. Ruth is sitting on the sofa with her in her arms. Their upper arms, breasts, are against one another. Lynn holds very still.

Lynn looks up into Ruth's eyes and Ruth looks down at her. "I do love you, Lynn," Ruth says, softly. Gently, Ruth strokes Lynn's hair, arms, hair. Lynn closes her eyes and breathes slowly, with care, listening to the cello sonata.

"Hey, there, what's going on in that dream?"

Lynn, startled awake, walks about the room. "I don't know," she says, "something about a truck. Boys in a truck.

It was going to crash."

Ruth watches her intently. "You were frightened. Do I frighten you, Lynn?"

Lynn shakes her head. "No. No, you don't ever frighten me."

Driving home to cook dinner, Lynn knows that she is scared. Of what she doesn't know. She follows the parts of the dream like a trap line through thick woods.

The truck was the pickup truck her brother Marsh owned before the war, the one in which they moved everything to the city from the farm. She sees her mother circling through the house choosing what to take, what to leave. She sees her brothers carting box after box to the enormous bonfire in the backyard.

But why am I shaky now? Lynn wonders, cooking dinner, clearing up, laying out Lori's clothes for school the next day. What happened?

Driving back to Ruth's she is still searching. Ruth, she thinks; and the familiar excitement makes her drive more quickly, impatient to be with her even though they have just been together.

At first, in her evening class, Lynn didn't notice Ruth, quiet in the back of the room. Then they did papers on similar topics. They met for coffee, Ruth read Lynn's writing and started writing poetry herself. After they spent an evening reading poetry together, something went crazy inside Lynn. She slept fitfully. All night she saw Ruth's face in front of her − every detail exact − black hair, dark eyebrows, hazel eyes pooling light and beauty, sharp cheekbones, hand quick in gesturing − all night in front of her like a vision. Lynn awoke the next morning at five o'clock, bolt awake, knowing she must see Ruth. That day Lynn phoned her and they went walking at the beach. After that there was no day without hearing Ruth's voice and almost no day without time together. Since that day Lynn has waited from one time together to the next and the time in between has been for marking time.

What is this shakiness? Lynn tries another route. What was new today was the holding one another. That has never happened with them before. There have been words − words

spoken, words written — and words are safe. Always there have
been women with whom there have been words and the words
have carried both intense meaning and muted mystery.
Today Ruth touched her. Not only the hands across the
void. Lying in one another's arms. Touch. Touch belonged to
something else. Touch belonged to Tony and before Tony to
Billy and Marsh.

*The long lace curtains on the stairway landing blow against
the sunlight in a sudden gust as the front door opens and Marsh
comes in. Lynnanne is crouching on the landing, in the cockpit of a fighter plane over Germany, diving, strafing. In front
of her is a paper airplane panel which she has memorized; an
instruction pamphlet came with it from Kellogg's.*

She knows how to take off, tilt ailerons, land.

*"Hey, kid, how you doing?" Marsh stands above her, tall,
grinning down.*

*"Okay," she says, awkwardly standing up, knowing he will
make fun of her new game.*

*"Been flying, huh? Maybe I'll go in the air force myself.
Then I'll take you for a spin."*

*His hand brushes her arm. "Come in my room. I'll show
you the kind of plane I'll fly."*

She follows him.

*He shows her an air force folder full of laughing boys in
air force caps. His arm circles her waist and he moves
against her slowly and then turns away to pull the blinds.
She looks once toward the closed door, once toward the
twilight pressing at the blinds. "You really want it, don't
you?" he says. She shakes her head. "What do you think
everybody's doing in parked cars and rooms all over town right
now, hmm? Just like this, they're doing it. Come on, admit it,
You want this cock, don't you?"*

She shakes her head. "Leave me alone."

*"Come on," he says, his voice moving from cajoling to a
sterner tone. "Look at that. I've got a hard-on. You have to
let me now. Just give in, enjoy." He moves against her more
insistently.*

"Okay," she says, remembering a Reader's Digest *article she's read that week in which the Japanese soldiers raped every nurse. "I'll be in the war and you be the soldier raping me." "No," he says, drawing back, disgust in his voice, "Look, what's so terrible about it? I'm telling you, everybody does it. You really want to, I can tell. Don't lie. Now hold still. He thrusts himself against her, shoving her down on the bed. "Uhnnnn," he says, "don't worry, I won't go in all the way . . . uhnnnnnnnnnnn." Lynnanne struggles away, in a single cockpit plane with a broken wing, somewhere over a European forest as night begins to fall.*

"I know why I panicked," Lynn says, coming into Ruth's house as she is putting on a record.

"Why?" Ruth leaves the needle off and looks carefully at Lynn.

"Touch has been with men before. My brothers. Tony. And words have been with women."

"The two don't overlap?"

"I don't know. I *said* they did with Tony. I *thought* they did. But when the kids were born I thought it was a miracle and I wrote poetry about the Word becoming Flesh and Love being the Word as though I bypassed the way our bodies acted. I guess I didn't have it all together. Until the therapy I guess I never did."

The room is quiet for a while. Then Ruth puts on Mozart, softly, and they sit together, holding hands. Lynn goes on, "And when I went to Tony from the therapy and tried to get it all together with him, he wasn't having any. With you everyting is different, Ruth."

"So what scared you?"

Lynn sits silently for a long time.

"Don't talk about it if you don't want to," Ruth says.

"That's all right. Ever since I was a little kid I've known how to get away — to leave my body lying there and go out the window in my head, you know? I can't even remember how it might have been before that. When you and I hold hands, I stay. Today, when you held me, I stayed."

Ruth nods.

Lynn goes on, "It's not sexual. I mean I don't want to make love with you and you don't with me. But it feels like all one thing — to touch your hand and to talk with you aren't two separate things. That feels safe. Today when you held me somehow it felt dangerous."

Lynn pauses. Ruth is silent and after a few minutes Lynn says, "I figured out the dream. The pickup was Marsh's truck, the one he turned the lights out in, remember? Once I saw a truck like that go off the road. It was loaded with boys in band uniforms and the side panel broke and spilled kids every which way and the driver lost control and went over in the ditch by our farm. I was sitting on the hill above the road and saw it happen — uniforms and drums and hats and batons — everything red and blue — kids upside down flying through the air.

"So always I've had this funny feeling about watching trucks, and in the dream it was my brother's truck, and I wanted it to crash — I must have always wanted my brother's truck to crash — not out loud but inside. Maybe the dream says if it had crashed I could have been whole then instead of now. When you touched me today I didn't split and run and that left me pretty shaky."

"Would you rather we didn't touch like that again?" Ruth's voice is very gentle.

Lynn says, "No, I wouldn't rather we didn't." She smiles, and they move together on the sofa.

14

Ruth pulls up to the curb just after dawn on a Sunday morning. Lynn gets in quickly, holds the door closed until they turn the corner, then slams it shut.

"Good morning," Ruth says softly, "anyone wake up?"

"Good morning. Here—" Lynn hands a freshly picked tulip to her. "I don't think so." Their hands meet and hold.

"The beach?"

"Sure." They drive for a long way in silence. Ruth's left hand tightens on the steering wheel. "What's up?" Lynn asks.

"I'm scared," Ruth says, flicking a glance sideways. "This is no ordinary friendship, Lynn. I *love* you."

"Hey, whoa. I love you too. Friends *do* love each other."

"Come off it. Friends don't hold hands all the time. Friends don't wake up at four a.m. and stay awake too excited to get back to sleep because they're taking a morning walk together!" Ruth laughs explosively. Her face darkens again. "No, I'm serious."

Lynn speaks from a script she's used before. "There are lots of kinds of love. One kind doesn't make the other go away. I don't love one kid less because I have another, or my husband less because I have kids, or friends. If anything, I'm learning better how to love and I can take that back to him, if he'll have it, and you can take it back to Neil."

Ruth looks at her in desperate disbelief. "I wish I thought you knew what you were talking about." She laughs a short soft laugh.

"Look, from the beginning, haven't we agreed that it's like sisters?"

"If your marriage blows, then what?"

"If my marriage blows, it has nothing to do with us." Lynn stares past Ruth. Her marriage is for her now like the spinning ride at a carnival. She stands pressed back against a flat somewhat familiar surface with her arms back, hands spread flat, dizzy from the speed of the rotating walls, and beneath her feet when she looks down to verify her own position, she sees only air where the platform fell away, to leave the grinding of the coarse, black, greased gears roaring up at her. She feels the air spin now beneath her feet.

"I feel like an intruder." Ruth swings into a parking lot near the ocean. She moves her hand from Lynn's and sits with both hands knuckle-white on the rim of the wheel, staring in front of her.

"You're in no way intruding, Ruth. If I've got marriage troubles, they're my own. You've made me happy this spring. God, you're the only thing that's happy. And we've spent half our time together working on my marriage — how to save it. For Christ's sake, what do you want? I *love* you, Ruth."

Ruth slowly turns her head to look at Lynn. Lynn puts out her hand toward her and abruptly they are in one another's arms.

"It *feels* so *right*," Ruth whispers. "Oh, Lynn, Lynn."

"I love you, Ruth."

They stay a long while close in one another's arms. A morning fog drifts across the windshield, sometimes penetrated by streaks of sunlight, sometimes swirled by gusts of wind.

Like searchlights probing the area two headlights swing across them, jarring them apart as though a crowbar crashes through the steel frame above their heads. It's a big truck. The driver turns off its lights.

"Let's walk," Ruth says, already out of the car.

"He just parked to nap," Lynn says.

"I know, but I have to move."

They hike the beach swiftly. After a long time, Lynn says, "Don't worry, Ruth. Look, loving you does make me better able to be a loving wife."

"You mean I'm good therapy? Training sessions?" Ruth's half-laugh grates.

Lynn smiles in conciliation. "Not that way. But sort of. I think we're both healthier than we were. Something about opening up and being free. I *feel* like I am. Don't you?" Ruth throws one rock after another far across the water. "It sounds right. But I smell a rat."

"You want to stop?" Lynn confronts her.

On the horizon a ship moves slowly south. Ruth's voice comes softly, desperate, to Lynn, "No, you know I don't. I can't manage when I don't see you. But let's not be dumb."

"It's all right, Ruth." Lynn, after a quick glance down the long expanse of empty beach each way, reaches toward Ruth, but Ruth breaks into a jogging run away from her, back toward the lot.

Lynn runs after her. She doesn't catch up until they are at the steps leading to the car. Some boys run past them, headed for the beach, and a fisherman goes slowly up, carrying his bucket and his rod.

In the car Ruth puts her head down on the wheel, breathing heavily. "I'll be all right in just a minute," she says. Lynn reaches to touch her shoulder. She shrugs her off. "No," she says. "Just leave me alone for a minute. I'll be all right."

Lynn goes alone to a wedding in the city; Tony, refusing to go with her, stays home with the children. Lynn stays overnight with friends. The next morning, after the couple leaves for work, there is a light knocking and Lynn runs barefoot to open the door for Ruth.

Ruth throws her sweater on a chair and goes to the window to look out across the city rooftops. The morning streams in around her. Lynn stands, staring. Ruth is etched in sunlight, black hair shining, outline tense. She turns, her back to the window, and her eyes are happy, shadowed. A sharp rush of feeling locks Lynn unmoving, unspeaking.

"It's a beautiful day," Ruth says, her voice beautiful to Lynn. Beyond her the blue sky sparkles, the branch of a locust feathers in the wind.

They are together then, holding. Lynn watches the tree's

branches where the wind moves the soft leaves in undulating waves. Cars parked below glint sunlight back at her. Following the bright streaks of light from the windshields there is quiet streaming light within Lynn's eyelids as she lets them close. "Come. We'll sit down." Ruth's voice acknowledges her own dizziness. They move to the sofa. Lynn is lying, her head in Ruth's lap, her arms around Ruth. In the building morning sounds proceed. Children wake, cry, turn on TVs; parents wake, run water down through pipes inside the walls, call instructions to their children. Lynn and Ruth look at one another and it is as though they can not reach the limits of looking into one another's eyes.

This looking, holding, are inseparable for Lynn from the Mozart, night after night, voice answering voice as hand holds hand. Their looking now is in pure balance, fragile and beautiful.

From the beginning they have wanted to know everything about one another. As though cycles of deepening understanding create new space which they then enter to explore together, they move in a sphere of time and space that is their own. One hour passes, then another and another. Lynn knows this because the numerals on the clock by the window register time. They have never been alone together, indoors, anywhere away from home before.

"I love you," Lynn says.

"And I love you."

The sunlight is the sunlight of all their morning walks, the sunlight that stroked the wings of gulls and streamed across the water toward the still darkened western edge, along the glistening froth where the waves drew back from their own bare running feet, the sunlight that struck into Lynn's eyes from above Ruth's face as Lynn looked up at her, lying next to her on the sand, unwilling to look away a moment though the sunlight speared her with its brilliant light. They, in one another's arms, motion within stillness, glide the bright waters deeper, where the underchannelings are streaked with underwater blue and green and orange from the penetrating light. Deeper they descend and the beauty of the silent stratum under stratum holds them away from the familiar air. Lynn knows nothing but the intensity of that place, more beautiful, more compelling than any moment she has ever known. Deeper, deeper, their bodies translucent, lightening with the last release of air, their lips touch, hold, and beautifully open to one another's lips.

They rise to the surface of their day in the late afternoon and leave before the friends come home from work. Driving home they are quiet, hand in hand. "I'm taking the long way home," Ruth says. "I can't go there yet."

They phone to say they won't be in until very late and they drive to the shore. Trees and sky and fields and the first smell of the ocean swirl them together. They stop at the shore, sit high on sand dunes, eating oranges, watching waves, gulls, one another. Lynn lies on the sandy cliff, looking out across the sunset, and up at Ruth who sits beside her, and says, "I am absolutely happy."

"So am I," Ruth says, smiling down at her, reaching to smooth the hair out of her eyes.

It's two-thirty a.m. when Lynn goes quietly in the door. She checks all sleeping children and lies, still clothed, on the sofa. Ocean, sky, sunlight whirl her as she sleeps, as though she swims with Ruth just off the shore, lifted by wave after wave until she scrambles up the beach and stands, shaking off seaweed and sand. Waking, she goes to make breakfast for Tony and the rest.

They sit together in Ruth's car by a lake where they often meet. It's ten o'clock at night. "What's up?" Lynn asks.

Their hands tighten as Ruth tries to speak. At last she says, "I can't do it, Lynn." She lights a cigarette. "I can't manage."

In the light from a street lamp the leaves of a maple twist night green in the wind.

"I don't know how you do it," Ruth goes on, "but I can't compartmentalize like you do. You say it's fine. You say it's not going any further. I'm going crazy. We drive around like two teenagers who have no place to be together. I love you,

Lynn. We draw lines, we kiss and hold and say that's as far as we go and then we go home and go to bed with Neil and Tony and I can't take it any more." Her face is tight.

"What can we do?"

"I don't know." Ruth looks at the cigarette, grinds it out as she answers. "Maybe we shouldn't see each other any more."

Lynn, who runs the tops of mountains when she is with Ruth, scarcely knowing how thin the air, seeing only meadows filled with wild flowers, plummets. She is racked with dry hard sobs.

"Lynn, don't." Ruth's arms come around her.

"What if I were a man?" Lynn asks, "How would it be different?"

"We've been there. If *you* were a man, if *I* were a man, we'd run away together. Right? What if I were a man?"

Lynn is quiet for a while. Then she says, "If you were a man I would never have seen you twice. But if I had, then I'd run away with you. I love you, Ruth."

"But I'm not a man. You're not a man. So where does that leave us?" Ruth traces Lynn's fingers with her forefinger. "I love your hands."

"If I were a man, would you leave Neil?"

"Yes."

A car passes and they separate, dodging the headlights, and remain apart, only their hands together.

"It's all crazy mixed-up, isn't it?" Lynn tries to laugh. "In the end, I'll probably leave Tony and you'll stay with Neil and we'll still want to be together. That's crazy."

"Look, I don't know the answer. But you're trying to keep your marriage, right? This is no help with that. Seeing you, makes me want to be with you all the time. It's torture this way, Lynn. We're nowhere."

Two kids walk beside the lake, arm in arm. Ducks are swimming in the water's center, moving across a placid circle of moonlight.

Ruth turns the key. "I'm sorry, Lynn. I'm sorry. Maybe I'm all wrong. Tell me I'm all wrong . . ."

Lynn shakes her head. "I don't know. I don't want to hurt you, Ruth. For me it's better seeing you." She starts to cry.

"But for you it's different, isn't it? Let's try it. Not at all?"
"I don't know. We'll try." Ruth's voice is sharp with pain.

When Ruth lets her out in front of her house and drives away, Lynn begins to walk instead of going inside the house. It's late and all the houses are dark. At home everyone will be asleep. She walks and the pain begins. She recognizes it from a distance. As she walks, it takes shape, like a familiar person, first out of sight, then a dim outline, then its own known shape. She thinks about not seeing Ruth. She doesn't know how a day like that would be. Not to wait for her voice on the phone, not to know that in the evening they would sit together, or that at dawn she would wake to walk with her: it is a kind of day she has forgotten. She doesn't know what would shape a day like that, what would move one hour into another. The pain is in her head. It takes over. Her legs move her along the street and the pain shrieks from within, from ahead, from behind, like a siren coming closer. She looks around to see where it's coming from. But there is no emergency for anyone but her. The siren is within her head.

She walks. Left leg, right leg, left leg, right leg, and no leg connected with herself. The pain stops vision and she walks by rote, listening for cars, but there are none.

Lynn walks and the pain is past her comprehension. As though her head's two hemispheres were joined together in Ruth's presence, overgrown with one great pleasant meadow, and now the earth split asunder, her head severs within itself and the two hemispheres push at the skull that holds them next to one another, striaining its boundaries, blasting its bone structure. Shaking she walks.

She thinks of the day she and Ruth first kissed and the pain crescendoes and ricochets through her head. She staggers and sits on someone's lawn, head in hands. Far away on the flat earth a dog barks at her and she rises and walks, stick puppet with a cracking head in the control of someone she once knew, until she is in the flat house that is her home.

15

Tony lies on his back, head tipped upward, eyes closed, face contorted in a kind of ecstasy, arms flung wide on either side, hands loose against the sheet. Lynn kneels astride him, working for his pleasure. She strokes his swollen penis with both her hands, dangles her breasts against its head, pushes it against a nipple again and again, and at last closes it between her heavy breasts and lowers her mouth to it. He shudders as she takes his cock into her mouth, flicks her tongue around, across, along the shaft, closes her lips tightly on the head and sucks.

She feels his orgasm gathering as she moves and works to further it. Her back strains from the position and her legs begin to cramp but she knows he will come shortly and she heightens her motions, working the shaft with her hand, the tip with her tongue, flicking, sucking, flicking, sucking. He is wearing a condom — she has never learned to let him come in her mouth without it, and he has never seemed to care — and she accelerates, until he spurts and with an almost painful jerking of his head lies back, limp, eyes still closed.

She swings off him and pulls on her clothes.

These days they are like two tired walkers on opposite sides of a Moebius strip, in which a magnetic current called a marriage courses, holding their iron weighted feet against it all the time. Sometimes one or the other walks ahead, runs ahead, or lags behind, and then they catch sight of one another around the gradual bends.

Their feet are caught in the magnetic field, anchored in such a way that they do not ever look into one another's eyes nor walk, holding hands, but move always in the same familiar path as apart as if in different orbits around different spheres breathing different air.

Sometimes Lynn glimpses Tony's hair as he disappears into a building or catches sight of his arm and hand reaching for a coffee cup from behind a newspaper and then she is suddenly catapulted backward into another time and place where the rest of him accrues, laughing, carrying Anthony on his shoulders, or bringing flowers to her where she lies with new-born Jon, or running beside her up the steps of Carnegie, late to a concert, hand in hand. But when they resolutely set out to talk, they are on different planes, and she reruns his words before she answers, looking for an interior translation that will remedy what she hears, that will make a connection possible.

Sometimes Lynn mines the early years, trying to find a vein that will not peter out. Each path through the twenty years comes to a neat blank wall; she turns, retraces, starts again. These explorations fill her drives to and from teaching and the middle hours of the nights.

At the spring concert at Lori's school, Lynn and Tony are standing in the hall at intermission in front of an exhibit of first graders' art, waiting for Lori to come out of the bath-room. The drawing closest to them shows an obviously pregnant woman with eight children, graphically presented in green and purple crayon. "Pregnant, is it, hmm, Lynn?" a neighbor quips.

"Christ! She'd better not be! I'd have her to the abortion-ist before the encore!" Tony snaps, grinning belatedly as the neighbor forces a laugh and moves along.

Tony walks casually toward the auditorium, saying thought-fully, "Though if we get divorced and I marry again, I think I want to have children with that other woman."

Lynn focuses on Jimmy Burns playing clarinet. She cannot believe that Tony said that. Halfway through the concert she remembers that Jimmy Burns was in her own elementary school thirty years before and that this is Lori's school and that dark haired boy is not Jimmy but someone else, some stranger to herself, and the son of strangers. When the concert is over she walks out thinking, this is Lori's father whose name is Tony and I am still his wife.

Lynn grades papers late and writes letters to Ruth that she does not send, rewrites them, tears them up. She cleans out Lori's room, staring at each crayon and stray Monopoly thousand dollar bill. She cramps whenever the phone rings. In the night, half-awake, searching through the history of the marriage, she waits for the phone, strains after every car that uses their street. Each morning when she wakes the first thing she knows is that Ruth did not call or come and will not call or come and each morning it is the same unexpected, total drop, the way her body plummets in her sleep sometimes without cause or anticipation, snapping her awake.

Early one evening she takes a long walk alone. Her legs move the way the hands on old electric clocks in her school rooms worked: click, freeze.

She comes to a lake. The lake is far from her own house. Click, freeze.

"Get in," Ruth's voice says. Her car is at the curb, door open.

Lynn's body doubles over inside her skin. She cannot speak.

"Shhh," Ruth says, "I know. I couldn't either. There's no way that I could."

They hold one another on into the night.

The air inside the house is thick. Tony moves sluggishly, from newspapers to books, from books to papers, occasionally charging out of his isolation to shout at the boys, or to scrape away at their lives as though they were barnacles on a hull, with discussions about the children or the summer or the coming year. Whenever Lynn enters, lungs filled with air from classes, teaching, therapy, time with Ruth, she holds her breath while she does her chores until at last her lungs cave in and she must go again to find new space to breathe. Tony goes to more conferences away from home, teaches at night, works late in the library. For the first time in twenty years she now sometimes goes away overnight without him. She marvels at how easily they let one another go until it strikes her, driving away one day, rolling down the window, breathing deeply of the spring smells of grass and wisteria, that the hard thing now for each of them is to stay.

16

"Did you ever touch a woman before?" Ruth breaks a leaf from a branch beside the trail and chews on it as she speaks.

"No. Did you?"

"No."

They are hiking around the lake in the state park. It's early May and there aren't many people on the trail. Lynn says, "Until I met you, I could count on one hand the times I touched a woman's hand or even hugged good night."

She thinks backward past Ruth to Jeanne and Marie and all the friends on all the campuses where they have lived and before that to college and before that to relatives. She ranges through comings and goings, parties and vacations, far into the night conversations. Words.

"Once my poetry professor had us over to her apartment and she got high and I was sitting next to her. We were talking about war and what was coming next and she said, 'You will live through times that try men's souls,' and she took my hand and held it for a long time. I worshipped her. She served sherry that night and I'd never had sherry before and I got so high that when I left I was barefoot. I walked into the elevator and I looked down and saw bare feet. There was a very reserved elevator man. I had to go back up and ring the bell and say, 'I forgot my shoes!' "

Ruth laughs and Lynn laughs and they break into a run, hand in hand, wind in their faces, sun on their backs. Out of breath, they sit to rest on a fallen tree. Lynn picks off a chunk of bark and crumbles it as she talks. "Now I think she must've been what I guess they mean by gay. Then I didn't know. She lived with another woman. I knew she loved that woman. And I knew she was sort of in love with a friend of mine — but I was sure there wasn't any sex involved in any way, you know?"

Ruth nods. "I knew a pianist like that once. She lived with another woman. I used to think about them — they seemed so complete and serene — I wondered how that would be. I liked to visit them. We did political mailings from their house; against nuclear testing, back then. And who else?"

"When Miss M. was dying, we spent one long evening with her in her house. She told us she'd signed retirement papers and we were beginning to understand that she was dying. She took my hand and held it the whole evening." Lynn watches the crows circling above the trees. "She kept me sane in high school. I wrote for her. She told me to take the scholarship test. That's how I got away to college — four years' tuition, room and board."

Ruth responds to the tears just under the rapid talk and puts her hand on Lynn's shoulder. "She did save your life then."

"Right."

They sit in silence a while and then Lynn comes back from remembering Miss M. Girls. Women. "When I was in labor with Anthony a nurse held my hand. How about you?"

Ruth looks at her carefully. "I never touched another woman before — not since my mother, and I didn't touch her if I could help it. She used to tell how, when I was three years old, she took me to stay with friends in the country for a week; when she left, she *wanted* me to cry. I didn't. I just waved goodby, turned my back and walked away."

Lynn stands and walks on, kicking a rock aside. "One of the reasons I wanted this weekend together was to prove a point."

"Being?"

"That we can be alone together and nothing more will happen. You aren't sure."

Ruth smiles at her. "I haven't known what was happening from the beginning — why should I be sure now? But I don't think we're lesbians." Ruth laughs a short laugh. "But then, I'm not so sure any more that I have any idea what that means either. Do you?"

"I've never thought about it before. I've always had friends I loved. What's new with you is wanting to touch. I don't know if it's the therapy that's made me whole so when I love I want to touch, because when I love, my body goes along, or if it's you that's made me whole, because you're so unsplit yourself that your body and you can't love in different ways, and I feel that and so I want to touch because you do."

Ruth makes an involved circle motion with her hand, following it with her head into a twisted pose. They both start laughing and break into a run which ends with a quick embrace behind a thick clump of sapling pine.

They hike and talk, talk and hike. The tapestry of our lives, Lynn thinks, is almost all filled in. Their conversation makes references, oblique, subtle, to old friends, important times, that each has come to know as though she had herself been there.

Ruth lies, looking up into the trees, watching a bird. Lynn sits next to her, watching her watch the bird. "Is it a warbler?"

"I think so. It's very high up there — I'm getting blind as a bat. So I married him. I guess I didn't think I had many choices. There'd been Rick and Johnny and that summer with Robert and when Neil came along he was sure of himself and sure of what was right for me, and that was one thing I wasn't, and he was all set. He knew what he wanted, had his career all laid out, was sure about *everything*. I hadn't even been in this country very long. I was still trying to get straight what the right things to do were, what the right ways to be were." Ruth pulls herself to a sitting position and lights a cigarette. "I couldn't think of any reason not to marry him. In a way I was in love. I married him."

Ruth stands, head tipped back, staring up into the trees, blowing smoke. "And after the kids were born and all, when I had time to look around and think it over, like when he'd get mad and not speak to me for weeks . . ." Lynn looks questioningly at her, and Ruth, glancing down at her, responds, "Oh, yes, he did that — he still does — I start to criticize or just talk about something that he's done; then he says I shouldn't say things like that and then he won't talk to me — for a week, two weeks, once it was for a month — nothing more than 'Pass the salt' until I get tired of living alone and break it by giving in. Then he rolls around in bed with me a while and thinks that everything is all fine. All taken care of."

"And is everything fine then?"

"You mean *is* he that terrific in bed? Hell no. Oh you know, like everybody, we've tried a lot of different things. He gets ideas and gets excited about trying them out — new gimmicks which usually don't work. He likes anal sex but I don't. I've let him sometimes but I don't like it." Ruth blushes.

"Christ!"

"That's not so terrible. He's curious, that's all. He's a playful boy. He likes to experiment. He doesn't like to touch my breasts — that's strange, isn't it? I think that's probably unusual."

Lynn flinches. "That's awful for you," she says.

"But I—" Ruth throws her cigarette down with an exaggerated dramatic motion of her arm and grinds it out with an equally exaggerated stamping circling of her foot — "*I* have always known how to COUNT MY BLESSINGS!" She laughs, repeats, "Yes, I count my blessings, and I stay with him. And *that* is enough of *that!* NO MORE!" She runs up the trail, shinnies halfway up a young oak tree, holds herself unmoving as high as she can go, shouts, "NO MORE OF THIS HERE CONVERSATION!" leaps down and runs on out of sight.

They have never been alone overnight before. Lynn puts on her pajamas in the bathroom anxiously. Ruth undresses in the bedroom and Lynn, who has at first looked away, looks at her. She stands naked by the bed. Her breasts are small and firm, her thighs like a foal's. Lynn is surprised to see her standing there: a woman. "Strange to be together like this?" Ruth asks.

Lynn nods. Ruth pulls on her pajamas and comes to sit beside her on the bed. "Don't be afraid," she says, and takes her hand gently.

"I'm not," Lynn says.

"Shall we sleep in separate beds?" Ruth asks. "We can if you like."

"No, I don't like," Lynn says, laughing. "I want you near me."

Ruth reaches to put out the lamp and they lie on the bed together. They hold one another in their arms. "It feels absolutely right," Lynn says.

Ruth sighs. "God, doesn't it?"

They lie a long time in silence, holding, being held. They kiss. "How come we fit so well?" Lynn asks. "I thought we'd bump into each other."

They giggle. "Tell me about the toys you had when you were little," Lynn says. "Did you have stuffed animals?"

"No. I had books. I had *Der Struwelpeter* instead. You know? Where the little boy sucks his thumb so they cut it off and the little girl plays with matches and burns herself up."

"That's awful!"

"Yes. *Awful.*"

They laugh and talk on into the night and fall asleep at last in one another's arms.

"AHHHHHHHHHH."

Lynn snaps awake. Ruth is twisting, mumbling, trying to speak. "Hey, Ruth, wake up! wake up!" She shakes her and then hits her arm lightly but she will not come awake.

"Hey, Ruth, Ruth!" Lynn taps her cheek.

"Huh? Okay, I'm okay. Oh, sorry." Ruth looks about, confused.

"What was that about?"

"Soldiers. Gestapo, actually. Sorry about that." Ruth laughs apologetically.

"Still those dreams?"

"Sure."

Lynn holds her close. "Come on, you're safe. Relax."

"I'm okay now. That was a bad one. They broke the door down and dragged everyone away. I braced myself against the bed but the whole thing went, springs, frame, everything. I'm sorry."

"Shhhhh. Now sleep, sleep."

"You could laugh, you know."

"What?"

"Neil always laughed. My nightmares are an old family joke. I used to wake up screaming quite a lot and everyone would laugh about it the next day."

"Shit." Lynn feels pure hatred for Neil-who-laughed. She folds Ruth closer in her arms. "Now sleep. I love you."

Toward morning Lynn wakes again. Ruth is sliding quietly, out of bed. "What's up?"

"Nothing. Go back to sleep."

Lynn, who has lain in total peace and happiness all night, stares at Ruth. "What's wrong?"

"Nothing's wrong, Lynn. Really. Go back to sleep."

"Nightmare again?"

"No nightmare."

"What then?"

"Nothing, really." Ruth smiles at her. "I just need to be alone a little while. It's just that I can't sleep right now that close to you."

Lynn does not understand. "I thought you were happy the way we were last night."

"I was, Lynn. I am. Really. Never mind. You're sleepy. Don't try to think. Just go to sleep. Okay?"

"I'm cold."

Ruth laughs at her. "All right, I'll come back in." Ruth comes close to Lynn again and Lynn falls back asleep in her arms, but when she wakes later, after dawn, Ruth has moved to the other bed. Puzzled, Lynn goes to her, bends to kiss her good morning. Ruth reaches up and pulls her down against herself and they lie, whispering, kissing, talking, until they get up to hike.

Neil goes to a convention in California the last week in May and Ruth goes too, taking a leave from school. Lynn does the arithmetic of Ruth's absence: ten days times twenty-four hours, but the tenth day is not a whole day because she will come back that day and the first day is not a whole day because she was here this day. Lynn breaks the time into clusters, for school, for Christy's birthday party, for a dinner she is giving for Tony's friends in the department; none of the arithmetic alleviates the pungent ache of the separation.

Ruth phones to say that Neil is staying for a second week but she must come back to teach; "Want to meet a plane Sunday afternoon?"

Lynn paces between the terminal windows which look out on nothing but tractors and garbage cans, and the racks of magazines and candy. She checks the arrival board for the eighth time. The plane is down. She goes to the gate and stares up the ramp. Boys with knapsacks and well tanned young couples stream past her and little children are enclosed by grandparents' arms. Two nuns find two nuns to greet them. A Japanese couple finds an old woman and two little girls.

And Ruth is there. Lynn sees her face far up the ramp and a glow immediately connects them as though it transcends distance to let them touch.

Ruth moves quickly toward her in the crowd. Watching her come closer but held back by the bar Lynn feels within herself a storm more overwhelming than any she has felt before. The feeling crescendoes and recedes, and the falling away is like being on the under side of a great ocean wave that comes crashing toward her in a high and wild surf. When Ruth touches her, Lynn is enveloped, thrown under to scramble through sand and seaweed to get her footing back, to catch her breath, so they can walk to the luggage place, walk to the car, drive to Ruth's house, where they find themselves alone.

There, in one another's arms, thighs against thighs, lips against tongue and tongue within lips, Lynn concedes that there is no longer any limit to be held. The line she has assured Ruth exists is gone.

"You've waited long enough," she says, placing Ruth's hand against her mons. "I love you, Ruth."

"Are you sure?" Ruth whispers, smiling at her.

"Yes," Lynn says. She doesn't know what difference it will make — she thinks not much — to let their bodies touch in new and unknown ways. She does know with certainty that there is no way now to hold back anything that is hers nor any way not to take whatever Ruth may give.

Shyly they touch one another with their hands, shyly move

their fingers against one another's warmth. Ruth's first orgasm is sharp and quick. Wide-eyed she makes a sound that is somewhere between a laugh and sob. Lynn stares at her, turns the sound over in her ear and mind. Lynn watches her. It comes to Lynn as an astonishment that Ruth keeps her eyes open all the time, just as it did that they slept together in the cabin face to face, and that whatever they may discover in this new way of touching is in no way set apart, is not a silent hidden desperate thing but open, light as the touch of hand on hand and she doesn't have to be afraid nor close her eyes nor shut her mouth to stifle whatever words may come from whatever joy.

17

And which brand of orange juice do you use for *your* family?"

Lynn spins to see Ruth laughing as their hands touch in the ice cold storage bin. "I grow my own," she retorts, laughing.

"Hey," Ruth says, glancing around, "it's indecent to feel this way in a grocery store."

Lynn laughs. "Got a minute?"

"Sure. Meet you in the car." Ruth wheels her cart away.

Lynn moves rapidly through the other aisles, piling her cart high, and waits impatiently at the checker's. Once outside she sees Ruth's car and after unloading the bags into her car, she goes to sit with Ruth. Inside the car their hands meet and they sit a few minutes silently, glad to be together.

"You coming over tonight?" Ruth asks.

"Actually, I guess I can't."

"What's up?" Ruth lights a cigarette.

"Tony wants to talk. Over dinner out, yet."

"One of those nights. Okay. Good, maybe you can get through to him." Ruth's voice quickens and she draws deeply on the cigarette. "He still wants you to go to Chicago with him?"

"Umhm."

"Maybe you should go. Give yourself a chance to see what it's like, away."

"The kids would go too, so away from what?"

"Away from us."

"I don't want to be away from us, Ruth." Lynn feels a
stubborn click inside herself as though the roulette wheel
spins free until it hits that point and then locks in, same number
every time. Any combination seems possible to her so long as
she and Ruth can still be together and no combination that
leaves that out seems possible.

"Maybe you have to be. Maybe that's the only way you and
Tony will get together for real. You do want that."

Lynn looks about the parking lot, watching women push
grocery wagons to their cars, watching a young woman lift a
small boy out of the cart and settle him in a car seat, hand him
a lollipop. "Tony and I had a weird conversation the other
night," she says, thinking as she says it that she shouldn't tell.

"Which night?"

"The night you and I went to hear Jon and Nate play and
then talked till two." Lynn smiles at Ruth, remembering the
quiet house, their long embraces and their new ways of fondling
one another whenever they have a chance.

"And?"

"Tony woke up that night when I got into bed." Lynn
stops, awkward.

"And?" Ruth's tone is poised, attentive.

"It was strange."

Ruth says nothing, grinds out her cigarette and lights
another, waiting.

"I was lying there, thinking that I'm becoming whole and
wondering if he ever will — and I was thinking about what we
said, how much our marriages could profit from what we take
back to them — and I was wondering if he will ever *want* to
touch me below the waist — and of course he didn't and I
thought to hell with it and . . ." Lynn stops, seeing herself in
the windshield talking to Ruth about Tony and herself in bed
and she stumbles, confused at the image. The car is quiet. The
only sound is the tap of Ruth's cigarette on the ash tray and the
cars going in and out of the lot somewhere outside the car.

"You don't have to tell me," Ruth says.

"I want to. Because I don't understand what he meant."
Lynn reruns the memory to get it straight. "We had sex, as

they say, and he finished and then he said to me, 'I won't be your dildo.' I said, 'What do you mean?' and he said, 'I'm not accusing you and Ruth of playing around, but I mean just that: I won't be your dildo.' So I said, 'I certainly don't want you to be a dildo.' And that was all the conversation."

"Has he ever said anything like that before?"

"No."

"Has he ever mentioned me like that before?"

"No."

"What do you think made him say it?"

Lynn is quiet for a long time. Finally, with difficulty, she says, "I think I was different — maybe softer, maybe a little wet." She blushes.

Ruth flashes a quick smile. "I'll bet you were. He doesn't like sex, Lynn. That's where it's at. He doesn't like you to be sexy. It scares him." Ruth starts the car and whips it around next to Lynn's car on the other side of the lot. "Go to your husband, mother-of-the-year. Hey, if you're busy tonight, I'll give Jon a ride home from rehearsal. Call me tomorrow?"

"Late tonight, if I can."

"Right." Ruth is gone, swinging into traffic and out of sight.

Lynn drives home slowly, puzzling. The event with Tony frightens her. For herself it has a certain unreality: guilt flashes like a comet across the stereoscopic image of herself but only flashes and disappears because the two images do not ever come together: the body that she takes to Ruth is in no way the body that she takes to Tony. This enables her, for the first time in their twenty years together, to lie to Tony. It seems to her no lie.

She replays his moves again, first the taking hold of her, and second, the entry, and third, his comment, almost before he came, as though he swung himself out of bed almost before the orgasm which he did have, did want. Anger? Jealousy? He was put off by what he found. Isn't he entitled then to rage? Put off. He should have found her exciting. He hadn't even touched her breasts. He *had* been angry then. But something else. She searches. Something familiar. Like what? Like what other time? Like the way he was the night he tried cunnilingus!

Going into a turn she gropes for it – anger? Hate? Repulsion? Her brakes whine as she holds to the road coming out of the turn too fast. Repulsion, that was it; repulsed and angered. That what? That I am the way a woman is? That I want him to touch me there? That I'm not parched and rigid, dry? That I don't close my eyes any more the way he does? And she sees him, eyes tight closed, mouth a tight and silent line, elbows locked, body moving like a piston, wanting to be through, to have proved that he can do it, to make it through the trial under fire once again, to drop, exhausted, on the safe side of the course and not to have to touch her after that. Fear. His 'I don't want to hurt you' has meant, 'Don't hurt me. I don't want to get hurt.' He's always been afraid.

He wants less of me, not more, she thinks, swinging into the driveway. That's why he calls me oversexed. He wants me less. She sits a moment in the car in shock, seeing his closed eyes and straining flesh, and knows why she was startled that she and Ruth slept facing one another, face to face, eyes open until sleep, and open again, face to face, whenever they were awake. I haven't slept facing Tony for twenty years, she thinks, and he hasn't slept facing me, nor does he make love to me with open eyes.

Lynn puts the pizza she has brought the kids on the kitchen table. She hears Lori somewhere in the backyard with the neighbor kids. She hears Jon's stereo in the basement. There's a note from Christy on the table and Anthony? As she unloads the groceries, mechanically putting frozen things away first, she tries to know where Anthony might have gone. There's a demonstration on campus tomorrow, she remembers; he must be over there, planning that; God, please let it be peaceful.

The phone's ring cuts off her thinking. It's Tony, calling from campus. "Ready to go?" he asks.

"Don't you want to come home first?" she asks.

"No, let's take off."

"Okay. I just got in. I have to put food away and stuff. I'll be there in twenty minutes."

"I'll be out front."

"Okay."

When he gets into the car Lynn slides across the seat to let him drive. He tells her about his meeting, and a letter from a press he has received. At the restaurant, with relief, she focuses on the menu. After the waiter has brought them drinks they have to see each other.

"The thing is," he says, "if we get a divorce and I go out and see you at a restaurant I'll want to ask you for a date." He laughs.

Lynn smiles and doesn't answer. Would I? She thinks. Would I want him to ask me out? She tries to see him as a stranger as he says he is seeing her. Thick black hair, streaked with grey, dark eyes under heavy eyebrows; that's what she liked first and likes last, except now he seems to look away even when he looks right at her. Most of the time they avoid one another's faces and certainly, one another's eyes. Keep him stranger, she thinks, and see what you can find. They never go to restaurants so it's easier here than elsewhere to see him as someone different from the Tony she knows. A strange man among the strangeness of the tables, draped windows, shining floor, and men's hands setting table, men's hands serving food. Men cook here, she thinks, men serve, men pay; without following out her thought she lets the strangeness of that identify him as different from the Tony with whom she came into the restaurant.

"Remember that little restaurant on Fiftieth street where we always had the antipasto?" Tony asks. She hasn't thought of that in twenty years. "And the place with the great veal scallopini where we went on our anniversaries?" Tony grins.

"And the pizza and chianti place on Amsterdam?" Without warning, the way gears slip in an automatic transmission going at uneven speeds, she finds they are in nostalgia now. Once far enough away from the places he has been, nostalgia drapes almost everything and everyone for Tony. She is remembering with him the places they once went so rarely that each occasion is filed away. Anniversaries. Always, until the past few years, on their anniversary they went out. She thinks about the last time, when, faced with his reluctance, she suggested heroes and a bottle of wine taken to the beach; it was contrived and devoid of fun, without romance; feeling awkward they went right home.

Tony hasn't recognized this reminiscing as evasion and is going on, pouring wine, "Remember when we took the presents to those poor kids on Christmas Eve?" She nods. That was the first year. They deluged each other with little gifts that year, living in the single walkup: share the bath, share the refrigerator.

"Remember when I hid and watched while strangers came and held the letters up to the light and took the ones with checks in them?" He nods and laughs.

There is silence. Tony tries a different way of measuring. "Our kids have had a pretty good life, you know. We gave them everything they wanted."

Lynn looks down at her plate and sees a kaleidoscopic whirl of sleds and trikes, dolls and puzzles, stuffed animals and models, that swirls around her in birthday paper, ribbons streaming through balloons while the birthday song was sung.

"And not just material things, either," he says, his voice expansive, pleased with his largesse. "We gave them a good home, lots of attention, trips, books, music."

"Yes," Lynn says, "we did, I think," remembering bedtime stories, zoos, parks, baking bread, carving jack-o-lanterns.

"So where do they get off?"

Lynn struggles for footing. She knows she can summon monster memories as well: the time Tony confined Jon to his room for throwing a book that missed Anthony and broke a window; Jon was left there to cry and scream for hours. Why is that the first memory that comes? Or the time Tony persuaded her to leave Anthony in his crib, crying, until he went to sleep; he was how old? A year? It only took one time; he never cried again at bedtime, slept in the dark. Why, Lynn wonders, am I so sure that Tony was wrong, that I should have held my ground? Something disproportionate. And the family was always wedged in the car, moving, the kids never having time to find their place, to make good friends. Moving from one state to another, they never found time to explore the state in which they lived; California and never Yosemite, never Mexico. Her fault? too risky? his fault? too what? Why did he reminisce with nostalgia, plan ahead with excitement, and have trouble with the moment at hand?

"They could have been anything they wanted."

"Maybe they will be."

"Hah! Anthony will be a marcher; that's if he evades jail. They may be locked up tomorrow, you know."

A warning light flashes at the tracks and the barrier drops down. Lynn snaps back from exploring the past to confront present danger. "Why would they lock them up? Isn't it just the usual demonstration?"

"They may stage a sit-in."

"So why lock them up?"

"The president is fed up with them. I don't blame him."

"You don't mean that."

"Yes, I do." Tony pours more wine. "It's those crazies. Anthony should know better than to get mixed up with them."

"He's young, Tony. Remember yourself in the '48 campaign? This is lots harder. Who knows which method of protest is most effective? I don't. You don't."

Tony rejects nostalgia now. "At his age I was in the army. I'm tired of indulging him. Maybe the army would be the best for Anthony, too."

"You don't mean that! You enlisted because you believed our side was right. This time our side is wrong. Kids like Anthony can't survive in this army and you know it. They didn't make this war."

As though in a pistol shooting chamber Lynn hears herself tell Tony what she thinks he must believe. Her words echo beside his calculated shots.

"They don't act responsibly. Loving isn't a one way street; it's a contract. They've broken the contract. Then they can't expect me to honor it and go on loving them."

"Tony! They're hurt and angry and confused – it's not just Jon and Anthony. Look around! All the kids their age are in trouble now."

"All the kids aren't mine. Look, they made choices. They cut me off. I didn't cut them off. But I won't be had. I won't give and give if they won't give back."

"You want to help them. You're so much stronger than they are, Tony."

He laughs a derisive laugh. "That's where you're wrong. They're much stronger than I am."

"They'll come back to being free to love us — this anger and loneliness is part of adolescence. You don't stop loving kids just when they need you the most."

"What do you want me to do? Look, I'll go over tomorrow and see what I can do, okay? Now let's take a walk. I want to talk to you."

"All right," Lynn says. While Tony is busy with the check, she looks at her watch carefully, for one privileged moment thinking about Ruth: I will not see her tonight, but I will call. Then as though sliding a trick panel back in place she turns her mind from Ruth and back to Tony.

They walk along the harbor. Ships pass far out from shore; most yachts and fishing boats are already tied up for the night. "I think I might buy a boat," Tony says. "Would you like that?"

She looks at the little decks, the little cabins, thinks of loading their family inside, compressing the static that can't be contained in the big house into that tiny space. "I don't think so," she says, sorry to be unable to join him in his myth.

Two kids race by, wearing cut-off jeans, and dive into the water between boats. Lynn smiles to see their gleaming bodies cut the air and Tony snaps, "Crazy kids!"

They are on a hill. Sophomore spring. It's hot and the grass is newly cut, strong smelling, slightly damp. Her roommate, Nancy, and Eric and Tony and herself have been picnicking. Nancy tips back her head, letting her hair hang down her back, staring at the sky, and says, "God, it's a beautiful day."

Lynn watches her, loving her, loving Tony, loving Eric, loving the day, hill, grass, sky.

"Hey, let's all roll down the hill," Nancy says, falling on her side. "Did you do that when you were kids?"

Lynn has never done it and suddenly wants more than anything to lie there and let the hill take her down. She watches Nancy and takes a deep breath, lying down next to her. "No, but it's a great idea."

"Hey, don't do that," Tony says.

"Why not?"

"It doesn't look right," Eric says. *"Come on, let's go to my place."*

Nancy sits up, confronting Eric. "Look right?"

"Yeah," Eric says, *you're not even wearing jeans for Christ's sake. Your skirts'll go over your heads."*

"This is a campus, not a carnival," Tony says impatiently.

"You are too much," Nancy says, *"you're right out of the dark ages."*

"You're in *nursery school,"* Tony snaps.

"Well?" Nancy says, looking at Lynn. *"Have we caucussed?"*

Lynn nods. Nancy rolls and Lynn follows her. The grass scatters as she turns, sky and ground run together in a spatter painting of strong smelling green. By the bottom she's out of control and she tumbles, laughing, scared and laughing, looking through a whirling sky for Nancy, who appears, crooked and unsteady, to pull her to her feet. Laughing, they climb back up the hill.

"That was an asinine thing to do," Eric yells. *"Look at all those windows full of guys watching you."*

"Let's go," Tony snarls contemptuously. *"Someday they'll grow up and learn how to behave."*

"Look," Tony says, taking her arm. "We have a lot of differences, but I think we can make it. I made an appointment with a shrink today. And when I'd done it, I felt all of a sudden really happy and I thought, by God, she's gotten me to do it. Let's give it a try, hmm?" He is pleased, expecting her rewarding smile.

She is harpooned. The spike point bites into her flesh and the line snaps taut. She twists in pain and rage. Too late, she thinks, too late. Four years too late. He draws her in, his arm holding her arm, his words the barb on the harpoon fastening her flesh.

"All right," she says. "That's good."

"I want you to come to Chicago with me," he says, "I want us to give it a try."

"All right," she says, losing blood too fast to keep her balance, feeling it gush out where the spike plunged in.

"Hey," he says, turning to her in the semi-darkness of the pier, "I feel good. Let's go home." He moves against her like a boy, letting her feel his hard-on against her thigh, pushing it hard against her groin, out of sight of people behind a high bow in the gathering night. "I can't wait," he says, "to get home and stick it in you."

"Now that they've been to war they're grown up men. I can't tell them any more what to do." Tears fill her mother's eyes. "But it breaks my heart to see them drink." She tells Lynnanne this on her way to bed. "It just makes me sick. Tell Billy I'm napping."

Billy watches her, a beer bottle in one hand. "C'mere," he says, "I wantta show you something."

She shakes her head.

"C'mon. I'm not gonna hurt you. C'mon. Mom said to show you how to shut off the furnace in case it gets fouled up when she's not home." He opens the basement door.

Lynnanne follows him down the stairs. The basement is not fully cemented and smells musty. Billy goes to the old furnace and swings open its heavy door. "If you have any trouble with it, just click off this switch right here." He puts his hand on a red switch on a post near the furnace. "See?"

She nods. In one step he is next to her, his hands holding her arms, swinging her against the post. He presses against her crotch. She twists to get away.

"C'mon. It don't hurt you none. The army wasn't a bed of roses, you know. Hold still a minute dammit!" He unzips his fly and lunges against her thighs. His hand goes up to pull the light string and the bulb above the stairs goes dark. "Nobody can see in. Just hold still a minute." He pulls her skirt up, claws her panties down and thrusts his cock, stiff and huge, into the warmth that is her thighs. He shoves it against her, throws back his head and pants, thrusting.

Lynnanne has gone past the roaring fire in the iron cage across the cellar out the sooty window to where the trees rise green into the sunset, to where the birds go low to nest for night.

Tony says, pulling into the drive, "They left the mower out. It looks like rain. I'll put it away and be right up."

Couldn't he have said, "Let's go make love"? Lynn thinks, going into the house. Couldn't he have said, "I want to be with you"? She checks the children: Lori asleep, Jon quiet with his books, willing to turn his stereo down so there won't be a clash; Christy reading sleepily; Anthony not yet home. Just time to call Ruth for a second before we go to bed, she thinks, dialing.

"Could I speak with Ruth, please?" she asks, thinking, damn, as Neil answers, how come he picked it up. "Hope I didn't interrupt your work."

"No, no," Neil says. There is a pause. "Ruth isn't home right now."

"Thanks. Just tell her I called. Nothing important."

There is another pause. Then Neil says, "Actually, I'd like to ask you something, Lynn. I found this note. She says she's left. 'Have to think a while. Ruth.' Do you know anything about that?"

Lynn reels, gasping; her voice holds smooth. "No. I don't know anything about it. When did she go?"

Neil sounds angry, puzzled. "She brought Nate home from the rehearsal and then left."

"That's strange," Lynn says. "No, she didn't say anything to me. Where do you think she is?"

"I don't know. Well, don't worry about her. She acts without thinking it through sometimes."

"Let me know if I can help."

"Sure. Thanks. Good night." Neil hangs up.

Tony comes in and beckons her to bed.

18

Lynnanne is crouching beside her father on the dry surface of the bottom land in July. He pulls a carrot for her from the row she planted in the spring, dropping the tiny seeds into the trench he'd made. Next to the row of filigreed carrot greens the corn rises dusty and tall. They stand, walk to the creek. It flows shallow now, that in the spring went deep, beautifully shadowed, channelled dark and cool, between the deep cut banks where ferns and grasses, brambles, mosses grow. Her father squats to wash the carrot and gives it to her to eat. They sit, cross-legged, by the creek. It's dammed up to force the water off into trenches that irrigate the corn, beans, cabbages, and the two long rows of sweet peas at the end. Lynnanne chews the carrot, crisp and sweet, watches the sunlight glinting on the creek, sparkling where the water barely covers the tops of rocks, glittering on mica where the edges of the channel lie dry and hot.

Another day the water witcher comes to the higher land. Lynnanne follows her father, watching the old man with the green willow bough as he talks, listens, looks around the land, and then appears to wander in a daze. Lynnanne sees the old man as coming out of Grimms', moving mysteriously to do his magic, trees to princesses, maple leaves to gowns, pumpkins to carriages, frogs into princes.

Somewhere in the house her mother hides, in tears, not wanting any well. Next to the house the water tower stands, tall as the house, covered with ivy and honeysuckle vines. On *its top are two barrels to catch the rain. Her mother is afraid they'll tear the tower down.*

The old man finds his way among the trees, circling that which no one else can see or smell or hear, until, all eyes focused on his hand, he stops. The green wand quivers, bends toward earth. A hushed roar rises from the small group following. They wait to see if he will hesitate, move on. He plants his feet like fence posts on the ground. His concentration yields to his voice. "Here," he says, "yes, here."

"Here," everyone repeats. "Here is the place."

The men drag the heels of their heavy workshoes to mark the ground to designate the spot. Lynnanne sees her father push his felt hat back from his sweating forehead, rub his hand along his silver-whiskered chin, size up the growth of fir and cedar near the spot. "Before you can say Jack Robinson," he says to her, "there'll be a well dug here. The water's running down there under us. Great rivers are down there somewhere, Lynnanne, just like the ones we fish in up on top, except there aren't any fish in them." He laughs and she laughs with him and he crouches, hoists her up on his knee, and adds, "The water's down there all right, and we're going to drill right down to it."

The drilling rig comes on another day. Lynnanne stays in the ferns nearby and watches, waits. The drillers can't strike through. "Hard pan," they say.

Lynnanne slithers, Indian, through the ferns, feathers in her hair, and thinks about the great rivers underground flowing dark and still, evading these hard-talking men with their giant cutting drill that whirls its shaft through earth and rocks and sand in search of them. Hard pan, she thinks, and takes the words away with her, the feel of the clay, the knowledge that its smooth cool strength can hold great rivers from the reach of men.

Lynn lies with Tony, reconciled, in their bed, and grips the green willow bough with all her strength. Tony sleeps. His contentment lies above them like an extra blanket too heavy in the early summer warmth. She wants to kick it off but lies, holding her aching legs still, arching each foot in turn, stretching each ankle, rotating each foot, stretching the muscles quietly, acceptably, so she will not lash out like a wild mare. She moves carefully through their twenty years, letting the willow dip toward earth anywhere she can, hoping she will strike through to streams if not directly to a river coursing in magic majesty in caverns underground.

The willow quivers and she lets it dip, follows it downward through swirling faces, voices, laughter, past tablecloths and Christmas trees, past picnics and parties, and thinks she has found the fountainhead, holds tight to the branch and tumbles underground where all is dark and the waters rushing past her carry her downward farther, faster, rolling her over sideward and tumbling her, scraping her raw on ledges, jagged overhangs, piercing shags and splintered rock. She has the willow in her hand and sees Tony's face, but every smile turns into a sneer and every loving word into a barb. "You have become totally self-centered," he is saying, and "To distance is to kill." "I do not love the children," he is saying, "and I do not love you. Don't tell me whom I love." "No," he is saying, "No, no, no, no, no, no," and he is lunging toward her, eyes closed tight saying, "I can't wait to get home and stick it in you, stick it in you, stick it in you."

Lynn is at the phone before the third ring has begun. "I don't know why I'm calling you," Ruth says from far away, from somewhere the other side of oceans, on some abandoned edge of a wartime air strip.

"Come home," Lynn says, "come home, Ruth. I love you."

"I shouldn't have called," Ruth says.

"Where are you?"

"That doesn't matter."

'But where *are* you?" Lynn thinks this is what it's like to bring in a pilot blind.

"I don't know. Upstate somewhere. Maybe Massachusetts by now. The parkway doesn't end till Canada — maybe not then. It doesn't matter anyhow." Ruth's voice is tight and clipped and on a fast track.

Lynn breaks in. "Ruth. Are you in a motel?"

"I'm in a car."

"Ruth. Find a motel and stay there tonight and tomorrow come back."

"No, no."

"No to what?"

"No, I don't belong there."

"What does that mean?"

"I don't."

"Ruth?"

"What?"

"Whatever you're doing, don't. Look, you have to come home." Lynn makes her voice matter-of-fact, circumventing her own panic.

"No, actually I don't. You're home where you belong. I don't belong at home – Neil doesn't give a damn – and I shouldn't have called you."

"Ruth!" Lynn feels the fog hover over the control tower from which she speaks, feels it close around the place where Ruth now stands. She shifts beams. "Neil phoned to ask if I knew where you are. Maybe you should call him."

"I don't want to talk to Neil."

As she hears Ruth's answer, Lynn realizes that it was she who called Neil, not Neil who called. Designating the moment an emergency she doesn't correct her error. "He's worried about you."

"No, he isn't. He figures I'm doing just one more crazy thing. Which I am. Good night, Lynn." For a flicker of time Ruth's voice sounds like her own voice, "Sleep well, Lynn."

The wire is dead. Lynn sits, holding the phone, warming it with her hands, but it doesn't ring again. At last she stands and walks slowly through the house, touching the window pane with her flat palm, looking at pictures hanging on the wall; she sits on the sofa, thinking, wide awake. She tries to hold her thoughts on Tony and his news. Her thoughts ricochet off him every time toward Ruth. She picks up the photograph album from the end table. At least, she thinks ruefully, there are no pictures there of Ruth. Lynn sits, turning pages slowly on into the night, searching for links between the Tony who holds a baby laughing in his arms and the Tony who wishes his sons would leave the house.

Toward dawn she goes to bed. Half awake, half asleep she moves in and out of memories and dreams: the face of the young Tony in the album appears, only to change into a boy in uniform who is then carrying a rifle. Awake she watches the early light come gently around the trees, begin to delineate the branches, the rich leaves. She wonders if Ruth is driving down a highway, headed out or headed home, sleepy or stark awake. Lynn dozes. They are crashing down the door of the house where Ruth and her mother are hiding out; Lynn is there with them but she is hanging onto the window ledge, watching, as the door splinters into pieces and the Gestapo plunge in, intent clear on their faces. Ruth thrashes as they drag her out but she is silent, face clenched against crying out. Lynn sobs, tries to climb in the window to help her but knows even as she tries that she too will be hauled away, and that she cannot pull herself in the window, lacking the strength in her arms to raise herself. Her own struggling stifled scream hangs between Tony and herself in the bed as he asks her what's the matter.

"Nightmare," she mumbles, "nightmare. Gestapo after Ruth."

His arm encloses her shaking shoulders. She is sobbing, still in the dream, trying to pull her own weight up to the sill, knowing they are going down the stairs inside and will be out, under her on the sidewalk, ready to shoot her as she falls. "Hey, hey," he says, sleepily, his voice low and comforting, "it's okay. Just a bad dream."

The stream for which she searched is found. The willow dips and stays. She holds her fear on her open palm toward him and he on his open palm offers back his real comforting. She sleeps.

The next afternoon Ruth calls again. "I'll be home tonight," she says. "I panicked. I'm okay now."

"Thank God," Lynn says.

"Nothing so dramatic — just thank credit cards and a well-tuned engine. Are you all right?"

"I'm fine."

"I'll just bet you are."

"Come home, hmm?"

"Right. And yes, I do love you."

19

"Started from the beginning with the shrink," Tony says, filling his pipe.

"Which beginning?" Lynn asks, thinking of their first deep problems when they were in Rome, thinking of Tony's early childhood, his father's death, his dream as an altar boy of entering the priesthood.

"How I was grateful to you from the beginning and that was a mistake."

The words hang before her eyes superimposed on her text like Chinese characters, running counter to the print. "Hmm?"

"You know that. You know I've always been grateful to you — at first overwhelmingly grateful to you."

"For what?"

"For saving me."

"From what?"

"You know."

Something here should be familiar, Lynn thinks. It's their marriage he's talking to her about. He says she knows. Lynn surveys the terrain she's been exploring now for several years but can find nothing that will fill this space. Once, in third grade, reviewing old number facts, the teacher asked her what seven plus five was and she, who always answered first and best and never missed anything at all, couldn't find any language in which she could reply, and so stood mute; for this failure she was made to stand, dumb, in the aisle until school was out. Lynn sits now, studying the past, ranging the silent darkness for a clue. "No, I don't know."

Tony lights his pipe and starts to read again, then lays aside his book. "I thought I couldn't."

"Couldn't?" Lynn finds nothing to correspond to his words.

"I thought I was lost and you were lost too."

She says nothing, listens, lets her mind spin, waiting to connect with some facet of his words.

"You remember. You helped me make it, to have sex. I couldn't get over being grateful to you for that."

Lynn narrows her search, remembering his exuberant glee at his success on their honeymoon.

"You did know that?" he says, momentarily unsure.

"No."

"But you *must* have. I threatened suicide!"

Lynn concentrates on remembering. He's changed the cue. She remembers: "I don't want to throw myself in front of a subway train!" She remembers: "If mankind destroys the cities, the hub of civilization, of the arts, then mankind does not deserve to survive and I don't want to survive."

She remembers her response: "Don't you want to be around to help rebuild? I sure do."

And his torn laugh in answer, "You would! But I wouldn't. That's the difference between us, Lynn." She wrote a three act play about a nuclear war in which there were only a few survivors, about despair and love and hope, and her college theater class put it on.

"Not over that! You threatened suicide over nuclear war and the futility of life!" Lynn says.

"Christ! Lynn, come on — I threatened suicide because I couldn't make it with you. You remember that night."

She works backwards in search of some night she has forgotten. Couldn't make it. Couldn't make it.

They are alone in his apartment. They are lying on his bed, listening to music. Until then they have only sat on park benches and kissed and he has sometimes stroked her breasts through her clothing and pressed himself against her. Lynn has thought for a long time that she shouldn't try sex until she's married. She's afraid it will take a while to erase what she remembers from her childhood. Lying there with Tony, stroking, kissing one another, she wants to go further; wishing he would take his clothes off, she loosens hers. It feels to her like all her former logic about marriage being the only right time and place, might be wrong. She wants to yield if he asks to go ahead. She presses herself more tightly length to length. But he does not ask. During the months after that they go to concerts and to plays but don't again find themselves alone in his apartment. But that can't be the night Tony means. Lynn doubts he ever thought of it again. So what night then? The first time they did have sex?

On the first night of their honeymoon, Lynn thinks Tony will carry her past her own anxieties with his loving passion. He comes to bed with his pajamas on to hide his penis which is hanging limp. Anxiously he tells her he is sorry. Quietly Lynn relinquishes her fantasy. She strokes his back, thighs, kisses him with long deep kisses, fondles his penis with her hands until it is erect and he can enter her.

Impatiently Tony interrupts her memories. "In my apartment the night before the wedding. You certainly remember."
He means a still different night then, Lynn thinks. She realigns her memory and concentrates on the night Tony has in mind, the night before the wedding.

They go with friends, laughing a lot, to dinner and a foreign film that night. Afterwards, to her surprise, Tony asks Lynn to come to his apartment.
Once there, he says, "Why not tonight?"
Lynn thinks it can't matter if they start this night or the next. "If you want," she says.
He takes her in his arms and she waits. She assumes he will open his fly, his stiffened penis will emerge, and he will move it between her legs, in and out, and she hopes his orgasm will make her feel good, make her come, too, the way it happens

*when she masturbates to a fantasy of a man's penis penetrating
her. Tony hasn't ever touched her below the waist.*

*He drops his pants. They are in one another's arms, kissing.
But his penis doesn't stiffen, doesn't enter her. "Let's wait,"
he says. "It's better if we wait."*

Nothing more occurs on Lynn's memory screen. That
evening was not active in her mind and finding it, she finds a
forgotten night and doesn't know how accurately she brings it
back.

"I threatened to jump in front of a train for God's sake!"
Tony's voice is testy.

"Not that night," Lynn says. "I don't remember that."

Tony is incredulous. "Of course you remember that!"

"No, I don't." She remembers the line, "I don't want to
throw myself in front of a subway train!" But Lynn cannot
connect it in her mind with the night they almost had sex.
The suicide threat has always been that vague darkness in him
against which she's always argued. But it never had anything to
do with sex.

Suppressing his anger, Tony draws slowly on his pipe. He
explains slowly, as to students in an unresponsive class: "Once
in the army a guy came down on me and after that I thought I
couldn't make it with a woman. I never tried until that night
with you. I thought I was ruined. I thought I'd always been
queer. You know how kids doubt themselves? I worried about
myself. When I found out about you I thought we might at
least save each other. You were damaged goods from your
brothers. I thought you'd be frigid at the least. I was afraid I
was in danger of being a homosexual. I thought we'd be better
off married to each other."

Lynn hears her voice move across the room from somewhere other than within herself. "Did you love me?"

"Not at first. I thought we could protect each other. You
saved me right away and I was exaggeratedly grateful. The
shrink thinks I needn't have been so grateful. He thinks I
really had no problem — I would have been okay anyhow. But
I was terribly grateful. And I guarded you. I kept you from

falling off the precipice. After a while I loved you; I came to love you very much." He takes the pipe from his mouth and smoke comes out in tiny swirls.

Lynn says nothing. Her hands grip her book. She sits very still. Precipice, she thinks. Guarded. She feels a wave of nausea, as though at the top of an extremely high and narrow peak.

"At first when we had sex I fantasied you were a man," the person across the room is saying, putting the pipe back into the narrow opening between the narrow lips.

Now she plummets and is swept under the earth down roaring currents that are cold and dark, locked out of reach of air. The room is still. He has asked her something. She casts up from below the earth to replay the question already put to her.

"Did you have fantasies of making love to women?"

"No," she says.

"You must be very inhibited then. Normal people fantasize sex with both men and women. And you've always been especially attracted to women."

"No," a voice says, "no I never was. I loved you, Tony. I never was attracted to anyone but you, not for twenty years."

For twenty years, she thinks, he's guarded me. Guarded me. And lied to me. Never told me. Never let me guess. For twenty years he's touched me out of fear. Fear that he wanted to touch a man. He *married* me out of fear. *Fear.* So he wouldn't touch a man or let a man touch him. The sentences within her mind slide into notches, tab matches tab, code matches code. Her mind clamps down. Fear. Lie. Fear. Lie. Many little teeth on many little gears engage and turn and home film strips year after year after year careen in order within the marriage archives in her mind. The missing frame slides finally into place. Click. Irrevocably seen in place. Locked in, once seen.

"And Ruth?"

Two separate sorts of creatures sit here now in separate places sending words back and forth. The base language has been changed. Word-truth does not apply. A different order of magnitude whirs in this rhetoric.

"Ruth is my friend," she says, "only my friend."

Lynn lays down her book and walks to the other room where she picks up the phone. She dials each digit with transcendent care. "Julia? Could you possibly see me for a while tonight? It's not an emergency, but I . . . if you could, I'd like to come on over."

20

Lies. Lies. "And if all the axes were one great axe and the great man took the great . . ." And all the lies were one great lie and the great man took the great lie and cut down the great marriage what a great great splash that great tree would make! Lynn is driving, not yet heading home, after seeing Julia. The guard rail on her right clicks past her zing zing and she thinks: guarded, guarded, guarded from the beginning: GUARDED! Damaged goods, ". . . married you out of pity . . . you were damaged goods . . ." Not pity, she thinks. That's a lie too. Fear, not pity. He was scared. He was terrified because he couldn't get it up with a woman. You helped him. He married you because he was in danger and you were no threat. You helped him all those years; now he decides he was only momentarily in need of help. Now he decides he married you out of pity.

An undercoating of fear glints through the early years as she reruns them now, showing in streaks here and there. He straightarmed friends, she thinks, whenever they got too close. In graduate school, Nancy and Eric were the first. He was afraid whenever people came in close — she remembers her own happiness when someone came close and how the ones with whom there began to be real feeling were rejected by him for the ones who held equidistant dinner party after dinner party.

Pulling me back from the precipice. Controlling. Limiting. Holding back. Fear of love. Fear he'd want a man. Eyes shut, pretending, afraid of what he'd do if he let go. As soon as someone got in close, that person had to be put down, kept away, cut down. He guarded against them for me and for himself.

Pretending our love to keep bad love, wrong love at bay. Hypocrite! Lynn thinks, you hypocrite!

In the little room on holiday that first married year, when he said there were things he wouldn't ever tell, this was the thing he wouldn't ever tell, this was the wall that closed me off, that he fought to keep inside, that he lied, denied, masked over to keep from the light of day. On that deceit our marriage stood, built on a base I thought was love — and it was fear.

It's late and there are almost no cars now. Lynn drives fast, words catapulting through her head: damaged goods. And he, afraid to trust himself, afraid he would go with a man, not letting himself have, not letting himself want, faking it with me — pretending I was the man. Not wanting me.

Don't you and Ruth wish the other were a man?

Not like that. The other way around. We love each other as we are. We didn't deny that love. We don't deny that love. We don't deny the other. Just for the world's set-up, just for letting us be together, we've said what if one of us were a man. But I love her and she loves me exactly as we are. How could you make love to someone wishing that person were not the person that she is, not having that person's eyes, arms, hands, breasts, thighs?

Closed eyes, is how. Never to touch where the legs part and the woman-opening, the woman-smell, the woman-moisture is, that's how.

Lynn steps on the brake and pulls off on the shoulder, feeling sick. She remembers herself sitting astride Tony, her mouth around his cock, his eyes closed, his hands flung passive on the bed. Did he daydream me away, daydream me into a man? She puts her head down on the steering wheel. Yes, she thinks, yes, he did; he willed away my softness, my shape, my openings and closings, and made me into a mouth that took his penis into it, so that afterwards there would be another penis wanting his own mouth. A hard straight penis outside a hard straight man with no woman's dark and terrifying inner caves.

Didn't *you* have fantasies with Tony? What's wrong with fantasies? Lynn challenges herself.

She remembers lying under Tony, thinking of lying naked in the wind, the sun, thinking of a man kissing her hand, wrist, arm, thinking of being thrust back then upon the grass and entered by Leon from *Madame Bovary* while actually above her Tony thrusts steadily, eyes closed, breathing hard.

What's the difference? Lynn asks herself. The answer snaps back, already indisputable: he denied my presence, wanted what I could not be. I only wanted to accentuate what he himself was, to make it better. He had to work so hard to make love to me. I thought the fault lay with me. I thought I should be able to transform the scene so I would excite him; then he would excite me.

Ruth and I know one another, she thinks, starting the car. Ruth and I have held back nothing of our fear, nothing of our love. We know one another absolutely. He closed his eyes and lied.

"Your eyes are wrecked," Tony says.

"What?" Lynn asks, thinking he said, "Your eyes are cracked."

"Your eyes are wrecked," he says again, quite distinctly. "It's too bad."

"What do you mean?" Knowing that he means they do not look at one another any more; remembering the first year they were married, his saying to her while they are sitting on the subway train, "You can't look at people that way, you know." Knowing that he means openly, nothing hidden. He wants her to look only at him that way. But she will not guard her look. And now, twenty years later, she will not guard her look except with him.

Back in traffic, Lynn's head is swimming and the lights of cars across the divider blur and spin; she focuses sharply on the taillights of a truck ahead and follows carefully.

Moving on. Always moving on. And you? Because he had

the job you let him choose. The decisions to move were always his. You never opposed him, never said, "Let the kids keep their friends this time; let us keep our friends; let's stay at this campus and become even closer friends with them." Afraid, he always wanted to move on. Suddenly Lynn feels a wave of sympathy for the man who had to hide, hold back, deny his feelings all his life; what a volcano he must be, she thinks. How awful that I kept reassuring him, kept saying everything was find.

The taillights zigzag in front of her and she rubs her eyes hard. God, why didn't I believe him the first time he said he didn't love me? Why didn't I say then, all right, go — why not? Why not then, before there were children, before there were twenty years of happy, happy marriage with me smiling, smiling, smiling? Because he didn't say it then, she answers; he only said it after there were children, you fool, only then, and you didn't believe him when he did. The children were already born, already growing up.

"Modern psychology has taken my authority away," Tony says, standing angrily beside her on the lawn. I can't call the truant officer, can't call the police."
"For your own children?"
"Yes."
"But you wouldn't want to. You want to help your own children, Tony."

It is himself he needed the police for, Lynn thinks; he was afraid he would himself lose control. Until they turned adolescent, Lynn thinks, he must have genuinely enjoyed the children. Did his adolescent sons make him more anxious about sex? Lynn feels a strong wave of nausea that he would let it all explode on his own sons' heads as if they had created his turmoil, as if they were the cause of his old agony.

Abruptly she sees as though for the first time that scene she has reviewed so many times: two bodies locked in combat rolling on the floor. In the back room her visiting mother is hiding, pretending none of it is happening at all. Tony is sitting on Anthony's thin chest, pinning him; Anthony is desperate, gasping like a fish thrown on the beach. Lynn herself is moving between her mother's practiced none-of-it-exists-long-suffering-smile and her own way of reassuring Tony, reassuring Anthony, and catches herself for once unable to reassure them both — splayed in her fixed uncertain smile.

Then she goes to Julia. The kids won't go and Tony won't go and Lynn goes, apologizing, saying, "I'm ashamed to take your time when there are others who really need it. For me it's a luxury," and Julia, answering, "I don't consider it a luxury for you." She goes then, to the little room she has just come from tonight, where no one denies. Together they search for truth.

The car returns to the garage, Lynn's body finds its way to bed. Tony is already there, asleep. Lynn eases in beside him quietly.

The highway lights still swirl in her head. She allows her eyes to close, her hands to release the wheel. "Damaged goods, damaged goods," erupts around her like depth charges as she sinks toward sleep.

She sees snapshots of herself the first year she knew Tony, graduating from high school, and again of Tony and herself, laughing in the waves. She sees one of herself graduating from college the first year they were married, in a white dress, on a lawn, and the charges explode, spattering her white dress with blood: damaged goods.

"Who the hell is that?" Tony says.

"What?"

"What woke us up. It's people."

She hears then the voices in the kitchen. "Must be Anthony — he wasn't in yet when I came in."

"Well for Christ's sake, where does he think he is?" Tony

swings out of bed and heads for the door. She watches his angry form disappear. Downstairs the laughter quiets. There is conversation. Tony reappears.

"He's got some bitch with him," he says, pulling on his pants, "and I'm getting rid of her."

"What are you doing?" Lynn asks, sitting up.

"I'm taking the lady home," he says, and heads for the bathroom. As he leaves the room he calls back to her, "You're turning this house into a fucking whorehouse!" And he is gone.

She thinks they should have stayed asleep. Or pretended to. Why not let Anthony, who has been lonely, be with a girl for a few hours while everyone's asleep. What harm? No one would ever know. He'd walk her home by dawn. He has no car to be with her in. The fields? Not in surburbia. And he is old enough. What was the rage in Tony's voice, the fury in his stomping down the stairs?

She considers his shout, "You're turning this house into a fucking whorehouse!"

Fear. Fear of her. Hatred of her. "Stop ravaging me," he said once after her therapy had taken hold and she had become thin and sexier than before. He laughed but she thought the phrase an odd one. Now she hears his voice above her, around her, like a blizzard blasting her bare body with its cold. "You're turning this house into a fucking whorehouse!" Then, she thinks, I must be the whore.

Very carefully, very quietly, as though she were frozen almost numb, Lynn stands up from the bed and pulls her bathrobe on. Very quietly she walks over to the door.

Whore.
Whore.

New York. Before they are married. Walking home from an evening with Tony; he goes to his job at the health club where he works, and she walks toward the dorm, alone. She hears a car pull to the curb. It honks. She ignores it. It follows her. She walks faster; it follows her. She looks to see if she knows the driver. He is big and heavy and about forty years old. She doesn't know him. He calls to her. Again and again and again.

She glances back. He is smiling and waving at her. "Hey, I want to ask you something." She walks on. "Just ask. Any harm in that?" She stops and goes over to the car. He laughs. "Are you afraid of me?" She shakes her head. "That's good. Christ, you've no reason to be. Where're you going?"

   "Back to school," she says.

   "Where's that?"

   "A couple more blocks."

   "Want to ride?"

   "No, thanks."

   "Hey, wait a minute. This is a damned unfriendly town, do you know that? Were you born here?"

   She shakes her head, hesitates.

   "Where then?"

   "Out west."

   "That's more like it. Hey, I have an idea. If I park the car and get out of it, would you just talk to me a little while? I'm damned lonesome."

   She hesitates.

   "You can walk away any time you want. Okay?" He laughs. "Or are you scared of me?"

   She shakes her head. He smiles, parks the car, gets out and walks near her. "Hey now, that's better, isn't it? I don't come to the city often. How long have you been here?"

   They walk a ways, talking. Near the college he asks her to go in and have a cup of coffee with him and she does. It's a bar and he orders whiskey sours. They talk and he orders another round. She's not used to liquor. In the dorm she drinks only wine. When they stand to leave she feels her feet heavily uncertain under her.

   "I think you need a ride back home, Lynn," he says. "It was nice of you to come with me a minute."

   In the car he goes on talking, drives around the block, and parks near to the campus but on a darkened street. He turns off the key and faces her.

   Lynn sits, waiting, knowing what will come. "Let's have a little pleasure before you go in," he says. "You're so fresh and young. You do me good just seeing you." He puts his hand on her leg, and bends his face toward her.

"*I don't want to,*" *she says.*

"*Look,*" *he says,* "*I need you. I'm in a bad way. I won't hurt you, Lynn. I promise I won't hurt you in any way. Just be with me a while.*"

She watches him. She shakes her head but she knows the plane is already down the runway and away. He pilots it with ease. She can't jump out now. She's responsible for him. He studies her. "*Do it with your boy friend, don't you?*"

"*No,*" *she says.* "*We only kiss.*"

"*Show me how,*" *he says.*

She shakes her head.

"*Come on, do something nice for me. He moves his hand back and forth along her leg. She watches him. He strokes her leg with his right hand. With his left he puts his zipper down and lets his penis out. It swells, white and long, beneath the steering wheel.* "*Put your hand on it then,*" *he says.*

She moves as he directs. Her fingers close around the shaft. Somewhere, she knows, the Lynn she sometimes is, has a room in which to sleep, legs stretched out safely, where no prowlers come. But here, she watches through a scrim as this girl does what she is told, moving her hand in a rhythm known to her longer than she has known how to speak in words. "*My God that's fine,*" *he says.* "*Do that for your boyfriend too, don't you? Up in his room?*"

"*No,*" *she says,* "*I don't.*"

"*Kiss me,*" *he says.* "*Come on, baby, let's feel that tongue of yours, come on.*"

"*No,*" *she says.*

"*Put your mouth on my cock then,*" *he says, voice urgent, eyes pleading, desperate, in touch with her own eyes which she does not know how to turn away from him.* "*Come on, baby. Suck me off,*" *he says.*

"*No,*" *she says.*

"*Then open your mouth and flick your tongue for me. It won't hurt you any. Come on, kid.*" *He is not rough with her. His hand along her thighs does not intrude.* "*Look — you can't stop now.*"

This Lynn that Lynn is watching does as she is told. She parts her lips and moves her tongue in sight, then opens her lips further as she feels his cock rise and stiffen more. She flutters her tongue. He arches his whole body, freezes for a final rigid moment and lets out a long long moan. "My God," he says, "you do that like a professional. Where did you learn? Where in God's name did you ever learn?"

She says good night. He says he wants her name, her phone. He will send her flowers every day, he says. He will take her out to dinner. She says good night and goes.

Back in her room she lies alone staring at the walls. The night careens around her out of control. She hides from it on her bed, holding very still. She sees grotesque faces that she does not want to see against her wall. She sees men's faces and she sees men's hands distorted on the wall and she feels all night a throbbing ever present quickening as of a man next to her wildly jerking off.

Whore.
Whore.
Lynn stands in the quiet house, in the doorway of their bedroom, thinking, waiting.
Whore.

After the war: open windows letting the smell of dogwood quiver through the house; Marsh, whispering urgently, "Come on. I need it. I need it really bad."

Lynnanne rages back at him, "No, no. Why don't you go to a prostitute?"

And Marsh, who always wins at everything he does, pushes a comb through his wavy hair as he answers with contempt, "Christ! Why do you think I come to you?"

Tony comes up the stairs, quickly. "That's one little girl that won't be back," he says.
"Where's Anthony?"
"I left him there. He wanted to walk home."
"I'll bet he did."

"They have to 'talk'," Tony says, mockingly. "Come on, let's go to bed."

Lynn is in the hall outside their bedroom. The house is very still. Tony is very wide awake. "Come on," he says, starting past her. "Let's go to bed."

"No," she says. "I'm staying up a while."

They stand, face to face. There is a smell around them, as of a grass fire, smouldering near, unstoppable.

"Don't stay up," he says. The rage has excited him, she knows. She sees it in his face. She knows that he would take her now with more force than he ever has. Force, like the force with which he hurled Jon's guitar. Force like the force with which he pulled Anthony to the ground. Like his heavy pounding down the stairs as he called back, "You've turned this place into a fucking whorehouse." She knows he feels his own power; he is excited by it, values it, thinks he is now free to treat her, when they have sex, the way he thinks she wants to be treated. Wordlessly, standing six inches from him, he in his pants pulled on over his pajamas, she in her bathrobe, she knows all that.

"No," she says again. "I'm staying up."

"Come here," he says, confidently. Certain she will come, eager, smiling, to put her hands on him, her thighs opening beneath him as he wants, he jerks his head toward the bedroom doorway, uses language new between them: "Come on, you cunt, I want to fuck."

"No," Lynn says.

His hand is back at his side again, almost before she knows that he lifted it to strike her: hard. But he does not touch her. She walks away and he, throttling his own rage within himself, goes alone into the bedroom and closes the door behind him.

Lynn walks slowly down the hall and opens Lori's door to check on her. The summer breeze stirs her hair, flutters a Peanuts poster on the wall. Lynn goes in, pulls the light blanket gently around her shoulders, stares at her face a moment, turns and leaves. She starts down the stairs but hears Anthony coming in and doesn't want him to think she's trying to intercept him so they can have a talk. She stands there three steps down and knows that there is nowhere for her to go.

She doesn't remember in twenty-five years of knowing Tony ever before saying no.

No.

No.

A fucking whorehouse. She sits on the third step. She has nowhere to go. She has never made a place for herself to go. Even her typewriter is in a corner of their bedroom. She would go outside but she is not dressed and she will not, even to get clothes, go into their bedroom again tonight. No. No. Fear curls in her gut. He wanted to hit her. He wanted to hit her hard. But he did not. And will not. The possible moment is past.

Outside, the first light of dawn catches the tops of trees. Young leaves glow softly yellow-green.

My mother raised me to be a whore, Lynn thinks. Perfectly to be a whore. Smile and all. And all and smile. "Always smile," my mother said, "when you meet a stranger. It can never hurt."

No.

Whore.

No.

Lynn hears the neighbor's dog begin to bark. A door slams. The morning is beginning. In the kitchen the refrigerator door goes shut. Not too miserable to eat, she thinks of Anthony; that's good. That gentle wild kid. And Jon in the heart of his night's sleep now, as other people wake up for their day, and Christy wanting peace, and Lori about to appear for an orange to eat in front of the TV. Her table-setting mothering self whips through her like a desert wind, leaving no relief. Damaged goods, he'd called her. She puts her hand on the rails of the bannister and stares through the space between.

Whore. Whore. Whore.

Smile.

Smile.

Tony and Lynn stand on a patch of lawn somewhere in the city watching pigeons. He confronts her, seriously, "I care about silver patterns and lace tablecloths, and I don't think you do."

She laughs, watching the sunshine on the cement walk, pushing her foot into the grass, watching the pigeons fly into the sun. "I don't, but that won't matter, Tony, if we love each other."

"No?"

"No. I love you, Tony."

"Lynn, Lynn, I love you, too."

The sunlight blinds her as the pigeons rise toward the summer sky.

PART III

21

Driving to school, Lynn swerves to miss the small white form, quiet, halfway across the road. All this spring she has seen them there along the road: opossums: dead. She asks her supervising teacher why there are so many. "It's because they freeze when the headlights hit them."

"I think I'm getting a divorce," Lynn says.

They have passed through giant locks. No one saw the gate rise but the currents throb and pull until the level shifts and she is on a different plane than he.

"The therapy has changed you totally," he says. "You are completely self-centered now."

"Send the children to the living room," Tony says, imperious. "I'll tell them we're getting a divorce."

"Why not wait until we know what we're doing," Lynn says, washing lettuce.

"Why wait? I'm moving out tomorrow. It's all quite clear."

"Aren't you going to Chicago in two weeks? Isn't that soon

enough?" Thinking, what is happening? How did we get here? Not us, not Lynn and Tony. Lynn's body contests itself, not knowing how to move. Her voice interrupts itself, not knowing what to say.

"No, that's not soon enough! I can't stand it in this place another night!" He looks at her with contempt and rage.

Because I haven't gone back into his bed? she wonders. Is that what he can't stand? She turns to the stove to stir the stew.

"Now send the kids in."

"Not Lori. Not yet."

"All right. Not Lori."

Lynnanne wakes to the strange flicker of orange light. The walnut tree outside her window twists against the light as it moves sinuously across the window ledge. Her door opens. Her mother says, "Come, hurry now, we're going outside," and they move down the stairway and out into the night-time yard. Lynnanne stands next to her mother by the silver maple, among strangers who trample the daffodils and primroses in the round garden there. The fire chief tells her mother she should go to some neighbor's house because he thinks the farmhouse is burning to the ground. "Take the child and go," he says, and returns to the other men.

"We're staying right here," her mother says.

The house is saved. All the upstairs wallpaper has water stains that spread in jagged patterns down the walls, across the ceilings, but the house survives.

"What do you want to do about Marty and Marie?" Lynn asks, packing lunches.

"Meaning?"

"We said we'd go out to dinner with them when they're in Manhattan for Marty's conference."

"When?"

"This weekend."

"All right."

"All right what?"

"All right, let's go."

Lynn, who has never cared much what she wears, can't decide which dress, which skirt, which blouse. She ends up with a new pantsuit that has a flowered collar. On the way out, telling Lori, "There are fudgesicles in the freezer and you may stay up for *My Friend Flicka.* Christy will watch that with you, won't you, Christy?" Lynn knows that all the children are stalwartly looking elsewhere so they won't be caught staring at what looks like their parents going out together.

Lynn is glad they are eating in a restaurant instead of someone's home. It's easier to talk to Marty with a waiter over his left shoulder than with the kids around. It's easier to say to Marie, aside, "We've been going around and around for a long time now," while the family at the next table argues over desserts, than in the house where she would see the tears in Marie's eyes and want to cry herself; here, in public, she drinks more wine instead. Lynn is dizzy as if they are on a stage, as if the stage hands and the orchestra have gone home for the night, and she and Tony, Marty and Marie, are left on a half-furnished stage, revolving in front of an audience already turned to go.

When the waiter brings the dessert menu and Lynn orders pie, Tony interrupts to say, "They have cheese cake; it's listed separately, down with the mousse." The familiarity stings and Lynn thanks him for pointing it out but doesn't change her order; swallowing the bites of pie, she knows her cheeks are flushed as though smarting from a blow.

"Okay, kids, I won't say try to work it out, but maybe you should try to work it out." Marty's eyes are dark with his concern beneath the laughter. "Maybe you should try to work out a way to try to work it out — I mean —"

"Oh, Marty, stop!" Marie smiles at him but takes his arm and turns him toward their car. "Can we give you a ride?"

Around them on the sidewalk strangers pass. An amputee rests on the sidewalk against the building wall, his hat upturned in front of him, playing his harmonica for money. "No, no thanks. Our car is in the garage across the street."

"Seriously, I hope the Chicago teaching works out well."

"Yeah, thanks. I'll see you at MLA."

A bus comes at them as they cross the street. Tony grabs her arm as they run out of its path. "Crazy Americano driver!" Tony says, imitating pedestrians in Rome. "*Ariverdicci!*" he says, and they both laugh and Lynn doesn't know where to put her arm that is in his nor how not to let the laughter strangle her.

"He's taken two suitcases and gone to the city. He's staying with friends," Lynn tells Ruth on the phone.

Ruth's voice is taut. "Because of me?"

"No, no. He may come back after Chicago. I don't know. I'll think in the summer while he's gone." Lynn feels all the words about Tony and herself roll hollow as egg shells blown out for Easter. "Now, how are you?"

"Okay."

"No, how are you really?"

"I don't know really. I'm going to try."

"Good."

"Maybe good. I don't know."

"Come by tonight?"

"If I can. I'll call later."

Tony phones his colleagues to tell them he has left, moved out. "Divorce," he says. Friends call friends and it circles back to Lynn that he is doing this.

"We'll need a lawyer," Lynn says into the mouthpiece of the kitchen phone.

"No way," Tony answers. "Once you go into legalese you stop being human. It's worse than therapy. You've analyzed us into this. That's bad enough."

Lynn moves as carefully as though his clothes, still in the closet, his books still on the shelves, have burst into flames past which she is carrying the children to safety, one by one.

"Anthony goes before the judge on Tuesday," Lynn says.

Tony's smooth voice wraps her; it loops in and out, around her legs, her arms. "No, I'm not going to court with him. You go, if you want."

"I think he needs his parents there."

"He doesn't *need* us. He may *want* his parents there. And *you* may *want* to go. But *I don't* want to go and I don't need to go and I'm not going to go." He laughs.

His voice has roped her. He pulls it tighter with his laughter. She tries to break away which only makes the rope bite deeper.

"Then I'll go. I'll let you know what happens."

"Don't get yourself locked up!" He laughs.

"No," she answers, and hears her own laughter sucked into the phone, appeasing him. "Maybe you'll change your mind and come."

"I have no intention, Lynn, of encouraging Anthony's behavior. Good-by."

Rope-burned, she leaves the phone.

Lynn stands in the rain outside Nora Daniel's office, staring at the plate glass window, the lettering across the glass: Attorney-at-Law. The door is locked. Go get coffee, she says to herself, go look at books in the bookstore across the street. She's late. Lynn stands against the window, rain soaking through her clothes, the awning next door spouting water in erratic spurts down on her shoulders, into her hair. If she walks away she will not know how to make herself come back again.

Inside at last she says, "I want to draw up legal separation papers."

"Is that what your husband wants?"

"No. But he'll sign, I think. He's already moved out."

"But he doesn't want a divorce?" The woman pushes back her chair to study Lynn.

"He tells everyone he's getting a divorce. But he won't see a lawyer."

"Why do *you* want it legal?"

Lynn ponders the older woman's face. It's kind and tough. She doesn't seem hurried. "I think we'll get a divorce in the end. We have four kids. I've been going to school and doing my practice-teaching. I'm job hunting for September. There are family debts. When he figures out that this isn't melodrama, that we really are getting a divorce, then I'm afraid he'll get mad and refuse to help and I'll need help with the kids. We better have something in writing to be sure he'll help them."

"What does your husband do?"

"He's a professor."

"And you right now?"

"I hope I'll get a high school teaching job. Right now I do some writing — stories, a novel —"

"Have you worked before?"

"Not for a salary." They both laugh.

Nora Daniels pulls her chair back to her desk. She picks up a pen. "I want you to go home and write down some things for me," she says. "But let's see what we can do today. Give me the children's names and ages, first."

"Anthony," Lynn says, "seventeen." How many times, for how many blanks in schools and doctors' offices, has she reeled them off? And each time she remembers the boys walking in the fields with her before Christy was born, and the trips to the little zoo in the park near which campus? And which was the campus with the river near?

Nora Daniels asks about each child. She has a grandchild Christy's age, she says. She has a lot of clients like Anthony, she says, "God bless them for their courage and their young conviction."

Lynn stares at her, aching for those words to have come from Tony, remembering sharply his standing with her the first time Anthony was arrested. That was the only time he did go into court. Having denounced the boy all the way to the court-house, when they stood before the judge, hands on the rail, looking far up into the judge's middle-aged blue eyes, waiting to hear his voice sentence their son to serve a jail term or to go free, then Tony put his hand over Lynn's hand, as though he were the loving father comforting the mother. Thinking of all the days and nights when he refused comfort or support to Anthony or herself, Lynn pulled her hand away.

They talk for hours. Nora Daniels listens, asks more questions, leans back to tell joking stories about other people she knows. Her eyes are sad and before Lynn leaves, Nora places both hands flat on the desk top and asks once more, "Are you sure this is what you want to do?"

Lynn says that she is sure. There is no smile on her face as she drives home, still damp from standing in the rain.

"We have no openings at present. You may leave an application if you wish." The young woman secretary smiles up at her and adds, "I can put you on the substitute list, if you'd like."

Lynn thanks her and leaves an application. She has an interview with the English Department chairman at the local high school. He talks about their core curriculum. She would be teaching five sections of composition, with an emphasis on grammar. He asks her if she could handle that. Hating herself for her dishonesty, Lynn fakes. She wants to argue that high school students need to be allowed to write freely, to do a lot of writing and improve that way, not to be constricted by grammar drills that do not help them write. She says that she could handle it, and hopes she fools him, hopes she gets the job.

Before she hears from the local school, Lynn gets a call from the university. It's the professor who taught one of her graduate courses in the spring. He has spoken of her to the administrators in a neighboring town's high school. He gives her a phone number. "I told them you're terrific," he says. "Let me know if you get the job."

Only after the interview, after signing the contract, after making her budget for the year, does Lynn begin to know how scared she should have been.

Lynn moves, a stranger to herself, apart from Tony. Torn edges seal. New blood circuits begin to flow.

Mobile, Alabama. Summer. Lynn is pressed against the window of a Greyhound, headed north again, back to college.

Hurricane warnings posted everywhere. Through the window she watches store owners, home owners, nailing boards across their windows. You either hammer down or you take off.

Tony's taking off. He hates me for the hammering down I've done, Lynn thinks.

"You've had an emotional pre-frontal lobotomy," Tony says.

22

"I hope this place is okay," Ruth says as they walk into the hotel lobby one evening in July.

"It's fine," Lynn says.

"How do you know?" Ruth laughs at her. "You're just afraid I'll make a scene!"

The desk clerk checks their reservations. "Twin beds or a double?" he asks, looking at Ruth.

Ruth glances at Lynn and says, "Do you care?" and then back at the clerk, "Twin but we wouldn't mind a double if that's what you have."

"We have either, m'am."

"Twin then." Ruth signs the register and they go to the elevator. "I didn't have the nerve to say we wanted the double bed!" Ruth grins.

Inside the room, Ruth closes the door behind them and they set down their suitcases, check the curtains, bath, lock. Ruth moves the bedside stand out from between the twin beds and slides one against the other. "There!" She turns, laughing, toward Lynn. "Now it's a double!" They stand facing one another. "Feel funny?" Ruth asks.

"More — happy," Lynn answers, and they turn into one another's arms.

All afternoon they stroke and kiss and doze, to wake kissing and touching and talking again. At five o'clock Ruth sits up and says, "Hey, we'd better think about dinner." Lynn lies, watching her, and lifts her hand to touch her face. Ruth falls back next to her, gathering her in her arms again.

At last Ruth takes her lips away and reaches for her watch. "Guess what time it is?"

"Six?"

"Eight!"

"You're kidding!"

"No. Eight. I'll be right back." Ruth pulls on slacks and a sweater and goes out the door. Lynn lies waiting for her to come back, unwilling to give up the smell, the feel of their lovemaking.

"*Voila!*" It's a French restaurant on the hoof!" Ruth puts two bags of groceries on the bureau, takes a bottle of wine from one, cheese and bread from the other.

"Shall I dress for dinner?" Lynn stands up.

Ruth circles her from behind and turns her for a long deep kiss. "Hurry up or I won't let you."

They eat, shower, turn on the TV, check all the channels and turn it off again. "I love you," Ruth says, as they lie together on the bed. Lynn moans as Ruth's hands touch her thighs and her lips kiss her arm.

In the muted daylight of early morning Ruth leans over to look out the window. "A beautiful day. Are we going to hit that exhibit, hmm? Are we?" And she moves toward the bathroom. "I'm starving," she says, coming back after a few minutes. "Want an orange?" She takes oranges and rolls from the bag. Lynn watches her peel the orange, standing naked by the bureau. Her body is lean and smooth and Lynn puzzles still that it has a woman's shape. She comes to the bed and pops a piece of orange into Lynn's mouth and then falls beside her for a long embrace. "The museum's not open quite yet, I guess," Ruth says, kissing her, "and checkout time's not until eleven."

Reluctantly Lynn says, "I'd better check with Christy and make sure everything's okay." She phones.

"They all right?"

"Yes. Anthony phoned to say the demonstration was rough and he got a little tear gas but he's on his way home. You'd think the government was at war with the children."

"They are. With some of them."

"I should be home early. Lori had a good time sleeping at

her friend's. Nate's there, practicing with Jon and the rest. It's the usual summer scene."

"What have you told Lori?"

"That her Dad is in Chicago for the summer and that she can go visit him the last week he's there and come back with him."

"That's all?"

"That's all. She's getting used to his being away right now. That's a good beginning. Besides . . ." Lynn's voice fades out.

Ruth picks it up. "Besides, what if you get together again. I think Tony wants you back, Lynn."

"Wants me the way I was," Lynn says, thinking, somewhere in the middle he did love me – not in the beginning and not in the end but somewhere in the middle like a streak of red in a tapestry, fading in and out again imperceptibly. "But not the way I am."

"I suppose."

"I won't change backwards."

"No, I guess you can't even if you wanted to. But I want you to be happy. Lynn, I wish I were my twin brother."

Lynn laughs and sits next to Ruth on the bed. "You're just fine the way you are. I love *you*, Ruth."

"Am I in the way? Would you go back?"

"No, it was never like that. You were never in the way. We're a given. I know you and you know me. Tony doesn't even know me any more."

"I guess it's sexist to wish I were a man."

"Why?"

"I think I shouldn't have you because I'm just a woman. You're too good for a woman. That's pretty sexist, all right." Ruth speaks ruefully. "But I want you to be happy. I can't make you happy. I *do* wish I were my twin brother. You won't believe what I would like to do right now."

"I might."

They laugh and roll together on the bed. Ruth is on Lynn, her tongue moving within her lips, against Lynn's tongue, her hands gliding everywhere on Lynn. Lynn moves her hands in circles on Ruth's back, holding her close against her, length to length. Ruth slides lower so her lips can reach Lynn's breasts and moves her thighs in gradual circles, mons on mons.

"Ahhhhhhh," Lynn cries out unexpectedly.

Ruth intensifies her movements, holds one nipple with her lips and flicks it with her tongue as the moment whirls them together higher and higher until they let go and fall, to lie gently touching, Ruth whispering, "I love you, I love you, oh my God, I do love you."

A month later they drive north through late August heat.

"Does Neil care when you go off like this?"

"He notices, I guess. He wants me to go with him to Buenos Aires."

"When?"

"Next week. We'd be back right after Labor Day. I'd miss the first two days of school."

"Going?"

"I guess I'd better. He says I don't try."

"Do you?"

"God, do I ever. One of my oldest friends told me she just closes her eyes; 'Just lie back and close your eyes,' she said; 'it's easy.'"

"Like the dentist," Lynn says, laughing.

"Right. But I have to be there when I'm making love."

"Do you love him, Ruth?"

"What's love? I have trouble letting him make love to me," she says, and adds softly, "and I only want to make love to you." She takes her hand away from Lynn's and lights a cigarette. "So how about you? Want to go back to Tony? Miss him?"

"Ready to throw in the towel?" Lynn grins. "No to all of the above. You know what it feels like? Like I'm in a canoe with the kids and someone big and awkward stopped thrashing around and stepped out and the canoe, which was about to tip over, steadied itself, lifted out of the water and is lighter, easier to move. I don't really miss him. That's crazy, isn't it? After twenty-five years?"

"You *weren't* married twenty-five years!"

"No. I've known him twenty-five years though and all that time he was the center of my life."

"It's a long time. I'll bet you wouldn't ever have broken up if he'd been decent to the kids."

"I don't know. Maybe not. I went into therapy because Anthony was in trouble and it went from there. I never would have gone just for myself. Once I started finding out about myself it was too late to stop — and I didn't want to stop."

"Neil is a good enough father. I've no excuse. When I think about leaving him, I feel like I haven't any right. He's just like he always was."

"And you?"

"I'm pretty much like I always was, too, except that I want to be with you all the time. And I don't want to make do any more. You used to think you had a really fine marriage . . ."

"Didn't you?"

"No. I thought it was all right. I didn't have much to complain about. That rose-tinted glass you saw everything through wasn't my style. It was pretty good for the kids, our marriage. When I saw them getting grown up I started teaching. I knew I'd better have something to do and quick. So where do I get off thinking about leaving Neil? Even you feel guilty, don't you? And you had lots of cause. Hey, this looks right." Ruth snaps the car into the parking lot for a motel built like a ski lodge, set among pines.

After they unpack, they take a walk. "How did we ever manage this?" Ruth jumps up to touch the leaves of a tree along the trail. "For three whole days? Three whole days? I'll even toast Tony every time he takes Lori for a week!"

Lynn laughs and nods. "The gods are with us."

"There's only today. And tomorrow. And the day after that. And that's all the days that I am going to think about. No more than that. Three is enough. Three whole days!" Ruth runs down the trail, now and then leaping into the air.

Their cabin is set off by itself under pine trees. It's clean and the wood, unfinished, smells fresh and wild. At bedtime Lynn stands looking out the window and then turns to the bureau and pulls off her wedding ring. She puts it in her purse. "I never had it off before," she says to Ruth.

Her hand feels strange, bare, cold. There is a pale circle — twenty years of being in the shade of that gold band. She flexes her fingers curiously, slowly, as though just removed from a cast. They do not hurt to move.

Ruth touches her arm lightly, comforting. Lynn bursts into sobs, wrenching and dry. Ruth takes her in her arms and holds her tight. "Cry," she whispers, "let it all out. Cry, darling."

Later, peaceful, Lynn says quietly, "I've almost forgotten how to cry."

"Sure."

"It's not easy."

"Want to go back to him?"

"No. I wish we hadn't messed the kids up."

"They'll be all right. Are you sure you don't want to go back to Tony?"

"Yes. I feel bad that I don't — surprised and in a way ashamed, sorry for him, you know, and as though I should make it right for him. I don't know. But *enough*. How come we spend all our time together talking about Tony and Neil?"

Ruth smiles. "Not *all* our time," and kisses her.

All night Lynn thrashes and all night Ruth wakes her, soothes her, lets her cry. Toward dawn in a dream Lynn stands below an open attic door. It's narrow, a trap door. Two husky teenage boys tower over her. One straddles the trap door; one swells to fill the opening. Lynn is on the narrow stairway underneath. They mock her, laughing, threatening. It's her responsibility to get them down the stairs. Giants, she thinks, in recognition, starting herself to slip downward on the stairs. Then, as though the reel shifts to a different film, she knows that she is older than they are and has control of them. Good-humoredly, she orders them to go down the stairs. Good-natured, respecting her authority, they go.

She wakes in Ruth's arms. Ruth is dozing. Lynn thinks about the boys in the dream, breathes peacefully and sleeps.

They hike hard all day. The woods are thick with summer green. In the distance the mountains, blue-grey, edge a sharp blue sky.

Returning to the cabin, they drink wine, eat bread and cheese, and fall asleep together.

Lynn wakes to moonlight on the pine paneling. She lies, listening to crickets, tiny creatures in the leaves, watching the moonlight, and Ruth wakes to kiss her, turning to her nearly in her sleep, mouth finding mouth. A long time later Ruth begins to kiss her breasts, her arms, back, thighs and inner thighs, and the smooth planes within that Lynn has never known were there. Lynn lies beneath her caresses as though she walks in a woods where all the foliage is new, where light shines through levels of light green, dark green, where tendrilled ferns blow in the wind and trees with various barks rise smoothly toward the sky, with strands of cloud lightly blowing over. She moves there with no effort of her own. She moves there as though she is herself the wind moving among flowers whose smell she has never known, whose colors blow before her and around her, under and above her, orange and yellow and tulip red, and there is no ending to it and no beginning and she doesn't understand nor need to know but only to be there and hear Ruth's voice and know that it is Ruth and that they are together entirely beautiful.

In the morning, in the light of waking, they laugh happily together. Lynn touches the bed and finds it wet and looks at Ruth, bewildered, knowing then from Ruth's smile that she has flowed and flowed. "Didn't you even know?" Ruth laughs gently.

Lynn goes to the mirror and looks at herself, expecting to see the image changed, taller, different. "I didn't know that I existed, was alive that way, before." She blushes. "Until now I was a virgin."

Ruth smiles, coming toward her. "You're beautiful," she says.

23

"So what's up?"

They're sitting in Lynn's car in the supermarket parking lot. Ruth doesn't answer. She's smoking and looking around the lot.

"Ruth?" Lynn's voice is gentle.

"It doesn't matter. Next week we'll be in Buenos Aires. They say it's magnificent. Shall I bring you an orchid?" Her voice is brittle, quick. She taps her cigarette hard to knock off the ash and then inhales.

"Where are you off to now?"

"Neil is waiting for me. We're going to shop together for camera stuff. I have to be back practically now." She checks her watch. "I shouldn't have asked you to come to meet me here. This is idiotic."

"So why did you? What happened?"

"Nothing much. He just decided that what I really wanted was for him to take me by force." Ruth spits the words out like cherry pits. She blows smoke, laughs a harsh short laugh, and says, "I have to go. Forget it. It's not his first mistake."

Lynn holds Ruth's hand in both her own, gently. She thinks what to say, not wanting her to bolt, not wanting to crack the thin ice on which Ruth is crossing toward her. "You'll be all right," she says, uncertainly.

"I'm all right. I'm just fine. I'm off to buy the latest paraphernalia so we can catch the mountain flowers and the southern equivalent of Alpine goats." Ruth opens the door and starts to get out.

"Hey, hey, wait a minute."

"Why?"

"Because."

Ruth swings back in, closes the door, grinds out her cigarette. "Lynn, maybe he's right. Maybe a good rape is what every woman needs?" She laughs but the brittle edge weakens and tears begin to glisten in her eyes.

"Maybe. We could take a survey," Lynn says laconically. Then, "I'm sorry you went through that, Ruth. Did you tell him it was a mistake?"

"Not yet."

"What did you do?" Lynn unwillingly sees a slide of Neil mounting Ruth, his heavy frame settling down on her slight one, his face closing in, lips open, moist. She looks away from it at Ruth.

"I closed my eyes." Ruth grins.

"Tell him." Lynn speaks urgently.

"I will. I think he really thought I'd like it. This morning he looked proud." She laughs. "Is he crazy or am I?"

"Maybe we shouldn't have gone away last week."

Ruth doesn't answer but for a second her eyes meet Lynn's and Lynn spins, dizzy as though touched, held, kissed. Then Ruth looks away and says in her normal voice, still tense but not about to break and fall, "Okay. I'm okay now. I probably shouldn't have told you, but I guess I had to or do something foolish. I'll go get the correct equipment now. It'll take forever. He'll have to examine eighteen kinds. Look, I don't think I can get away tonight. Meet me tomorrow afternoon at the lake at three?"

"Fine. Call tonight if you can."

"I will."

"Ruth?"

"Um?"

"I love you."

Ruth is gone, moving swiftly, taut, snared.

Lynn drives out of the parking lot and down one street after another until she finds herself entering the highway. Once on it, going fast, she begins to think, he shouldn't have done that — he made a BIG mistake — if there's one thing he shouldn't have done, that would be it.

Lynn clenches her hands on the rim of the steering wheel as she watches a huge truck bear down on her. In the mirror it seems to mount her as it swerves to pass, its throbbing engine roaring, its hurtling weight shaking her own car. She hears her own voice say, "You bastard! Get off her! Who gave you the right? You think you own her? She's got feelings, you stupid oaf! You cocky primitive brute!"

Lynn hears the chung, chung of passing cars and the approaching roar of a towering truck, its sucking thunder as it passes, and its retreating drone. She shouts, "Fuck you! You bastard! You take and take and take, and then when it isn't given like always — not that you ever let her know you cared —" Remembering Ruth's, 'Neil isn't demonstrative. He doesn't like to hold hands. He doesn't do anything about birthdays or anything. He didn't bring me flowers when Mark was born,' Lynn shouts: "You fucking fucking fucking selfish pig! You conceited son-of-a-bitch! Screw you! Screw all of you! You come down heavy just because you can! You think God gave you women with your Tonka trucks to screw any time you want! Screw you! Fuck you, you fucking fucking fucking sons-of-bitches! God damn you to hell and back!"

Lynn swerves out of her lane into the far right lane and pulls off on the strip of green. She takes paper and pen from her purse and begins to write: "Ruth, Ruth, dearest Ruth, that was a terrible thing that Neil did to you. Even if he did think it was a good idea, it was a terrible thing. You are so gentle and beautiful and direct in your feelings that for him to land on you by force is worse than for most people. It was tantamount to giving you a beating. He is really a bastard — or was last night. And if he feels proud of himself, then he is a fucking brute. If he thinks he can fuck you into submission he has another think coming, and more important, he doesn't know you at all — not even a little tiny bit. When you said he doesn't know — or care — who you are, I didn't believe you quite. But my God he *doesn't* know you at all.

"How could anyone who knows you — and how beautifully, sensitively, feeling every nuance of your lover's mood and body, you move in making love (when we lay together last week I felt nothing separated us one from the other, as though wherever you were I was also and wherever I was you knew to be) — how he, who must know how immediate your feelings are, how direct your sense perceptions — how he could come and pound into you, fuck you heavily, heavily like that and think you'd like it? Not possible. FUCK HIM! DAMN HIM! FUCK HIM THE FUCKING BASTARD!

"I want to hold you and talk to you and walk in the sunlight with you until you forget what happened and until your voice is beautiful and yours again and not strained and tense and touched with fear. I love you, Ruth. If you can work things out with Neil I'll be happy for you but force isn't the way and you must tell him that! I'll see you tomorrow at the lake. Three o'clock. I'm writing this on the highway where I found myself booming along shouting FUCK YOU! I don't believe it either. My God I do love you. It freaked me out to think of him not being gentle with you, who more than anyone I've known need gentleness. I love you."

Lynn signs and folds the letter and puts it in an envelope with Ruth's name on it. She leaves the highway and drives by Ruth and Neil's house. Their cars aren't there. She slides the letter into the mailbox, puts up the flag, and takes herself home.

As she enters the familiar parking space beside the lake the next afternoon, even before she turns off the key and pulls on the brake, Lynn smells the acrid stench of fear coiling up from beneath the car like smoke. Ruth's car is not there, nor is it at the gas station across the street.

Lynn goes through their conversation once again. Something about not being able to get out no matter what last night, and meeting today at three here at the lake. Lynn flicks on the key and the radio to get the correct time. It is 3:05.

A young father stands on the grass strip beside the lake with three small kids, feeding ducks which swarm in toward them on the quiet water. A teenage girl sits cross-legged, head bent deep into her book.

No phone call last night. But Ruth had not promised one. Lynn turns to the news station, listens a minute, shifts to music, deliberately leans back, breathes deep, looks at the placid lake, the sunshine on the trees. She's late, she thinks, so what? Never been late before? Of course she's been late before. He's locked her in? First rape, then lock-up? Don't be silly. She'll come. Relax. Flat tire? You can cruise and look for her. Then she'll come and you won't be here and she'll leave again.

Lynn waits. She settles deeper in her seat, stares at the children, watches their arms rise and fall with bread crumbs flying from the little fists into the midst of squawking ducks, watches the father handing the bread out from a paper sack, watches the little one, about three, lose his balance as he throws; he falls awkwardly to the grass, cries, waits for his father, who tells him to get up again.

At 3:30 she knows that something has gone wrong. She gets out of the car and walks slowly along the shore, looking for a note stuck in a tree, wedged on a post. She finds nothing. The young man puts his children in their car and drives away.

Think, she tells herself. Think. Where would Ruth be coming from? It's the last day before the flight to South America. Passports? No, they got them in the mail last week. Clothes? No, she would've waited. Doctor appointment? Shots? No, all done already. Neil needed something? Neil tied her up with car repairs or picking up plane tickets or some errand like that. She's with him and can't get away. But nothing fits. Lynn leaves the lake and checks several gas stations nearby, the supermarket lot, the travel agency's parking lot, and then goes home to look for a letter — none — and to ask Jon, who is playing with his group in the basement, if she had any calls — not that he would have heard. Lynn sits a moment, hand on phone, but doesn't dial. She tells Jon she's going out for groceries, and she drives toward Ruth and Neil's house. Halfway there she feels the air thick with that smoky heaviness; she gasps and turns to go by the lake once more. No Ruth.

Lynn's neck hurts from yanking it after cars in search of Ruth's blue Dodge. Not that one she thinks. Not that one. That? Down the side street? No . . . no. Think. Ruth would have driven from their house toward the lake. She would've dropped Neil off somewhere and then driven to the lake. But she couldn't come and couldn't call for some reason and expects you to phone her? Expects you to know better than to phone while she and Neil are so tense and wants you to go home and wait? Lynn cruises, head snapping, trying to plot Ruth's day from the beginning.

Breakfast with Neil. Travel arrangements. List of errands to be done. Neil to school. Nate to practice at the high school, Mark? Mark was working. Mark to his job in the park. Lynn changes direction, drives by the park, thinking as she does so that it's too early for Ruth to be picking him up from work. Back to their breakfast. Drop the kids off. Drop Neil off because the other car is at the garage? Maybe. Or maybe pick up the other car at the garage? Lynn cruises past the Dodge place but sees neither of their cars.

She pulls in at the lake again. It's now 4:30. I will phone, she thinks. To hell with this. Ruth got busy, Neil trapped her into drinks with colleagues? Lynn is sweating and her shoulders are hunched tight. She starts to pull out again and Ruth is there. The air for a split second clears, is pierced with silver, clear as a distant horn sounding across the lake.

And then the smouldering smoke that has shortened her breath all day bursts into suffocating clouds of heat and ash: "Neil found out." Ruth, without leaving her car, speaks tersely through their rolled down windows. "Let's get out of here. He read your letter. He knows. I'll park my car at the supermarket and we'll go in yours somewhere to talk."

Ruth guns off in front of Lynn and Lynn follows her, saying over and over to herself the words Ruth flung at her through the open windows: Neil found out. Neil found out. He read your letter. Letter. Fuck you, fuck you, you fucking fucking bastard. What else was in the letter? What else? Not, please God, not something explicit about them. What was in that letter? All she can remember is the rage, so rare for her. A thousand letters, she thinks, gentle, thoughtful, solving the problems of her marriage or mine, or about the kids, or just hello, and which letter does he find? Oh Christ!

Ruth has locked her car already and is standing, waiting, in the supermarket lot. She gets in immediately.

"Where to?" Lynn asks.

"Away. Far. I don't want to be seen."

Lynn heads out of town for a beach an hour away. "When should you be back?"

"By eight."

"Okay, we're fine."

"Every time you say that it frightens me. We are not fine. Neil found it."

"How? In the mailbox?"

"No, no, he wouldn't open my mail. No, I had read it quickly and shoved it in my purse to re-read later; and he went to get our plane tickets out of my purse to check our departure time and saw your letter there, ripped open, and he read it."

"What did he say?"

"He said now he understands what's been going on."

"And?"

"And he wants me to see a shrink, stop seeing you, and try to make our marriage work. He thinks you seduced me and I didn't understand until too late. He says you obviously hate men."

"Oh."

"I feel sick."

"Shall I stop?"

"No. No, I just feel very sick."

Lynn reaches for Ruth's hand, but Ruth is lighting a cigarette and does not take Lynn's hand when she is through.

"Are you leaving as planned?"

"Yes. And he intends us to have long talks while we're away." Ruth grinds out the cigarette. "Maybe you should just take me straight on home."

"I won't see you again before you go. Let's have a minute."

"All right." Ruth lowers her head as under a weight.

Lynn stares attentively at the road ahead. "What was in the letter?"

"Everything."

"Like?"

"Like how it was for us making love together —" Ruth interrupts her panic for a second to smile at Lynn. "I liked that part —" and then she is gone again into the rigid fear.

"Out of a thousand letters, why that one?"

"That's what I thought too. Why that one?"

"Where are the other letters?"

"I burned them all last night after he was asleep."

Nausea swamps Lynn but she stares ahead, turns the wheel, depresses and releases the gas pedal appropriately for the curve. "Shall I burn yours?"

"Absolutely."

Lynn doesn't speak for a while, in shock at the loss of their written words, a shock separate from the rest. Then she says, "It's custody that's bad."

"And everything else. Like jobs."

"They won't let me keep Lori if that comes out. Do you think Neil will tell anyone?" The smoky fear has settled in Lynn's lungs.

"No, not now, he won't. He'll lecture me all week in Buenos Aires. 'This is a rare species of violet orchid, and Lynn is more sophisticated than you are. It was clear from the beginning but you didn't understand.' " Ruth laughs her short hard laugh. "Oh God, do I ever not want to go."

"Will he leave you?"

"No. Too much trouble. He'll claim me. You know I think it excited him. Last night he was all frantic to have sex. But he didn't try to rape me again. He was just turned on." Ruth snorts. "Isn't that crazy? I mean really crazy."

"And you?" Lynn asks, gently, frightened.

"I was numb. N-u-m-b spells Ruth. I'll be numb all week. Totally asleep on my feet. I'll send you a postcard — wish you were here — signed, Numb."

"Hey, take it easy, hmm?"

"Oh, right. Take it easy. We're about to be ruined together — how many kids? How many jobs? Only two jobs? Only six kids? Nothing to get uptight about."

"I know, but we'll make it somehow." Lynn parks at the beach. "Want to walk a little?"

"I don't know if I can. Okay, better than sitting, I guess."

They walk in silence for a ways. "I don't believe it really," Lynn says at last.

"Neither do I. Except I did when I burned your beautiful letters, the whole carton of them, one by one smashing them into the fireplace, making sure no shriveled up page was left with your words on it. We should have burned them from the start."

"Would have made a good book, our letters."

"Yes, they would. I never wrote so much in my whole life." Ruth laughs ruefully.

The beach is deserted where they're walking. The cliffs rise toward trees and shrubs, thick along their crest. They turn into one another's arms and stand a moment casting a single shadow on the still warm beach, stroked by the evening wind as it stirs the darkening sand. Then they break apart and walk back toward the car. The water stretches grey and blue with a long slash of brightness wedged out from the setting sun.

24

The day Ruth leaves, Lynn walks the beach alone. Once she took Neil and Ruth to the airport for a flight to California. Against the blaze of blue, Lynn remembers the airline terminal that day: Ruth resolutely walking behind Neil, shoulders bowed by the weight of her suitcase, head set for the long trek. Lynn sees the sliding doors close behind them and hears the plane gather its horrendous sound and then begin to move, accelerate, lift. Under it this time the water of the bay and then the ocean and then? Clouds and space and inside the steel shell, Neil next to Ruth, arm against arm; and Neil talks.

Already it's too long, Lynn thinks. It's been half a day since I heard her voice, saying, "I'll try to write or phone or something, but if not, I'll be back next Wednesday night and then we'll see." That voice was a seine which allowed only massive facts (flight time and routes) to be caught, while it let all the real things (their love, their being scared) slip through to lie in the water near the bottom.

"Travel well," Lynn had said.

"Good luck with your new classes," Ruth had said.

"Call me when you get back," Lynn had said. "Please."

Hours slide in between the hours. Lynn takes Christy shopping for school clothes and helps Jon have a summer's-end beach party. She plans her first week of full-time teaching, class by class, day by day, possibility by possibility, the way she would play a complex game of chess. She puts the house in order and shops for the week. Each day is interminable and each night is a steeplechase.

Tony phones to say he will bring Lori home from Chicago on Saturday.

"Where will you stay?" Lynn asks, knowing already what he has in mind.

"I'm coming home to talk things over."

"You're staying here?"

"That's home, isn't it?"

"We have a legal separation, remember?"

"I don't care."

"Well, I do."

"Then that's your problem, isn't it? Let me say hello to Christy."

Lynn arranges to bunk at the home of friends for Labor Day weekend while Tony stays in the house with the kids. They agree to invite Tony to come stay with them on Monday night, so Lynn can be back home to get herself and the kids off to school the next morning. And, Lynn thinks, to be there for Ruth's phone call when their plane gets in from Buenos Aires on Wednesday night.

"Staying with Neil and Ruth?" Tony asks her, his voice leashed.

"No. I'll be at the Curtisses until Monday. They've invited you to come there Monday night since I have to be here to get ready for school on Tuesday. They'll be glad to have you the rest of the week."

"Okay," he says. "But I'll be back here Friday night to stay for good so plan accordingly."

Tony stands across the room from her, pipe in hand. His words come at her as though accented wrong and in inverted order. She replays his sentences before she answers them.

"It will be cheaper," he says, "if we go on living together."
He looks around the living room, noticing and disapproving
in one glance each change: a poster on the wall that Anthony
brought home from one of his marches, her own stacks of
books and pamphlets. "It will also be better for the kids."

"Not if we're unhappy," Lynn answers. "Not if it's not
working, Tony."

"Working? Is that Julia's lingo?" he asks mockingly.

"You know what I mean. Children aren't happy if their
parents aren't."

"Come off it. Who's happy? What's this 'happy'?"

"You don't particularly like me any more, Tony."

"So?"

"So how can we live together?"

"It's better than a divorce." He edges away from her as
he talks, turns his face away to look at the old coffee table,
the scattered newspapers, the worn rug.

"You don't even like to be in a room with me. Why would
you want us to live together?"

"It's not as bad as pulling the family apart."

"Are you serious?"

"Yes."

"But all year you kept saying that you don't love me —"

He shrugs. "Look, at our age what do you want?"

"More than two people tolerating each other."

He looks just beyond her as he speaks. She tries to think
what is on the wall behind her shoulder. She wants to turn
but holds very still. He says, "Incidentally, I'm finding things
out in therapy, too. Our sex problems weren't my fault. In
the beginning I always thought they were. I thought for
instance that my prick was too small. But it wasn't. When I
have an erection it gets very large."

Lynn watches him as through a telescope turned the wrong
way around. He is far away and his voice comes hollow through
the tube.

"It was your vagina that was too big. Your brothers

stretched it. There are mechanical things to use when that's a problem."

His voice goes on and she backs warily away from him as from a threatening animal, until she is in the car on the way to her friends' home.

In the car Lynn thinks, I'll ask my brothers. We'll be around a Thanksgiving Day table somewhere, and I'll say, "Pass the turkey, please, and by the way, Billy, when you used to horse around with me, did you penetrate? I remember it as though you beat against me, sort of like a clubbing. But Tony thinks you rammed it home and stretched me out of shape. What's the story anyhow?"

The students come at her like breakers at the beach that she leaps with some new energy and ease. She gets them to start writing the first day and eagerly reads their words during her lunch hour and at night, late into the night, already changing her lesson plans for the next day to match what she is learning from their work. When she has turned out her light at two a.m. she feels a sudden jolt: "Ruth, Ruth," she whispers, "tomorrow night," and sleeps.

"Lynn?"

"Yes." It's Wednesday night after midnight.

"I'm sorry it's so late."

Within her body boulders crash downward, starting a landslide that frees her path of what has blocked her way. For a long moment she cannot hear anything. "It doesn't matter. My God, it's good to hear your voice. Hello, hello."

"Lynn?"

And then she knows that Ruth's voice is pilloried. "Where are you?"

"We're back. I wasn't going to call tonight. I'm sorry, Lynn."

"Sorry what?"

"I love you." Lynn listens, knowing the voice comes from a bright canvas, slashed and torn: Breughel's harvesters shredded to ugly barren canvas underneath. "I've agreed not to see you." There was a long silence between them while they listen to one another there. "For two months," Ruth says.

"Can we write to one another?" Lynn presses against the bare cliff, one hand gripping an exposed tree root, the other curled on a tiny ledge of rock, her weight pulling downward.

"No," Ruth's voice retreats.

"Nothing?"

"Nothing. I promised. For two months. And then we'll see. Maybe by then I'll know."

"Know?"

"Whether I'm leaving Neil."

"Ruth?"

"I'm sorry, Lynn. Oh God I'm sorry. I should have stayed away from you from the beginning."

"Don't be crazy. Are you all right?"

"Sure."

"The hell you are. Listen — I may be moving out."

"Moving out?"

"Yes. Tony came home and he won't leave the house."

"God. Is he there now?"

"No. He's coming back Friday though. It's weird. He thinks we should live together. Not that he loves me. He agrees he doesn't even like me. He stood there and told me, so help me God, that it would be cheaper." Lynn laughs, desperation in her voice.

"This is a hell of a time for me to do this to you."

"Are you all right?"

"I'll be all right. It's all crazy. But I agreed."

"Okay."

"Lynn?"

"Yes."

"Lynn."

"I love you, Ruth."

"I'm sorry. I told you I'm destructive. I told you I'd ruin everything."

"Hey — hey — come on. It's all right. Try it. See if you can think your way through. I'll be here. Not *here*, but somewhere." Lynn laughs. "And I'll count the days. Now go to sleep. I'm glad you called even so. I was waiting."

Ruth's voice, saying, "Good night," suddenly goes dead. Lynn knows Neil has entered the room.

"Good night."

The root Lynn has been gripping pulls out from the bluff's sandy wall and she falls, rocks and dirt clods pelting down on her from above as she falls and falls into the deep gully far below.

"The car is mine. I'll be glad to lend it to you occasionally so you can go food shopping."

Lynn doesn't look up from packing. "Will you give me some money for my share? I'll have to buy one to get to work."

"No. That's your problem, isn't it?"

Anthony moves in with friends, sharing the rent, working part-time. Jon and Christy and Lori go with Lynn to the newly rented house. It's old and too small and the noise from the neighbor's party the first night keeps them all awake, but Lynn goes through the move almost without doubt. Once, putting Lori's dolls in a carton, she panics, and crouches, staring at the straw-colored hair, the nubby fingers curled to hold a bottle. What am I doing? she thinks, what is this all about?

Then she remembers lying next to Tony in bed and watching him across the breakfast table, and she knows that she must go. Funny, she thinks, near the end I couldn't watch him eat. I couldn't stand to be at the table across from him. After twenty-five years of eating together every day. Strange, she thinks, remembering how she moved about the kitchen constantly so that she never had to sit down at the table with him those last months.

Days whirl all around her. From teaching to lawyer to grocery to PTA to band practice to packing lunches to getting

Lori up and off to school to teaching to meetings to night classes to teaching to laundromat to sleep. Sleeping is the hardest and she does it very little.

Lynn picks Jon up from band. "Give Nate a ride home, Mom?"

"Sure." Nate's face, an echo of Ruth's own, knocks all Lynn's defenses down, as though her school, kids, house, car, were styrofoam miniature models and Ruth's son has yanked the earth away, scattering them at will. She drives the familiar route, hoping Ruth will be there, hoping Ruth will not, hoping to sneak in and out the driveway, hoping Ruth will run out and take her in her arms. Turning in their driveway, she sees one car is gone. Are they both out? Is Ruth home alone?

"Thanks," Nate says, hauling his instrument case out of the car.

"You're welcome, Nate," she says. "Good night." Backing out the wide driveway, listening to Jon's account of the idiocy of the new members of the band, Lynn plays it through: Ruth runs out the door and says to Jon, "Go in a minute — there's a chocolate cake —" and as Jon disappears into the house leaving them alone, they meet in one another's arms, Ruth's lips take hers, and Ruth is saying, "I love you, I love you, I love you," into her hair.

"Watch out, Mom, their car's just turning in," Jon says.

Lynn hits the brake. Should she back on out or let them drive in first? She watches their headlights fracture in her mirror as though they spatter her with shards of glass.

The car pulls in beside them. She sees Neil at the wheel like the oarsman carrying Ruth across the River Styx. She is clearly chained, veiled, drugged. No one moves.

"Are you going in?" Jon asks.

Her foot lets up the brake and jerkily her car moves out the drive. "No," she says, "no, I have work to do for school tomorrow. We'll just go home."

Lynn sits at the kitchen table, adding, subtracting, adding, subtracting. There is no way. He'll give her nothing more than the child support which the separation agreement stipulates, which was set low because he was on summer salary. There is the rent, double for security on moving in, and the car payments, and the utilities (deposits: "But I've had a telephone for twenty years and never missed a payment; I'm not a new customer." "Your husband had the phone, ma'am. You will have to establish credit. The deposit will be refunded if you pay regularly for one year. Just send a check for one hundred dollars and service will begin.") and tuition.

"Look, Tony, there are family debts and initial costs I think that we should share."

"You moved out, not me. Your choice — you pay." He grins, leers, mocks. "What a dump!" he snarls, taking Lori off to lunch from her newly rented house. "Christ! What a dump!"

He guns the motor and drives off. Later Lori tells her, "Daddy doesn't like our new house, Mommy."

Driving home from school Lynn thinks, if I could just touch her hand. Just for a moment, touch her hand.

She tries to put the thought away, tries to roll herself in the cotton bunting of what must be done: get food, gas, pick up Lori from Brownies, Christy from orchestra, cook dinner, wash up, pack lunches, drop off Jon, phone Anthony to arrange to give him cash for food, grade papers, wash a blouse, pay the late light bill. Nothing holds. The thought of Ruth is a laser beam and she is struck.

A blue Dodge turns onto the street a block ahead. Lynn presses the gas pedal. The Dodge turns off. Lynn takes the same turn and accelerates. "Hey, Ruth," she says, "Wait, wait!" She passes an intervening car, going faster than she ever goes. She's not gaining on the Dodge. She goes faster, faster, but it keeps its distance. Into town they go. At a red light a string of cars come between. At another corner Lynn loses sight of it. Out of town it speeds up again. Lynn is some ten cars behind. When a red light stops the line of cars, Lynn passes them on their right, ignoring the blasting horns. "Sorry!" she yells back at them and charges on.

The blue Dodge stops at a gas station. Lynn careens in behind it, flicks off the ignition, throws open her door and runs toward the gas pumps. A strange woman in the Dodge glances idly up at her, pays the attendant for her gas and drives away.

"Can I help you, ma'am?" The boy drags his greasy fingers down his jeans' leg twice.

"No, thank you. I thought that was a friend of mine in the Dodge."

He walks away.

Not Ruth, she thinks. Back in the car driving home, hurrying now, late to shop and cook, late to pick up Lori and Christy, she says very quietly, "Not Ruth. That wasn't even Ruth. Just for a minute, dammit. Couldn't you let me see you even for a minute? I can't take it, Ruth. Just to sit for a minute, touching hands. Nothing more. Not even words." Almost got killed driving like that. Maniac. You are a maniac. See there, it wasn't even Ruth. After all that craziness, you maniac, it wasn't even Ruth.

25

Thrust and parry. Thrust and parry. We should have seconds hidden in the bushes, Lynn thinks. Tony is walking with her in a park.

"It's time we had a conference," he said by phone.

"All right," she said.

"Come to the house?"

"No. I'd rather not."

"A restaurant?"

She groped for a place of no eavesdropping and a place where she would not be closed in with him. "How about the park by the lake?" she said.

Now, walking together there in the dark, she is afraid. Absurd, she says to herself, I can't be afraid of him. We've lived together for twenty years. A trickle of tightening nerves traces its way along her shoulders, up her neck, as he speaks.

"I'm not sure who should have the children," he says, his voice heavy with moderation.

"By the time the divorce goes through, the boys will both be eighteen or older," she says, "and that's too old for formal custody. The girls should stay with me."

"You're assuming an uncontested divorce?" His voice is . . . it eludes her; is it his attempt at rationality that thickens his tone this way?

"Yes, I am. We have a separation agreement. In a year we can have a divorce based on that agreement without any kind of blame attached."

"What if I won't give it to you?"

No, she thinks, it's the judge about to condemn after due

thought, that's the tone. "Why wouldn't you?" she asks, voice quiet, interested.

"I think I should keep the girls."

"Why?" Steady, steady, left leg, right leg, walk easily forward, left leg, right leg.

"No court will think a lesbian is the best parent for a child." The shock waves inside must not show even by an extra moment's silence, Lynn thinks, responding, "So who's a lesbian?" This word has not been spoken by them before.

"You are lesbians. You and Ruth." He laughs, tossing his head as he does so. "She and I fought it out," he says, sand in his throat, "and the best man won, as it were." He laughs again.

"Would you lower your voice," Lynn says. "You're saying some pretty wild things and I'm a teacher now." She glances into the bushes, hearing a rustling, knowing it's squirrels or mice, not human beings.

"Now that I know you're a lesbian, we're through. I don't wish you any harm. I understand we have different routes to go."

Or his voice is that of the dedicated priest, she thinks, wishing the witch Godspeed as he lights the kindling that will ignite the stake.

"You can certainly understand that it would be better for little girls to have a parent who leads a normal life. Think about Jon and Anthony. Would you like me to take them for their initiation to a gay bar?"

Tony turns his jurist's face toward her. Lynn moves her legs, right, left. She moves her mouth, word, word. "Look, I don't think you intend to take the boys to a gay bar and I don't go to bars at all, let alone gay bars. We're talking about our daughters, and they would be better off with their mother."

"Not if she's a lesbian. No court in the country will give them to you."

"I'm not a lesbian."

"Don't lie to me. You could at least be honest. I've always thought you were the most honest person I have ever known."

Accused of witchcraft she is tied and gagged and taken to the water to be tested. If she escapes the ropes and rises to the surface she proves the demons are in league with her and she must be burned, for witch she surely is. If they are not in league with her, she will quite simply drown.

Left, right, left, right, voice calm, move steadily — there is a way out if you keep on going, left, right.

"We have lived together for twenty years and before that, for five years I never saw anyone but you. We've had four children together. Just because we're not staying married doesn't suddenly change us into different people than we've always been," she says, thinking, even the sentence came out all screwed up. He is not the man I lived with: this creature dragging me toward the stake, righteousness shining in his eyes. He is the high priest, chanting, with that depraved judicial voice.

"Don't put me on," he says, his voice a rope winding around her legs, her arms, "I knew from the beginning you were in great danger. If I hadn't been there you would have gone sooner is all. Don't you think I knew? You and your women friends! Nancy. Jeanne. Marie. Sandy."

"You're crazy," Lynn says.

"Shut up!" he snaps, yanking the rope tight. "It's you who ran off. It's you who's spent the year 'walking beaches—' " His voice tilts into sarcasm, rope burning her arms, her legs. "I sat with my books and watched. Don't think I didn't see you two. You couldn't take your eyes off her. Snuggling down to the phone to purr into it hour after hour. Don't give me any of that crap! Maybe you went off with all the others too and I *was* fooled — I don't know."

"You know better. Christ, I was never out of the house, Tony. I was never without a baby in my arms. What *is* with you?"

"What *is* with me is that I want to salvage whatever protection I can for my little girls."

"Protection? You think I'll hurt them?"

"Not deliberately. But you will hurt them. I hope I will remarry and then I can give them a normal home. Meanwhile, I think I would be better for them than you are. I don't think you actually even want them."

"Of course I want them."

"Why? What are you trying to prove?"

"Tony, I think they'll be better off with me. I think girls should live with their mother."

"Girls *should* live with their *mother and father.* You know, incidentally," he laughs, "I think I'll lead the corrective movement to the women's movement."

"The what?"

"The corrective movement. It's swinging all one way now — ERA and all — and there will have to be a counter-movement to restore perspective — sanity—" He grins at her.

"I'm supposed to laugh and it's all supposed to be all right, she thinks. Left, right, steady, steady. "We had a long and in many ways good marriage. We changed and it won't work any more, Tony. We can't agree on reasons or whose fault. Could we just agree to move for a divorce after a year's separation? It's very simple to do that."

"I won't agree to anything. And don't think you're going to get any money from me!" His voice thrusts for a moment bare, glinting ugly in the dark.

"I don't want any of your money for me, Tony," she says. "You'll have to help support the children."

"The boys don't need support," he snaps. "They're as old as I was when I was on my own."

Somewhere long ago Tony's boy-voice saying, "My mother put me out — 'You are old enough to be on your own,' " his voice mocking his mother's tone and accent, " 'so *be* on your own,' she said; if she'd helped me maybe I would have tried music seriously, maybe I would have gone to Harvard Law. Who knows? Who cares? She wouldn't that's all."

"And you always wished someone *had* helped you."

"I've changed my mind. Just don't think *you're* ever going to get any of my cash, lady!" he snarls.

Lynn glances around at the water, astonishingly calm, at the moonlight sifting through the leaves. "I don't want your money, Tony," she says.

"You'll want it all right," he says. "But you won't get it. Not a penny. You deserve to live in a garret. Like that dump you're in now only worse – cold and decrepit. And you will. But I don't want my daughters growing up deprived because you choose to debase yourself."

"I don't tend to deprive them," Lynn answers. "Now let's head back."

He pivots as she turns and she braces herself not to flinch, not to let him sense her fear.

"If I marry can you see that it would be better for them to live with me?"

"I can imagine that happening." Thinking, if he finds someone.

She remembers their bed, one night near the end, him peering down at her, leaning on his elbow, fingering her genitalia like assorted shell specimens for display, saying, "I know how to make a woman happy sexually. I'll find another woman if we get divorced."

And her saying nothing, thinking, let him think well of himself, leave him that, shut up.

They are at the parking lot now. Their car, now his car, stands next to her newly bought used car. "Good night," Lynn says, unlocking the door of her car.

"Good night," he says, unlocking his. "Think it over. I think they might be better off with me."

Lynn does not intend an answer. Tony seems to be leaving calmly. She sits, closes the car door. Safe.

Tony walks over to her car, leans against her door. "And if I decide you'll mess them up," he says, shoving the words in her open window, "then I'll take you to court and that'll be the end of you and your dyke friend!"

"Shut up, Tony. There are people around here. I'll sue you for libel."

"Try it." He leers at her, turns away toward his own car, turns back. "What do you girls do anyhow?" He curves his raised voice into her car as she pulls out, eager revulsion slung to hit her as she goes: "Suck cunt? Do you?" shouting after her: "Is that what you do? Suck cunt?"

26

Lynn sits at the kitchen table. The house is late night quiet. Even Jon's stereo is off. Outside trucks pass and an occasional noisy car full of partying kids. It is three a.m.

She picks a letter from the stack in front of her, takes it from the envelope, drops the envelope in the wastebasket on her right, reads it slowly, twists it into a long tight wad, touches the tip to an open flame in the gas range on her left, lowers it slowly to a kettle on the floor, and watches it burn out inside the scorched aluminum. Then she takes another, reads, destroys.

Ruth's voice comes from the page: "Sometimes I wonder what it would be like if we were to enter that place we choose not to go. Sometimes I think about it as a vast cavern with beautifully grained wood for walls and great windows to let the light flow in and peace in the space there. We would be together in harmony and it would be like Mozart and sunlight and all the beauty that we already know." That was before we even kissed, Lynn thinks, and puts her head down on the table for a moment, moves her hand along the ripped vinyl cloth that covers it, scratches idly at a jagged edge, then lifts her head, picks up another and twists and burns.

"One minute I think we're insane. Raving mad. We want our marriages to last. We keep working to improve them. So what are we doing? Who will be hurt? Everyone? And the next I think, why is it so confusing? It's simple. I love you. You love me. If either were a man we'd be together. Even if we are women, if we were free we would be together. By now we both know that. I gave Neil twenty-five years and you gave Tony twenty-five years and it's so hard to make things work with them. With you and me nothing is hard. Between us every-thing is easy. So why don't we leave them? Why don't we come together if we both want it?"

Lynn twists and burns and watches the cinders flutter around in tiny circles in the bottom of the pan. She takes a stick and prods to make sure every word is burned. The scorched paper disintegrates when she touches it with the stick. Scorched transparencies, she thinks — good opening line for a poem sometime. To hell with poems, to hell with everything. She puts her head flat in her arms and waits for the pain to dull. At least keep her words, she thinks, touching the letters with her fingertips, feeling shivers against the sur-face of her skin as from a bad sunburn.

Hide them. He won't find them. He doesn't come here. Hide them. They may be all you ever have of her. Keep them. Hide them.

Burn them, she answers herself back. Burn every word. There are six kids involved. There are our jobs. Burn them. Hurry up and burn them. You shouldn't have waited until now. What if he found them?

You have to get up to teach in three hours. Hurry up. Get to it. Want the kids to find you here, slumped like a drunk? Get busy. Her head is suddenly too heavy for her to lift. Her eyes are closed. She drifts between swirling knots of air where tornadoes smash down houses, lift up towns. She drifts in darkening circles, down, down, down.

Outside a car careens, brakes screeching, past the house. Lynn jerks her head up, looks at the window, thinking, Tony? Heart pounding, gathering the letters in her arms as though to burn them all before Tony crashes through the window to snatch them from her hands.

Hey, wake up, wake up. No Tony. No smashed glass. You're just sleepy. Burn them. Quick. Don't read them. Just burn them. Get it over with.

No. This is crazy. I want these letters. They're mine. Her words. Hers. And my letters. Mine. He has no right. He wouldn't anyway. He's a decent man.

"And if I don't hear from you that you have . . . ." comes

into Lynn's mind, like a fragment of a song, the opening of some oath she had to take. 'As a girl scout I will do my best to serve my country at all times . . .' 'Thou shalt not covet thy neighbor's wife nor his ox nor his manservant . . .' 'I am not now nor have I ever been . . .' What the hell? she thinks, twisting one more sheet into the flame, singeing her fingers as she drops it down into the kettle, watches it smoulder, flare, die out. In the New York room? First year married? It clangs urgently like an emergency vehicle's repetitive warning bell — the memory coming up behind her swerving in and out of books and classes until it passes her and she sees it, clearly there before her, sharp as a tableau carved into rockface, glimpsed through a sudden rift as boulders shift to let her see through by the light of flashing torches from below: "I told him that if he didn't resign and if I didn't hear from him that he had resigned and if he didn't send me a copy of his resignation letter, I would write to his congregation myself and inform them." Tony stands, face stiff, voice strained. "Here's his letter. He resigned."

The torches flicker out. The crevice closes. The boulders stand dark and firm.

Lynn goes to the bathroom, leans, one hand on each side of the toilet tank, nausea in her like a tidal wave. Nothing happens. She slowly wipes her sweating face and returns to the table. The gas flame flutters blue and yellow by itself in loops and tongues of flame.

Blackmail. Blackmail. Blackmail. My God, she thinks. And you, what did you do? What in the name of God did you do to stop him? Did you argue? Did you tell him he wasn't God? WHAT DID YOU DO?

But the rock wall is shut. There is not the tiniest finger-hold for her to use to pry it open, to force the rocks apart.

Didn't you argue? Did you try to stop him? She searches for a protest, a fight, entreaties. She searches for estrangement coming after such a fight, entreaty, protest. She finds nothing but a smooth bluff, dark and unscathed.

"After we were married, we never fought," Lynn remembers saying again and again to friends and to the children. It had been a claim, an assertion of a marriage that was stable.

Now she squirms, remembering the sunlight of her past content where she would brook no discontent within herself, as though the first eighteen years of marriage were one long pastoral symphony, recorded that way in spite of any cacophony that might intrude. She executed the excisions so adroitly she barely knew any menace intervened.

"I never knew I wanted to cross him," Lynn says out loud, staring at the cinders in the kettle. "I thought that I agreed with him. Always I found a way to see what he was doing so that it was right, so that he meant well, so that I could be supportive and not challenge him."

Dizzy with her confusion, Lynn shuffles the remaining letters on the surface of the table. "Your marriage has been quite different from mine," Ruth wrote, "in that I knew what was good and what was bad and chose to stay because of what was good. You seem not to have seen anything bad. I guess you couldn't handle any anger . . ."

I didn't know it was there, Lynn thinks. I denied that it was there?

Close around the table the friends lean on their elbows, playing with the candle wax, reminiscing. Miss M. is serving pie. Lynn, holding Anthony in her arms, remembers her desk in Miss M.'s classroom, the way she sat staring at Miss M., to soak up the wonder of those dark and loving eyes, to watch the grace of her hands' movements, the shy awkwardness of her walk, her forward thrusting shoulders, Lynn's aching shock when Miss M. came into the room.

"You gave me Katherine Mansfield and Eudora Welty, Carson McCullers . . ." Lynn remembers the rush of recognition she had for Welty's small town voice, McCullers' young girl's urgencies. "And I wrote and wrote and you kept saying, 'yes' and 'write some more.'" Lynn laughs, mellow with remembering and love.

Tony interrupts. "You should have given her Shakespeare. High schools should train people in the classics. It's criminal that we graduated not knowing the difference between Keats and Yeats—" He reverses the pronunciation and everyone roars with laughter. Lynn wants to interrupt, to say she sat in on the Shakespeare class sometimes, but not for Shakespeare, just to breathe deep, to covertly love Miss M. Tony goes on. "We were ready for that kind of training; the European schools give it to their students; you never catch up here. Lynn shouldn't have gone to college without a better background in English literature. We were all cheated of our heritage, actually."

Miss M. sends one lightning glance at her, hoping that Lynn will counter Tony's accusation. Lynn recognizes Miss M.'s wish. Lynn also knows that Miss M. realizes that Lynn can not challenge Tony; that Lynn can do only what she does, gather up the baby and go home with Tony, with whom Lynn does not disagree, now that they are married.

Remembering Miss M.'s face, her quickly covered hurt, Lynn aches with guilt. I choked my disagreements off in my throat, she thinks. I was hypnotized into smiling and agreeing. My own fault. Why? Why? It showed to everyone. Once in a village, in Italy, visiting Tony's distant relatives, the old women watched Tony and Lynn and the children, and nudged one another, whispering, laughing. One of them asked Tony a question, gesturing toward Lynn where she sat nursing Lori. Tony grinned and translated it for Lynn, "She wants to know where I found one like you in America?" Lynn smiled and blushed and laid aside the complexity of the question, choosing to view it as a compliment. Tony later quoted it with pride.

Even when Miss M. died, Lynn thinks. Even then I let him tell me what to do. Lynn is spinning, crashing through the sunlight of the marriage, past shining motes to pitch black moments never allowed to fully register before, as though they were repelled on contact with the cornea, reflected off by the ubiquitous sunshine that registered continuously there.

"The doctor says there's nothing he can do," Miss M. says to Lynn on the telephone.

"Doctors! I hate doctors!" Lynn responds.

"I'd rather he told me the truth," Miss M. answers. Lynn refuses to let herself know for another year. Then she understands. They're living near to Miss M. then. She puts the words on paper one afternoon, knowing she can gather all her love into written words and that they will be infused with power as her spoken words never are. She shows the letter to Tony in the evening. He tells her not to send it.

"It would only upset Miss M. to know we think that she will die."

Lynn does not send the letter.

Before Miss M. goes into the hospital Tony and Lynn take the children to visit her at home. Lynn sits beside her, holding her hand, as long as they can stay. Later, when she is in the hospital, Tony stops often on his way home from campus. Lynn asks him to keep the kids so she can go, but he can't find the time. Lynn hasn't ever left the children with a sitter. Lynn finally gets Tony to agree to keep the kids on a certain Tuesday afternoon. She will go and put her letter in Miss M.'s hands; she knows she wants to let her know fully how deeply she is loved; spoken words have been inadequate; only the words on paper can explosively and beautifully connect.

The morning of the day of Lynn's appointment, Miss M. dies. Later Tony says that he is sorry. Subconsciously, he says, perhaps he wanted to keep Miss M. to himself.

Lynn flips three of Ruth's letters in the kettle, lights the bunch, fuzzily watches the fire leap, its light shimmering against tears.

What did you think would happen if you broke the bond? What if you opposed him?

Fifth grade. 1940. The teacher carries a piece of rubber hose in his pocket. When he lectures the class he takes it out and taps it on his palm. He wears a tweed jacket and is the first male teacher Lynnanne has ever had.

Out back in the school playground there is an enclosed

space between the stairway, the brick sides of the building, and the gym. After school, waiting for the bus, students fight there. The class tomboy fights with the boys there and once she asks Lynnanne to do standing wrestling with her. Lynnanne does.

Hands locked on one another's arms they sway, body to body, strength to strength.

In class the next day Mr. Hammond marches the aisles, tapping the rubber hose, tap, tap, tap, telling the class how one of the boys was caught and disciplined for fighting after school in the playground, and how any other boys who get caught will be given the same punishment — tap, tap, tap — and how he has even heard rumors that there is in this class a certain girl — he pauses to let the ominous weight of that unbelievable statement crawl beneath their desks like poison gas — a girl who has been fighting there — and everyone's head holds still while each thinks about the tomboy who is the wild girl in class, the girl who hits boys back when they hit her — while the hose goes spat spat spat against his palm — and if a girl were to be caught, he says, she also will be disciplined by him. Tap tap tap.

What if you didn't agree, understand, anticipate Tony's needs, get there first to reassure him before he even knew he wanted reassurance? What if you didn't head yourself off at the pass before you knew you were about to square off with him? Was it "abnegation" of yourself as Mill says, and as Miss Campbell in the fourth grade, who had never heard of Mill said: "We are here to make the world a better place to be; think about the other person's need; it won't hurt you." Lynn stands and walks back and forth through the house, trying to shift ground to take comfort in the theoretical. But no matter what she tries to use to keep her distance, the dark magnet of these newly unearthed memories draws Lynn irresistibly to it.

Blackmail. Did you argue? Did you? I didn't understand, she defends herself, clawing at the bare rock face; I didn't understand. She tries to find an escape route by starting at the beginning.

Tony worked nights in the health club before we were married. Then he worked there days. He told you there were homosexuals there, didn't he? Yes. Did you know what that meant? No. What did you think it meant? I don't know. You liar. All right, it meant men who had sex with other men. And what did Tony do about them? He threw them out. Why? To protect the club's clients. From what? I didn't know. What did you think? I didn't think; he said that was his job; he said they were sick; he said there should be counseling for them, but nobody cared, so they just threw them out.

The boulders shift a second and through the crack Lynn glimpses Tony and two friends from work; they're leaning together in a subway car swaying their way home; she is sitting looking up at them, hearing half of what they say. "So sadist number one . . ." and the train makes its roaring noises and she can't hear. The torches flame up and the tableau frays away into fire and drifting ash rising above the mountains into smoke.

What is the rest of that subway scene? I can't remember; I don't know. Guess! I can't. No, you can't. You didn't even know the right words then. But you're not an idiot, weren't even then. Why didn't you learn the vocabulary? "Sadist:" did you know the word? Did you look it up in the Oxford Unabridged? Or even the student Webster? Two years Tony worked there? Two years of his jokes and laughter, sometimes desperate, sometimes entertained. You heard all right. You had to, you, with your empathetic ears. What did Tony do there for two years? Watch? Dream? Mock? Or help sadist one and two torment?

WHY DIDN'T YOU STOP HIM?

I didn't understand. That's what the Germans said. Didn't know? Didn't see the smoke? He BLACKMAILED that minister. Did you understand that much? Did you? Were you an illiterate slave who would be shot if you learned to read, to understand? Did he own you?

Tony talked about protecting children. He said it wasn't right for a man like that to be a minister. He said children were entrusted to his care. Tony said he would abuse them. And you believed him? "A man like that?" Did you know the man? Did *he know* the man?

No. I trusted Tony. That was marriage. To trust him, help him, support him.

You make me sick. You helped him get it up. You told him he was great, no matter what; you told yourself he was great no matter what. What did you think he was doing when he black-mailed that man?

Protecting children. That's what he said. He said someone had to protect the children.

From what?

From abuse. I didn't understand.

You didn't understand, Lynn repeats scathingly to herself.

No. I really didn't understand. There were lots of things I didn't understand when I first knew Tony. I didn't know how to find my way in the subway or how to get tickets or about politics. I didn't understand that game where he whistled a single note and his friend guessed which symphony or quartet it was; I believed there was really only one right answer. I didn't understand history or economics. I understood poetry. I understood novels. And I understood that children needed to be protected from people who would use them for sex.

But you didn't understand blackmail. Poor baby. Well, begin to understand. You wanted an airtight marriage. Secure. Safe. Safe at all costs.

Safe for our children.

Okay. Safe for the children. Safe. And anything that threatened that private safety you kept out. You collaborated all the way. Shave your head, Lynn snarls at herself, shave your head, you all-supporting wife, you whore.

Lynn pushes the last letters into the pan and lights them. The flames leap up out of the kettle. She runs to the sink for water but by the time she turns back to drown the flames, they have subsided and the water sizzles in the pan and runs along the floor, black with scattered ash. She mops it up, puts the charred kettle in the sink, turns off the gas flame, and goes to her bed, where she lies, fully clothed, for the last hour before her alarm will ring.

Lynn lies alone in the dark and swings on a vine, back and forth from one side of a gully to the other. Tony is not the monster that I'm making him, she thinks; it will level out, right now all I can see is the worst he ever was. I'll tell Julia how that is, how I'm dizzy, want balance. I had a pretty happy marriage, she says to herself, just short of sleep. "I had a pretty happy childhood," she said to Julia, first time there. You never told on Billy and Marsh and until you told Julia all about it, you said you had a happy childhood. Happy childhood, happy marriage. You never even told on Tony to yourself.

The clanging whirr of the alarm wakes Lynn from a city fire where buildings fall like stage scenery and she is running, running as papier-maché people drift in the glowing air like a million translucent ghosts.

27

Lynn, one dark Friday afternoon, turns into the driveway of her rented house and finds the trees have blown almost bare. Brown leaves, orange, yellow, red tinted leaves swirl around the yard, pile against the fallen fence, burrow in droves behind the shrubs against the house. There are no lights on in the house. For the first time this fall it's already dark enough to know then that there is no one home. She takes the mail from the mailbox by the front door and goes inside to put it and her books down before beginning to unload the groceries. Her hand goes up to pull the string that works the hanging shaded bulb that is the kitchen light, and standing, arm raised, shadows thickening around her, she says out loud, "When did my mother die?"

What did I send her for Christmas last year? Nothing. She was already dead. She didn't know we separated — that was already summer. When Tony said Anthony didn't deserve a birthday present? She was already gone. When Christy broke her leg and lay on the sofa from Thanksgiving through the holidays? Yes, she was there then. So when was that?

The years swirl like the blowing leaves outside the window and Lynn cannot locate the day her mother died. It was in the fall. Funny how I still start to phone her in my head, sort the things to tell her. She never knew most of the trouble. I only wrote the good things: Jon's practicing, Anthony's playing basketball, Christy's in orchestra, no, chorus — she was already dead before she got to orchestra.

"My mother only had one dress." Lynn's mother, seventy years old and ill, lying, propped up with pillows, watching a TV quiz show, tells her this. "When she died, we went through her closet. There was only one dress hanging there. No one had ever noticed. She never mentioned it and we never thought about it. Imagine — only one dress. I can see it still . . ."

Lynn goes out to the car. She stands, watching the blowing leaves. You have no family at all, besides your own children, she thinks, seeing a hose from summer still lying in the grass. Should roll that up. Should turn the outdoor faucets off so they won't freeze. Tomorrow I'll do that sort of thing. No storm windows in this house. Half the screens useless. Half the windows stuck shut and one stuck open. Have to hammer it down for winter. Next summer I'll find a better house. This is okay for now.

"I remember once — we'd just moved from the log cabin in the valley to the big house on the hill — the house you grew up in—" Her mother's voice is heavy with nostalgia. "My mother said I could ride to town with her. Nothing could have made me happier. Later that day, I was down in the orchard, picking apples. I heard her call and I ran toward the house. She didn't see me coming and thought I'd forgotten and she drove away without me. I stood watching the horses pull the wagon until it was out of sight, crying and crying. I couldn't believe she went without me."

Lynn opens the door and carries two bags of food into the house. Had her with us every year until the last two; let her stay four months, six months, every year. The guilt is thickening in her veins; she feels it crowding through her arms and legs, heading for her heart. Should have gone.

Lynn goes back outside, walks around the house just to breathe air that isn't thick with chalk dust, like the school's, to let her arms hang useless for a Friday moment before beginning to clean, cook, taxi, shop for Lori's shoes, grade papers, get ready for next week. The neighbor's phone rings. Lynn hears it far, encased in someone else's cooking-dinner smells, home-from-work weekend hug. No, Ruth will not call. But it's been five weeks. She said two months. But five weeks. Thirty-five days. Thirty-five nights. And then she may decide to stay with Neil, you know. You idiot, go find some people. Don't sit home alone. Too much to do. Liar. Don't want people; want to touch Ruth's hand, hear her voice. I could call. I could call just to ask her and let me know if she's made a choice. So I won't wait after that. That's all. Not to talk. That wouldn't break the agreement. Just to say, "Don't let me wait two months listening for the phone, turning off the shower halfway through to make sure the phone's not ringing, running to the window every time a car pulls up in front thinking it might be you" — I'll call, just to say that, not to break the silence, just to say not to torture me. Shut up.

Why didn't you go see your mother before she died? Simple. Drive to the airport, fly out, stay two days. Fly back. Could've. Tony didn't object. "Go," he said, "if you want to go. I'll give you the fare. You decide." Sitting in his big chair in the corner, pipe in hand, he spoke as if in a Victorian novel, where the husband is called Mr. by the wife and the wife is called Mrs. by the husband and they speak to one another across some void that is as tangible a furnishing as the ornate carpet, were it to be squared and held vertically between them. There was nothing to go for after she was dead. They didn't even have a funeral. No memorial service. Nothing.

But earlier. You knew that she was dying. Why didn't you go then? Couldn't leave the kids. You wouldn't leave Ruth, you mean.

Late evening. The first April. Ruth and Lynn sit in the car outside Ruth's house, poetry in their hands. "I can't go in," Ruth says.

"What's the matter, Ruth?"

"I don't know. I'm afraid."

"Shall I come in with you?"

"No, thank you, no. I'll be fine in just a minute."

"Is Neil away?"

"No, he's asleep."

It's dark in the driveway where they sit. Trees and bushes obscure the lawn and street. Lynn feels Ruth tense and looks through the darkness toward the place where her eyes must be darkening with fear. "What are you thinking about?"

"I don't even know."

"About Germany again? Did you ever go back to your boarding school again?"

"Yes. Neil had a year in Paris and we went to The Netherlands and I saw where it had been. A few months after I left, the Germans came and killed everyone who was still there."

"My God." Lynn takes Ruth in her arms, feels her trembling, takes off her own sweater and folds it around Ruth's shoulders. They sit in silence a long time. Ruth speaks in a low voice.

"You cannot spend your time this way. I think you shouldn't see me any more. You have a life, a family, a husband. Don't let me destroy that."

"You won't destroy anything."

"You're starting to take care of me. Look at you." Ruth's smile is in her voice. "You take care of everyone. That's why everyone loves you. But you're not going to take care of me."

Lynn tightens her hold on the slender body in her arms. "Shhh. You have a right to live, a right to be known."

There is silence for so long Lynn thinks Ruth is asleep. "When I went back to Germany after the year in school in Holland, we kept moving. Families had to move in with other families. Because I was only half-Jewish I got a different food allowance and a fuel allowance until the end; but what was worse was that I could go to concerts when my mother couldn't. My piano teacher was afraid to teach me though. Funny. I can hardly remember the sealed train we escaped in, but I can remember sitting in the opera hall listening to Mozart when Mother had to stay at home. That was just before we got away. I think our train may have been the last train out."

The night turns cold around them. Ruth makes a slight

*motion to go. Lynn tightens her arms around her and says,
"Not yet. You're not ready yet."*

"Okay. In a little while."

*Toward morning a light snow begins to fall. It coats the
trees with white just before the dawn works its gradual brightness across the sky.*

*"I'll go in now. Thank you. But you mustn't do this. This
is just what I mean. You have to go through a long day now
without any sleep." Ruth sits up straight.*

*"I'm not tired. An April snow. Reminds me of Housman
and his cherry trees — and through these woods I'd better drive
and right now to see them hung with real snow. Good morning,
Ruth," Lynn says. "Call me tonight," and she drives home
singing Housman to herself.*

Afraid to leave her, stayed to take care of Ruth. You
should've gone. No. That wasn't it. Even Julia said maybe I
shouldn't go. Jon shoved Anthony through the kitchen
window. Lynn flinches: shattering glass, blood and slashed
flesh; Anthony's eyes dark with disbelief and fear. Remember,
every time you drove up to the house, turning off the key and
listening, hoping there wouldn't be a scream or crashing glass
or that weird silence that meant it had already blown and no
one dared to move. Remember that?

You could've gone for a day or two. Didn't feel safe to do
it. Didn't feel safe to go to the grocery store unless Tony was
home. Found time to be with Ruth. She came to the house.
Or Tony was home and I went to her house, but not for days
and days, just for a few hours.

You got away with her, to the city, overnight. That was
later.

So I should've gone, no matter what. You make mistakes.
Everybody makes mistakes.

She didn't go when he died.

He died in the Old Soldiers' Home. Felt hat. Milk bucket.
Saw on shoulder. Snapping off dead roses in the snow. Stroke,
they said. Lynn's always hoped it was outdoors, that he was
walking in the morning in the prison yard they called a soldiers'

home, thinking about spring when the rose bushes he tended would bloom again, watching the snow fall gently on the trees — there were hardly any trees in that God-forsaken place. Travelling through she'd gone to see him once. Golf course. For the doctors? Snow on that open expanse of green turning it soft and white, like the fields of the farm he wanted to own and work. They found a lot of money he'd saved up to buy that farm rolled up in the drawer beside his bed. He needed her mother's signature before he could buy land or leave the soldiers' home. She wouldn't ever sign.

Years later, in the therapy, Lynn first wonders whether or not it was necessary to keep him there. The hospital discharged him ten years before he died, then reassigned him to the soldiers' home because her mother could not, would not, did not live with him. Lynn wonders why she stayed married to him if she wouldn't live with him. If she wouldn't live with him, why didn't she divorce him and let him be free to do whatever the doctors decided he could do?

In her detective work with Julia, Lynn traced from the beginning. She found the commitment paper in the court archives and studied it at Julia's. Less than two pages long, it quoted the two witnesses against him: one, her mother, said he was talkative, aggressive, irritable, suicidal, and couldn't keep a job because he thought they thought he was a secret agent; the other, her father's sister, said, "Tore his fence down about the place and allowed the cow to come in and destroy things. Took a boat to town and came looking for a job at midnight." That was all there was to ponder, trying to understand what happened when Lynnanne was seven months old. When she was almost three the doctors sent him home again, and when she was eight, he went away for good.

In the city neighborhood near the narrow house, Lynnanne watched a dancing man with a rangy setter, black and white, that followed him around. The kids hopped from foot to foot to imitate his dancing; they put their circling fingers at their brows, signalling "crazy man, crazy man." The index finger moving in a little circle while pointing to one's temple meant "insane" in school yards all of Lynnanne's life. In seventh grade Lynnanne thinks she will be crazy when she grows up;

she thinks she can't ever marry or have a family; she decides to be a psychiatrist instead.

The commitment document concludes with an itemized bill. "Cost of insanity: $10.00." The line burned itself into Lynn's mind beside another line imprinted there when she was seventeen. Her mother let her go along to see her father, in the hospital, after a nine year separation, unbroken by news or visits. Lynnanne expected it to be a strange nightmare with a man past all recognition.

Once there, the felt hat is the same. The overalls, suspenders, lace-up work shoes are his. The hands that point to flowers and to birds are also his. She knows the silver stubbled face, the blue eyes, the silver eyebrows and the slightly pursing mouth. They picnic.

He talks about the farm that he will buy, where he will live with her mother while he farms. Lynnanne begins to know that her mother holds him in the hospital. Before they leave the grounds, her father points to the name of the hospital engraved above the gate. He reads to her, "Abandon hope all ye who enter here." She kisses him goodby, the line imbedded in her brain the way his old man's hug is pressed into her flesh, both indenting her like links of a chain fence she has pressed her whole body against long and hard.

When their father had his stroke, only Billy went. He phoned their mother, who was at Lynn and Tony's for the winter. "Should I go? Do you think I should?" she asked of Lynn.

Lynn, Lori a baby in her arms, said to her mother, "No, of course you shouldn't go. You're not strong enough for that long a trip. You'd just make yourself sick again." All true. Her mother had already then had several heart attacks. Relieved, her mother lay back down. She did not want to go.

Billy made the arrangements. No one else even made the trip. Lynn walked the streets alone the day of her father's funeral a thousand miles away. Lynn walked alone, to stay out of the house; she hated her mother for not wanting to be there. She walked and she remembered. She remembered the orange turning in his great hand, as he says, "The earth is like this orange and it turns around the sun. China is here. We are here.

If you dug a hole deep enough you'd come out in China."
Digging sometimes in the yard Lynnanne wondered how much
deeper she would have to go to break through to rickshaws
and colored fans. She remembered playing croquet on the
grass behind the farmhouse. "Now hit your ball right to here,"
he says, and deadeye, she does. "Now I'll hit Billy galley west
for you," he says of her brother's ball, and leaves her safe to
follow him back through the wickets to the home stake and
out.

In his pocket when he died they found his knife for whit-
tling; he made her whistles from the alder by the creek.

And my mother did not want to go even when he died.

Lynn scuffs the leaves around her feet, remembering herself remembering. She carries in the last of the groceries and
puts the frozen foods away, then the fresh vegetables, the
fruit, and then the cartons, cans. All summer on the farm the
froth boiled high above the giant canning kettles on the wood
range that made the kitchen hotter and hotter. My mother
canned everything, Lynn thinks, and baked all our bread,
cake, pie, cookies. And she churned the cream into butter,
made cottage cheese from the milk. She thinks with shame that
she has never given credit to her mother for the prodigious work
she did.

Lynn washes a chicken and puts it in the oven. She sees a
mound of towels on the dryer at the end of the kitchen and
gathers up others, from Lori's bed, from Christy's doorknob,
from Jon's floor, and puts in a load. My mother washed the
clothes down in the cellar where the floor was half dirt and
half concrete. The washer had a wringer hooked on its side.
The sheets and towels came winding through, coming out in
a flat squirmy line. My mother then carried them in buckets
out past the maple tree where she propped up the lines with
long sticks with forked ends and hung the sheets in billowing
rows. Lynnanne tried to help and once, age four, she tripped
and catapulted down, bucket rattling, far down to the concrete at the bottom of the stairs. Blood matted her hair and
streaked her face and dress. Her mother wouldn't let her carry
the bucket after that.

"Soon afterwards a little daughter was born to her, who was as white as snow, as red as blood, and with hair as black as ebony, and thence she was named 'Snow White,' and when the child was born the mother died.' If you cry when I read it, I won't read to you," her mother says, and Lynnanne forces her tears to stop.

So I should have gone to see her before she died. But I can't go now. So get on with it. Hearing a car pull up and start again, Lynn goes to the window to see if Lori has been brought home from her friend's, but she has not. The street is empty. Lynn pours herself a glass of wine and sits at the table to go through the mail.

The legal envelope is very white and thick. She opens it. It's from Tony's lawyer. The legal language winds it like a great ball of twine: ". . . alleges and contends . . . that the party herein named . . . has on numerous occasions . . . at the address below . . ."

Lynn gropes for a minute, trying to make sense of the address. Not this rented house she lives in now. "Maple?" In which town was there a Maple? An avenue with trees . . . "307. 307 Maple . . ." Abruptly the number and the street register in her mind as though imprinted there by some huge metal stamper.

". . . with one Ruth Martinson . . ."

What has Ruth to do with our divorce? What is Tony doing? Lynn sees the lawyer's signature and she sees Tony's name. She reads again and hits the words: ". . . committed adultery . . ."

The ball of twine spills to the floor, undone.

28

"One thing you could just do," Nora Daniels says, with a twinkle in her eye, "is give the girls to him, and see how long he lasts."

Lynn quickly laughs. "Two weeks?"

"Less!"

"But I don't dare gamble." Serious again, Lynn speaks, "I think he'd be too proud to admit he couldn't handle them and by the time he gave up, he would have somehow managed to get both of them all messed up. I don't want to take that risk."

"You're sure, aren't you?"

"Yes. I've thought about it a lot."

"All right then. Now, what's your guess? You know him better than I do. Will he go through with this adultery suit?"

Lynn pauses. "I don't know. He's like a man I've never met before. But I don't think he will. For one thing I think he's scared of me."

"What do you have on him? Other women?"

Lynn thinks, what has he done to us? To make us tell strangers what we once told each other in love and closeness, to make us play cops and robbers with each other. "No," she says, swamped with the guilt of telling what she has never told anyone before. "When he was young he blackmailed a minister." She tells the story.

Nora Daniels makes an expression of disgust. "What a thing to do! That's enough to ruin him. He wouldn't want his colleagues to hear that. What else?"

"That's about it. As a kid he was afraid he would be homosexual. He had an experience that scared him . . . in the army, I think."

"That may explain why he's so worried about you. A frightened man is a menace. He knows you might talk?"

"He knows."

"Good. Now. What does he have on you and Ruth? Level with me, Lynn. I've got to know. I'll fight, but when I get into court, if it comes to that, I don't want any surprises, understand?" Nora plants her hands, palms down, on her desk and sighs, waiting.

"Maybe letters. Ruth's husband found one letter and at that time she burned all her letters from me and I burned all mine from her." Lynn starts to cave in. Shouldn't have, she thinks; it's all you've got of Ruth. You don't believe that, she retorts to herself, you're waiting for Ruth.

"Anything else?"

"We've taken trips together."

"That letter Ruth's husband found. Does he have it?"

"No. He gave it back."

"Would he have xeroxed it?"

"I don't think so."

"Would he testify?"

"I don't know."

"I wonder if he would. They're on the same campus, aren't they?"

"Yes."

"Ask Ruth what she thinks."

Lynn nods. I could call her to ask, she thinks. I practically have to call her to ask that. Forget it. Give it up.

Nora Daniels studies her. "I hope it will never get to court, Lynn." She sighs. "God, do I hope it won't. But if it does—" She leans forward. "I don't see what they can prove. You and Ruth are the best of friends. You help each other; you support each other. You help each other when your kids are sick. Women friends, you know? If a man and a woman go into a motel together and spend the night, the law says that's presumptive evidence. We assume they went to bed together!" Nora chuckles. "But if two women spend the night together we don't assume anything except that they talked a lot!" She lets out a belly laugh. "That's because the laws were written by men and that's all they think women can do!"

Lynn tries to think what else Tony might use against her. "He objects to *Ms.* magazine!" She laughs. "I can't think of anything else."

"Unless he has pictures of you two doing cunnilingus!" Nora Daniels laughs again at the thought, preposterous to her, "I don't see really how he could win." Her eyes sharpen and she snaps, "Find out if he and Ruth's husband — what's his name — have gotten their heads together, will you? I'll need to know."

Pressed hard against the pay phone wall, Lynn dials for help. They are closing in to kill. No answer. Waking, she knows this is the day of the first lawyers' conference.

They sit at a heavy wooden table, Tony's lawyer on his side, Nora Daniels on hers. Strangers to the years they touched one another, they watch as each child, each aspect of their lives, is held up target flat. Tony, penny arcade rifle in his hand, sights unsteadily. Riddled and spun, each target is hauled down, contracted where it falls, or set aside to be raised when they have reloaded at a later time.

"We have written in a clause that stipulates that your client will not share housing with anyone." His lawyer savors the sentence, rolls it smoothly in his mouth. "I think we all understand the reason for this protection."

"I won't agree to such a clause," Lynn says. "Do *you* intend to live alone the rest of your life, Tony?"

Tony looks at his lawyer who studies the shining table top a moment, then replies, "We, of course, do not mean to exclude remarriage. We mean to exclude cohabitation with someone of the same sex."

"You mean I can't rent out a room?"

"It would depend to whom."

Nora Daniels interrupts. "The future housing arrangements

of my client do not concern your client. They are being divorced.

"There are certain existing conditions, of which I am sure you are aware," he gives Nora an unctuous flicker of a smile, "which make it imperative that my client be guaranteed a certain degree of control over his wife's behavior, in the best interest of the children." He looks toward Tony who nods.

"You cannot control my life," Lynn says to Tony, "nor I yours."

"I can protect my children," Tony says, voice rising, "from a reckless woman."

His lawyer leans forward. "We are concerned here with custody." His voice toughens. "After the children are all over twenty-one we don't care if you live with red or purple or yellow polka-dotted creatures from outer space." He smiles condescendingly.

It registers in Lynn's mind that racists always use bizarre colors to describe the people they are allegedly not prejudiced against. "I'll live as I choose just as my ex-husband will," she says.

"The hell you will!" Tony yells. "You don't have the right any more to live as you choose, lady. You are supposed to be a mother and you are too self-centered and irresponsible to keep my children safe so if you want them you'll have to be watched. Not by me but by the court. You are too incompetent to be a mother! Incompetent and reckless!"

The lawyers intervene and quiet him. The voices go on firing across the smooth glow of the conference table. He will give modest child support for Lori and Christy until they are eighteen. Half of their equity in the house is hers by law; that's about nine thousand dollars. Nothing else. Their only savings are in retirement funds which he claims as exclusively his own. He will not agree to pay any legal fees. He will not accept any responsibility for past family debts, for the boys' support, for Lynn's re-training costs or moving or her car. Nora Daniels expostulates about the horrendous financial burden Lynn has assumed. Tony's lawyer interrupts to say, "No court will award your client custody, you know, if we bring charges against her as my client has every right to do." Disbelieving, Lynn starts to realize that Tony and his lawyer are trading custody for money.

"We'll sue you for libel," Nora retorts, gathering up her papers.

"Will you?" his lawyer leers at her, mocking.

"We will. Furthermore, there are other things that will be damaging to your client's reputation if you force a confrontation." She slams shut her briefcase and goes out the door.

Lynn, right behind Nora Daniels, says to Tony, "Don't take away the children's parents, Tony. They still have two parents who love them. We'd destroy each other in court and leave them orphans. Don't do that, Tony."

In the parking lot, Nora says, "You did very well. They're bullies, those two bastards. They're blackmailing us. It makes me want to fight. But I'm scared we'd lose the kids for you. If you don't insist on any alimony — or any help with debts or with the older kids — they'll let you go. Can you manage?"

"I'll manage," Lynn answers, flint in her voice.

"Yes, I'll bet you will. You were great. I was sweating, I'll admit. Yes, you'll be fine. That man doesn't know what he's losing when he loses you. Too bad."

At night, before they catch me, closing in, sweating and wild, I am not dead after all, alone in my waking bed, Lynn thinks, and gets up to walk around.

In the kitchen, still half-caught by the dream, she reaches for the light string. It brushes her arm. Pulling it on, thinking, like the basement light on the farm, same dangling string, she checks her arm for crawling spiders. She opens the refrigerator door. Milk? My mother always had hot milk at night and the thought of hot milk makes me nauseous. Cocoa, yes. She made you cocoa when you came home from school when you were little, she says accusingly to herself. For what price? she challenges herself back. That you wouldn't tell. My mother sold me to my brothers off an auction block. Why do I always think 'my mother,' never 'mother?' I went to school unable to say 'mother.' No other speech defect at all, only that — could say father, brother, smother, other — but not mother.

Lynnanne, age seven, is in the bathtub, being bathed. She is going to the hospital for treatment of a urinary infection. Marsh whispered to her the night before, "It's 'cause of what Billy does to you."

Her mother hands her the washcloth. "Sometimes the boys . . ." Lynnanne says.

Her mother abruptly takes back the washcloth and scrubs her with it, hard. "Have to be good and clean," she says. "The boys have enough trouble," she says. "Don't ever make life harder on them, Lynnanne. You have it easy. You don't know how it is for them. Now hold still. Hold still."

The nurse who wheeled her to a room with bright hard lights stands by her head and says, ether makes people sick and has an awful smell and Lynnanne instead of asking to breathe it, should lie still, hold still, be good, hold still. Her mother is also there and says, lie still, hold still, be good.

Lynnanne makes her body lie still, keeps it from crying out, as the doctor cauterizes the urinary tract that is a part of the body they call hers.

Lynnanne herself rides her wooden stick horse with the barn-red head toward where her father swings the scythe through the tall and blowing grasses, mowing hay.

Years later, Lynnanne, bringing bread and milk home to the narrow house, says, "There was a man in the doorway by the store with his pants open and he was rubbing himself up and down."

"No, no, he wasn't," her mother says. "I'm sure he wasn't. Forget about it now and let's have supper."

Denial after denial, year after year, until she got to Julia where, denying the importance of what she told, Lynn told.

"I don't think it matters much, but my brothers bothered me sexually when I was young," Lynn says, ready to go on with contemporary things.

"Oh, yes?" Julia intervenes. "Tell me more about that, why don't you?"

Then Lynn begins to tell and to remember what more there is to tell. That night Lynn dreams: she is at the foot of a wildly cascading waterfall which rises high above her; she is crying with a consuming intensity; the sobs hurtle through her; still in the dream she is then in a room with Julia who is sitting on a sofa; Lynn reaches toward her, wanting, desperately wanting, to take her hand across the sofa back. Lynn wakes with sobs still erupting from her throat.

Eluding Billy, Lynnanne edges into the living room. Her father lies sleeping on the sofa. His work shoes, with their high lace-up tops and their thick mud-stained soles, stand on the floor, side by side. The tips of his black socks show outside the brown and orange blanket under which he sleeps. He sleeps hugely, his chest rising and falling with deep breaths. His cheeks, rough and red beneath a silver stubble, move with his breathing, and his mouth is slightly open. His arms are under the blanket except for one hand which hangs out under the brown fringe that edges the blanket. Lynnanne stands, staring at that hand, wanting to wake him, wanting to run to him to be held.

"Come on," Billy says, "come on or you'll be sorry. You'll really get it if you wake him up."

Lynnanne knows she will not tell. She sits on the floor, tracing with her finger the patterns in the rug, within the circle of his breathing. Wanting to awaken him, wanting to tell, she is edging near him when he awakens, but she does not tell.

Lynn remembers writing in a college paper: "Education is essential because no human being will hurt another if he understands that he is being hurtful. Understanding is what is needed to sustain civilization. No one would knowingly hurt another person. Education is the route to such understanding." The philosophy professor marked the essay, "An interesting position to hold — A—" and argued with her in his benign way. Her friends argued with her in total disbelief. Underneath what she presented as intellectual beliefs, the music thundered: if they had known they wouldn't have hurt me; IF SHE HAD KNOWN THEY HURT ME SHE WOULDN'T HAVE LET THEM HAVE ME, HURT ME.

Lynn stays at the table, studying the vinyl cloth, drawing lines on it with the handle of the spoon. That last year my mother stayed with us, she told me how she tied me down. I didn't tell her then how Marsh and Billy used that tied down two-year old. In college I wrote that story about abuse and she read it and said it was very good except for the part about the boy bothering the little girl; she said that seemed unreal. I told her it happened quite a lot; girls at college told me, I said, and let it drop. That was the last time I ever tried to tell her.

Lynn draws with indentations in the cloth the single word: Lysol. She etches each letter deeper.

" 'May I go swimming, Mother dear?' 'Why, yes, my darling daughter. Hang your clothes on the hickory limb and don't go near the water.' " I'd forgotten that one, Lynn thinks, and is flooded with bits of songs her mother sang to her, wearing her housedress and apron, sitting at the old piano, eyes sad, face like a Botticelli virgin's overcast with melancholy rue. "My darling Nellie Grey, they have taken you away, and I'll never hear your singing any more," and "The north wind doth blow and we shall have snow, and what will poor robin do then? Poor thing! He'll sit in a barn and keep himself warm, and hide his head under his wing. Poor thing." In the song book on the piano were pictures that she memorized while her mother sang: the muted colors of the falling leaves that matched "Poor babes in the wood, poor babes in the wood," as the little boy and girl, hand in hand, lay down under the blowing, falling leaves, "and they laid down and died, poor babes in the woods."

"Don't touch the keys. Don't cry, don't cough, don't talk

so loud — it makes my head hurt; don't scowl — you'll get lines across your forehead; don't touch yourself; keep your hands folded in your lap."

Why, Lynn taunts herself, did this mother who didn't love you rub your aching legs and tell you stories in the middle of the night? Rheumatic fever. Couldn't hold still. Thrashing because you slept with your legs hunched in a knot, a terrified little animal guarding yourself by curling around yourself into a cramping knot? Your bed? Did she come to comfort you in your bed where you lay in fear? No, her bed, their bed. And where was he? He pulled on his trousers. He went into the bathroom where his razor strap hung next to the little sink and he slept then in some other bed. She was left alone with me. And her magazines. She braided her hair in a long braid down her back at night; I lay and watched; then she came to bed and read and I read over her shoulder. She had big amber hair pins and silver clips that I made airplanes out of when I was sick in bed. She must have wanted him out of the bed. Very young, standing by the ironing board where my mother ironed, her visitor looking me up and down, laughing, saying, "And how's Daddy's pet, Daddy's little surprise for Mommy, doing today?" And the visitor laughed and laughed.

Still there were stories in the middle of the dark night: "Solomon Grundy, born on a Monday, christened on Tuesday, married on Wednesday, tool ill on Thursday, worse on Friday, died on Saturday, buried on Sunday. This is the end of Solomon Grundy." And knowing the next words, already protesting, already thrashing against the hopelessness: "No, no—" "Told you the story of Solomon Grundy and now my story's begun; I'll tell you another about his brother and now my story is done." No, not that one, not that one." Brothers and marriage and death.

"If she has your brothers there, she doesn't need you. She won't miss you," Julia said. Before that, in the ambulance, her last year with us, hearing the siren that was our progress through the night, watching her breathing, I looked my question at the attendant who shrugged his doubt back at me through the night. Later, at the hospital, I leaned down, my heart doing skin-the-cats in my chest, to tell her how great she'd always been, that I loved her; Lynn rehearses it like a litany to chase away the guilt for not going at the end. Twenty years I had her stay six months, four months, every year, nursed her, drove her, joked with her, and never told her, never let her know what I found out, never let her know how she'd declawed me, left me in the wilds without a way to fight.

Lynn swirls backward, dizzier and dizzier as she goes.

Train tracks; 1952; putting her mother aboard the train for the West Coast after a long visit.

Her mother, smiling bravely, waves goodby. Under the smile is the rue. Under the rue is the coveting.

Lynn turns into Tony's arms and sobs. "It isn't fair," she says, "she's had such a hard life. I have so much happiness, such an easy life. She should have more. It isn't fair."

The train carries her mother down the tracks, away, leaving her unvoiced coveting trailing like a scarf she holds from the window, wrist turned just so, face averted, tears surfacing just enough to reflect Lynn's guilt-streaked eyes as she watches where her mother slowly disappears.

Lynn goes to boxes stacked in the corner of the living/dining room. She starts hunting through them for letters from the past. Seeing her mother's writing on a packet of envelopes she takes off the rubber band and starts to read. After several pages she stops. She coveted everything I ever had, Lynn thinks. She kept reminding me how she wanted to be a writer, how she wanted to go to college. But she had a year of college and chose to leave to go to work as a secretary instead; she could have written, but she chose to do other things instead. She chose not to write. Lynn squats by the boxes, letting the logic of history well up in her mind. I went to college because I won a scholarship, she thinks: full tuition, room and board. I wrote because I forced myself to stay awake and do it after the kids were sleeping. She had a hard life. But I didn't give it to her, that hard life. And she didn't give an easy one to me.

Lynn's legs cramp and she sits beside the boxes, stretching out her legs in front of her. Orphaned then. Old enough to be an orphan, that's for sure. Strange though. I always thought of myself as surrounded by family, living among family. Weird. And spoiled. I always thought I grew up spoiled and happy. I wrote Billy and Marsh about the divorce. They could have answered, could have offered help — they have money. Neither offered anything, she thinks. Finished, that.

Funny though. No one to phone if anything happens. Dial a relative: this is Lynn; I have some bad news for you. Operator interrupts: deposit ninety cents for the next minute of this recording, please. Or, alternately, this is Lynn; I have some exciting news for you. Operator: deposit one dollar and eighty cents for the sound of a champagne bottle opening, please.

Lynn rummages further through the carton. Maybe a letter from Ruth is here among the rest, misplaced, left back when the rest were burned? The sudden craving for the shape of Ruth's handwriting drives her to search deeper in the box, reaching in the crevices at the side for a scrunched envelope. But there are none. Instead she pulls out a thick manila folder full of old letters of her father's that Aunt Nell sent to her before she died.

From France. 1918. Lynn browses through comments on camps and friends, weather and cathedrals. She reads: "In Brittany there used to be a good many skylarks but down here in this part of France I don't or rather haven't seen even one. They seem to sing more (contrary to my impression) while they are dropping back to earth rather than when they rise . . ."

Lynn walks to the window, leans her head against the pane and cries. The headlights of strangers' cars passing on the highway through the little town spray against her face like tracer fire, her tears splitting every ray of light into a million facets, cold and clear as starlight, distant and unknown.

In the fierce thrust of interrogation that Lynn evinced in therapy, she asked her mother, seventy years old and letting down her guard, questions and more questions, and one day, without noticing particularly, her mother told her that she didn't want her to be born. It was 1930 when Lynnanne was conceived. Her father was out of work. There was no money. Produce couldn't be given away. "You couldn't get fifty cents for a crate of apples, even if you took it to the city to try to sell them," her mother said. "I tried everything I knew," she said, thoughtfully. "I filled the enema bag with Lysol and used it for a douche again and again. It didn't work."

"Then they laid down and died, poor babes in the woods," Lynn hears in her mother's singing voice, remembering the curled up children hidden underneath the russet leaves that bury them deeper and deeper, falling and blowing over them on into the night.

Lynnanne is riding high on her father's shoulders. She is three years old. Her face is right against his tan felt hat, its good hair smell in her nose. Beyond it she sees bright berries on a bush. His workshirt is rough and warm against her legs. He lifts her down and she stands close against his grey twill pants while he talks to an old man. They have walked far up the road from home. Lynnanne studies workshoes and pants' legs, suspenders and denim shirts, and beyond them birds and squirrels in the trees.

"What'll you take for her?" the old man with the grizzled face and wild white hair asks.

Lynnanne knows he's offering to buy her. Not their cow. Not their eggs this time. She knows that she is the thing they're talking about selling. She focuses on her father with a fierce expectancy.

"I wouldn't sell her for all the tea in China — and not for all the gold and silver either," her father says.

29

"Why don't you ever come to the happy hour with us, Lynn?" Her colleague stashes his briefcase behind the seat and quirks an eyebrow at her, smiling.

"I don't have time is all," she answers, getting in behind the wheel.

"You teach at night?"

"Two nights a week. And two nights I take classes. I have to get certified by next September to keep this job."

"God – you never *seem* harried. I don't know how you do it."

She stops in front of his house. "Say hi to Lucy," she says, smiling.

"Right. Have a good weekend. Thanks for the ride."

Driving away, her mouth hurts from a day of tired smiles. Okay, she thinks, groceries first; try to get Lori to go see Tony; grade papers; call the lawyer. Still list-making she parks near the supermarket. Halfway across the lot she sees Ruth's car. It's empty. Watching for Ruth's car is like breathing; just to see it is to gulp pure oxygen. Her head is light, her legs buckle, and she doesn't know what to do, how to move her body.

"Come. Let's get out of here." Ruth is next to her. "Get in my car."

Lynn slides in beside Ruth who turns on the ignition, then turns to face her, takes her hand in her own. "I can't do it," she says. "Lynn, Lynn, Lynn. I love you."

Lynn, unable to speak, stares at Ruth. The dammed up

feeling of the forced weeks apart rages between them. Ruth drives out of town to a quiet country road where she stops the car and takes Lynn in her arms.

Lynn balances on the high wire. Week after week she has waited, wanting to step off onto the tower platform where Ruth would wait to claim her, to take her in her arms, to find their way together; and Ruth has not been there. Week after week she has resisted stepping off onto the platform at the other end where she would need to find her way alone, where new people and new adventures wait for her, one by one, until she might find someone new to share herself with, some-one not Ruth to love.

Now Lynn starts to put her foot on solid boards, starts to let herself begin to know she's safe, past the open fall space where no net hangs — and catches herself, teeters, checks it out in words: "Are you leaving Neil?" and before words answer, knows from the tension in Ruth's arms and the narrow tight-ness of her lips that she is not. Lynn pulls back her foot, care-fully retains her balance and backs off, stands midway again, arms steadying her stance, readying herself to move toward either end.

"No, no, I don't know. You shouldn't come near me. I'm driving you crazy, I'm driving Neil crazy, or so he says. He says I'm very destructive and I think he may be right. Why don't you both forget me? I should have gone away when I started to." Her voice accelerates. Her eyes are a trapped creature's, beautiful and wild.

Lynn has pulled away, listening. Ruth's hand lies lightly on her own. Ruth is most like some exotic bird, barely light-ing, about to take flight at any caging move, Lynn thinks, and does not speak, does not move.

"I can't manage without seeing you. I know that. I've tried. I can't." Ruth pulls her hand away, lights a cigarette. "But that doesn't seem to mean that I leave Neil. Is that crazy? Maybe it is. He says, choose. You say — without saying any-thing — choose. You chose — why don't I?"

"I left Tony because it wasn't working. We weren't happy together anymore. I can't live with him, Ruth. That's aside from us. I think knowing you has made me see things clearer — but I left him to live alone. And if you go off to the Yukon

I'll still live without Tony. I'm not going back to him."

"But I'm not in the Yukon, am I? And I want to see you, touch you, love you — so why don't I leave Neil?"

"I don't know. Maybe you don't want to hurt him?"

"I'm hurting him now, God knows."

"Why don't you leave him?"

"I don't know. I'm a coward."

"I don't think you're a coward."

"Well, I am." Ruth rams out the cigarette. "We'd better go back."

"Will I be seeing you?"

"Yes."

"I'm glad. I'm awfully glad."

"Maybe you shouldn't be. Maybe you'd be better off not ever seeing me again. Go find a decent man and marry him."

"I love *you*, Ruth."

"Then you're an idiot." Ruth flashes a half-smile through tears and starts the car.

"I think the roads are too bad to go out tonight," Lynn says, putting her briefcase on the kitchen table.

"You promised!" Lori turns, leaving the refrigerator door open, to accuse her. "It's practically Christmas. Everybody has their tree by now, Mommy."

"Okay, we'll try." Lynn closes the refrigerator door. "Get Christy and Jon and let's go."

"This one?" Jon shakes the snow off a tall pine.

"That's too prickly. Look, Mommy, look." Lori runs to a giant fir.

"That's too big for our house!" Jon says, laughing at her. Lori starts to cry. "I want it, Mommy."

"It's beautiful but it really is too big to get in the door," Lynn says.

Christy wistfully points to another pine and Lynn thinks how easy it would be if only one of them had come to choose. Lori has run ahead to a taller spruce.

Eventually Jon and Lori agree on a very tall and bushy spruce and Christy concedes defeat. "It's a beautiful tree," Lynn says, driving home, "isn't it?" She wants all three to be happy, to agree that it's the best tree they could have found. She starts to sing *The First Noel* and Christy joins her.

"To be just like the Waltons, Mom?" Jon quips.

"Oh come on," Lynn says, grinning, "be a good John-boy, Jon."

"John-boy Jon-boy John-boy Jon . . ." Lori starts in.

"Cut it out, you little imitation of a Barbie doll!"

"Sing! Quick! Sing!" Lynn shouts and they all humor her. The snow is falling heavily again and as she turns a corner near their rented house Lynn is suddenly lost in white. She doesn't know which street they're on nor which turn leads to the house. She starts to go left and then veers back to continue straight ahead. Which state? Which town? Which campus? Which house? "All is calm, all is bright," the children sing and Lynn focuses on the car in front of her, and waits for its bumper sticker to lead her back to a familiar street in a familiar town in time present where she can find the house they stay in now, the house in which this Christmas tree will stand.

Ruth walks quickly around the living room, measuring the windows. "Why don't you put Lori and Christy in one room?" she asks, writing down figures.

"Because they're too far apart. Lori would drive Christy crazy. And Christy would keep Lori awake."

"So what about you?"

"I'm okay."

"You are not okay. You're working much too hard and you don't even have a bedroom of your own."

"*Voila!*" Lynn points to the alcove where she sleeps, on a sofa bed. "It's only for a while."

"Who says?"

"I say. I'll move in the summer."

"Where to?"

"Who knows?"

"Right now you have no privacy." Ruth snaps her tape

measure back into its case. "Which means *we* have no privacy."

Lynn puts the stack of papers she's been grading in her briefcase and goes to Ruth. "Hey, what would you do if we had some privacy right now?" She smiles.

"Who knows?" Ruth laughs and turns away. "It's crazy. We can't be at my house. We can't be alone at your house. We might as well be in different countries." Her voice has a desperate tone.

"I'm sorry."

"It's not your fault — but it *is* bizarre."

"It'll be better with the curtains around the alcove." Lynn tries to be reassuring but watching Ruth's face shifts tone. "We could rent a pad?"

"Don't think I haven't thought about it."

Lynn starts to put her arms around Ruth but Ruth glances around and pulls away. "Too many unseen eyes!"

"Nobody's here right now," Lynn says, and as if on cue, the kitchen door bursts open and Lori and two neighborhood kids come in and go to the refrigerator. Lynn laughs but Ruth has turned away and without smiling picks up her coat to leave.

"I can't see renting any longer," Lynn's colleague says, biting into his hamburger. "But I don't know how to come up with a down payment."

"Where's the summer school sign-up sheet?" another says.

"Yeah, right, but even so."

Lynn takes an apple from her lunch bag and cuts it into quarters. "What do you figure you'd need?"

"For a down payment? Fifteen thou!" He laughs. "I make twenty. They'd let me buy for forty-five and they'd probably want fifteen down. So it don't compute nohow!" He laughs again and reaches for the salt. "You rent, right?"

"Right."

But I want to buy, she thinks, going to the restroom. It's empty and she stands, combing her hair, thinking. I want "a room of my own," anyhow; I'm forty-one years old and Miss M. gave me Woolf's *A Room of One's Own* to read when I was seventeen. Did I understand a word of it? Maybe not. Actually now I want a room that is Ruth's and my own. So did you leave Tony to be alone or to be with Ruth? You sound so logical and convincing when you say you left him for yourself, for the children, because the marriage was no longer tenable. All true dammit. So all true. Now do you want a room of your own? she taunts herself. I want to live with Ruth, she answers, with sharp recognition. I don't want to see her in stolen moments in the car or in the house if the children all happen to be out or sound asleep. I want to be with her day by day, peacefully, in broad daylight.

The door opens and a colleague enters. "How are they doing with Twain?" she asks.

"They don't get the humor! I didn't realize that would be hard for them," Lynn answers.

"Yes. I have a lead-in that helps with that, if you want to take a look; I'll put one in your box."

"Thanks. I'd like to see how you do it. See you later." Lynn goes to class, thinking, but Ruth is a married woman, fool; Ruth lives with Neil or had you forgotten that?

"I could join the Peace Corps," Ruth says. "Do you have any Scotch?"

"What did Nora say?"

"To stay married and inherit lots of money in the end." Ruth laughs. "No, actually she said to stay put and try to get Neil to move out. She said it prejudices my case if I'm the one to leave."

"Desertion?"

"But he won't leave." Ruth pours herself a glass of bourbon. "You don't like Scotch, do you?"

"Sorry. Do you want a divorce?"

"Who knows? We're going to a counselor next week and to Hawaii spring vacation. It's Neil's Reconciliation Plan, stages two and three."

Spring vacation, when Lori and Christy are scheduled to go to Tony's, snaps like a broken flower stem in Lynn's plans.

"Hawaii?"
"Hawaii."

Lynn house hunts all spring. She checks on apartments near the school and within an hour's drive. On the map she has drawn a circle around Tony's town and x'd it out. She finds two-bedroom apartments she can't quite afford. Jon will be off to college in the fall. Christy and Lori could share a room, she thinks, or I could sleep in the living room again. She goes to a realtor and checks out houses. She would need ten thousand as a down payment on anything she could buy and with her beginning salary of ten thousand she could only get a mortgage on something for twenty-five. Houses for that price depress her more than the apartments. She gets a letter from her landlord that her one year lease will not be renewed; he wants to sell the house. She sits at the kitchen table juggling figures. She owes for the car, on charge accounts, the bank for a personal loan that she used for tuition and for moving. Tony has not paid a bill for anything since he left the June before and he will never contribute anything toward any of those bills. She owes the lawyer and the doctor and the dentist. She will need summer tuition; Christy needs braces; Jon needs tuition; Tony might help with that? Anthony needs subsidizing every month. She owes her therapist. Lynn adds and subtracts and says to herself at last: take a small apartment, get as many night classes to teach as you can, run a workshop next summer, and don't panic.

"Mark will be gone to the Academy in September. And Nate is spending his senior year in England; some new exchange program which is mostly for juniors but he wanted it so much and ranked so high among the applicants that they're letting him go." Ruth stares at the candles between them on the table as she speaks.

Lynn waits, saying nothing. Ruth gets up to change the record and to pour more wine. "Want to come over to the house with me later?"

Lynn hesitates. "Are the boys home?"

"They'll be in and out. They don't care. Neil won't be back until Sunday."

Lynn feels like a thief in the night sneaking into Neil's house when he's gone. It's Ruth's house too, she thinks; it's her choice what to do. "Sure," she says, "I'll come over for a while. Wait till I get Lori to bed. Let me check with Christy to see if she'll be home tonight."

Toward morning, leaving Ruth's bed, Lynn whispers, "No matter what happens, Ruth, I wouldn't trade the time we've had together for anything. Not for anything."

Ruth's hand tightens on her own. "Neither would I."

"I've bolted!" Ruth's voice on the phone startles Lynn.

"Where are you?"

"The Cape!"

"What Cape?"

"Cape Cod. North of you."

"What are you doing there?"

"I'm housesitting."

"You're what?"

"I'm taking care of a house while some old friends go to Italy for opera at La Scala et cetera." Ruth's laugh catches Lynn but under the laughter Lynn is remembering another phone call when Ruth suddenly drove away.

"Are you alone?"

"Absolutely. Want to visit?"

"How long are you there for?"

"Forever."

"Hey, are you drunk?"

"No. I had to get off by myself. I had to, Lynn."

"Okay."

"I'm going to walk the beach a while. Maybe in a week or two I'll know better what's what. They called me on the long shot chance we'd want to vacation here and it was too good to turn down. Just me. No family."

"For how long?"

"July. Crazy? Crazy."

"Well, I'll see you around."

"Hey, you're not mad?"

"No. Not mad."

"Come see me."

"I have to go to summer school, remember? And teach a workshop. And I have these kids, remember?"

"I know. Come in between. Will Tony take the kids next weekend?"

"Probably."

"Come, Lynn. There's a whole house and it has a beach of its own. I'll meet the plane if you want to fly up. I'll treat."

The door closes and they are in one another's arms. "My God," Ruth says, twirling out of her embrace, "You mean it's just us? No kids? No passing headlight? A whole house that's just for us? I did good, did I? Did I do good?"

Lynn nods, laughing. "I think you did good. The place looks terrific."

"You mean I can do this—" she comes to Lynn and kisses her — "any time I want?"

Lynn pulls her toward the sofa where they kiss and stroke one another for a long time. Ruth says, "Let's shed our clothes. I'll show you the way around."

Washed and naked they lie together in the bed. Lynn lays her head on Ruth's shoulder for a moment of free peace.

"That's where you belong," Ruth says.

"Umhm."

"It feels so *right* , doesn't it?"

"Yes."

Funny, Lynn thinks, how I wanted to lean on Tony's shoulder and never could. Wrote a story about that once in college, something about the act creating the reality, but it never did. This is real. I can trust Ruth's strength, give up to her, let her hold me.

"It's turn and turnabout we do, isn't it?" Ruth whispers to her, lips close to her ear. "I take from you and you take from me. You shelter me and then I shelter you. This is the way for us — would be every night if we lived together — yes?"

Lynn cannot speak but nods into Ruth's neck and turns to kiss and be kissed, their bodies sliding against the smooth sheets as they turn together.

"You're marvelous," Ruth says.

Lynn feels Ruth's leg on hers, her foot cross and recross her leg. The skin along her thigh unexpectedly tightens. Lynn thinks of moving her leg away but does not change position. Sharply and against her will, she is remembering Tony's touch, night after night, her own tactile alertness, like hairs on end in her juxtaposed unwilling flesh as she willed it to be willing against his.

"Hey," Ruth says gently, "I'm not expecting anything," and the tension slides out of Lynn's body and flows away into the night. Sometimes she can feel it drain downward until it hangs heavy in her thighs and then in her calves where the charleyhorses come and at last out the feet and away into the semi-darkness of the room in which they lie. Tonight it disappears upward like a vapor rising from the bed.

"I love you," Lynn says. "I love you." Their mouths meet and their arms circle one another and everywhere there is smooth skin and the flow of fingertips and lips, tongue against tongue lashing like warm waves.

Ruth moves her head to Lynn's breast and kisses, then closes her lips on the nipple, holds them there pressing and twisting, sometimes flicking her tongue between them at the stiffened nipple, while one hand caresses her other breast and one hand strokes her thigh.

Lynn turns on her back, giving up to the crescendo which grows almost to climax. She moves her hands on Ruth's thighs and back and arms but does not match her as Ruth slides one hand across her mons to stroke the plains and draw that warm wet smoothness toward her lips and tongue.

"Oh God, God, I love you, Ruth," Lynn cries out, arching her body upward in delight.

Resting, her head on Ruth's shoulder again, Lynn says, "Funny. I used to think there was a little slit between my legs — a narrow slit."

"Sure. Girls do. Think of what it's called. Cunt. And fuck. A quick fuck. How would you have known?"

"Now it's like the great plains." They laugh quietly together. "With blowing grasses and streams and wide skies and spaces . . ."

"And a waterfall?" Ruth giggles.

"You've no respect for rhetoric, damn you." Lynn grins at her and draws her tongue lazily across Ruth's breast, then snaps her lips together on the nipple, erect and hard.

"Does my loving you make me a lesbian?" Ruth strokes her hair gently as Lynn continues kissing her. "I used to think gays see men and women differently — like from a somersault, you know — but now I don't know what I think. I love you, I don't think I love all women though."

"You mean you don't want all women kissing you like this?" Lynn moves her tongue languidly down Ruth's thighs, circles her vagina slowly.

"Hey, you come here, you're trying too hard, you," Ruth pulls her upward and they lie, side by side, holding hands, at peace. "No, really. What about you?"

"I guess for me I can only think that I love you. An individual loves an individual. So you are a woman — it seemed funny at first but now I don't think about it any more. I want you. I love to be with you and touch you and let you touch me and—"

"And we *do* talk too much?" Ruth smiles and turns to her again, gently at first. They move together far into the night.

Toward dawn, Ruth whispers, "Sometimes I think . . . when we're like this, sometimes I think this is how I want to die."

"I know," Lynn answers, tightening her arms around Ruth's slender shoulders, fierce against the night. "I love you, Ruth." Lynn knows that she will hold her this way when that time comes as she will want herself to be so held. It has been that way from the start.

Lying there with Ruth sleeping against her, Lynn watches the first light of dawn soften the darkness and begin to be a discernible glow against the window blind. A car passes and stops and she tightens her hold on Ruth. A detective? No, certainly not. Then who? Way out here away from every place.

Silence. What if it is a detective? What can he do? Nothing. Break in the door and snap snap snap pictures of us naked together in the bed. Listen.

Footsteps. A metallic sound. Car trunk. Car door. Footsteps on sand fading out. Fishing, idiot. They're going fishing. No detective. Lynn breathes deeply, slowly, kisses Ruth lightly and Ruth smiles in her sleep as Lynn's lips brush hers.

Christ, Lynn thinks, what an irony that Ruth should have to be on guard. No more Nazis. Now detectives? Christ. Would Neil send detectives? Would Tony? Yes, Tony might if he knew where we were. We should stay apart until my divorce goes through, Lynn thinks. To hell with that. I won't. They can't manipulate us like that. But the kids? I'll scare him out. I'll have Lori and Christy. He wouldn't last a month with them. They need me. I'll let him keep the money. Blackmailer.

Ruth speaks in her sleep, speaks again. Sometimes Lynn sees the straight-haired child watching her Nazi teacher, forcing herself to excel at swimming, diving, running, hurdling, going home to hear talk about leaving, talk about tightening restrictions, to sit on the boarder's lap listening, her eyes wide and dark, to his stories and to the bombs as they began to fall.

"Wait, wait!" Ruth thrashes herself awake.

"It's all right, it's all right," Lynn says softly, moving her arms gently to hold her safe.

"There was this train station. I was running down the platform and the train was leaving. It was full of vacationing workers going to England for the holidays and on the platform there was a ticket taker and myself, and in the back of the train a tall man with a beard tipped his hat to me as the train went into a tunnel, leaving me there with the ticket taker coming toward me, hand held out, and I knew I had no ticket and it didn't matter anyway because the train was gone. How's that?"

"That's a good clear dream, I'd say," Lynn kisses her lightly.

"My father died after a vacation, standing on the platform, waiting for a train to take him away again. Back to his other family."

"How old were you?"

"Eight, nine, maybe."

"That's hard."

"I don't know. It was before the Nazis took over entirely. Maybe it was best that way. He wouldn't have saved my mother and me." Ruth's voice is strained. "He was a coward."

"Not to marry your mother?"

"Yes. Not to leave his wife and marry mother. His own father was a minister. He intimidated him, I suppose."

Lynn's arms tighten around the little girl with the skinny legs who knew her own father did not ever tell the world she was his nor give her his name to have for her own.

"I wish I could shout from the rooftops that I love you, Ruth. I wish I could make it easy for you. I wish I could make everything peaceful and beautiful and . . ."

Ruth lays her fingers gently on Lynn's lips. "You do, you know. It's strange, but you do."

The letter, from Ruth's house, is not from Ruth. Lynn opens it slowly, the strangeness of it making her careful as she handles it. It's from Neil.

"Give Ruth back to me," he writes. "She will not find a happy life with you. You cannot provide her with the things she needs for happiness. She needs a stable home and the security I provide. You have broken up a long and happy marriage. Give her up. I promise you I will cherish her."

Lynn goes directly to the phone. "Ruth. Neil wrote me a letter."

"Neil?"

"Yes."

"Saying what?"

"Saying to give you back."

"You're kidding."

"No. What does he think you are? He wants me to give you back like stolen goods."

"What did you do?"

"I wrote him that I can't give you back, that you are your own person, that he should talk to you. They think we're property."

"Did it upset you – the letter?"

"Yes. It upsets me that he thinks you're something to be handed back and forth. He doesn't know you at all–"

"I think he may not know me at all. I'm coming home soon, Lynn."

"Where to?"

"I don't know yet. Don't sign any leases yet, though."

"I have to be out of here by October first."

"I know. I haven't forgotten that. Give me until the end of July. Can you come up again?"

"I don't know."

"Try. Lynn. I love you. I do know that."

"Sleep well. I love you, too."

Lynn hangs up the phone and looks again at Neil's script, old fashioned, polite. "Give her back?" Her own person. Her own person. She makes her own choices and is her own person.

I wish that she were mine and I were hers.

30

It's three thirty a.m. The rain hits the windshield in hard uneven bursts and jagged streaks blow crosswise to obscure her view. Lynn tenses her leg to keep the speed down. Lightning flashes beside the road. She brakes for a red light. The engine throbs. Above the intersection a wire has torn loose; the wind whips it against a cable and there is a wild flare of flame and then the sheets of rain again and black. Lynn leans forward, following the narrow beams of her headlights down the road.

"You shouldn't have gone," she says to herself out loud. "You shouldn't have gone." They're all right, she answers. Maybe the storm isn't even there yet; it blew in from the east, maybe the northeast; you may break out of it before you get there even. They're asleep just like every Sunday night. And if they're not? If the power went out? If Lori woke up and there weren't any lights? What if there's a short circuit or a wire breaks loose and starts a fire? Lynn puts more weight on the gas pedal and strains to see ahead as the car goes faster down the roadway where the water flows in billowing sheets flecked by her headlights' glow.

Pulling into the driveway Lynn sees the house intact, the lights as usual in the upstairs hall and by the door. She goes in quickly, turns out the porch light, runs upstairs to check the kids.

At the door to Lori's room she stands to catch her breath. Lori lies peacefully asleep, arm casually beside her stuffed dog, hair spread loosely against the fairytale sheets. Thank God, she thinks, breathing hard. I'll never do that again. Never. She walks softly to the bed, pulls the sheet gently around her shoulders, and goes out. Down the hall Jon is sleeping, still wearing his jeans, his radio pounding rock into the first light of dawn; he never pulls his shades. Christy's door is closed; Lynn opens it a crack just to make sure she's really there.

In her alcove downstairs, Lynn pulls off her jeans and shirt. Two hours and you have to get up to teach, she thinks. Sleep, woman, sleep. Her closed eyes bring her rolling visions of roofs split apart by lightning and the sound of Lori's cries, frightened and alone. She's fine, she thinks. They're all fine. Christy would have gone to Lori if she woke up scared. You've never left her alone, not once. Never. Tony's face intervenes. He taunts, "Reckless." He accuses, "Incompetent." I'm not incompetent, she answers. That *was* reckless, she accuses herself. Chasing all over the country to be with Ruth. Yes. Reckless. Besides, tomorrow you'll be out on your feet. I don't care, she retorts. I don't care. It was worth it anyway. But she cannot sleep.

"I can't come up there again," Lynn says on the phone. "I really can't. It's crazy."

"I know."

"If you do leave Neil, Ruth — if you do, would you want to find apartments next to each other? Then we could be together without my leaving the kids alone. I'll have a kid at home forever, you know."

"I know." Lynn waits out the silence. "I don't know if I can handle it."

"Which?"

"All the years you've got left of raising kids. I'm through with it. The boys will be out of the house next month and that's the end of that. If I leave Neil I don't want to rerun what I already did. I want to travel, explore the world. I don't want to ever get trapped again."

"Do I make you feel trapped?"

"Not *you* — never you. That's the trouble. I want to be with you. But I don't want to do any more mothering. You have a long time of mothering ahead of you. I haven't *left* Neil yet, have I?"

"Next week July is over."

"I noticed."

"Have you made up your mind?"

"I'll probably decide when I hit the toll gates at the south end of the bridge." Ruth laughs. "I can't imagine coming back to Neil. But I don't know how to do anything else either. I'm still walking the beach, I guess. How is that for you? What would you like, Lynn?"

"I want us to live together. I mean next to each other. I've known that for a long time now. All of a sudden I knew that if you were ever free I wanted to live with you. It was more than loving you–" Lynn feels a rare shyness as she speaks. She pulls the honest words from deep inside: "–it was knowing that if we could be together, I wouldn't be looking for anyone else, I guess."

"You want me to promise, Lynn. I can't. I'm sorry, but I can't. I can only do it day by day if we do it at all."

Lynn feels tears rise in her eyes and she is glad they're on the phone instead of face to face.

Ruth says, "Don't, don't. I don't want marriage but I *do* love you. I *love* you. I love you more than I've ever loved anyone in my life. We'll find a way. Don't worry, darling, we'll find a way. I'll be back Sunday. I'll come straight to you whatever I decide. Be home."

"Why, Mommy? I don't want to go. I won't go! You can't make me! I won't go!"

Lynn thinks for a second, why make her? Why not let her stay home? Then she says, "You have to go, Lori. Daddy is expecting you. And you really want to see him, I think. Why don't you ask him if you can bring Susie next time? I'll bet he'll say yes."

"No! No! I won't go!"

Tony's hand pounds on the door. "Hi, Lori," he says, smiling. "Let's go. Want a Carvel?"

"Okay," she says, picking up her bag and going out the door. "Bye, Mommy," she says.

"Bye, Lori." Lynn leans down to kiss her lightly, not to deflect her from her dignified route to her father's car.

"You be in this dump at six tomorrow?" Tony turns to sneer at her behind the child's back, "or will you be busy elsewhere?"

"I'll be here," Lynn answers, and then adds, "and whenever I'm not here when you bring her back, Christy or Jon will be. Could you call me about Jon's tuition?"

"Um," he says and goes, his features rigid, all mobility withdrawn, like a death mask taken before the man began to die.

Lynn hears the roar as he guns off down the driveway and she sees through the window his car bumper rip out part of the hedge as he tears off. A shiver runs through her as she turns away.

Lynn tells Julia, "Every time he looks at me that way."

"We can be glad we left no stone unturned to save that marriage," Julia answers, "it's hard enough as is."

"I wish he wouldn't hate me so."

"You can't protect him from his own hatred, Lynn. You used to rescue him. Now he's stuck with it."

"What are you doing tomorrow morning at ten?"

Lynn shakes her head, holding her hope firmly in check. "Nothing."

"We have an appointment at the realtor's." Ruth sets her suitcase down inside the door.

Lynn's smile is released and they embrace. "Are you sure?" Lynn asks between hugs.

"I'm sure. I tried heading the car for Neil and it wouldn't go that way. That's how I know. It always comes to you."

Lynn lets the intense presence of Ruth's happy voice after the long uncertainty enter her quietly. "I'm glad, Ruth, very glad."

"Me too."

They settle at the kitchen table with coffee and cigarettes to talk. "Tell me everything you've learned about local housing and tell me how much money you can spend." Ruth laughs. "We've never been businesslike before."

"I've looked at apartments and they're pretty bad. I haven't got any money right now and I'm heavily in debt. When the divorce goes through he has to give me my half of the equity in the house – that's nine thousand. That will just about pay off the debts that he won't help me with – kids' medical bills, my moving out expenses, tuition, et cetera. Then I'll start even and I'll have to get a loan for a down payment if we buy. But I'm through with my courses now and I've already lined up two night classes to teach and one workshop for teachers in the afternoon. I'm a terrific risk."

Ruth sips her coffee, thinking. "Okay. I have the money I inherited from my mother. I'll give you a loan for the down payment if we buy and if we rent, there's no problem?"

"No."

"That's where we start then. Side by side apartments. And I don't want to live near Neil!"

"I don't want to live near Tony!" They laugh, and their hands reach out to one another. The house is late night quiet. They go together to the alcove where Lynn's bed stands. "Will you stay over?"

"Let's see how it feels." Ruth takes her in her arms and they lie down together. The richness of their feeling radiates through the length of Lynn's body and she breathes deep as though she has not had full access to the air for a long time.

"Good rentals are hard to find," the agent says, "but I have some fine mother/daughter houses that sound just right for you."

"Have you looked at any of these?" Ruth asks Lynn. "No."

"The one we'll see first was built by a family whose parents stayed active until they were nearly eighty. It's beautifully engineered." The realtor settles his tweed suit behind the wheel of the Buick and talks steadily as he drives. "You girls work near here?"

"No," Ruth says. "We teach but not near here."

"I see," he says. "I admire teachers a lot. My brother-in-law teaches. I tell him to get out and do something lucrative—" he laughs apologetically — "but he's devoted. Devoted. Nice guy too. Now here we are. The lady with the family — that's you, right?" he looks at Lynn and goes on without waiting for an answer, "would live in this section: kitchen, two baths, living/dining room; and the lady whose kids have flown the coop," he laughs and winks at Ruth, "would live back here. Beautiful little studio with a patch of lawn all your own out back. Separate entrance. Laundry in the cellar. Take your time, look around."

"We want something where each of us has approximately the same sort of space — perhaps two apartments would be more likely."

"I know just the thing. Exactly matching. It's a marvelous investment. I'd buy it myself if my cash flow was a little different right now. I really would. They might rent it if you don't want to buy, but if I were you, I'd buy it."

It's a brick two-story structure that reminds Lynn of an illustration of a factory in a text book. The backyard is square, fenced in with cyclone fence, and has three trees and a patch of grass. The inside is two apartments, side by side, brand new.

"What do you think?" Ruth asks. "I guess it'd be a good investment. We could always rent it out."

"I guess so," Lynn says. "Nora Daniels would approve. The entrances are certainly totally separate. There's that." She grins laconically.

"How much are they asking?" Ruth takes out her pad and pencil. Lynn wanders away to consider how that would be. It feels cold as the new brick. "Okay. We're off to another mother/daughter. Don't worry, we're just getting started," Ruth says, smiling at Lynn.

The man offers them each a cigarette as they walk back to the car. Ruth takes one and says, "What else?"

"A lovely bright ranch — actually painted yellow, I believe. The mother's section of this is incredibly designed."

Emerging from the yellow ranch, Ruth shakes her head in exasperation, saying quietly to Lynn, "Awful. Absolutely awful. I have the classified in my car. Let's ditch this guy and check out the rentals in Sunday's listings."

"Right."

Lynn walks up the steps of an apartment building. The musty carpet smell that comes at her when she opens the front door rules it out before she has talked to the pleasant woman in the office or climbed the stairs to check out the empty suite. She cannot imagine fitting Lori and Christy into the little rooms nor can she imagine Ruth staying even overnight. "Thank you anyway," she says, writing down the figures, crossing off the address.

Ruth is at Nora Daniels', asking about divorce. She hasn't seen Neil, only spoken to him by phone. "He asked me to have dinner with him next week," Ruth said. "I'd like to see the lawyer first."

Lynn goes to three more buildings before she meets Ruth at a restaurant near Nora's. "How'd it go?"

"You first."

"Nothing. Musty carpets and very expensive places that you wouldn't like."

"And you?"

"I wouldn't like them either." Lynn grins. "But how did it go with Nora?"

"As I thought. She wishes I hadn't left the house. She thinks you and I had better stay apart. She thinks Neil may not give me a divorce and she thinks it'll be extremely hard to get any sort of fair settlement from him."

"You want to give up on our house hunt?"

"No, I don't. Do you?"

"No."

"Let's drink to that. Do you ever drink at lunch?"

"Never." Lynn smiles across the table and says, "Well, hardly ever, and you'll get us thrown out if you look at me like that in broad daylight."

"So what's next?"

"We have appointments with two agents this afternoon."

The first shows them more mother/daughter places of which there are apparently an unlimited number. They see three story arrangements, back and front ranch houses, one with a small attached unit that was once a large garage. The second agent is a woman. They sit at her desk a while, talking about their jobs, their kids, before they leave the office. "I think I have the place for you," she says quietly. "It's been on the market a while — it's not suitable for most people. It may be exactly right for you two. It's a duplex."

"How much?" Ruth asks.

She answers, without hesitation, giving a larger figure than they've ever considered.

"That's a lot more than we were thinking about," Ruth says. "We don't want to see it."

The woman doesn't argue and takes them through another batch of single houses in the same neighborhood, apartments, and mother/daughters. She shows them one that is being re-modelled that they could buy and then finish in any way they want. It's late when she leaves them back at the office.

"Thanks a lot," Lynn says.

"You're welcome. I hope you find what you want. If you change your minds, call me and I'll be glad to take you to see that duplex. It's in a beautiful wooded area with lots of trees on the lot itself. I have a hunch it's what you're looking for."

Lynn is at the lawyer's, planning the next conference with Tony and his lawyer. "Look," Nora says, planting both hands palms down on the wood, speaking in an even tone, "Do us all a favor, will you two? Don't move in together until both divorces are accomplished."

"That may take years," Lynn says.

Nora nods. "May take a while. I have to warn you, Lynn, if you two move in together now, they'll use it. You'll both pay for it."

"Just for living next to each other?"

"Just for living together certainly."

"What about adjoining apartments?"

"Separate entrances?"

"We could put up a barricade if you'd like that."

"It's not what I'd like, Lynn. It's what will protect your

interests. I wouldn't be a damned bit of good to you if I didn't warn you. You might not take my advice but I have to give it. You're such beautiful women — I'd hate to see either one of you hurt. The odds are against you. Even ten years from now it might be different. But right now it puts you both in jeopardy. Ruth with her assets — they have quite a large estate between them, you know, and he'll claim it all — and you with your children. It's custody you might lose, not money, because Tony doesn't have a lot of money and because you're only asking child support, not alimony. It's rotten, but you're better off waiting."

After two more weeks of hunting they've seen innumerable places and none of them have been right. They're back at the woman agent's for the third time. "Let's at least look at the duplex in the woods," Lynn says.

"Okay. We can look. But it's too much money, Lynn."

The agent turns in the driveway to the duplex without saying anything. Lynn feels the trees surround her. The thick green of August encloses the house on all sides. Walking toward the house from the car, Ruth beside her, hands nearly touching, Lynn knows that to be there, alone together in the woods, is to come home.

Inside there are two apartments, just alike. Out of every window there are trees. They ask the right questions about plumbing, wiring, roofs and floors. It can't be faulted. The woman living there, a widow, offers them coffee, shows them the yard.

Leaving, Ruth says, "It's fine, it is, but it really *is* too expensive."

"They'd give you a mortgage on your combined incomes," the realtor says. "It's a sound investment. And actually, it's not that much more than other stuff you're considering and it will hold up much better. I don't want to pressure you but think about it."

Lynn stares at the trees and shrubs, delighting in the green foliage.

"Would they rent?" Ruth asks.

"I'll find out for you," the agent says.

Lynn walks around her living room anxiously. They have not yet found a place to live. Ruth is having dinner with Neil. Maybe she's gone home with him, Lynn thinks. Maybe they've gone to the house to talk and he's persuaded her to make love with him. Her flesh tightens at the image and she goes to the window to look out.

"He says I am going to live in a morass." Ruth comes in the door talking. "A degenerate swamp. I will sink in it, he says." She goes to the kitchen to pour herself a drink. "What was it Tony told you?"

"I should live in a garret. Starve in a garret, I think he meant. So how was it?"

"Strange. First he was very nice and wanted me to come back. Then he was very distant and polite. Finally he told me in a matter-of-fact way that he's seeing another woman and doing very well with her and that if I'm determined to go off with you, I'll enter a life of dissolution and sink in a morass." Ruth's laugh is short and ragged. "And he says he has no time to think about our property right now. When he has time, he'll see a lawyer. He's put everything in his name. That's what he's done. If he hadn't already. I'm such an ass. Why are women such asses? I never thought about any of that. The house is in both our names and I drove off in one car so I'll keep it, I suppose, but everything else is in his name. I've been teaching full time for fifteen years and he says all the savings are his, all the investments are his, all the retirement is his. I did without household help always so we could save for our old age. It's all his. I've been a fool. If he decides to marry, he'll arrange for a divorce. If not, he won't bother. He's got all the cards. And he's like a businessman, studying investments. I wanted to hit him, to knock some feeling into him. He sat there entirely analytical, measuring his chances to make off with a little more. That new woman. Me. All the same to him. Interchangeable!"

"Do you want to live with him until you get the divorce

like Nora recommended?"

Ruth shakes her head. "I can't. Probably I should. But I can't." She empties her glass. "Tomorrow we find a place to live, young lady. Enough of this dallying around."

"Let's start with that mother/daughter I saw last week. The price is right," Lynn says.

It has a tiny sun deck and a patch of yard; inside everything is neat and closed in, measured and adequate like an expensive rest home would be. Ruth turns to her when they are in their car again with a mix of rage and panic in her voice, "Why did you bring me here? The part I would live in is a cramped miserable little prison tacked on as an afterthought. I can't live like that, Lynn!" Her voice explodes in desperation.

"I know."

"So why the hell are we here?"

"Because this is all we're going to find. This or apartments that are cruddy and completely separate. Or the duplex in the woods."

"Lynn, it costs too much. We were crazy to even look at it."

"It's solid. It's on two acres. It's a beautiful place. It's right for us, Ruth. It's *really* right. And it's an investment. It won't go down in value."

Ruth laughs. "All right. Let's drive by it and I'll think about the money part again."

They cruise slowly by the house. Lynn wants to live there with Ruth so much she can't speak. Ruth takes her hand and neither of them says anything. The woods extend all around the house. The house has simple graceful lines. The woods are right for Lori to grow up in, Lynn thinks. For us to be together every day in a place of beauty, to wake up to the trees around us every morning, is to come home, she thinks. "Remember your poem?" she asks.

"Which one?"

"The one that ended 'with you I am come home'?"

Ruth nods.

"This is the right place."

"I'll think about it, Lynn."

That night they sit up late, each figuring her own accounts. They remind one another of all Nora's warnings. Then Ruth says, "We both want to do it. Shall we for once do what we both want? Let's buy the duplex, Lynn."

Jon comes home late from practicing with Nate. Christy comes home with her boy friend; they go to her room where they argue until midnight; he leaves, angry, not saying good night. Lynn goes up to see Christy but she doesn't want to talk, tells her through the door, "I'm okay, Mom. Tomorrow we can talk, maybe, okay? Not tonight."

At four a.m. Lynn wakes stark awake. She has seen against the light of dawn a girl's slender figure hanging with a broken neck. Under the figure was a crudely lettered placard that read: PRICK-TEASE. A cold terror rakes her flesh. She forces her eyes open. She forces her hand out to touch the lamp. She lifts herself from the bed and stands, dazed, looking around the room.

Ruth, as every night, has moved from her bed to sleep on the sofa in the living room. The house is silent. Down the street there is the disappearing screech of brakes. She goes quietly upstairs to check the children, each of whom is sound asleep and safe. At Christy's door she stands the longest time. Then she goes to Ruth. She puts a hand gently on her arm.

Ruth smiles sleepily. "Hi," she says.

"Ruth, hold me a minute. I'm scared," Lynn says.

"Hey, what's up?" Ruth pulls her close, stroking her shoulder, her hair.

"Nightmare." Lynn begins to shake.

"Hey, hey." Ruth tries to wake up to listen. "Tell me," she says, and sleeps again.

Lynn lies quietly, trusting in the safety of Ruth's arms. For Christ's sake, she thinks, first gangster dreams and now this. She studies the details of the ceiling, the molding, as daylight filters in to delineate each object separately. 'Prick-tease,' she thinks. I haven't heard that since I was little. Because Christy and her boy friend had a fight, is that why?

As the light makes the room plain and familiar to her eyes, Lynn turns the nightmare back and forth, letting the terror dissipate with the gradual coming of daytime. Now they say cock-tease. That had nothing to do with Christy, she thinks. That was me. That was me hanged by my brothers and hanged again by Tony. I think I will be killed for saying no. I think I will be killed for telling and for saying no. To buy the house is to say no to them and to come out in the open and say yes to Ruth and me and to our love. My God.

Lynn lies, waking but holding still, in Ruth's arms till seven o'clock. Then she wakes her so they will have a few minutes together before Lori comes running down for juice and toast and morning cartoons. "Let's call the woman at the realtor's and say we want to buy the house," Lynn says.

"You're terrified, darling, aren't you?"

"Yeah. Especially asleep."

"We don't have to do it, Lynn. We can rent and then later, after the divorces, take our time and find a place together. That would be the wise thing to do."

"Do you want to be wise? Do you? I want to be with you, Ruth. Now. You?"

Ruth holds her close. "Yes," she says very softly. "Yes."

"Then let's do it. We can't build our whole lives on fear."

PART IV

31

The moving van takes back into itself the hand trucks and ropes, the canvas and the loading ramp, like a turtle pulling its parts into its shell, foot after foot. The man asks her to sign and as she does so and then turns to see the new house, now Ruth's and hers, and then turns back to watch the truck drive out, Lynn is spun through the hazy summer air to all those other moving days, all those driveways down which vans backed at the end of the unloading time.

The first van moved them away from the little student rowhouse she loved, the first home that was not a school's, not their parents', but their own, where Lynn filled the rooms with the smell of baking bread and sat on the tiny porch with Jon a baby in her lap to watch Anthony pedal his trike around the circle where all the children rode; and when the rains came Anthony stood on the little porch and threw bread to the ducks who swam by in the yard. They had no car, no TV, no sitters, nothing but themselves; Lynn argued with the other wives, watching children in the common yard, and they said any man would be turned on by a naked model or a nude work of art, and Lynn argued that sex was integral to love and couldn't exist apart so a good man would not be turned on except by the woman he loved. When she took around an anti-nuclear testing petition, her neighbor wouldn't sign because "Christians needn't be concerned with things like that, because when the world ends *we'll* all be saved, Lynn"; and then her neighbor cried because she loved Lynn and she couldn't bear to think of her in hell, where she knew from their discussions Lynn was probably going to go. They'd been moved in there by friends with cars. In graduate school no one ever hired movers. But when they moved away, two years later, a van came.

And a van came a year after that, and another two years after that, and another one year after that and another three years after that, and never have they stayed anywhere longer than the place where they broke up and there they stayed four years, and there he planted a flowering peach for her, and Lynn shakes off the haze and turns back to the house to get to work.

In the same way that her mother walked into the kitchen, pushed stove wood through the open cast iron door to fire up the cook stove and begin the canning, Lynn walks toward the house. Neither of us, she thinks, would count the seasons and neither of us would falter at the work. If Tony and I moved seventeen times, if seventeen times the kids had to be tuned in on new doctors, schools, neighbors, friends, then that was the way it was. Lynn, in her blue jeans, starts just as her mother in her faded washdress turned each summer to the great oval canners full of jars, to the table of knives near the cartons and buckets of fresh fruit, to begin to wash, peel, core, boil, sweeten, cool, skim, pour into jars, seal, cool, store, without ever questioning her strength, only sizing up the order of the harvesting, the size of each successive crop, so that there would be enough jars, paraffin, sugar, boiling water, always assuming she would herself possess enough strength. As my mother always, season after season, lined the basement shelves with jars, so I've always, season after season, lined the new rooms with curtains, rugs, furniture, toy boxes, bookshelves, for their bright colored animals, dolls, models, puzzles, games, books and papers, paints and crayons, guns and wagons, cars, trucks, horses, trikes and posters. That I got from her, Lynn thinks, turning to the boxes to begin.

Jon has already left for college. Ruth is away, driving Mark

to the Academy. Nora Daniels sighed and said, "Do have the
common sense not to move in on the same day at least." Lori
and Christy went to their father's for the weekend. Lynn
straightens up, holding a picture in her hand, and thinking,
where should I put the vase, hang the picture, set the chair,
she recognizes that she is listening for a voice to say, "How
about putting that here," or, "Did we remember to turn off
the phone?" Now all the voices and all the answering nods are
inside her own head. The silence of the house envelops her.
She sits on a box and looks around.

Which van on which cross country run lost the box in which
my spinning top that grandfather brought me from the Chicago
Fair was packed along with my big baby doll and my favorite
little rubber doll, Bobby, named after the first boy I liked?
She thinks, the faucets in this sink have straight stainless steel
handles, one on each side, and the left is hot and the right is
cold and the water comes out of a single long stainless steel
spigot which can be swung from side to side. Which house had
the sides reversed? And which had the two spigots so I couldn't
wash my hair in the kitchen sink, and that was before we could
afford shampoo, so I used the soap in the shower, letting the
warm water flow down my swollen belly where which baby
kicked? Now, inside, the only thrashing is a misbegotten hair-
ball from the healing licks I've used to try to heal all the hurts
he's done to all the children and me, stroking with words the
way a cat laves with her tongue, until the words are all massed,
enmeshed, knotted in my insides into a heavy ball.

The wooden drainborad was at the farm and there was hot
water only if the fire in the woodstove had been going long
enough. We didn't wash up there anyway but in the enamelled
basin in the backyard near the porch, where they shot the flying
ants with squirt guns, until the call came to come in. "Wash for
supper," she called and we sloshed the cold water on our hands
and shared the single towel. That was before I knew Tony was
alive. Will Tony come by to jeer, to attack? To destroy? She
is alone. Did Jon choose to go for freshman orientation which
he had spurned before so that he wouldn't have to watch her
settle in with Ruth?

"Who are your best friends, Mom?" Christy leaned in the

doorway, speculating.

"Ruth," Lynn answered, "Ruth is my closest friend. And Julia and Jeanne and Marie."

And another time, "Are you and Daddy going to marry other people now?" Lori watched her as she walked past *Father Knows Best* on television.

"I think Daddy might," she answered, "but ask him. I don't think I will. I have this good friendship with Ruth, you know. We help each other a lot and we love each other a lot. I'm happy with that."

Lynn says to Ruth, "I hate not having it in the open."

"If we tell them, we have to ask them not to tell anyone," Ruth says, "and that's impossible."

"I know."

"Actually, what don't they know? They know we're moving in together; they know we spend all our time together. All they don't know is that we make love and that's our own private business anyhow."

"I know. It'll be okay."

Lynn sets a carton of books in Lori's room. She hesitates, wonders if Lori would rather find the books already shelved or find them waiting for her to arrange herself. Lynn carries in boxes of dolls and toys, decides to hang the curtains, make the bed, and leave the rest for Lori to decide. Seeing a Raggedy Ann slumped in the corner of a carton she perches it on the bed, adds a few other dolls and animals, and leaves the room.

Doors locked, dog and cat brought in, lights left on, Lynn goes to bed. When the girls, at Tony's for the weekend, are asleep and Tony starts thinking about returning them to this new house, will he come by? When he sees that it is not a garret, what will he do? Has he already seen it? Did he drive by with them and make derogatory comments? Have they told him Ruth is going to live in the other apartment? The questions clog Lynn's head so she can't read, and she gets up to walk around the new space, to let the restless dog out and in again, to have some milk and cake. She considers brandy but decides against it.

Lying awake in the three o'clock stillness, Lynn ranges faces she has loved around her in the unfamiliar darkness to shield her from harm. Lying in hard labor the first time she placed Miss M.'s face against the perforated soundproof paneling of the labor room and beside her she put Dr. Swenson, her poetry professor; Lynn and Nancy and another student, Gerri, used to follow Dr. Swenson about, taking her to lunch, hoping for a chance to talk; she lived with another woman. Strange, Lynn thinks, of how little consequence that seemed to me. Or did it?

Lynn remembers the dorm, sophomore year, June, Nancy going to marry Eric the next day. Roommates, Nancy and I were kept awake by a pain we did not understand; Lynn thinks, I loved her and she loved me and words were what we had. I'd walked in the park thinking that I loved her as a friend, that wild and beautiful girl who read poetry with me all night and walked along the river talking about life; I walked alone thinking that she loved me, that we knew one another as no one else had ever known us, as Tony and Eric had not yet begun to know either one of us. We knew girls must marry boys and boys must marry girls and though understanding and feeling flowed naturally between Nancy and me, that was not enough for marriage, because she was a girl and I was a girl and we couldn't marry each other and have children, which is what we had to do. All that night before her wedding I sat on the floor beside her bed. All night, the hurt that we were doing what we believed must be done, filled the room with the candlelight and wine and poetry, and even our hands didn't touch and only our words attempted to hold one another in one another's presence for the years we had not yet begun to recognize or understand. Twenty years later I watch Ruth tilt her head listening to Bach and I recognize in her hairline, her shoulder's slant, an echo of the girl I loved with words when I was seventeen.

And if, Lynn thinks, if in that dark night in that candle-lighted room I took that girl I loved in my own arms and told her, and let myself be told, that we loved one another and did not have to marry men . . . Lynn turns restlessly, wanting Ruth, trying to avoid the vast emptiness of the bed. Nancy, Nancy she thinks, wondering what time has done to her, what pain, what joy she found, not having turned that night to Lynn with more than words. She knew then more than I ever knew till now, Lynn thinks. She knew what she wanted, but she didn't know if she could ever have it; she married before I did because she understood she had to block off what was incipient between us before it flowered; I had no notion of everything she knew. Nancy. But the name is crossed with static that is twenty years of children's voices. I can't begin to think how it would have been if they weren't there: they are: the children. I can think how it would have been if Tony had been other than Tony or not there at all, but then what children would the children be? I would have found a way to have the children that I wanted, whatever else.

Gerri never understood. Gerri and I in that southern rooming house on the trip we took that summer, after Nancy and Eric went away. Waitressing for twenty-eight dollars a week, forty-eight hours, buy your own uniform, buy your own food and eat on your own time. Chicory and hominy grits and on the counter noise machines, *Good Night, Irene*, all day long. Lynn remembers a particular morning when she stared at a delivery truck outside the restaurant, watching the uniformed man carry in case after case of after-dinner mints; she burst into laughter at what struck her as a patently absurd instance of reality. Lynn pointed, laughing, but Gerri did not see anything to laugh about and was cross. Lynn thought then that Nancy would have tuned in and laughed spontaneously with her; abruptly Lynn knew how mean she'd been to Gerri for not being the Nancy that Lynn loved.

The corridor between the counter section of the drug store and the dressing room/bathroom, where the waitresses change into uniform and have a cigarette on their break, is short and dark. The druggist puts his arm around Lynn's shoulders as he walks with her after work, saying, "How did a little girl like you get such big boobs? Did you work at it or did they just grow like Topsy's?"

Trying to remove herself from his armhold and failing,
Lynn answers, "Just grew, I guess," blushing, smiling.

A Black man comes in one day to order a sandwich to go.
Only whites eat there. Lynn sees that he is ill and gives him a
glass of water, asks him to sit down; he refuses to sit but drinks
the water.
The manager calls her over: "We don't encourage their
trade," he says to Lynn.
"He wasn't well."
"I don't care," the manager says. "Don't smile at them."
"I'll smile at whom I please," she says, enraged, and
marches back to the counter.

Same manager, Lynn thinks, remembering, whose arm I
couldn't keep off my shoulders, whose eyes I couldn't keep
off my breasts, whose words I couldn't field when they dealt
with what he'd like to do with me; for all that I could only
smile. But for the Black man I could snarl at the manager. No
problem fighting for what I believe in. Unless it's me, my body,
that's at stake. My mother trained me to understand my
brothers' needs and not to get mad at them. If I couldn't get
mad at them how could I get mad at anyone else? Who ever
did something worse than that to me? Nobody. So I never got
mad at what people did to me. "Sexually abused children hurt
themselves"; Julia told me that once. Not others, themselves.
Attacking self is the only self-defense they allow themselves, I
suppose. Empathy was the only route to survival. What were
the manager's needs? Wasn't I supposed to be good and satisfy
them? That's why I smiled instead of belting him one. Ruth
would have punched him out. I *was* declawed when I was little
and then sent out into the wilderness. "But don't you ever
get *mad* at anyone – not to rescue someone else, but for yourself? Just *mad*?" Ruth asked. "Well, learn, baby, learn. Though
when you do, you'll probably practice it on me. Well, go
ahead, see if I care." She put her arms around Lynn and hugged
her hard.
Thinking of Ruth's touch Lynn suddenly cramps with

wanting her. She reaches down beside the bed for a note Ruth left and holds it in her hands. She doesn't need the light; she knows the words.

Abruptly lights careen across the wall, gears grind, the dog begins to howl and bark. Lynn runs to the window. An apparition moves noisily down the street, lights flashing, its steel jaws extended, bending down to snap up prey, pausing to chew, crunching glass and tin, rocks and paper, then stretching its neck toward the sky to swallow the whole mess. Men run from side to side along the street, scooping up the garbage cans and dumping them in. No other dogs in the neighborhood are barking; they recognize this creature. "It's okay, girl," she says, patting Pal's head, "it's okay."

Gerri and I got so sunburned, Lynn thinks, on our day off, that we couldn't wear clothes at all. I had a fever of 104 and Gerri moved the beds under the ceiling fan and we lay there all night, skin throbbing. There was just tap water and Gerri got us ice from a machine on the landing down the rickety old stairs.

Lynn listens as a car turns down their street. She is in that room on Canal Street. The dull blades of the fan circle with aggravating slowness, stirring the heat-rippled air.

THUMP! THUMP! THUMP! "Let me in!"

"Who the hell is that?" Gerri whispers.

"Shhh," Lynn answers.

"Let me in, goddammit! Listen you mothers, my gear is in there! Now open up!" Thump! Thump! Thump!

The walls shake with the pounding. One hard kick and the wall will splinter, Lynn thinks. One lunge of that shoulder against the door and it will fall flat, leaving nothing but a ragged hole where the hinges pull apart the frame.

Lynn looks around for suitcases but sees nothing that is not theirs. THUMP! THUMP! THUMP! "I'm gonna knock this fucking wall down if you don't unlock this door!" Then muttering.

"Is it all right to lock him out?" Lynn whispers.

"What? Are you crazy?"

"Turn off the fan so we can hear."

Gerri pulls the cord from the socket beside her bed. The blades settle sluggishly into one place. Wet air drapes Lynn's thighs and arms immediately, trickles along her searing skin.

"Wanna make me miss my ship? Jesus Christ!" A bottle hits the stairs. Silence.

Only distant night sounds enter the room. A car drones to a stop, a door slams, the car goes away, gears moving from first to second, third. A horn blasts far away. There are muted voices in a downstairs room. Her skin burns, radiating heat into the space around that settles back on her like pools of dust, each particle generating heat which doubles with the friction caused by her careful breaths.

Gerri's whisper barely trembles across the air to her, "Do you think he's gone?"

Lynn puts her finger to her lips in the near blackness. She listens for thickened breathing outside the door. She listens for mouth sounds on a bottle's lips. She hears the current coursing through the neon sign in a window opposite.

Quick steps go up the board sidewalk. Music blares incongruously from an upstairs window. An angry voice follows, "Shut it off! Let's get some sleep!"

Lynn's skin tightens, her breathing shallow, quick.

THUMP! THUMP! THUMP! The thick voice whines, "Come on now, I need my gear. Just let me in a minute!" Silence. Then a shattering of glass and the voice exploding, "You mother fuckin' asshole! I'm gonna ram this up your royal rear!" Crash! THUMP! THUMP! A body lunges at the door. There is a sliding sound and a dull thud as he hits the hallway floor.

Lynn lies still. She wonders if the man will really miss his ship. She wonders if his gear is in the room, if they should have let him in, where he will go next, what he will do to earn his way. Sweat coats her flesh, smarting the scorched parchment that is her skin. She stares at the vibrating door, the silent fan. She listens, waits. She does not move.

At dawn the sunlight sprays silver through the trees around the duplex. The grass shines green under glistening dew. Birds trill, moving swiftly from tree to tree. He did not break in. Lynn watches the dawn drift into morning. She hears the neighbors' cars go off to church, to the beach. None of those cars is Tony's car, she thinks. Today Ruth will come home. Tonight the girls will both be here. This is our home now. Ruth and I are together now in broad daylight, and I am still alive. I am alive.

32

Tony's lawyer has four secretaries who sit typing and talking incessantly in the front office. There is a narrow space, where clients sit, waiting, between them and the door. Tony sits in the chair next to Lynn. Nora Daniels has not yet come.

If he were a stranger, Lynn thinks, I could show him a cartoon or make a remark about the noise of the typewriters. If he were a stranger we could exchange a glance, a laugh, to ease it a little for us both. He is a stranger that I know. I cannot speak. He cannot speak. If words come between us, they won't be in English.

Inside his lawyer's inner office, they fire pointblank.

Twenty years before they went once to Coney Island. There was a giant tower with a long, high slide. They bought their tickets and climbed a narrow circular stairway to the top where there was a platform on which to sit from which to slide down the long smooth slide.

Tony's lawyer escorts Lynn to the metal staircase and drives her at gunpoint before him as he climbs: "Your client's reckless actions leave us no alternative. We will sue for divorce and ask that she be denied custody on the grounds that she is an unfit mother."

"Unfit mother" echoes down the steel stairwell. "Unfit. Unfit. Unfit."

Lynn speaks by rote. "I am a good mother."

"You *used* to be the best mother I know," the strange man, Tony, says across the table. "Now you've forfeited the right to be a mother."

"My client and I were very clear at our last meeting. It is not acceptable to him that you raise his children in the environment you have chosen to enter."

Nora speaks. "Your client is getting a divorce. He has no right to legislate behavior for my client, any more than she can for him."

"We are speaking of that which most directly affects the well-being of the children: the deportment of the mother."

Nora's eyes are afraid.

"He has not only every right, but the obligation, to protect his children. Any judge in the land will rule in his favor and against your client, Ms. Daniels." The "Ms." slithers mockingly off his tongue. He glances toward Lynn as though she will rot out his eyes.

For Lynn, the "to protect his children" is the glossy varnish on the slide. She watches the lawyer pour it on. He talks about healthy children, normalcy, the sanctity of motherhood, the inviolability of childhood; he talks of children's needs for role models and stability.

Lynn observes them, as at a formal affair of state, sitting side by side on the high platform, having climbed step by step from health to sanctity. Tony is wearing an academic gown, his lawyer a judge's robes and wig; they sit, arms linked, pouring varnish down the shining slide.

For a moment Lynn, driven by pointblank fire, the sacred needs of children, bang, bang, bang, stands, dizzy, before them on the platform, ready to plummet. Lori is on one side on her bright red birthday bike, and Christy on the other, poised on horseback, face happily open to the wind. Both of them are looking toward her with trusting children's eyes. Behind them Anthony's dark watching eyes look up from a demonstration and Jon is playing, "Turn, Turn, Turn, to everything there is a season . . ." but for her and Ruth no season is acknowledged by anyone, Lynn thinks.

The lawyer fires volley after volley: so long as the children need the safety of a home, to stay within the bounds of propriety, to provide a healthy atmosphere, responsible motherhood, he repeats, demands . . . He and Tony, eyes shining, evangelical, lean forward, arms raised for the final thrust.

A loving mother? For twenty years since Anthony's first
trembling flutter let her know there was life within her womb,
Lynn has been first and last a loving mother. Even her new
administrator wrote into her evaluation that she is an Earth
Mother, nurturing every student in an atmosphere of intelligent
affection. She has put the children first for twenty years, without once faltering. Thinking this she hesitates, confused.

Far below her the slide ends in mid-air. Below it the ocean
thrashes over rocks and if she stands passive one more second
they will with utter sanctimoniousness and all due deliberation
shove her off to hurtle down and smash herself to smithereens
on the sharp rocks of selfless motherhood.

Their hands are lifted. The chant is in full sway. Forfeit
Ruth. Forfeit Ruth. Their eyes are excited and triumphant. She
teeters, giddy with the height, with her own doubt, hearing in
the surf a child's cry in need.

Then she hears: Jon: "He wants me to go to Harvard but
he won't pay my tuition at Podunk Community."

Then she hears: Tony, to colleagues, by the fireplace at the
party: "I marched in Washington with them . . ." and then,
Tony, to Anthony, in his room: "You phoney! What will you
do if the war ends tomorrow?"

A banner unfurls over the wigged head of the lawyer, above
the mortar board that Tony wears in the vision she is having.
The banner unfurls to a fanfare of trumpets and drums, its
letters gold on royal blue. The banner whips in the wind: it
reads: HYPOCRISY.

"I am a good mother," Lynn says quietly, and walks back
past their flailing arms, their emptied rifles, to the stairway
again, pushes past the guard who points back up, excuses herself to the people flowing upward, and climbs safely down, step
by metal step. "It's not healthy to focus exclusively on
children. I have a right to my own life, my own relationships.
I am a better mother because I am a writer and a teacher and
because I have close friends and good relationships with adults."
Lynn feels the real and quiet strength and dignity of her life,
her work, her love.

"We are not talking about good relationships. I only wish
we were." The lawyer's unctuous voice settles like fetid smoke

under the cigarette haze that lies along the table. "We are talking about sickness. We are talking, I fear, about deviant behavior." Having come almost to the word itself, the lawyer lets a tiny illicit smile underscore the irony in his smooth tone.

"We'll sue for libel," Nora Daniels says.

"We have conclusive evidence, *Ms.* Daniels, about your client and her so called 'friend.' " His tone makes the word 'friend' a gutter term.

Lynn carefully takes a rifle from the lawyer's polished gun rack, steadies her arm and sights along the barrel. "If you start making accusations I'll tell things about you, Tony, that I don't think you want the world to hear. I don't want to do that, but if you force me to, I will. You can take the money, but Lori and Christy need me and I intend to keep them. You want to start it, go ahead. You won't come out alive though. I'm warning you." In a gentler, parenthetical voice, Lynn says, "You're their father. I'm their mother. The kids have us both now. If we kill each other off, they won't have anyone. You don't want that. Let it be, Tony." She watches him waver. Twenty years of trusting him to be a loving father rise up in Lynn and for a second she sees a Tony who loves his children and wants them to love him back. "Let them love you, Tony," she says and the words are private between a woman and her husband and she thinks he hears her, thinks he will not hurt the children, will stop short of causing them to lose their mother and their father. She sees the lawyer's sneer begin, his mouth ready to spout obscenities again, and especially for him, she adds, "Don't make the mistake of thinking I won't attack you if you force me to. I will." Her arm does not tremble. Her trigger finger does not flinch.

Afterward, outside, Nora embraces Lynn. "My God, that was tough. You did it yourself. I was more scared than you! Didn't you tell me Tony went to counseling with you?"

"Yes. He asked me to — at his therapist's."

"And you did, right?"

"Right. That's why I was surprised just now at how long they went on threatening."

"That sanctimonious creep didn't help matters any — well,

it cost us money but we got the girls. And we got child support; we'll make sure he sends that. But I think he will. I think he really loves the girls. It's you he wants to bully!"

Lynn nods. She wants to get out of the parking lot.

"Look. I have just half an hour. Let me get you a drink or a cup of coffee. Come on." Nora puts her arm around Lynn and takes her in her car. "What ugly men they are! We had nothing to bargain with, you know. The equity in the house — thank God for that state law — they can't change that! — that's enough to pay your debts, right? And you'll start out even-steven. With four kids and child support coming in for two. How old are you?"

"Forty-two."

"You know, I had to warn you and Ruth, but I admire the two of you. You've got spunk!"

Driving home later Lynn thinks she has forgotten something. She checks to make sure she released the emergency brake. She has her purse, her jacket. She asks herself if she should have signed something more, left some form, made an appointment with Nora for next week. There is nothing. It is finished. There will be a routine court appearance. Nora says it will be only a formality. Tony agreed. He will not go through with the adultery charge. He will not charge her with being lesbian and unfit. He will not contest.

Lynn stops for gas and feels closer to the friendly student who pumps the gas than to the stranger at the lawyer's office. She gropes for whatever is forgotten, whatever is eluding her. The candles she used to light every night when she and Tony held hands a minute before they began dinner flash before her eyes. No tears form. Only her mind contracts. Legalities do dehumanize, she thinks. True. The whole process of extrication (therapeutic, legal, financial, practical) blunts us, turns off feelings, and makes us function like strange robots toward each other. But it was his own damned fear, his tormented suspicion, kept from the air year after guarding year, that festered and gradually snuffed out that candlelight. I tried, Lynn thinks, I tried. There was no way to breathe life back into those blackened wicks.

33

"Hey — how many women are there in this bed?" Ruth asks, peremptorily.

Startled, Lynn stops lovemaking; laughing, she answers, "Two."

She is catapulted by Ruth's challenge back to a scene with Tony, in which she kneels astride his thighs, holding his penis between her breasts, bending her head to bring him to orgasm with her mouth; her back hurts from bending toward him as she strains to make him come.

"Remember that and stop thinking about me." Lazily Ruth pulls her toward her and they lie pleasantly together, waiting for intensity to come or not to come their way again, without obligation on anybody's part.

In the morning, Ruth, waking, encloses Lynn in her arm. Lynn lies, her head on Ruth's shoulder, letting the morning light break into her sleepiness, letting the warmth of their bodies fill her until she turns her face toward Ruth's. They kiss. Waves of feeling rise in Lynn; they move swiftly together and delay relinquishing the sharp crescendo. Hands move every-where and lips and tongues. Lynn knows she wants to lie with Ruth's tongue like water lapping and Ruth's hands like summer breezes on her breasts, and at the same time she moves to lie heavy, on Ruth, breast against breast, hands gliding thighs, mouth moving smoothly on arms and neck. The passion in their fingertips and lips whirls length to length through them so Lynn does not know whose joy, whose flesh. Their lips, held open wide, touch long. Their tongues within that wild vacuum wait, wait, and as their thighs move together in a throbbing beat, their tongues, light and sharp as blades of wild grass, touch on an exquisite plane and each cries out.

"I love you," Lynn says.

Later, dressing and going to fix breakfast for the girls, Lynn thinks, in my married life, I said I love you, first, and then I touched him, let him touch me. With Ruth it is a circle: we touch and then I know we love; we love and then we want to touch.

Lynn walks the beach with Jeanne, who has come East to a psychology convention. The wind whips the water into white-caps and sanderlings dart along the foam. They've talked about Jeanne's research and Jeanne has read some of Lynn's new stories in manuscript. They've gone to the theater with Ruth and they have all three picnicked at the ocean with all the kids. It's the last day of her visit and Lynn wants to tell Jeanne about Ruth and herself.

Lynn clears her throat. She starts to tell. "We tell most people we're renting, that we share a house for convenience." The two paths are identified as splitting here. She's on the truthful path. This is Jeanne, to-be-trusted-friend. What if Jeanne balks?

"It's hard because of custody and because of teaching. We can't tell at school; we can't tell the kids because we don't want to lay that on them: 'Keep this secret, kid, or it's all up with our jobs!' This isn't something either Ruth or I expected to happen. We went from being friends to being lovers."

Each time Lynn tells this to someone she feels the gap spring open between the listener and herself. She waits for a bridge to be begun or for flight. She looks at Jeanne now, to see if she will call back from across the wide ravine. A tern breaks its flight to plummet into the waves and then rise again with a small fish glinting silver in its beak.

"You're happy. That's easy to see. I'm glad for you. Ruth is a delightful woman. Thank you for telling me." Jeanne's smile glistens tears from feeling, not shock or awkwardness. Lynn smiles back and talks on, eager to tell everything. "I hate the secrecy!" she says, walking beside the flashing blue of sky and water.

"Ruth's a pretty private person anyhow, isn't she?" Jeanne's voice is uncertain.

Lynn answers quickly, "It's fine to keep quiet about your private life if you're reticent and don't want to blurt out your feelings. But to have to keep quiet out of fear is something else — to have to hide a marvelous part of our lives—"

Jeanne nods. "Must be simply maddening. You do have to, I suppose?"

"We might be fired if we came out."

"It's a conspiracy. When I think how many single women teachers I had — or anybody had — and they must have been mostly . . ."

"Right. But who would ever know?"

Ninth grade. Just after Christmas vacation. Lynnanne watches the math teacher, Miss Allen, move briskly to the blackboard to write equations there. The gym teacher, who shared a house with her, died in the fall. During vacation, Lynnanne mailed a Christmas card to Miss Allen with a note on it, saying how sorry she is and that she knows Miss Allen must be especially lonely this Christmas time. Lynnanne watches her; she wonders how it is for her, wonders if the loneliness goes away.

Miss Allen finishes putting the equation on the board, calls Lynnanne to her desk, thanks her for the card, tells her, with a deep and thoughtful glance, that no one else in the school realized that she was lonely this Christmas time.

"Are there people here with whom you *can* be open?" Jeanne frowns thoughtfully, kicking sand.

"Not many. I have to be especially careful because Tony threatened a custody fight."

"Was that just noise because he was hurt, do you think?"

"No. He actually had the papers served on me — charging adultery."

"That's wild."

"Most judges still deny custody to lesbians. If he'd won, the kids would be denied access to me. I thought it essential to keep that from happening."

"My God, yes. He could never raise them."

"That's what I think. This way the kids can be with him as much as they want — if he's willing and able."

"You've done the right thing for the kids. I wish you didn't have to pay such a heavy price though." Jeanne takes her arm. "Thanks for trusting me, old friend. I wish you happiness."

They walk quietly along the beach, arm in arm.

Lynn sets an armful of wood down on her hearth. "It's been a long, long time, Sandy," she says, straightening up to face the young woman.

Sandy, wearing jeans and a denim shirt, puts the log she's carrying into the fireplace. "May I lay a fire?"

"Sure. Now: *where* have you been?"

"Since Tony kicked me out?"

"What?"

Sandy crouches, arranging the wood. Her back is to Lynn. There is a silence before she answers. "Remember the last time I stayed with you?"

Lynn searches her memory for the visit among the many visits that, unknown to her, was the final visit. It is there somewhere in that stretch of time that she finds impossible to order. "No," she says, "not exactly." She speaks to Ruth, "Sandy was our babysitter and then a visiting member of the family. And then she disappeared!"

"He told me not to come around any more. Remember, I came out with Vivian? Tony took me outside and told me that he hated everything I am and everything I stand for and not to come to his home again."

"Christ!" Lynn puts her hand on Sandy's shoulder, tears in her eyes.

"You didn't know that before?"

"No."

"I thought you must."

"How?"

"I thought Tony would tell you."

"No. We didn't tell each other much during those last years. I'm sorry, Sandy."

"It's not your fault," Ruth says softly. "You didn't tell her not to come."

"That's why I didn't call," Sandy says quietly. "I thought you probably felt the same way Tony did."

"And I thought you were hitching through Europe or something and would turn up some time."

"I ran into an old friend who teaches and she had heard about Tony and you splitting up or I never would have called."

"You're living in the City?"

"Right."

"You and Vivian?"

"No." Sandy gets up from working on the fire and sits opposite Lynn. "I live alone right now. I'd like you to meet a woman I know. We're thinking of moving in together."

"Want to bring her out for dinner next Saturday?"

"You come in. It's your turn."

"Okay. I'll talk Christy into staying with Lori. She's almost as good a sitter as you were!" They laugh. The fire blazes up around the backlog.

Lynn, pregnant with Lori, is driving Sandy, the babysitter, home. "Guess?" she says to her.

Sandy looks questioningly back, "You're going to Moscow and I'm going with you?"

"Not quite."

"I give up."

"I'm pregnant."

"You're kidding?"

"Nope." Lynn laughs at her.

"Why?"

"I want another baby. I like them!"

Sandy looks out the window and then back at Lynn.

"That's great. I never knew anyone before who was glad *about it!"*

"You're kidding?"

"No, I'm not. You're really happy about it, aren't you?"

"Yes, I really am."

They sit in the car in front of Sandy's place for a long time, talking. Sandy says she doesn't want to marry, doesn't want to have babies. Lynn tells Sandy, "You'll find the right man some-day. You'll see. And I want to be there when it happens."

"Do you know what I just thought of? The night I told you I was pregnant. Remember?"

"Yeah, I remember." Sandy studies the fire. "I believed you, you know."

"Believed what?" Ruth asks.

"Sandy told me she didn't want to ever get married or have kids. I told her she did," Lynn says.

"I believed her," Sandy says. "It took a lot of affairs with a lot of men before I figured out that I was right and Lynn was wrong. I didn't think she'd be wrong."

"She's a very persuasive woman," Ruth says, smiling rue-fully. "And she was the believer of all believers! I think you could go back, Lynn. You could be a true believer again!"

Lynn pushes Ruth on to the floor and pins her there. "Take it back!" They all begin to laugh. Lynn sits up and looks again at Sandy. "I still can't believe that Tony did that."

"He did though. He *hates* homosexuals, Lynn. We scare him shitless."

"Not just me?"

"Not just you. But what about you two? Tell me."

"Want some brandy?" Ruth asks.

Sandy nods and Ruth goes to get glasses. Lynn starts to tell, "I met Ruth in a night class — and we kept on seeing each other — every day after that."

Sandy grins. "Like that, huh?"

"Like that."

Ruth pours the brandy. Lynn says, "I used to feel like you were almost my daughter. Here's to being sisters instead!"

"Hear! Hear!" Ruth says.

Sandy has tears in her eyes as she lifts her glass.

"Actually," Ruth says, "that's why I'm so good for Lynn. I never listen when she waxes pedagogical."

"Never?" Sandy laughs. "That's terrific! God, I've missed you, Lynn."

"What a bastard that man is!" Ruth says.

"Speaking of bastards," Sandy says, "whatever became of your brothers? I'll bet you're still sending them Christmas presents, aren't you?"

"Only cards," Lynn answers, laughing awkwardly.

"And she thinks she's mean!" Ruth says, "But I'm working on her."

"Hey, I'm glad you're here." Lynn goes to Sandy. They meet in a big bear hug.

"Me too," Sandy says.

"About time, I'd say," Ruth says.

34

In the teacher's cafeteria, paying for lunch, Lynn sees in her purse a button Sandy gave her: "A woman without a man is like a fish without a bicycle." She sits next to the one friend there who knows, says quietly to him, "Look what I'm going to wear to Parents' Night," and opening her purse, flashes the button at him.

"Don't you wish?" he says, and they laugh together before joining the general conversation.

At the dinner party at Sandy's apartment in the city, Lynn stands in front of the bookcase, reading titles. "Look, Ruth," she says.

"Interesting?"

"Um*hm*."

"Borrow whatever you want," Sandy says across the room. "There's a lot more than the *Well of Loneliness* to read by now!"

Several women laugh in agreement. Lynn takes several books and sits down with a group. "You teach?" someone asks.

Another voice answers, "I'm in the psych program at NYU. Where are you?"

As they drive toward home, Lynn says, "Hey, there's a world out there!"

"It did feel good to be with new friends. We've been cut off too much, I guess." Ruth takes Lynn's hand. "Shall we come in every weekend?"

Lynn moves closer to her, saying, "Why didn't you hold hands there?"

"Maybe next time. I'm the shy type." They both laugh.

"I didn't know how good it'd feel to have everyone in a room know — and what interesting women — what does Lorraine do?"

"Computers. We talked a long time about the new system she's designing. If I were young again I think I might do that."

"Just leave me out," Lynn retorts. "Want to go to the lesbian poetry reading in November?"

"Sure, if you want."

"Do you think lesbians are smarter than other women?" Lynn laughs as she asks.

"Stronger, maybe. If you don't want to be dependent on a man you need strength. But actually, I think most women have great strength."

"Maybe it's that women who choose to be women identified women refuse to forfeit their own strength . . ."

"And who don't love men as much as they love women," Ruth smiles. "Though I'd hate to leave men out altogether."

"We'll let a few in. Just not the ones who abuse their power."

"Now that we know six lesbians you can formulate lots of theories . . ."

"Okay." Lynn laughs. "But there is a lot to think about. You have to start all over again thinking about marriage and everything! Besides, six will lead to six will lead to . . ."

". . . sex?" Ruth kisses her hand and arm lightly again and again.

"Hey, cut that out while you're driving — you'll go off the road!"

"*I'll* go off the road?"

"*You're* driving."

"You mean we get to go home to bed together just like that?"

"That's what I mean."

"In our own house?"
"In our own house."
"Hey, how did we ever accomplish that?"

"Then I'll drive you there tomorrow morning?" Lynn watches Anthony's face darken as he tries to maneuver within the boundaries the law has set.
"I guess I have to, huh?"
"Hey, Anthony, come play catch with me!" Lori summons him to the lawn.
"Yes, you do. But they won't take you, Anthony."
"What happens if I don't show up?" he asks automatically.
"You get locked up," she answers on cue.
"Hey, Mom, where do you want the table?" Christy is standing with a stack of paper plates and cups, scanning the yard.
"Right there is fine. I'll help you in a minute."
"Lynn, I'm bringing pie," Ruth calls from her doorway.
"Okay, thanks. We'll eat in half an hour. Go play catch with Lori, Anthony. Don't think about it any more today."
"Yeah, I guess." He lopes off and Lynn sits, watching him, controlling her own anxiety. She watches his tense body move across the lawn.
Ruth comes to join her. "Everything okay?"
"I'm taking Anthony for his army physical tomorrow morning."
"I forgot. He knows they'll exempt him for his eyesight, doesn't he?"
"Umhm, but he's still scared – and angry."
"Sure. What about tonight? Can we duck out a while?"
"I don't see how. He's edgy and I told him to sleep over. I'd like to hang around anyhow because Christy's new friends are coming over and I'd better be here to keep an eye on them. I don't want them to think they can come here and smoke pot whenever they want."
Ruth shakes her head. "It's not all so easy for you, is it?"
"What do you hear from Nate?" Lynn says, to divert the conversation.

"He's having a fine time. He's already been invited home with a new friend for Christmas in Kent!"

"That's good luck. Jon sounds lonesome."

"So does Mark. Let's send them each a friend."

"Do I smell pie burning?"

"Oh damn!" Ruth runs back to her kitchen.

"Mom, we need ice cream." Christy stands in front of her. "Give me your car key and I'll go pick some up."

"Dream on."

"Oh come on. Everybody else's mother lets them drive."

"Without a license?"

"I know how."

"Well, not this mother. So spread the word. Also, tell those new kids that your mom's tougher than she looks and they're not to bring alcohol or drugs into this house."

"Oh mother!" Christy gives her a strong disapproving look and goes inside. Rock music comes on, loud.

"Turn it down, Christy," Lynn calls.

Easy, she thinks, no, it's not so easy. Watching Anthony dive after a low throw, Lynn thinks of all the demonstrations he's been at and of all the other boys who have been killed and hurt and who have done the hurting and the killing in Vietnam. She wonders if it will be finished before Jon gets called. She feels as though she should phone Tony about Anthony but can't think of anything good that might come of it. He knows Anthony's going in the morning. "Let him do it by himself," he said. Lynn goes into her study to check on the folder of doctor's reports that Anthony will need. She looks around her study, savoring the privacy, a place to work entirely on her own. I'll build a bookcase here after a while, she thinks, and get another file.

"Mom, hurry up, the hamburgers are burning!"

"Well, take them out!"

"Mommy, can I turn on the sprinkler and run through?"

"Not until after dinner, Lori! Wash up now and let's eat."

"Mom?"

"What honey?"

"Are you okay?" Christy stands, considering her.

"I'm fine, Christy." She gives her a hug. "A little worried

about Anthony tomorrow, is all. But it'll be all right. Are *you* okay?"

"Yes. This is a nice house, Mom."

"I'm glad you like it. I think it's terrific, myself. Go call Ruth, will you? Tell her to bring some pickles if she's got any."

Lynn pauses in the doorway, seeing the sunshine filter through the trees. "It's a beautiful day," she starts to say, to Anthony on the lawn, to Lori in the house, to Christy in Ruth's kitchen, to Jon in the letter she will write to him that night, and to Ruth as she joins them at the table.

"What a good place for a picnic," she says out loud, sitting down. "Who's hungry? There's plenty more where that came from."

"Now hold that pole up."

"This one?"

"Right. Easy now."

Lynn holds the tent pole carefully, watching Ruth tie the ropes that hold it in place. "You know, I always wanted to go camping but Tony never would."

"Okay, a minute more — there. You can let go."

"Shall I unload the car?"

"Why not? I'll start a fire. We did that right; we've got another hour of daylight."

"Look at that!" Lynn points to a large maple with scarlet and yellow leaves caught in the almost level rays from the setting sun.

Ruth comes to stand with her a minute. "God, it's beautiful, isn't it?"

"Love me?"

"I'll let you guess."

"Watch," Lynn says, wiggling her fingers between the flashlight and the canvas so a shadow rabbit meets a shadow wolf. "My father showed me in the barn by lantern light."

Ruth smiles, watching, and then clicks off the light and

pulls Lynn to her for a long slow hug. "Only trouble with a tent is that you can't see the stars. Think we can manage?" "I'm willing to try." Lynn puts her lips on Ruth's and savors the way feeling encompasses their whole bodies, pressed length to length.

"Yes," Ruth says quietly, "I love you, Lynn. I do love you."

Later Lynn drifts the darkness down toward sleep, sheltered by Ruth's arms. The moonlight outlines branches on the tent. The shadows feather gently, moving in the wind.

At night, back home again, Ruth encircles Lynn with her arm. "I wish things were easier for you," she says, holding her close.

"I'm fine," Lynn says. Letting her head lie against Ruth's shoulder, she adds, "I love you."

"I love you, too," Ruth says.

The warm luxury of lying together envelops Lynn. "You know, there's a poem . . . about lovers lying together all night long . . . at peace . . . alive within the night . . ." Lynn realizes Ruth is already asleep. Lying quietly, savoring their peace, words run through Lynn's mind. Ruth is wholly beautiful to me, she thinks, and I am — cherished is the word. I've never felt this way before. I trust Ruth to hold me safe, to cherish me. Lovers in the night. We only know we're writers when we're actually writing . . . I heard someone say that once . . . and I only know we're lovers when we lie like this, body against body, natural together. Process, she thinks. There is no accomplishment, only process.

To write, to love, to live. Poets know. Lovers know. Julia enables process. It's when the process fails that people get in trouble. Rigid on the ice. Skidding stiff legged, pretending to produce a figure eight. Product. Happy family. Success. Tony was afraid of the process of being alive and I lived with him out of good intentions. Spinning on the ice. His fear, my denial of his fear. Nauseous. Dizzy. Now I lie with Ruth and it's natural. That moves out into whatever else I do. The process flows. This is my place, here on her shoulder, this is where I find myself — the starting point — until dawn, when the waking process begins again.

So what if people see that we are lovers. Or even guess that we were making love all night. Sometimes in the candlelight we read Millay all night long, Lynn thinks, remembering her college dorm. And that year there was still the 125th Street ferry — 126th? Somewhere around there, to ride over to Jersey and back and over again and we are like the lovers in her poem who gave the old woman all their money and all their, was it apples? Sweet crisp Gravensteins we found lying in the high grass underneath the trees in the orchard on the farm. From the farm we took a stage and then a ferry and then an old street car and Ruth, the little girl with the wide eyes was right then looking out the window of a street car in Berlin . . . buttercups in the ravine along the stream and I'll ask her in the morning if there were buttercups where she played when they went to the mountain meadows, and primroses . . . and Ruth and I wandered on the cliff by the water and found wild roses where we walked.

Home from school one day in early September, Lynn parks the car in their garage and walks toward Ruth, who stands near the forsythia, pruning shears in hand. Lynn imagines Ruth's dark hair framed by the brilliance of yellow petals as it will be in spring. "Hi," she says, "I love you. Did you know that?"

"Even when I cut back the shrubs?"

"Even then," Lynn says, helping her to gather up the trimmings and toss them on the compost.

"How was your day?"

"Long. Yours?"

"Of equal length." They laugh. "Ready for wine?"

"I am. Where's Lori?"

"She went to the neighbors, I think. She left you a note."

They walk together back to the garage. "Sometimes I want to shout from the rooftops that I love you. I want to say, I'm a lesbian. I love a woman and her name is Ruth. Sometimes at school I feel like that."

I know you do and sometime you will, but don't until you've decided that's what you're ready for, okay?"

"I wouldn't unless you agreed, anyhow."

Ruth puts the shears on the tool rack and they stand still a minute in the shelter of the garage doorway. Lynn takes Ruth's hand. High up in a dead oak a woodpecker beats the bark.

"In spite of everything . . ." Ruth pauses, "or maybe because of everything − I don't know − with you I am come home."

They walk together back through the yard and into the house. Afternoon shafts of sunlight strike the doorway as they move through.

Lynn sees as in a photo album Ruth and herself. They carry forsythia in one snapshot, the bright yellow petals spilling like sunshine from their arms. In another Ruth shovels snow, wearing a jacket with a crimson hood flung back, her black hair flecked with melting snow, as snow falls lightly on her arms. her head. Near her, Lynn, taller, lighter, cheeks reddened by the cold, cuts wood for their fireplace, loads her arms high with it, and pauses to watch Ruth in the thickening snow.

Their voices break the silence of the house with laughter and with the new things they are bringing home to say, not in the coming winter, not in the coming spring, but in the sufficient beauty of the present afternoon.

A few of the publications of
THE NAIAD PRESS, INC.
P.O. Box 10543 • Tallahassee, Florida 32302
Phone (904) 539-9322
Mail orders welcome. Please include 15% postage.

PARENTS MATTER by Ann Muller. 240 pp. Parents' relationships with lesbian daughters and gay sons.
ISBN 0-930044-91-6 $9.95

THE PEARLS by Shelley Smith. 176 pp. Passion and fun in the Caribbean sun.   ISBN 0-930044-93-2 $7.95

MAGDALENA by Sarah Aldridge. 352 pp. Epic Lesbian novel set on three continents.   ISBN 0-930044-99-1 $8.95

THE BLACK AND WHITE OF IT by Ann Allen Shockley. 144 pp. Short stories.   ISBN 0-930044-96-7 $7.95

SAY JESUS AND COME TO ME by Ann Allen Shockley. 288 pp. Contemporary romance.   ISBN 0-930044-98-3   8.95

LOVING HER by Ann Allen Shockley. 192 pp. Romantic love story.   ISBN 0-930044-97-5   7.95

MURDER AT THE NIGHTWOOD BAR by Katherine V. Forrest. 240 pp. A Kate Delafield mystery. Second in a series.   ISBN 0-930044-92-4   8.95

ZOE'S BOOK by Gail Pass. 224 pp. Passionate, obsessive love story.   ISBN 0-930044-95-9   7.95

WINGED DANCER by Camarin Grae. 228 pp. Erotic Lesbian adventure story.   ISBN 0-930044-88-6   8.95

PAZ by Camarin Grae. 336 pp. Romantic Lesbian adventurer with the power to change the world.   ISBN 0-930044-89-4   8.95

SOUL SNATCHER by Camarin Grae. 224 pp. A puzzle, an adventure, a mystery—Lesbian romance. ISBN 0-930044-90-8   8.95

THE LOVE OF GOOD WOMEN by Isabel Miller. 224 pp. Long-awaited new novel by the author of the beloved *Patience and Sarah*.   ISBN 0-930044-81-9   8.95

THE HOUSE AT PELHAM FALLS by Brenda Weathers. 240 pp. Suspenseful Lesbian ghost story.   ISBN 0-930044-79-7   7.95

HOME IN YOUR HANDS by Lee Lynch. 240 pp. More stories from the author of *Old Dyke Tales*.   ISBN 0-930044-80-0   7.95

EACH HAND A MAP by Anita Skeen. 112 pp. Real-life poems that touch us all.   ISBN 0-930044-82-7   6.95

SURPLUS by Sylvia Stevenson. 342 pp. A classic early Lesbian novel.   ISBN 0-930044-78-9   7.95

PEMBROKE PARK by Michelle Martin. 256 pp. Derring-do and daring romance in Regency England. ISBN 0-930044-77-0   7.95

THE LONG TRAIL by Penny Hayes. 248 pp. Vivid adventures of two women in love in the old west.   ISBN 0-930044-76-2   8.95

HORIZON OF THE HEART by Shelley Smith. 192 pp. Hot romance in summertime New England. ISBN 0-930044-75-4   7.95

AN EMERGENCE OF GREEN by Katherine V. Forrest. 288 pp. Powerful novel of sexual discovery. ISBN 0-930044-69-X — 8.95

THE LESBIAN PERIODICALS INDEX edited by Claire Potter. 432 pp. Author & subject index. ISBN 0-930044-74-6 — 29.95

DESERT OF THE HEART by Jane Rule. 224 pp. A classic; basis for the movie *Desert Hearts*. ISBN 0-930044-73-8 — 7.95

SPRING FORWARD/FALL BACK by Sheila Ortiz Taylor. 288 pp. Literary novel of timeless love. ISBN 0-930044-70-3 — 7.95

FOR KEEPS by Elisabeth Nonas. 144 pp. Contemporary novel about losing and finding love. ISBN 0-930044-71-1 — 7.95

TORCHLIGHT TO VALHALLA by Gale Wilhelm. 128 pp. Classic novel by a great Lesbian writer. ISBN 0-930044-68-1 — 7.95

LESBIAN NUNS: BREAKING SILENCE edited by Rosemary Curb and Nancy Manahan. 432 pp. Unprecedented auto-biographies of religious life. ISBN 0-930044-62-2 — 9.95

THE SWASHBUCKLER by Lee Lynch. 288 pp. Colorful novel set in Greenwich Village in the sixties. ISBN 0-930044-66-5 — 7.95

MISFORTUNE'S FRIEND by Sarah Aldridge. 320 pp. Histori-cal Lesbian novel set on two continents. ISBN 0-930044-67-3 — 7.95

A STUDIO OF ONE'S OWN by Ann Stokes. Edited by Dolores Klaich. 128 pp. Autobiography. ISBN 0-930044-64-9 — 7.95

SEX VARIANT WOMEN IN LITERATURE by Jeannette Howard Foster. 448 pp. Literary history. ISBN 0-930044-65-7 — 8.95

A HOT-EYED MODERATE by Jane Rule. 252 pp. Hard-hitting essays on gay life; writing; art. ISBN 0-930044-57-6 — 7.95

INLAND PASSAGE AND OTHER STORIES by Jane Rule. 288 pp. Wide-ranging new collection. ISBN 0-930044-56-8 — 7.95

WE TOO ARE DRIFTING by Gale Wilhelm. 128 pp. Timeless Lesbian novel, a masterpiece. ISBN 0-930044-61-4 — 6.95

AMATEUR CITY by Katherine V. Forrest. 224 pp. A Kate Delafield mystery. First in a series. ISBN 0-930044-55-X — 7.95

THE SOPHIE HOROWITZ STORY by Sarah Schulman. 176 pp. Engaging novel of madcap intrigue. ISBN 0-930044-54-1 — 7.95

THE BURNTON WIDOWS by Vicki P. McConnell. 272 pp. A Nyla Wade mystery, second in the series. ISBN 0-930044-52-5 — 7.95

OLD DYKE TALES by Lee Lynch. 224 pp. Extraordinary stories of our diverse Lesbian lives. ISBN 0-930044-51-7 — 7.95

DAUGHTERS OF A CORAL DAWN by Katherine V. Forrest. 240 pp. Novel set in a Lesbian new world. ISBN 0-930044-50-9 — 7.95

THE PRICE OF SALT by Claire Morgan. 288 pp. A milestone novel, a beloved classic. ISBN 0-930044-49-5 — 8.95

AGAINST THE SEASON by Jane Rule. 224 pp. Luminous, complex novel of interrelationships. ISBN 0-930044-48-7 — 7.95

LOVERS IN THE PRESENT AFTERNOON by Kathleen Fleming. 288 pp. A novel about recovery and growth.
ISBN 0-930044-46-0 — 8.95